ALEXANDER: THE SANDS OF AMMON

Dr Valerio Massimo Manfredi is an Italian historian, journalist and archaeologist. He is the Professor of Classical Archaeology at the University of Milan, and a familiar face on European television. He has published seven novels, including the bestselling Alexander trilogy, for which the American Biographical Institute voted him Man of the Year in 1999. He is married with two children and lives in a small town near Bologna. He is currently at work on a screenplay for a major Hollywood studio.

Iain Halliday was born in Scotland in 1960. He studied American Studies at the University of Manchester and worked in Italy and London before moving to Sicily, where he now lives. As well as working as a translator, he currently teaches English at the University of Catania.

Valerio Massimo Manfredi

ALEXANDER

THE SANDS OF AMMON

Translated from the Italian by Iain Halliday

PAN BOOKS

First published 2001 by Macmillan

This edition published 2001 by Pan Books
an imprint of Pan Macmillan Ltd
Pan Macmillan, 20 New Wharf Road, London N1 9RR
Basingstoke and Oxford
Associated companies throughout the world
www.panmacmillan.com

ISBN 978 0 330 51859 8

A CIP catalogue record for this book is available from
the British Library.

Typeset by SetSystems Ltd, Saffron Walden, Essex
Printed and bound in the UK by
CPI Mackays, Chatham ME5 8TD

Visit **www.panmacmillan.com** to read more about all our books and to buy
them. You will also find features, author interviews and news of any author
events, and you can sign up for e-newsletters so that you're always first to hear
about our new releases.

TO CHRISTINE

ALEXANDER

THE SANDS OF AMMON

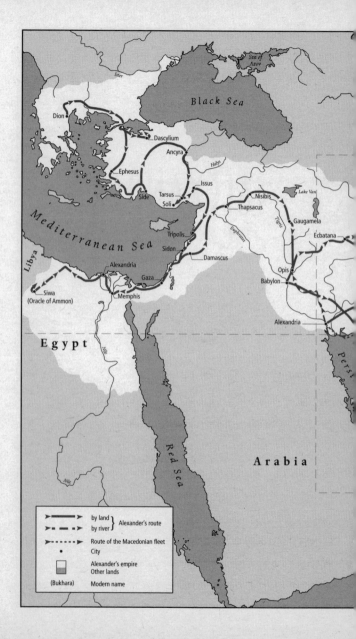

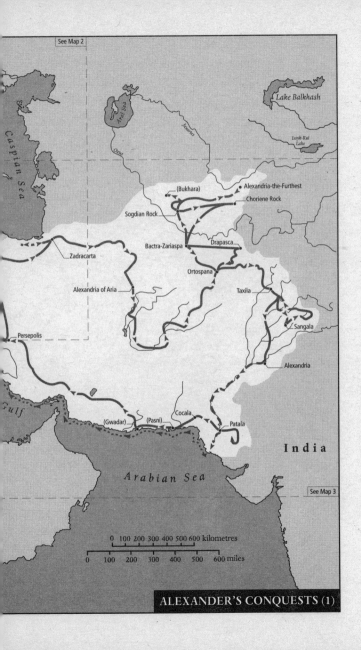

Lake Balkhash

Caspian Sea

Aral Sea

Jaxartes

Oxus

Issyk-Kul Lake

(Bukhara) • Alexandria-the-Furthest

Choriene Rock

Sogdian Rock

Bactra-Zariaspa — Drapasca

Ortospana

Zadracarta

Alexandria of Aria

Taxila

Sangala

Persepolis

Alexandria

Gulf

(Gwadar) (Pasni) Cocala

Patala

India

Arabian Sea

See Map 2

See Map 3

0 100 200 300 400 500 600 kilometres

0   100   200   300   400   500   600 miles

ALEXANDER'S CONQUESTS (1)

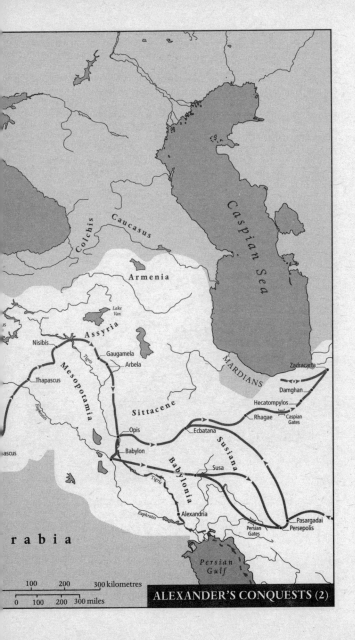

ALEXANDER'S CONQUESTS (2)

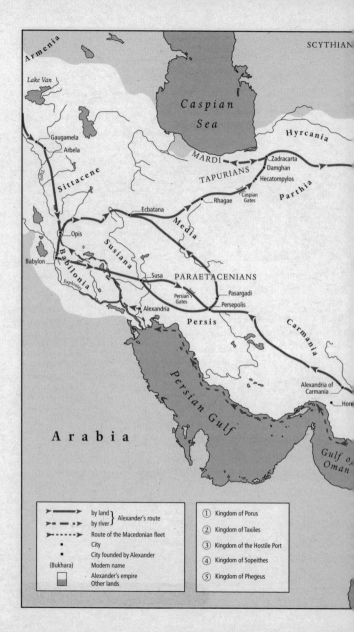

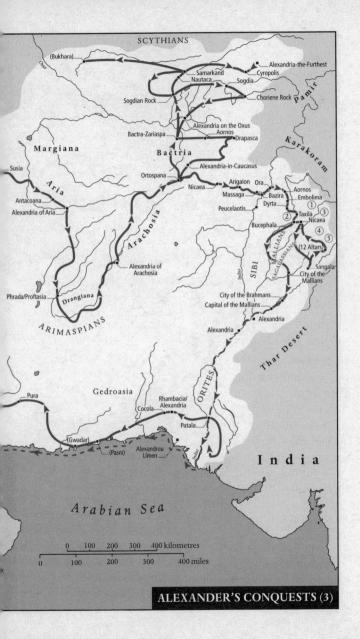

SCYTHIANS

(Bukhara)
Oxus
Samarkand
Nautaca
Cyropolis
Alexandria-the-Furthest
Sogdia
Sogdian Rock
Choriene Rock
Pamir

Margiana
Bactra-Zariaspa
Alexandria on the Oxus
Aornos
Drapasca
Bactria
Karakoram

Susia
Alexandria-in-Caucasus
Aria
Ortospana
Nicaea
Arigaion
Ora
Aornos
Antacoana
Massaga
Bazira
Embolima
Alexandria of Aria
Peucelaotis
Dyrta
① ③
Taxila
Nicaea
②
④ ⑤
Bucephala
Arachosia
Alexandria of
Arachosia
(12 Altars)

Phrada/Proftasia
Drangiana
ARIMASPIANS
SIBI
MALLIANS
SAGA...SIANS
Sangala
City of the
Mallians

City of the Brahmans
Capital of the Mallians
Indus
Alexandria
Alexandria

Pura
Gedroasia
Rhambacia/
Alexandria
Cocola
Alexandria

ORITES
Thar Desert

(Gwadar)
(Pasni)
Alexandrou
Limen
Patala
Indus
India

Arabian Sea

0   100   200   300   400 kilometres
0   100   200   300   400 miles

ALEXANDER'S CONQUESTS (3)

ANCIENT GREECE

1

FROM THE TOP OF THE HILL Alexander turned towards
the beach and beheld a scene that was almost an identical
repetition of one that had been played out a thousand
years earlier. Hundreds of ships were lined up along the
coast, carrying thousands and thousands of soldiers, but
the city behind him – Ilium, heir to ancient Troy – rather
than preparing for years of siege and resistance, was
now getting ready to open its gates and welcome him,
descendant of Achilles and of Priam.

He saw his companions coming up towards him on
horseback and spurred Bucephalas on towards the top.
He wanted to be the first to enter the ancient shrine of
Athena of Troy and he wanted to do it alone. He
dismounted, handed the reins to a servant and crossed the
threshold of the temple.

Inside, objects glimmered in the darkness, difficult to
make out, draped deep in the half-shadow. Their shape
was indefinite and his eyes took some time to become
accustomed to the gloom because up to just a moment
before they had been coping with the dazzlingly bright
sky of the Troad region with the sun at its highest.

The ancient building was full of relics, of weapons
displayed in memory of the war described by Homer in
his epic of the ten-year siege of the city built by the gods

themselves. On each of the time-worn souvenirs was a dedication, an inscription: Paris's lyre was here, as were Achilles's weapons and his great storied shield.

He looked around, his eyes resting on these mementoes which unseen hands had kept shining for the reverence and the curiosity of the faithful over the centuries. They hung from the columns, from the ceiling beams, from the walls of the cella – but how much of all this was real? And how much was simply the product of the priests' cunning, of their will to exploit it all for their own ends?

At that moment he felt as though the only genuine thing in the confused jumble – more like the clutter of objects displayed in a market than fitting décor for a sanctuary – was his own passion for the ancient blind poet, his boundless admiration for the heroes who had been reduced to ashes by time and by the countless events that had taken place between the two shores of the Straits.

He had arrived out of the blue, just as his father Philip had done one day at the temple of Apollo, at Delphi, and no one was expecting him. He heard some light footsteps and hid behind a column near the statue of Athena, a striking image of the goddess carved in stone, painted in various colours and bearing real metal weapons: this primitive simulacrum was sculpted from a single block of dark stone, and her mother-of-pearl eyes stood out starkly from a face darkened by the years and by the smoke of the votive lamps.

A girl wearing a white peplum, her hair gathered into a headdress of the same colour, moved towards the statue. She carried a bucket in one hand and a sponge in the other.

She climbed up on to the pedestal and began wiping the surface of the sculpture, spreading as she did so an intense, penetrating perfume of aloe and wild nard throughout the temple. Alexander moved up to her silently.

'Who are you?' he asked.

The girl jumped and the bucket fell from her hand, bouncing once and then rolling over the floor before coming to a halt against a column.

'Do not be afraid,' the King reassured her. 'I am only a pilgrim who seeks to pay homage to the goddess. Who are you? What is your name?'

'My name is Daunia and I am one of the sacred slaves,' replied the young girl, intimidated by Alexander's appearance, which was certainly not what one would have expected of an ordinary pilgrim. His breastplate and greaves glinted under his cloak and when he moved there came the noise of his chainmail belt clanking against his armour.

'A sacred slave? I would never have guessed. You have fine features – aristocratic – and there is such pride in your eyes.'

'Perhaps you are more used to seeing the sacred slaves of Aphrodite: they really are slaves, before being sacred, slaves of men's lust.'

'And you aren't?' asked Alexander as he picked up her bucket from the floor.

'I am a virgin, like the goddess. Have you never heard of the city of women? That is where I am from.'

She had an unusual accent that the King had never heard before.

'I had no idea there was such a place as the city of women. Where is it?'

'In Italy, it bears the name of Locri and its aristocracy is exclusively female. It was founded by a hundred families, all originating from Locris in Greece. They were all widowed and legend has it they formed unions with their slaves.'

'And why are you here, so far from home?'

'To atone for a sin.'

'A sin? But what sin can such a young girl have committed?'

'Not my sin. A thousand years ago, on the night of the fall of Troy, Ajax Oileus, our national hero, raped Princess Cassandra, daughter of Priam, right here on the pedestal bearing the sacred Palladium, the miraculous image of Athena that had fallen from the heavens. Since then the Locrians have paid for Ajax's sacrilege with the gift of two maids from their finest aristocracy, both of whom serve for a full year in the goddess's shrine.'

Alexander shook his head as if unable to believe what he was hearing. He looked around while outside the cobbles surrounding the temple resounded with the noise of horses' hooves – his companions had arrived.

Just at that moment, however, a priest entered and immediately realized who the man standing before him was. He bowed respectfully.

'Welcome, most powerful lord. I am sorry you did not let us know of your arrival – we would have given you a very different welcome.' And he nodded to the girl to leave, but Alexander gestured for her to stay.

'I preferred to arrive this way,' he said, 'and this maid

has told me such an extraordinary story, something I could never have imagined. I have heard that in this temple there are relics of the Trojan War. Is this true?'

'It certainly is. And this image you see before you is a Palladium: a likeness of an ancient statue of Athena that fell from the heavens and granted the gift of invincibility to whichever city held it in its possession.'

At that moment Hephaestion, Ptolemy, Perdiccas and Seleucus entered the temple.

'And where is the original statue?' asked Hephaestion as he came nearer.

'Some say that the hero Diomedes carried it off to Argos; others say that Ulysses went to Italy and gave it to the King, Latinus; and then others again maintain that Aeneas placed it in a temple not far from Rome, where it is still housed. However, there are many cities which claim the original simulacrum as their own.'

'I can well believe it,' said Seleucus. 'Such conviction must be a considerable source of courage.'

'Indeed,' nodded Ptolemy. 'Aristotle would say that it is conviction, or the prophecy, which actually generates the event.'

'But what is it that distinguishes the real Palladium from the other statues?' asked Alexander.

'The real simulacrum,' declared the priest in his most solemn voice, 'can close its eyes and shake its spear.'

'That's nothing special,' Ptolemy said. 'Any of our military engineers could build a toy of that kind.'

The priest threw him a disdainful look and even the King shook his head. 'Is there anything you believe in, Ptolemy?'

'Yes, of course,' replied Ptolemy, placing his hand on the hilt of the sword. 'This.' And then he placed his other hand on Alexander's shoulder and said, 'Together with friendship.'

'And yet,' the priest said, 'the objects you see here have been revered between these walls since time immemorial, and the tumuli along the river have always contained the bones of Achilles, Patroclus and Ajax.'

There came the sound of footsteps – Callisthenes had joined them to visit the famous sanctuary.

'And what do you make of it all, Callisthenes?' asked Ptolemy as he walked towards him and put his arm around him. 'Do you believe that this really is Achilles's armour? And this, hanging here from that column, is this really Paris's lyre?' He brushed the strings and the instrument produced a dull, out-of-tune chord.

Alexander no longer seemed to be listening. He was staring at the young Locrian woman as she now filled the lamps with perfumed oil, studying the perfection of her figure through the transparency of her peplum as a ray of light came through it. He was captivated by the mystery that glowed in her shy, meek eyes.

'You well know that none of this really matters,' replied Callisthenes. 'At Sparta, in the Dioscurian temple, they have an egg on display from which Castor and Pollux, the two twins, brothers of Helen, were supposedly born, but I think it's the egg of an ostrich, a Libyan bird as tall as a horse. Our sanctuaries are full of relics like this. The thing that matters is what the people want to believe and the people need to believe and need to be able to dream.' As he spoke he turned towards Alexander.

The King moved towards the great panoply of bronze, adorned with tin and silver, and he gently stroked the shield carved in relief, with the scenes described by Homer and the helmet embellished with a triple crest.

'And how did this armour come to be here?' he asked the priest.

'Ulysses brought it here, filled with remorse for having usurped Ajax's right to it, and he placed it before the tomb as a votive gift, imploring Ajax to help him return to Ithaca. It was then gathered up and housed in this sanctuary.'

Alexander moved closer to the priest. 'Do you know who I am?'

'Yes. You are Alexander, King of Macedon.'

'That's right. And I am directly descended, on my mother's side, from Pyrrhus, son of Achilles, founder of the dynasty of Epirus, and thus I am heir to Achilles. Therefore this armour is mine, and I want it.'

The priest's face drained of all colour. 'But Sire . . .'

'What!' exclaimed Ptolemy with a grin on his face. 'We're supposed to believe that this is Paris's lyre, that these are Achilles' weapons, made by the god Hephaestus in person, and you don't believe that our King is a direct descendant of Achilles, son of Peleus?'

'Oh no . . .' stammered the priest. 'It's simply that these are sacred objects which cannot be . . .'

'Nonsense,' said Perdiccas. 'You can have other identical weapons made. No one will ever know the difference. Our King needs them, you see, and since they belonged to his ancestor . . .' and he opened his arms as if to say, 'an inheritance is an inheritance.'

'Have it brought to our camp. It will be displayed before our army like a standard before every battle,' came Alexander's orders. 'And now we must return – our visit is over.'

They left in dribs and drabs, hanging on to look around at the incredible jumble of objects hanging from the columns and the walls.

The priest noticed Alexander staring at the girl as she left the temple through a side door.

'She goes swimming every evening in the sea near the mouth of the Scamander,' he whispered in his ear.

The King said nothing as he left. Not long afterwards the priest saw him mount his horse and set off towards the camp on the seashore, which was teeming with activity like some giant anthill.

*

Alexander saw her arrive, walking briskly and confidently in the darkness, coming along the left-hand bank of the river. She stopped just where the waters of the Scamander mixed with the sea waves. It was a peaceful, calm night and the moon was just beginning to rise from the sea, drawing a long silver wake from the horizon to the shore. The girl took off her clothes, undid her hair in the moonlight and entered the water. Her body, caressed by the waves, glowed like polished marble.

'You are beautiful. You look like a goddess, Daunia,' Alexander said quietly as he came out of the shadow.

The girl went in deeper, up to her chin, and moved away. 'Do not harm me. I have been consecrated.'

'To do penance for an ancient act of rape?'

'To do penance for all rapes. Women are always obliged to endure.'

The King took off his clothes and entered the water, as she crossed her arms over her chest to hide her breasts.

'They say that the Aphrodite of Cnidus, sculpted by the divine Praxiteles, covers her breasts just as you are doing now. Even Aphrodite is demure . . . do not be afraid. Come.'

The girl moved towards him slowly, walking over the sandy bed and, as she came nearer, her divine body emerged dripping from the water and the surface of the sea receded until it embraced her hips and her belly.

'Lead me through the water to the tumulus of Achilles. I don't want anyone to see us.'

'Follow me then,' said Daunia. 'And let's hope you are a good swimmer.' She turned on to her side and slipped through the waves like a Nereid, a nymph of the salty abyss.

The coast formed a wide bay at that point, the shoreline already illuminated by the campfires, and it ended in a promontory with an earthen tumulus at its tip.

'Don't you worry about me,' replied Alexander as he swam alongside her.

The girl struck out offshore, cutting straight across the bay, aiming directly for the headland. She swam elegantly, graceful and flowing in her movements, almost noiseless, slipping through the water like some marine creature.

'You are very good,' said Alexander, himself breathless.

'I was born on the sea. Do you still want to go as far as the Sigeus headland?'

Alexander did not reply and continued swimming until

he saw the foam of the breaking water in the moonlight on the beach, the waves stretching up rhythmically to the base of the great tumulus.

They came out of the water holding each other by the hand, and the King led them closer to the dark mass of Achilles's tomb. Alexander felt, or he believed he felt, the spirit of the hero penetrate him and he thought he saw Briseïs with her rosy cheeks when he turned towards his companion, who was now standing before him in the silver moonlight, searching for Alexander's gaze in the darkness that enveloped him.

'Only the gods are allowed moments like this,' Alexander whispered to her and turned towards the warm breeze that came from the sea. 'Here Achilles sat and cried for the death of Patroclus. Here his mother, the ocean nymph, deposited his arms, weapons forged by a god.'

'So you do believe in it after all?' the girl asked him.

'Yes.'

'So why in the temple . . .'

'It's different here. It's night and those distant voices, long silenced, can still be heard. And you are resplendent here before me – unveiled.'

'Are you really a king?'

'Look at me. Who do you see here before you?'

'You are the young man who sometimes appears in my dreams while I sleep with my friends in the goddess's sanctuary. The young man I would have wanted to love.'

He moved closer and held her head on his chest.

'I will leave tomorrow, and in a few days' time I will have to face a difficult battle – perhaps I will be victorious, perhaps I will die.'

'In that case, take me if you want me, take me here on this warm sand and let me hold you in my arms, even if we will regret it later.' She kissed him long and passionately, stroking his hair. 'Moments like this are reserved for the gods alone. But we are gods, for as long as this night lasts.'

2

ALEXANDER UNDRESSED BEFORE his assembled army and, as required by the ancient rite, ran three times around the tomb of Achilles. Hephaestion did the same thing around the tomb of Patroclus. Each time they completed a lap, more than forty thousand voices cried in unison: '*Alalalài!*'

'He certainly knows how to act the part!' exclaimed Callisthenes from their corner of the camp.

'You think so?' replied Ptolemy.

'There's no doubt about it. He doesn't believe in the myths and the legends any more than you or I do, but he behaves as though they were more real than reality itself. This is how he demonstrates to his men that dreams are possible.'

'It's as though you knew him like the back of your hand,' said Ptolemy, his voice full of sarcasm.

'I have learned to observe men, and not just nature.'

'In that case you should be aware that no one can ever claim to know Alexander. His actions are there for everyone to see, but they are not predictable, and neither is it always possible to understand their deeper significance. He believes and he doesn't believe at the same time, he is capable of great expressions of love and of uncontrollable rage . . . he is . . .'

'What?'

'Different. I first met him when I was six years old, and I still cannot say I truly know him.'

'Perhaps you're right. But now he has all his men believing he is Achilles reincarnate and that Hephaestion is Patroclus.'

'At this moment the two of them believe it as well. After all, wasn't it you who established, on the basis of your astronomy, that our invasion took place in the same month in which the Trojan War began, exactly one thousand years ago?'

Alexander in the meantime had dressed again and put his armour on. Hephaestion too got ready and they both mounted their horses. General Parmenion ordered the trumpets to be sounded and Ptolemy, in his turn, leaped on to his charger. 'I must join my division. Alexander is about to inspect the army.'

The trumpets resounded again, repeatedly, and the army lined up along the shore, each division with its own standards and insignias.

There were thirty-two thousand foot-soldiers in total. On the left-hand side were three thousand 'shieldsmen' and then seven thousand Greek allies, one tenth of the number which a hundred and fifty years previously had taken on the Persians at Plataea. They wore the traditional heavy armour of Greek frontline troops and sported massive Corinthian helmets protecting their faces completely, right down to the base of their necks, leaving only their eyes and their mouths exposed.

In the centre were the six battalions of the phalanx, the *pezhetairoi* – some ten thousand men. On the right-hand side, instead, were the auxiliary barbarians from the north

– five thousand Thracians and Triballians who had taken Alexander up on his offer, attracted by the money and the prospect of looting. They were brave men, capable of the most reckless of feats, indefatigable, and they were able to bear the cold, the hunger and the ordeals of battle. They were a frightful sight with their red, bristly hair, their long beards, their fair, freckled complexions and their bodies covered with tattoos.

Among these barbarians, the wildest and most primitive were the Agrianians of the Illyrian mountains: they had no Greek and an interpreter had to be called to communicate with them, but their unique talent was their ability to climb any rocky face using ropes made of plant fibres, hooks and grappling-irons. All the Thracians and the other auxiliaries from the north were equipped with helmets and leather corsets, small crescent-moon shields and long sabres that were used both with the point and the blade. In battle they were as ferocious as wild beasts and in hand-to-hand combat they had been known to bite lumps of flesh out of their opponents' bodies. Behind them, almost as a sort of barrier, came seven thousand Greek mercenaries – light and heavy infantry.

Out on the wings, detached from the infantry, was the heavy cavalry, the *hetairoi* – two thousand eight hundred of them in total. To these were added the same number of Thessalian horsemen and some four thousand auxiliaries, plus the five hundred special horsemen of the Vanguard, Alexander's squadron.

The King, astride Bucephalas, inspected his troops division by division, accompanied by his entourage. Eumenes was present as well, armed to the teeth and proudly sporting a breastplate of crushed flax, decorated and strengthened with polished plates of bronze, shining like mirrors. The secretary general's thoughts, however, as he passed before the multitude, were not at all grandiose – he was making mental notes of how much grain, how many vegetables, how much salted fish, smoked meat and wine would be required to keep all these men going, and how much money he would have to spend every day to purchase all those provisions. During the inspection he worked out how long the reserves they had brought with them would last.

Despite these worries, however, he still had some hope of being able to offer the King some suggestions for a successful expedition.

When they reached the head of the line-up, Alexander nodded to Parmenion and the general gave orders for them to set off. The long column began to move – the cavalry on the flanks two by two, the infantry in the middle. The direction was northerly, along the seashore.

The army slithered forward like a long snake and Alexander's helmet, crowned by two long white plumes, could be made out from far away.

Just at that moment Daunia looked out from the main entrance of the temple of Athena and stood there at the top of the steps. The young man who had loved her on the shore that fragrant spring night now looked as small as a child, his overly polished, overly resplendent armour glinting in the sun. He was no longer that young lover; that young lover no longer existed.

She felt a great emptiness open up within herself as she watched Alexander disappear towards the horizon. When he had left her sight completely, she dried her eyes with a rapid movement of her hand, entered the temple and closed the door behind her.

*

Eumenes had dispatched two messengers under escort – one to Lampsacus and the other to Cyzicus, two powerful Greek cities along the Straits: the former stood on the coast while the latter was on an island. The dispatch was a renewal of Alexander's offer of freedom and a treaty of alliance.

The King was enchanted by the landscape as it unfolded before him and at every bend along the coast he turned to Hephaestion to say, 'Look at that village . . . see that tree? . . . look at that statue . . .' Everything was new for him, everything was a source of wonder – the white villages on the hills, the sanctuaries of the Greek and the barbarian gods in the midst of the countryside, the fragrance of the apple blossom, the lucent green of the pomegranate trees.

With the exception of his exile in the snow-capped mountains of Illyria, this was his first journey out of Greece.

Behind him came Ptolemy and Perdiccas, while his other companions were all with their own soldiers. Lysimachus and Leonnatus were at the end of the long column, their role to lead two rearguard units, separated somewhat from the rest.

'Why are we travelling northwards?' asked Leonnatus.

'Alexander wants control of the Asian shore. This way no one will be able to enter or leave Pontus without our permission, and Athens, which relies upon grain imports that come through here, will have every reason to remain our ally. What's more, this way we isolate all the Persian provinces that overlook the Black Sea. It's a clever move.'

'That's true.'

They continued at a walk, the sun shining down as it climbed high in the sky. Then Leonnatus started up again. 'But there is one thing I don't understand.'

'We can't understand everything in life,' joked Lysimachus.

'You can say that again, but can you explain to me why everything's so calm? We land in daylight with forty thousand men, Alexander visits the temple of Ilium, completes the rite around Achilles's tomb, and there's been no one waiting for us. I mean, no Persians. Don't you think it's a bit strange?'

'Not in the least.'

'Why not?'

Lysimachus turned to look over his shoulder. 'See those two up there?' he asked, pointing to the silhouette of two horsemen proceeding along the ridge of the Troad mountain range. 'Those two have been following us since dawn and they were observing us all day yesterday – the countryside must be crawling with them.'

'In that case we'd better inform Alexander . . .'

'Don't worry. Alexander's perfectly aware of the situation and he knows that somewhere along the road the Persians are preparing a welcoming party for us.'

The march continued without any problems throughout the morning until the midday break. The only people to be seen were peasants in the fields, intent on their work, or groups of children running along the road, shouting, trying to attract attention.

Towards evening they set up camp not far from Abydos and Parmenion had them post guards all around, at a certain distance. He also sent light cavalry patrols out into the countryside so as to avoid surprise attacks.

As soon as Alexander's tent was pitched, the trumpet sounded for a council meeting and all the generals gathered around a table while supper was served. Callisthenes was there too, but Eumenes was absent and had left instructions for them to begin without him.

'Well, lads, this is much better than Thrace!' exclaimed Hephaestion. 'The weather's excellent, the people seem friendly, I've seen a fair number of pretty girls and boys and the Persians are keeping to themselves. It reminds me of Mieza, when Aristotle used to take us all out together into the woods to collect bugs.'

'Don't delude yourself,' replied Leonnatus. 'Lysimachus and I spotted two horsemen who followed us throughout the day and they certainly won't be far away now.'

Parmenion, with his old-general style, respectfully asked for permission to speak.

'There is no need for you to ask for permission to speak, Parmenion,' Alexander replied. 'You are the most experienced of us all here and we have much to learn from you.'

'Thank you,' said the old general. 'I only wanted to know what your intentions are for tomorrow and for the near future.'

'To push towards the interior, towards all the territory controlled by the Persians. At that point they will have no choice – they will have to face us in the open field and we will beat them.'

Parmenion said nothing.

'Don't you agree?'

'To a certain extent. I fought the Persians during the first campaign and I can assure you they are fearsome opponents. What's more, they can count on an excellent commander – Mcmnon of Rhodes.'

'A renegade Greek!' exclaimed Hephaestion.

'No. A professional soldier. A mercenary.'

'And isn't that the same thing?'

'It's not the same thing, Hephaestion. Some men fight many wars and ultimately find themselves emptied of all conviction and ideals, yet full of ability and experience. At that point in their lives they sell their sword for the best offer, but they remain men of honour and Memnon is one of those. He keeps to his word, whatever the cost. For these men their homeland becomes the word they give, and they maintain and respect it with absolute resolve. Memnon is a danger for us, so much the more so because he has his own troops with him – between ten and fifteen thousand mercenaries, all Greek, all well armed and formidable opponents on the open battlefield.'

'But we defeated the Thebans' Sacred Band,' said Seleucus.

'That doesn't count,' replied Parmenion. 'These are professional soldiers – they do nothing else but fight, and when they are not fighting, they are training to fight.'

'Parmenion is right,' said Alexander. 'Memnon is dangerous and his mercenary phalanx is equally so, especially if flanked by the Persian cavalry.'

At that moment Eumenes came in.

'The armour suits you,' Craterus laughed. 'You look like a general. It's a shame you're knock-kneed and your legs are so spindly and . . .'

At that point everyone burst out laughing, but Eumenes started reciting:

> 'I don't like an army commander who's tall, or goes
>   at a trot
> or one who has glamorous wavy hair, or trims his
>   beard a lot.
> A shortish sort of chap, who's bandy-looking round
>   the shins,
> He's my ideal, one full of guts, and steady on his
>   pins.'*

'Well said!' shouted Callisthenes. 'Archilochos is one of my favourite poets.'

'Let him speak,' Alexander shut them all up. 'Eumenes brings us news, and I hope it is good.'

'Good and bad news, my friend. You decide where I should begin.'

Alexander barely concealed his disappointment. 'Let's begin with the bad news. Good news is always easier to digest. Give him a chair.'

Eumenes sat down, somewhat stiffly because of the breastplate which prevented him from bending the upper half of his body. 'The inhabitants of Lampsacus have replied that they feel sufficiently free already and they

---

* Archilochos, fr. 114, translation by M. L. West.

have no desire to become involved with us in any way. In a word, they don't want us meddling in their affairs.'

Alexander's face had darkened and it was clear there was an explosion of temper on its way. Eumenes immediately started speaking again. 'There is good news, however, from Cyzicus. The city agrees and will join us. This really is good news because the wages of the Persians' mercenaries are paid in coin from Cyzicus. Silver staters, to be precise – like this one . . .' and he threw a splendid-looking coin on to the table which began rotating on itself like a spinning top until the hairy hand of Cleitus the Black came down to stop it with a short, sharp blow.

'And so?' asked the general as he flipped the coin across his fingers.

'If Cyzicus blocks the issue of coin for the Persian provinces,' explained Eumenes, 'the governments of these lands will soon find themselves in difficulty. They will have to tax themselves, or they will have to find other forms of payment, an expedient which the mercenaries will not appreciate. The same goes for their provisions, for the wages of their naval crews and all the rest.'

'But how did you manage that?' asked Craterus.

'I certainly didn't wait until we landed here in Asia before getting things moving,' replied the secretary. 'I've been negotiating with the city for some time now. Since . . .' and he bowed his head, '. . . since before King Philip's death.'

At those words a silence fell in the tent, as if the spirit of the great sovereign who had fallen to the dagger blows of an assassin at the height of his glory were suddenly with them.

'Good,' said Alexander. 'In any case this does not change our plans. Tomorrow we head for the interior – our mission to coax the lion out of his den.'

*

Throughout the known world, no one had such accurate, well-made maps as Memnon of Rhodes. It was said that these maps were the product of thousands of years of experience of the sailors of his island and the skills of a cartographer whose identity was a jealously guarded secret.

The Greek mercenary opened the map on the table, held down its corners with lamp-stands, took a pawn from a games set and placed it on a point between Dardania and Phrygia. 'Alexander, as I speak, is more or less here.'

The members of the Persian high command were standing around the table, all in battledress, with leggings and boots: Arsamenes, governor of Pamphylia, and Arsites of Phrygia, then Rheomithres, commander of the Bactrian cavalry, Rosakes and the supreme commander, the Satrap of Lydia and Ionia, Spithridates, a gigantic Iranian with olive-coloured skin and deep, dark eyes who was leading the meeting.

'What do you suggest?' he asked, in Greek.

Memnon looked up from the map. He was about forty, the hair above his temples slightly greying, his arms muscular, his beard tidy and neatly shaped with a razor, which made him look like one of those characters represented by Greek artists on relief work or on the decorations of their vases.

'What news do we have from Susa?' he asked.

'None for now. But we cannot expect any substantial reinforcements for the next few months – the distances involved are huge and the time required extremely long.'

'So we can only count on the forces we have now.'

'In essence, yes,' confirmed Spithridates.

'But there are more of them.'

'Not so many more.'

'In this situation that fact means a lot. The Macedonians are organized formidably for fighting, they're the best there is. In open battle they have defeated armies of all types and nationalities.'

'So?'

'Alexander is trying to provoke us, but I think it would be better to avoid any direct conflict. Here is my plan: we must deploy a great number of horseback reconnaissance troops who will keep us constantly informed of his movements, together with spies who will somehow discover his intentions. Then we will retreat before him, destroying everything in our wake, leaving not one grain of wheat or drop of drinkable water.

'Groups of light cavalry will then undertake continuous incursions against the sorties he will inevitably send out to look for food for his men and his animals. When our enemies are on their last legs, exhausted in their hunger and in their fatigue, then we will strike with all our strength, while a naval force will land an army in Macedonian territory.'

Spithridates studied Memnon's map in silence for a long time before rubbing his hand across his thick, curly beard. Then he turned and walked towards a balcony that overlooked the countryside.

The Vale of Zeleia was truly a natural wonder: from the garden surrounding the palace there came the slightly bitter fragrance of hawthorn flowers together with the sweeter, more delicate perfume of the jasmine and the lilies; the white canopies of the blossoming cherry and peach trees – plants worthy of gods which grew only in their *pairidaeza* – shone brightly in the spring sunshine.

He looked over to the woods which covered the mountains and the palaces and the gardens of the other Persian nobles gathered in the meeting and he imagined all those delights being torched by Memnon, that emerald sea being reduced to an expanse of black carbon and smoking ash. He turned suddenly.

'No!'

'But, my lord . . .' said Memnon in objection as he moved nearer. 'Have you fully considered all the features of my plan? I feel that . . .'

'It is out of the question, Commander,' the satrap cut him short. 'We cannot destroy our gardens, our fields and our palaces and turn tail. In the first place it is out of character, and then it would truly be a crime to inflict on ourselves greater damage than our enemy would ever inflict upon us. No. We will face him and we will chase him back to where he came from. This Alexander is nothing more than a pretentious little boy who must be taught a lesson.'

'Please bear in mind,' Memnon insisted, 'that my own home and my own property are in this area and that I am prepared to sacrifice everything for victory.'

'We do not doubt your honesty,' replied Spithridates. 'I am simply saying that your plan is not feasible. I repeat, we will fight and we will force the Macedonians to turn back.' He now spoke to the other generals: 'From this moment onwards all troops will be on permanent alert and you must call up every possible man capable of fighting under our flag. There is no more time left.'

Memnon shook his head, 'This is a mistake, and you will come to realize it, but I am afraid it will be too late when you do.'

'Do not be such a pessimist,' said the Persian. 'We will seek to face them from a position of advantage.'

'That is to say?'

Spithridates leaned over the table, putting his weight on his left arm, and began to explore the map with the tip of his right index finger. He stopped at a blue snake-like feature, indicating a river that flowed north towards the Propontis inland sea.

'I would say here.'

'On the Granicus?'

Spithridates nodded. 'Do you know the terrain, Commander?'

'Quite well.'

'I know it because I have been there hunting several times. The river, just here, has steep, clayey banks. It is difficult, if not impossible terrain for cavalry, and heavy infantry would also find it extremely heavy going. We will crush them on the Granicus, and that very evening you will all be invited back here, for a banquet in my palace at Zeleia, to celebrate our victory.'

3

DARKNESS HAD FALLEN when Memnon returned to his palace, a magnificent construction, eastern in style and located on the top of a hill. Its grounds were inhabited by wildlife of every imaginable type and contained an enormous estate with houses, livestock, wheatfields, vines, olives and fruit trees.

Memnon had lived for years among the Persians as a Persian, and he had married a Persian noblewoman, Barsine, daughter of the satrap Artabazos. She was a woman of incredible beauty – dark-skinned, with long black hair and a graceful, shapely figure, as lithe and beautiful as a highland gazelle.

Their two sons, one fifteen and one eleven years old, both spoke their father's and their mother's tongues fluently and had been brought up in both cultures. Like Persian boys they had been educated never to lie, for any reason whatsoever, and they practised archery and horsemanship; like Greek boys they observed the cult of courage and honour in battle, they knew the Homeric poems, the tragedies of Sophocles and Euripides and the theories of the Ionian philosophers. Like their mother they had olive complexions and their hair was black. But their muscular bodies and green eyes came from their father. The firstborn, Eteocles, bore a Greek name; the second, Phraates, a Persian one.

The villa stood at the centre of an Iranian garden, cultivated and looked after by Persian experts, with rare plants and animals including the wonderful Indian pea-cocks of Palimbothra, an almost legendary city on the Ganges. Within the garden there were Persian and Baby-lonian sculptures, ancient Hittite reliefs which Memnon had collected from an abandoned city on the highlands, splendid sets of Attic symposium pottery, bronzes from Corinth and far off Etruria, sculptures in Paros marble painted in bright colours.

On the walls were images created by the greatest painters of the day: Apelles, Zeuxis, Parrhasius, depicting not only hunting and battle scenes, but also mythological representations of the legendary adventures of the heroes.

Everything in that house was a mixture of different cultures, yet the impression received by visitors was of a singular, almost incomprehensible harmony.

Two servants came to meet their master, helped him take off his armour and led him to the bath chamber so that he might wash before supper. Barsine came to him with a cup of cool wine and sat down to keep him company.

'What news is there of the invasion?' she asked.

'Alexander is marching on towards the interior, prob-ably with the intention of provoking us into a head-on conflict.'

'They chose not to listen to you, and now the enemy is almost upon us.'

'No one believed the boy would ever dare take on so

much. They thought the wars in Greece would keep him busy for many years, depleting his resources – a completely mistaken view.'

'What type of man is he?' asked Barsine.

'It appears difficult to define his character: he is very young, very handsome, impulsive and passionate, but it seems that when danger rears its head he becomes as cool as ice, capable of judging the most delicate and intricate situations with incredible detachment.'

'Does he have no weak points?'

'He likes wine, he likes both boys and women, but it seems he has only one constant love – his friend Hephaestion, much more than a friend. They say they are lovers.'

'Is he married?'

'No. He has embarked on this invasion without leaving an heir to the throne of Macedon. It seems that before leaving he gave all his property away to his closest friends.'

Barsine gestured to the handmaids to leave them and she personally attended to her husband as he left the bath. She took a cloth of soft Ionian linen and wrapped it round his shoulders to dry his back. Memnon continued to tell her what he knew of his enemy.

'They say that one of these close friends asked him, "What are you keeping for yourself?" and he replied, "Hope." It's not easy to believe, but it is obvious that the young King has already become legendary. This is a problem – it's not easy to fight against a legend.'

'Does he really not have a woman?' asked Barsine.

A handmaid brought a damp cloth and another one helped Memnon dress for supper – a long chiton, down to his feet, blue in colour and embroidered in silver around the edges.

'Why are you so interested in him?'

'Because women are always a man's weak point.'

Memnon took his wife's arm and led her to the dining chamber, where the low tables were arranged in the Greek manner before the dining beds.

He sat down and a maidservant poured him some more cool wine from a magnificent Corinthian crater, two hundred years old, which sat on the central table.

Memnon indicated a tableau by Apelles hanging on the wall before them, depicting a highly erotic love scene between Ares, the god of war, and Aphrodite. 'Do you remember when Apelles came here to paint this?'

'Yes. I remember it well,' replied Barsine, who always stretched out to eat with her back to the painting because she had never got used to the Greeks' forwardness and the way they represented nudity.

'And do you remember the model who posed with him as Aphrodite?'

'Of course. She was stupendous – one of the most beautiful women I have ever seen, a worthy model for the goddess of love and beauty.'

'She was Alexander's Greek lover.'

'Really?'

'It's true. Her name is Pancaspe and when she disrobed in front of Alexander for the first time he was so taken by her that he called Apelles to paint her in the nude. But then he realized that the painter had fallen in love with her – such things happen between artists and their models. Do you know what he did? He gave Pancaspe to Apelles in return for the painting. Alexander never lets himself be shackled to anything, not even to love, I'm afraid. I tell you, he's a dangerous man.'

Barsine looked him in the eyes, 'And you? Have you let yourself be won over by love?'

Memnon returned her gaze. 'Love is the only opponent I accept defeat from.'

Their sons arrived to say goodnight before retiring and they kissed both father and mother.

'When can we come with you into battle, Father?' the eldest asked.

'There will be time,' replied Memnon. 'You must grow first.' And then, when they had moved farther off, he added, lowering his head to his chest, 'And you must decide which side you're on.'

Barsine remained silent for some time.

'What are you thinking of?' her husband asked.

'Of the next battle, of the dangers that lie waiting for you, of the anguish of waiting and looking out from the tower for some sign of the messenger who will bring me news of whether you're dead or alive.'

'This is my life, Barsine. I am a professional soldier.'

'I know, but knowing it doesn't help. When will it take place?'

'The clash with Alexander? Soon, even although I am against it in principle. Very soon.'

They finished supper with a sweet wine from Cyprus, then Memnon lifted his eyes to Apelles's painting on the wall in front of him. The god Ares was depicted there without his weapons, which lay on the ground, on the grass, and the goddess Aphrodite was sitting alongside, naked, holding his head in her lap while his hands lay on her thighs.

He turned to Barsine and took her by the hand as he said, 'Let's go to bed.'

4

PTOLEMY RETURNED FROM his reconnaissance patrol along the perimeter wall of the camp and headed towards the main guardhouse in order to ensure that the night watches were properly organized.

He saw there was still a light burning in Alexander's tent and walked towards it. Peritas dozed away in his kennel and did not even bother looking up. He walked past the guards and stuck his head in the tent as he asked, 'Any chance of a cup of wine for a thirsty old soldier?'

'I knew it was you as soon as your nose appeared,' Alexander joked. 'Come on, help yourself. I've already sent Leptine off to bed.'

Ptolemy poured himself a cup of wine from a jug and took a few sips. 'What are you reading?' he asked as he looked over the King's shoulder.

'Xenophon, *The March of the Ten Thousand.*'

'Ah, Xenophon. He's the one who manages to turn a retreat into something more glorious than the Trojan War.'

Alexander scribbled a note on a sheet, put his dagger on the scroll to keep his place, and lifted his head. 'It's actually an extraordinarily interesting book. Listen to this:

As soon as it came to be late in the afternoon, it was time for the enemy to withdraw. For in no instance did the barbarians encamp at a distance of less than sixty stadia from the Greek camp, out of fear that the Greeks might attack them during the night. For a Persian army at night is a sorry thing. Their horses are tethered, and usually hobbled also to prevent their running away if they get loose from the tether, and hence in case of any alarm a Persian has to put a bridle and other tack on his horse, and then has also to put on his own breastplate and mount his horse – and all these things are difficult at night and in the midst of confusion.'*

Ptolemy nodded, 'And do you think their army is really like that?'

'Why not? Every army has its own customs and is very much used to them.'

'So what have you been thinking about?'

'Our scouts tell me the Persians have left Zeleia and are moving westwards. This means they're coming towards us to block our way.'

'Everything would seem to suggest that.'

'Indeed. Listen to me now ... if you were their commander, where exactly would you choose to block us off?'

Ptolemy moved towards the board on which a map of Anatolia had been spread open. He took a lamp and passed it backwards and forwards from the coast towards

* Xenophon, *Anabasis* 3.4.34–5, translated by Carleton L. Brownson.

the interior. Then he stopped. 'There's this river . . . what's it called?'

'It's called the Granicus,' replied Alexander. 'They will probably lie in wait for us there.'

'And you are planning to cross the river in the dark and attack them on the opposite bank before dawn. Am I right?'

Alexander continued poring over Xenophon, 'I told you, this is a very interesting work. You ought to get yourself a copy.'

Ptolemy shook his head.

'Anything wrong?'

'Oh no, the plan is excellent. It's just that . . .'

'What?'

'Well . . . I don't know. After your dance around Achilles's tumulus and taking his weapons from the temple of Athena of Troy, I rather thought there might be a battle in the open field, in full daylight, ranks against ranks. What we might call a Homeric battle.'

'Oh, it will be Homeric,' replied Alexander. 'Why do you think I'm having Callisthenes follow us around? But for now I have no intention of risking the life of even a single man, unless I have to. And you will have to adopt the same line.'

'Don't worry.'

Ptolemy sat down to watch his King continue taking notes from the scroll there in front of him.

'Memnon will be a hard nut to crack,' he started again after a short while.

'I know. Parmenion has told me all about him.'

'And the Persian cavalry?'

'Our spears are longer, the shafts stronger.'

'Let's hope that will be enough.'

'The surprise factor and our will to win shall do the rest: at this stage we simply have no choice but to defeat them. Now, if you want my advice, go and get some rest. The trumpets will sound before dawn and we will march all day.'

'You want to be in position by tomorrow evening, is that right?'

'Exactly. We will hold our war council on the banks of the Granicus.'

'What about you? Are you not going to sleep?'

'There will be time for sleep . . . may the gods grant you a peaceful night, Ptolemy.'

'And you too, Alexander.'

Ptolemy went back to his tent, which had been pitched on a small rise on the land near the eastern wall of the field. He washed, changed and prepared himself for the night's rest. He gave one last look outside before lying down and saw that there was still light in just two tents – Alexander's and, far off across the field, Parmenion's.

*

The trumpets sounded before dawn as Alexander had ordered, but the cooks had already been on their feet for some time and had prepared breakfast – steaming pots of *maza*, semi-liquid oatmeal enriched with cheese. The officers instead had a type of flat bread, sheep's cheese and cow's milk.

At the second fanfare the King mounted his horse and took his place at the head of the army, near the eastern gate of the camp, accompanied by his personal guard and by Perdiccas, Craterus and Lysimachus. Behind him came the phalanx of the *pezhetairoi*, preceded by two units of light cavalry and followed by the Greek heavy infantry and the Thracian, Triballian and Agrianian auxiliaries, all flanked by two lines of heavy cavalry.

The sky was turning red in the east and the air was filling with the chirping of sparrows and the whistles of blackbirds. Flocks of wild doves rose from the nearby woods as the rhythmic noise of the march and the clanking of the weapons woke them from their slumber.

Phrygia lay there before Alexander, with its rolling landscapes covered with fir trees, small valleys crossed by clear-flowing streams along which grew rows of silver poplars and shimmering willows. The flocks and the herds came out to pasture, guided by their shepherds and watched over by the dogs; life seemed to be proceeding peacefully along its daily path as if the threatening sound of Alexander's army on the move might just blend in perfectly with the bleating of the sheep and the lowing of the cattle.

To the right and the left, in the valleys parallel to the army's forward movement, groups of scouts, without insignia, camouflaged, also moved forward. Their job was to keep Persian spies as far away as possible. But this was in fact a pointless precaution because any one of the shepherds or peasants might have been an enemy spy.

At the rear of the column, escorted by half a dozen Thessalian horses, came Callisthenes, together with Philotas and a mule with two panniers full of papyrus scrolls.

Every now and then, when they stopped, the historian pulled out a stool, took a wooden board and a scroll from the panniers, and sat down to write under the curious gaze of the soldiers.

News had soon got round that the official chronicler of the expedition was to be this bony young man with the knowing air, and everyone hoped to be immortalized in his words at some stage. On the other hand no one was bothered about the very ordinary stories of daily life recorded by Eumenes and the other officers who had the job of keeping the march diary, keeping a tally of the various stages of the expedition.

They stopped to eat around midday and then later, very close to the Granicus by that time, they stopped once more on direct orders from Alexander below a range of low hills, to wait for darkness to fall.

Shortly before sunset the King called the war council in his tent and presented his battle plan. Craterus was there as head of a division of heavy cavalry and Parmenion as leader of the *pezhetairoi* phalanx. Cleitus the Black was also present, together with all of Alexander's companions who made up his bodyguard and were in the cavalry: Ptolemy, Lysimachus, Seleucus, Hephaestion, Leonnatus, Perdiccas and even Eumenes, who continued to attend meetings in full military dress – breastplate, greaves and wide belt. He seemed to be enjoying playing the part.

'As soon as darkness falls,' began the King, 'an assault group of light infantry and auxiliaries will cross the river and move as close as possible to the Persian camp to keep them under observation. One scout will come back to let

us know how far away the river is, and should the barbarians change position for any reason during the night,
others will return to bring us news.

'We will light no fires and tomorrow morning the
battalion commanders and team leaders will give the
wake-up call without trumpets just before the end of
the fourth watch. If the coast is clear the cavalry will cross
the river first, line up on the opposite bank and when the
infantry has also crossed, they will all set off.

'This will be the crucial moment of our day,' he said,
looking around him. 'If I'm right, the Persians will still be
in their tents, or in any case they will not be lined up in
formation. At that stage, our distance from the enemy
front lines calculated, we will unleash our attack with a
cavalry charge that will wreak havoc in the barbarian
lines. Immediately afterwards, the phalanx will let fly with
the final hammer blow. The auxiliaries and the assault
units will do the rest.'

'Who will lead the cavalry?' asked Parmenion, who up
until that moment had listened on in silence.

'I will,' replied Alexander.

'I advise you against it, Sire. It is too dangerous. Let
Craterus do it – he was with me during the first expedition
into Asia and he is truly very good.'

'General Parmenion is right,' Seleucus intervened. 'This
is our first clash with the Persians, why should we risk
jeopardizing the King's safety?'

Alexander lifted his hand to mark the end of the
discussion, 'You saw me fight at Chaeronaea against the
Sacred Band and on the River Ister against the Thracians

and the Triballians – how can you imagine that I might behave otherwise now? I will lead the Vanguard personally and I will be the first Macedonian to come into contact with the enemy. My men must know that I will be facing the same dangers they face and that in this battle everything is at stake, including our lives. I have nothing else to tell you, for now. I will see you all at supper.'

No one had the courage to protest, but Eumenes, sitting alongside Parmenion, whispered in the old general's ear, 'I would put someone particularly experienced next to him, someone who has fought against the Persians and knows their techniques.'

'I had already thought about it,' the general reassured him. 'The Black will be at the King's side – everything will go well, you'll see.'

The council was brought to an end. They all left and went to their divisions to give the final briefing. Eumenes remained behind and approached Alexander. 'I wanted to say that your plan is excellent, but there is still one unknown factor, an important one.'

'Memnon's mercenaries.'

'Exactly. If they lock up into a square formation it'll be a hard job even for the cavalry.'

'I know. Our infantry might well find themselves in trouble, perhaps it'll come to hand-to-hand combat – swords and axes. But there is one other thing . . .'

Eumenes sat down, pulling his cloak over his knees, and the gesture reminded Alexander of his father, Philip, whenever he was losing his temper. But for Eumenes the gesture was different – simply the result of his feeling the cold in the cool evening; he wasn't used to wearing the short military chiton and had goose-bumps all over his legs.

The King took a papyrus scroll from his famous box, the one containing the edition of Homer's works which Aristotle had given him, and he unrolled it on the table. 'You know *The March of the Ten Thousand*, don't you?'

'Of course, it's studied in all the schools now. The prose is very readable and even youngsters can manage it without any difficulty.'

'Good, listen to this then. We are on the battlefield at Kunaxa, some seventy years ago, and Cyrus the Younger orders the commander Clearchus:

> . . . to lead his army against the enemy's centre, for the reason that the King was stationed there; "and if," he said, "we kill him there, our whole task is accomplished." '

'So you would like to kill the enemy commander with your own hands,' said Eumenes in a tone of complete disapproval.

'This is why I will lead the Vanguard. Then we will take care of Memnon's mercenaries.'

'I understand. And now I must take my leave because no matter what I say, you aren't going to pay any heed to my advice.'

'Exactly, Mr Secretary General,' laughed Alexander. 'But this doesn't mean that I love you any the less.'

'I am fond of you too, you stubborn old sod. May the gods protect you.'

'And may they protect you too, my friend.'

Eumenes left and went to his own tent, where he took off his armour, put something warm on and set about reading a manual of military tactics while he waited for suppertime to come around.

5

THE RIVER RAN FAST, its waters swollen by the melting snows on the Pontus mountains, and a light westerly wind stirred the leaves of the poplars which grew along the banks. The sides of the banks themselves were steep, clayey, sodden after the rains.

Alexander, Hephaestion, Seleucus and Perdiccas were all positioned on a small rise from which they could see both the course of the Granicus and a certain extent of the territory beyond the eastern bank.

'What do you think?' asked the King.

'The clay on the banks is very wet and slippery,' said Seleucus. 'If the barbarians take up position along the river they will let loose a rain of arrows and javelins and wipe out many of us before we reach the other side. As for those of us who do get across, our horses will sink up to their knees in the mud, many of them will be lamed and we will be at the total mercy of our enemies once more.'

'It is not an easy situation,' Perdiccas commented dryly.

'It's too early to begin to worry about it. Let's wait for the scouts to return.'

They waited in silence for some time, and the gurgling of the flowing water was drowned out only by the monotonous croaking of the frogs in the ditches nearby and the chirping of the crickets just beginning in the peaceful evening. At a certain point there came a call, like an owl.

'It's them,' said Hephaestion.

They heard the noise of men walking through the sodden clay and then the gurgling of the river around two dark figures who were fording it – two of their scouts from the shieldsmen battalion.

'Well?' asked Alexander impatiently. The two looked terrible – completely covered in red mud from head to toe.

'Sire,' said the first of them, 'the barbarians are three or four stadia from the Granicus, on a small hill which dominates the plain right up to the banks. They have a double row of sentries and four teams of archers patrolling the area between the camp and the banks of the river. It is extremely difficult to cross without being seen. What's more, there are bonfires burning all around among the guard units and the sentries are using the concave sides of their shields to project the light outwards.'

'Fine,' said Alexander. 'Go back and wait on the other bank. At the slightest movement or sign from the enemy camp, hurry back to this side and raise the alarm with the cavalry guard behind those poplars. I will be told almost instantly and I will decide what is the best thing to do. Go now, and make sure no one spots you.'

The two slid back down into the river and crossed it again in the waist-deep water. Alexander and his companions walked to their horses to ride back to camp.

'And if tomorrow we find them waiting for us on the

banks of the Granicus?' asked Perdiccas as he took his black horse by the reins.

Alexander ran his hand quickly through his hair, as he always did when he had a lot on his mind. 'In that case they will have to line up their infantry along the river. What sense is there in using the cavalry to hold a fixed position?'

'That's true,' agreed Perdiccas, increasingly laconic.

'So they will line up their infantry and we will send out the Thracian, Triballian and Agrianian assault troops, plus the shieldsmen covered by a thick rain of arrows and javelins let loose by the light infantry. If we manage to dislodge the barbarians from the bank, we'll push the Greek heavy infantry and the phalanx forward, while the cavalry will protect their flanks. Anyway, it's early yet to decide all this. Let us return now, supper will be ready soon.'

They went back to the camp and Alexander invited all the commanders to his tent, including the chiefs of the foreign auxiliaries, who felt very honoured.

During supper they all wore their weapons, as called for by the tense situation. The wine was served in the Greek manner, with three parts of water, meaning that they could approach the discussion with the necessary clarity of mind, and because drunken Agrianians and Triballians were dangerous.

The King briefed them with all the latest news regarding the situation and they all breathed a sigh of relief; at least their enemies were not yet in direct control of the river.

'Sire,' said Parmenion, 'the Black asks for the honour

of covering your right flank tomorrow. He fought in the front line during the last campaign against the Persians.'

'I fought alongside your father, King Philip, more than once,' added Cleitus.

'In that case you will be at my side,' said Alexander.

'Are there any other orders, Sire?' asked Parmenion.

'Yes. I've noticed we already have quite a following of women and merchants. I want them all out of the camp and kept under surveillance until the attack is over. And I want a detachment of light infantry ready for battle stationed on the banks of the Granicus all through the night. Naturally, these men will not fight tomorrow – they will be too tired.'

Supper finished in due time, the commanders retired for the night and Alexander did too. Leptine helped him take off his armour and his clothes and washed him, having already prepared his bath in a separate area of the royal tent.

'Is it true that you yourself will fight, my Lord?' she asked as she rubbed his shoulders with a sponge.

'These things do not concern you, Leptine. And if you eavesdrop again from behind the curtain, I will have you sent away.'

The girl looked down at her feet and stood in silence for a while. Then, when she realized that Alexander was not angry, she started again. 'Why does it not concern me?'

'Because nothing bad will happen to you should I ever fall in battle. You will have your freedom and sufficient income for you to live your life.'

Leptine stared at him intensely and sorrowfully. Her

chin trembled and her eyes brimmed with tears – she turned her head so that he wouldn't see.

But Alexander spotted the tears running down her cheeks. 'Why are you crying? I thought you would be happy.'

The girl swallowed her sobs and said, as soon as she was able, 'I am happy as long as I can be with you, my Lord. If I cannot be with you then there is no light nor breath nor life for me.'

The noises of the camp faded away. All they could hear were the calls of the guards shouting to one another through the darkness and the barking of the wild dogs scavenging for food. For a moment Alexander seemed to listen out, then he stood up and Leptine approached, ready to dry him.

'I will sleep fully dressed tonight,' said the King. He put on fresh clothes and chose the armour he would wear the following day: a helmet of bronze, laminated with silver and in the shape of a lion's head, its jaws wide open and adorned with two long heron feathers, an Athenian breastplate in crushed flax with a bronze heart-plate in the shape of a gorgon, a pair of bronze greaves so shiny they seemed to be gold, a sword-belt of red leather with the face of the goddess Athena at its centre.

'You will be easy to spot from a great distance,' said Leptine, her voice trembling.

'My men must see me and must know that I risk my own life before risking theirs. And go to sleep now, Leptine, I no longer need you.'

The girl left, her steps rapid and light. Alexander arranged his weapons on the stand near his bed and extinguished his lamp. His armour, his panoply could be made out in the darkness nonetheless – it was like the ghost of a warrior, waiting motionless for the first light of dawn to bring him back to life.

6

ALEXANDER WOKE UP WITH Peritas licking his face and he jumped to his feet to find two servants standing there before him, ready to help him put on his armour. Leptine brought his breakfast on a silver tray – Nestor's Cup, raw egg beaten with cheese, flour, honey and wine.

The King ate standing up while they laced up his breastplate and greaves, hung his sword belt across his shoulder and attached his scabbard, complete with sword.

'I don't want Bucephalas,' he said as he left. 'The river banks are too slippery and he would risk his legs. Bring me the Sarmatian bay.'

His attendants went to prepare the chosen horse and Alexander joined them in the centre of the camp, carrying his helmet under his left arm. Almost all the men were already lined up and there was constant movement from those running to take up position alongside their companions. Alexander mounted the steed and rode to inspect first the Thessalian and Macedonian cavalry squadrons, then the Greek infantry and the phalanx.

The horsemen of the Vanguard waited for him at the far end of the camp, near the eastern gate, perfectly lined up in five rows. In silence they lifted their javelins as the King passed by.

The Black took up position alongside Alexander when

the King lifted his arm to give the order to move off. There came the rumble of thousands of horses setting off, together with the muted clanking of weapons as the foot-soldiers began their march in the darkness.

At just a few stadia from the Granicus they heard the noise of horses galloping, and a patrol of four scouts suddenly came out of the darkness and stopped in front of Alexander.

'King,' said their leader, 'the barbarians have not yet moved and are encamped at some three stadia from the river, on a slight rise. On the banks there are only patrols of Median and Scythian scouts who have our side under observation. We cannot take them by surprise.'

'No, of course not,' said Alexander, 'but before their army covers the three stadia between them and the eastern bank, we will have crossed the ford and we will be on the other side. At that point most of our work is done.' He nodded to his bodyguard to move nearer. 'Tell all the divisional commanders to be ready to cross over to the other bank as soon as a suitable landing site is identified. At the sound of the trumpets we will rush towards the river and ford it as quickly as possible. The cavalry will go first.'

The guards moved off. Shortly afterwards the infantry stopped to let the two columns of horsemen on their flanks move forwards and line up before the Granicus. A pale light was just beginning to fill the sky to the east.

'They thought that we would have the sun in our eyes, but instead not even the moon will be bothering us,' said Alexander, indicating the bright crescent that was just setting to the south behind the hills of Phrygia.

He lifted his hand and guided his horse into the river, followed closely by the Black and by the entire Vanguard squadron. At the same time they heard a shout from the other bank, then ever louder calls culminating in the drawn-out, plaintive sound of a horn accompanied by other signals. The Median and Scythian scouts were sounding the alarm.

Alexander, who was already half-way across the ford, shouted, 'Trumpets!' and the trumpets sounded one single, sharp, piercing note, which sped like a bolt to the other side and mixed with the deeper sound of the horns so that the mountains echoed repeatedly with all the various signals.

The Granicus seemed to boil with foam as the King and his guards crossed it as quickly as they possibly could. A shout was heard and a Macedonian horseman, wounded, fell into the water. The Median and Scythian scouts were grouped together on the banks and were firing wildly into the approaching group without even taking aim. Others were hit in the neck, in the belly, in the chest. Alexander undid his shield from its bracket and spurred his bay horse forwards again. He had reached the other side!

'Forward!' he shouted. 'Forward! Trumpets!'

The sound of the trumpets became even sharper and more piercing and in response came the neighing of the steeds, excited by the confusion and the shouts of the horsemen kicking them on and even making use of the whip to urge them on against the strong pull of the current.

The second and third rows had crossed the centre of

the ford now, and the fourth, fifth and sixth were just entering the water. Alexander with his squadron were now climbing up the slippery bank. Behind them came the booming, rhythmic marching of the phalanx as they advanced in their regular lines in full battledress.

The enemy scouts, having run out of bolts, turned their mounts and spurred them on at full speed towards the field, from which came a terrible, confused din of weapons, while the indistinct shadows of soldiers ran everywhere in the darkness, torches in their hands, filling the air with calls and shouts in a hundred different languages.

Alexander had the Vanguard assume formation and took his place at its head, while two squadrons of the *hetairoi* and two of the Thessalian cavalry arranged themselves behind and on the flanks, in four rows, under orders from their own commanders. The Macedonians were led by Craterus and Perdiccas, the Thessalians by Prince Amyntas and the officers Oenomaos and Echekratides. The trumpeters waited for a signal from the King to start sounding the charge.

'Black,' called Alexander. 'Where are our foot-soldiers?'

Cleitus trotted over to the end of the line and looked out towards the river. 'They are scaling the banks now, Sire!'

'Then sound the trumpets! Forward!'

The trumpets sounded again and twelve thousand horses galloped off together, head to head, panting and neighing, their pace dictated by Alexander's massive Sarmatian bay.

In the meantime, on the other side, the Persian cavalry

was gathering together at full haste and with considerable confusion – those already lined up were waiting for a signal from their supreme commander, the satrap Spithridates.

Two scouts arrived at top speed. 'The Macedonians are launching an attack, Lord!' they shouted.

'Then follow me!' ordered Spithridates without any further delay. 'Let's send these *yauna* back where they came from, we will throw them back into the water as fish food! Forward! Forward!'

The horns sounded and the earth shook under the hammering gallop of the fiery Nysaean steeds. In the front line were the Medians and the Khorasmians with their big double-curved bows, while behind came the Oxians and the Kadusians with their long curved sabres, finally the Saka and the Drangians brandishing enormous scimitars.

As soon as the cavalry was under way, the heavy infantry of the Greek mercenaries, already in battle trim, followed at a march and in close formation.

'Mercenaries of Anatolia!' Memnon shouted to them, raising his spear. 'Your swords are sold! You have neither home nor homeland to which you may return! For you it is either death or glory. Remember there will be no mercy for us because even if we are Greek, we fight for the Great King of Persia. Men, our homeland is our honour, our spear is our daily bread. Fight for your lives – for our lives are the only thing left to us '*Alalalài!*'

And he set off, forwards, briskly at first and then at a run. His men responded: '*Alalalài!*'

They ran up behind him, maintaining the solid formation of their front line, a terrible din of iron and bronze clanging as each foot touched the ground.

Alexander saw the cloud of white dust at less than a stadium and shouted to a trumpeter – 'Sound the charge!' The trumpet sounded, unleashing all the fury of the Vanguard as it galloped into battle.

The horsemen lowered their spears and lent forwards, their left hands gripping the bridle and mane of their steeds, right up until the impact, up until the frightful, violent tangle of men and animals, of shouting and neighing that followed the first clash of the long shafts of ash and cornel wood and the deadly rain of Persian javelins.

Alexander spotted Spithridates off to the right, fighting furiously, his sword red with blood, covered on the left by the giant Rheomithres, and he spurred his horse in that direction. 'Fight, Barbarian! Fight against the King of Macedon, if you have the mettle!'

Spithridates spurred on his steed in his turn and let fly with his javelin. The point tore into the shoulder-piece of Alexander's breastplate, grazing the skin between his neck and his collarbone, but the King unsheathed his sword and galloped at full tilt towards Spithridates, crashing into him head on. The satrap, knocked off balance by the shock of the impact, had to grab wildly at his steed to avoid falling, exposing his flank in the process. Alexander wasted no time in sticking his blade into his opponent's armpit, but by this stage all the Persians were homing in on him. An arrow brought his horse to its knees and Alexander failed to duck in time to avoid Rheomithres's axe.

His shield only managed to deflect the blow in part, so that it hit his helmet, splitting the metal, cutting through the felt lining and reaching his scalp. Alexander was on the ground now, with his horse, and from the head wound the blood flowed copiously, covering his face.

Rheomithres raised the axe again, but the Black broke in just at that moment, shouting wildly and brandishing a heavy Illyrian sword which cut clean through the barbarian's arm with a single blow.

Rheomithres fell from his horse screaming and the blood spurted from the truncated limb, taking his life even before Alexander, on his feet once more, delivered the final blow.

Then the King leaped on to a steed that was running free on the field and threw himself into the reel of the battle again.

The Persians were utterly devastated by the deaths of their commanders and they started to fall back, while the impetus of the Vanguard was added to now by the considerable weight of the four squadrons of *hetairoi* and the Thessalian horsemen, led by Amyntas.

The Persian cavalry fought valiantly, but their ranks had been thrown into disarray not only by the Vanguard, which penetrated ever deeper now, but also by the lateral action of the light cavalry which struck their flanks in waves. These were Thracian and Triballian warriors, as ferocious as wild beasts, and they galloped along the flanks unleashing swarms of arrows and javelins, waiting for the right moment to launch themselves into hand-to-hand combat as soon as it was clear the enemy were exhausted and on their last legs.

Alexander's companions – Craterus, Philotas and Hephaestion, Leonnatus, Perdiccas, Ptolemy, Seleucus and Lysimachus – following their King's example, were all fighting in the front line and seeking direct combat with the enemy commanders, many of whom fell wounded or dead. Among them were many relatives of the Great King.

Then the Persian cavalry turned in retreat, chased by the *hetairoi*, the Thessalians and the very fast light cavalry of the Thracians and the Triballians, now wildly engaged in furious hand-to-hand fighting.

Now came the clash between the phalanx of the *pezhetairoi* and Memnon's mercenary infantry, who continued to advance compactly, shoulder to shoulder, protected by their large convex shields, their faces covered by light Corinthian sallets. The two armies called out: '*Alalalài!*' and rushed forward brandishing their weapons.

Memnon gave the signal and the Greek mercenaries let fly with their spears in a single swarm of iron-tipped shafts and then they unsheathed their swords and threw themselves into the battle before the phalanx had time to reorganize itself. Great blows were unleashed, right, left and centre, as they sought to cut through the shafts of the *sarissae* to open up a breach in the enemy front line.

Parmenion realized the danger they were in now, and he called up the savage Agrianians and directed them towards Memnon's flanks. The Greek mercenaries had to hold back to defend themselves.

The phalanx re-formed and the front line started throwing short spears again. Memnon's troops were completely surrounded now, even from behind, with the Macedonian cavalry approaching on its return from having chased the Persians. But they fought valiantly to the bitter end.

The sun now flooded the plain, illuminating the bodies which lay heaped one upon another. Alexander had Bucephalua brought to him, while the vets took care of his wounded bay, and he inspected his victorious troops. His face was red with blood from his head wound, his breastplate torn by Spithridates's javelin and his body covered with dust and sweat, but to his men he looked like a god. They beat their spears on their shields just like the day on which Philip had announced Alexander's birth to his troops and they all shouted: '*Aléxandre! Aléxandre! Aléxandre!*'

The King turned his gaze off to the far right of the line-up of the *pezhetairoi* and saw Parmenion there. The general was almost seventy years old now and he stood, fully armed, the marks of the battle he had just fought clearly on his body, his sword in his hand, just as solid as any of the young, twenty-year-old soldiers.

Alexander guided Bucephalas over to him, dismounted from his horse, and embraced the old general while his soldiers' cries rose up to the heavens.

7

THE TWO AGRIANIAN WARRIORS leaned over a group of bodies and started stripping them of their best weapons – bronze helmets, iron swords, greaves – which they then threw on to a nearby cart.

In the now fading evening light one of them suddenly spotted a gold bracelet in the shape of a serpent on the wrist of one of the dead bodies; he moved nearer, while his friend's back was turned, with the intention of keeping this small treasure for himself. But as he bent over to grab hold of it, a dagger came flashing out of the tangle of bodies and cut his throat from ear to ear in a single movement.

The man dropped to the ground in silence. His companion, intent on loading the weapons on to the cart, was making so much noise he did not even hear the sound of the body falling. When he turned round again he found himself alone in the twilight and started calling out for his friend, thinking that he had perhaps hidden himself away as some sort of joke.

'Come on . . . come out, stop being so stupid and give me a hand here with this stuff . . .' He didn't even manage to finish the sentence – the same weapon that had slit his friend's throat flew blade first into the space between his collarbone and his neck, plunging right up to the hilt.

The Agrianian fell to his knees and instinctively grabbed at the dagger, but he didn't have the strength to pull it free and he fell face first into the dirt.

Memnon got up then, freeing himself from the pile of bodies in which he had remained hidden up to that moment, and he swayed on his unsteady legs as he moved. He was in a bad state, consumed by fever and losing blood from a large wound on his left thigh.

He took a belt from one of the Agrianians and tied it tightly around his leg just below the groin, then he ripped a piece of chiton to use as a bandage, stemming the bleeding. When he had completed this makeshift dressing, he dragged himself as best he could under a tree, where he waited for night to fall.

He could hear the cries of joy from the Macedonian camp, muffled in the distance, and off to his left, some two stadia away, he could see the glow of the flames in the Persian camp, now completely ransacked by the enemy.

He cut a branch with his sword and set off at a limp, while out of the darkness came packs of wild dogs to feed from the limbs of the Great King's soldiers, their bodies already beginning to stiffen in death. He dragged himself on, gritting his teeth against the pain and against the tiredness that threatened to drag him down. As he moved forward he felt the wounded leg grow heavier and heavier, almost a dead weight.

Suddenly he saw a dark shadow there in front of him – a lost horse that was returning to the camp to look for its master and which in the darkness now did not know which way to turn. Memnon shuffled towards it slowly, calling gently and reassuringly, and carefully he stretched out his hand to take the bridle that hung from its neck.

He moved even closer, caressed it and then, with an almighty effort, dragged himself up on to its back and urged it on slowly with his heels. The steed set off at a walk and Memnon, holding on to its mane, guided it towards Zeleia, towards home. He almost fell off more than once during the night, exhausted as he was and having lost so much blood, but the thought of Barsine and his children kept him going, gave him the strength to continue right to the very last spark of energy.

In the first glow of dawn, as he was about to collapse altogether, he saw a group of men in the half-light, armed men cautiously skirting the edge of the wood. Then he heard a voice calling him: 'Commander, it is us.' They were four mercenaries from his personal guard, out searching for their leader. He barely recognized them as they moved closer, then he lost consciousness.

When he opened his eyes again he found himself surrounded by a patrol of Persian horsemen on a reconnaissance mission to see how far the enemy had penetrated.

'I am commander Memnon,' he said in their tongue, 'and I have survived the Battle of the Granicus together with these valiant friends. Take us home.'

The leader of the patrol jumped to the ground, moved nearer, and then signalled to his men to help him. They laid Memnon under the shade of a tree and gave him something to drink from a flask – his lips were cracked with fever, his body and his face dirty with dried blood, dust and sweat, his hair stuck to his forehead.

'He has lost a lot of blood,' said the eldest of his men.

'Have a cart brought here as quickly as possible,' the Persian officer ordered his soldiers, 'together with the Egyptian doctor, if he is still a guest of the nobleman Arsites. And send word to Commander Memnon's family that we have found him and he is alive.'

The man leaped on to his horse and was swiftly out of sight.

'What happened?' the officer asked the mercenaries. 'We have received conflicting reports.'

The men asked for water, drank and began to tell their tale. 'It was still dark when they crossed the river and they sent the cavalry against us. Spithridates was forced to counter-attack even though many of his men were simply not ready. We fought to the bitter end, but they overwhelmed us – at one stage we had the Macedonian phalanx in front of us and the cavalry behind us.'

'I have lost many of my men,' Memnon admitted, lowering his eyes. 'Battle-hardened veterans, valiant soldiers I was most fond of. These here with me are among the few I have left now. Alexander did not even give us a chance to negotiate a surrender – it was clear his men had orders to show no quarter. Our massacre was an example for all those Greeks who dare to oppose him.'

'And what do you think his plans are exactly?' asked the Persian officer.

'If we are to believe what he says, the liberation of the Greek cities of Asia, but I really don't think that's it at all. His army is a formidable machine, made ready for a much bigger undertaking.'

'What would that be?'

Memnon shook his head. 'I do not know.'

A deathly weariness filled his eyes, a grey pallor lay on his face, despite the fever. He trembled and his teeth chattered.

'Rest now,' said the officer, covering him with a cloak. 'Soon the physician will arrive and we will take you home.' Memnon, completely exhausted, closed his eyes and fell asleep – a tormented slumber, wracked by pain and nightmarish visions. When the Egyptian finally arrived, Memnon was delirious, shouting out nonsense, in the grip of frightful hallucinations.

The doctor had him laid out on the cart, washed his wound with vinegar and straight wine, sewed it up and bandaged the thigh with clean cloth. He also had him swallow a bitter drink that helped relieve the pain and induced a deeper, more restful sleep. It was then that the Persian officer gave the order for them to start off and the cart moved, creaking and swaying, drawn by a pair of mules.

They reached Zeleia in the dead of night. As soon as Barsine saw the convoy at the end of the roadway, she ran to meet them in tears; but the children, remembering all their father had taught them, stood in silence by the door while the soldiers carried Memnon bodily to his bed.

The whole house was illuminated and there were three Greek physicians in the antechamber waiting to examine the commander. The one who seemed to be the most expert of the three was also the oldest. He came from Adramyttion and his name was Ariston.

The Egyptian physician spoke only Persian and Barsine

had to interpret during the consultation, which took place at Memnon's bedside.

'When I arrived he had already lost a lot of blood and had spent the whole night on horseback. There are no bones broken, he passes water normally and his pulse is weak, but it is regular and this at least gives us ground for hope. How will you proceed?'

'Compresses of mallow on the wound and some drainage, if it becomes infected,' replied Ariston.

His Egyptian colleague nodded. 'I agree, but have him drink as much as possible. I'd give him some broth as well . . . it's good for the blood.'

When Barsine had finished translating his words, she led him to the door and put a bag of money in his hand. 'I am most grateful for all you have done for my husband – without you he might have died.'

The Egyptian accepted the payment with a bow, 'I have done very little, my Lady. He is as strong as a bull, believe me. He lay there all day hidden among the bodies, losing blood from that wound, and then survived the night in terrible pain – men of such temper are few and far between.'

'Will he live?' Barsine asked anxiously, and even the soldiers who looked on in silence had the same question in their eyes.

'I do not know. When a man's body receives such a serious wound the vital humours flow and carry with them his soul – this is why his life is in danger. No one knows exactly how much blood Memnon has lost and how much is left in his heart, but make sure he drinks as much as possible because even watered-down blood is better than no blood at all.'

He left, and Barsine returned to the room where the Greek doctors were busying themselves with their patient, preparing herbs and infusions and arranging their surgical instruments in case it proved necessary to drain the wound. The handmaids had undressed him and they cleaned his body and his face with cloths soaked in warm water perfumed with a mint essence.

The children, who up until that moment had stood there in silence, came closer and asked for news of their father.

'You may come to see him,' said one of the doctors, 'but do not bother him because he must rest.'

Eteocles, the eldest, was the first to move forward and looked at his father hoping he would open his eyes. Then, seeing there was no movement, he turned towards his brother and shook his head.

'Go to bed now,' said Barsine, trying to reassure them. 'Tomorrow your father will be better and you will be able to speak to him.'

The children kissed the hand that hung motionless from the bed and left with their tutor.

Before they reached their room, Eteocles turned towards Phraates and said, 'If my father dies I will find this Alexander wherever he may be and I will kill him. I swear I will.'

'I swear it too on our father's life,' repeated the younger brother.

Barsine watched over her husband all night, although

the three physicians took turns like guards on watch. Every now and then they changed the compresses of cold water on his forehead. Towards dawn Ariston examined the patient's leg and saw that it was swollen and reddened. He woke one of his assistants.

'We must apply leeches to relieve the pressure of the liquids inside. Go to my room and fetch all the necessary equipment.'

Barsine spoke. 'Forgive me, but during your consultation with the other doctor no one spoke of applying leeches. You spoke only of draining the wound if it became infected.'

'But my Lady, you must trust me. I am the doctor.'

'The Egyptian was Spithridates's personal physician and he has treated the Great King himself. I trust him as well, so please do not apply the leeches before I have sent for him.'

'But you really should not listen to that barbarian,' Ariston let slip.

'Remember that I too am a barbarian,' Barsine said, 'and I am telling you that you will not be putting those disgusting animals on my husband's skin if the Egyptian doctor is not in agreement.'

'If you put it like that, then I will take my services elsewhere,' said Ariston resentfully.

'Off you go then . . .' came a response in a voice that seemed to be from some place beyond life, '. . . off you go and fuck yourself.'

'Memnon!' Barsine shouted, turning towards the bed. Then she turned to Ariston. 'My husband is better now, you may leave us. Tomorrow I will have your payment sent to you.'

Ariston had no intention of having them repeat their orders and he called his assistants. On his way out he said to Barsine, 'I have warned you, however, without the leeches the pressure will become intolerable and . . .'

'I will take all responsibility, don't worry.'

When the Greeks had left, she sent a servant to call for the Egyptian physician, who arrived at full tilt in a carriage from the palace of the satrap Spithridates.

'What has happened, my Lady?' he asked as soon as he came out of the carriage.

'The *yauna* physicians wanted to use leeches, but I objected – I wanted to hear your opinion first. They have taken offence and have left.'

'You did the right thing, my Lady. The leeches would have worsened the situation. How is he now?'

'The fever is still high, but he is awake now and is speaking.'

'Take me to him.'

They entered Memnon's room and found him still awake – despite the pleas of the handmaids and the swearing of his men who had kept watch all night outside the door, he was trying to get out of bed.

'Put any weight on that leg and I will end up having to amputate it,' said the doctor. Memnon hesitated for a moment then lay down again, grumbling as he did so. Barsine uncovered his thigh for the examination and the Egyptian began inspecting it – it was swollen, irritated and evidently painful, but there were no obvious signs of infection as yet. Then he opened his bag and emptied the contents on the small table near the bed.

'What is this?' asked Barsine.

'It's a type of moss. I have seen Oxian soldiers treat their wounds with it and very often it results in rapid healing. I do not know how it works, but the important thing for a doctor is the cure, not his own convictions. I'm afraid that the mallow compresses on their own will not be enough.'

He moved over to Memnon and applied the moss, securing it in place with a bandage. 'If by tomorrow morning he has a terrible itching, almost unbearable, then that means he's on the mend. But don't let him scratch it, even if you have to tie his hands together. If he has more pain and it becomes more swollen, then you must call me because if that happens we must amputate. I have to go now – there are many wounded to take care of at Zeleia.'

The doctor's carriage, pulled by a pair of mules, moved off. Barsine allowed her husband's soldiers to see him for a short time before she climbed to the highest tower of the palace, where she had had a small shrine built. A priest awaited her there, praying intensely, his gaze fixed on the sacred flame.

Barsine knelt on the floor in silence, watching the tongues of flame dancing in the light breeze that came down from the mountains, and awaited the response. In the end the priest uttered these words: 'This is not the wound that will kill him.'

'Can you tell me no more?' asked the woman anxiously.

The priest again stared into the eyes of the flames that

gained strength now with the rising wind. 'For Memnon I see a great honour, but with this honour comes a grave danger. Stand by him, my Lady, and make sure his children stand by him too. They still have many things to learn from him.'

8

ALL THE SPOILS taken from the Persian camp and the weapons and armour stripped from the dead had been piled up in the centre of the Macedonian camp. Eumenes's men were busy taking the inventory.

Alexander arrived with Hephaestion and Seleucus and sat down on a stool close by the secretary general.

'How's your head?' asked Eumenes, indicating the large bandage, handiwork of Philip the physician.

'Not so bad,' replied Alexander, 'but I was lucky. If it hadn't been for the Black, I wouldn't be here today. As you can see, Eumenes,' he continued, pointing to the rich pile of loot, 'there's no longer any reason to worry about money. There's enough here to keep our men going for at least a month, and even to pay the mercenaries.'

'Don't you want to keep something for yourself?' asked Eumenes.

'No. But I'd like to have the purple cloth, the rugs and the drapes sent to my mother, and something for my sister as well ... those Persian clothes, for example. Cleopatra appreciates exotic things.'

'I'll take care of it,' said Eumenes, and he gave orders to the servants to prepare the selected items. 'Anything else?'

'Yes. Choose three hundred sets of armour, the finest

of the lot, and have them sent to Athens as an offering to the goddess Athena in the Parthenon. With a dedication.'

'A special dedication?'

'Of course. Please write: "From Alexander and the Greeks, with the sole exception of the Spartans, having stripped this armour from the barbarians of Asia."'

'A fine insult for the Spartans,' said Seleucus.

'No less than they inflicted on me by refusing to take part in my expedition,' replied the King. 'It won't be long before they realize that they are no more than a small, insignificant village. The world moves with Alexander.'

'I have arranged for Apelles and Lysippus to come here to depict you in poses on horseback,' said Eumenes. 'They should arrive somewhere along the coast in a few days' time – Assus or Abydos. In any case we'll know in good time so that you can pose for both the statue and the painting.'

'I'm not really concerned about that sort of thing,' said Alexander. 'What I do want is a monument to our men who fell in battle, something that has never been seen before, something that only Lysippus is capable of creating.'

'Soon we will have news of the effects of your victory on both our friends and our enemies,' said Seleucus. 'I am interested to know what the people of Lampsacus will have to say, the ones who didn't want to be liberated.'

'They will suddenly say that they are most grateful to you for their liberation,' laughed Hephaestion. 'The winner is always right, the loser is always wrong.'

'Has the letter for my mother been dispatched?' Alexander asked Eumenes.

'As soon as you gave it to me. At this point it will already be on the coast. With a favourable wind it will reach Macedonia in three days at the most.'

'Has there been any contact with the Persians?'

'None at all.'

'That is strange . . . I had my surgeons take care of their wounded and I had their dead buried with full honours.'

Eumenes raised an eyebrow.

'Are you trying to tell me something? Because if you are . . . by Zeus, speak!'

'That's exactly what the problem is.'

'I don't understand.'

'The Persians don't bury their dead.'

'What?'

'I didn't know either. One of the prisoners explained to me yesterday. The Persians consider the soil sacred and they consider fire sacred, while for them a corpse is simply refuse – to bury a corpse would contaminate the soil, and if they were to burn it as we do then it would contaminate fire, which for them is actually a god.'

'So . . . what happens?'

'They put the corpses up on plateaux or high up in towers in the mountains, where they are eaten by the birds and are slowly consumed by the elements. They call these buildings their "towers of silence".'

Alexander said nothing. He got up and started walking towards his tent.

Eumenes understood what sort of mood the King was in now and gestured to their companions not to detain him. 'He feels humiliated for not having understood the customs of a people he esteems and for having offended them, albeit involuntarily.'

It was only after sunset that Eumenes went to see the King after having had himself announced. Alexander had him enter the tent.

'General Parmenion has invited you to supper with all of us, if you wish to come.'

'Yes, tell him I'll be with you shortly.'

'You mustn't take it badly. You could never have known . . .' said Eumenes, seeing how despondent he still was.

'That is not the reason why. I was thinking . . .'

'About what?'

'About this custom of the Persians.'

'It seems to me it must be a rite they have preserved since the time when they were nomads.'

'This is the great thing about the rite – it is a custom of their ancestors and it has not been forgotten. My friend, should I ever fall in battle, perhaps I too would like to sleep for ever in a tower of silence.'

9

THE FOLLOWING DAY Alexander sent Parmenion to occupy Dascylium, the capital of Pontic Phrygia, a fine city on the sea with a great fortified palace. The general also had orders to take possession of Zeleia.

The Persian nobility had fled, taking with them only their most precious things. Parmenion interrogated the servants at Zeleia to discover where they had gone and to have news of Memnon, whose corpse had not been found on the battlefield.

'We have not seen him since then, my Lord,' said one of the palace administrators. 'Perhaps he was wounded and managed to drag himself far away from the site of the battle only to die later, hidden away somewhere. Perhaps his servants and his soldiers found him and buried him to make sure the dogs and the vultures did not get to him. But we have not seen him.'

Parmenion sent for Philotas, his son.

'I don't believe a word I've been told by these barbarians, but it is anyway likely that Memnon was wounded. Our information is that he had a villa here, where he lived like a Persian satrap. Have squadrons of light cavalry search the area – this Greek is the most dangerous of all our enemies. If he is alive, he will create many problems for us. Last night I saw the flashing of light signals up on the mountains – news of our victory is surely travelling far and wide and at great speed. The response will not be long in coming, and it certainly won't be with a message of welcome.'

'I will do everything I can, Father, and I will deliver him to you trussed up at your feet.'

Parmenion shook his head. 'You will do nothing of the sort. If you find him, treat him with respect: Memnon is the most valiant warrior east of the Straits.'

'But he is a mercenary.'

'And what does that mean? He is a man whose life has stripped him of all illusions and who now believes in his sword alone. For me this is reason enough to respect him.'

Philotas scoured the countryside stone by stone, searching the villas and the palaces, interrogating slaves, even resorting to torture, but he obtained nothing.

'Nothing,' he reported to his father a few days later. 'Nothing at all. It's as if he'd never existed.'

'Perhaps there is a way to root him out. Keep an eye on the doctors, especially the good ones, and find out where their work is – you might just find yourself at the bedside of an illustrious patient.'

'That's a good idea, Father. It's strange, but I had always thought of you as a soldier, as a man capable only of thinking up ingenious battle plans.'

'Winning a battle is never enough – the difficult part comes afterwards.'

'I will do as you have advised me.'

From that day onwards, Philotas began distributing money and cultivating friendships, especially among people of more humble station, and he was not long in learning who were the best physicians, and who was the best of them all – an Egyptian by the name of Snefru-en-Kaptah. He had attended to King Darius at Susa and had been the personal physician of Spithridates, the Satrap of Phrygia.

Philotas had a series of observation posts set up and one evening the Egyptian was spotted leaving his home by a small rear door, after which he climbed aboard a cart drawn by a mule and headed off into the country-side. Philotas, with a patrol of light cavalry, followed him at a safe distance and off the road. After a long ride in the dark, in the distance they spotted the lights of a fine dwelling – a palace with battlements, porticoes and balconies.

'This is it,' he announced to his men. 'Stand by.'

They dismounted and moved closer on foot, holding the animals by their bridles. But just as they were approaching the palace, they were welcomed on both flanks by a furious barking – a pack of ferocious Cappa-docian bulldogs was attacking them.

They had to use their spears to keep them at bay, but in the dark they could not take aim properly and to use bows and arrows was even more difficult so that they found themselves having to engage in close combat, using daggers. Some of the steeds, frightened terribly, bolted, neighing and kicking, into the night and the horsemen, when they finally got the upper hand over the pack that had attacked them, found the number of horses almost halved.

'We must continue all the same!' ordered Philotas in a fury.

They leaped on to their mounts, those who still had them, and rode to the courtyard of the palace, which was lit by lamps arranged all around the portico. There before them was a most beautiful woman, dressed in a Persian gown with long golden fringes.

'Who are you?' she asked in Greek. 'What do you want?'

'I am sorry, my Lady, but we are looking for a man who has sold his sword to the barbarians and we have reason to believe he is in this house, probably wounded. We followed his doctor.'

The woman was obviously shocked by these words and turned pale with rage, but she moved to one side to let them past. 'Come in and look anywhere you wish, but I beg you to behave appropriately in the women's quarters. If you fail to respect my wishes I will make sure your King is informed. I hear he is a man who cannot bear any abuse of power.'

'Did you hear that?' Philotas asked as he turned to face his men, covered in wounds and dirt from the dogs.

'I am sorry,' Barsine then added, as she realized exactly what a state they were in. 'If you had had yourselves announced, you could have avoided meeting the dogs. Unfortunately the area is rife with brigands and we have to take measures to protect ourselves. As for the physician, I will lead you to him immediately.'

Together with Philotas she entered the atrium and then started off along a long corridor, behind a handmaid who held a burning lamp.

They entered a room where a youth lay on a bed. Snefru-en-Kaptah was examining him.

'How is he?' asked Barsine.

'It is only indigestion. Have him drink this infusion three times a day and have him fast all day tomorrow. He will soon be fighting fit.'

'I must speak to the doctor alone,' said Philotas, 'with only my interpreter present.'

'As you wish,' Barsine agreed, and showed them both into a nearby room.

'We know that this is Memnon's home,' Philotas began as soon as the door was closed.

'Indeed, it is,' the Egyptian confirmed.

'We are looking for him.'

'In that case you must look elsewhere, because he is not here.'

'And where is he?'

'I do not know.'

'Have you treated him?'

'Yes. I treat all those who require my services.'

'You are of course aware that I can . . . *oblige* you to speak if I so choose.'

'Of course, but I will not be able to tell you any more than I already have. Do you think that a man like Memnon would ever tell his doctor where he was planning on going?'

'Was he wounded?'

'Yes.'

'Seriously?'

'Any wound can be a serious one. It depends on how it progresses.'

'I have no need of a medical lesson. I want to know what state Memnon was in the last time you saw him.'

'He was on the mend.'

'Thanks to your treatment.'

'And those of some Greek doctors, including a certain Ariston of Adramyttion, if I remember correctly.'

'Was he in any condition to ride?'

'I really have no idea. I know nothing of horses. And now, if you will excuse me, I have other patients who are waiting for me.'

Philotas could not think of anything else to ask the doctor and let him go. Back in the atrium he met up with his men, who in the meantime had searched the house.

'Well?'

'Nothing. There's no sign of him. If he has been here, he certainly left some time ago, or he is hidden somewhere we can't think of, unless . . .'

'Unless what?'

'Unless we set this place alight – if there are any rats hidden away they would have to come out at that stage, don't you think?'

Barsine bit her lip, but she said nothing. She simply lowered her eyes so as not to meet the gaze of her enemies.

Philotas shook his head in disappointment. 'Let's just leave it and clear off – there's nothing here of any interest to us.' They left, and shortly afterwards the galloping of their horses faded into the distance, followed by the barking of the dogs. When they were three stadia away, Philotas pulled on the reins of his mount.

'Blast! I bet right now as I speak he's crawling out of

some hole and he'll be speaking peacefully with his wife. A beautiful woman . . . beautiful, by Zeus!'

'I don't understand why we didn't grab her and . . .' said one of his men, a Thracian from Salmydessus.

'Because she's too rich for your palate and if Alexander were ever to find out he'd cut your balls off and give them to his dog for supper. Indulge yourself with the camp whores if you really don't know where to put it. Let's go now, we've been riding around for too long.'

At that very moment, over on the other side of the valley, Memnon was being transported towards another refuge on a stretcher suspended between two mules, one behind and one in front.

Before crossing through the pass that led to the Vale of Ephesus and the city of Azira, he asked the mule driver who was leading the first animal by its halter to stop. Memnon sat up and turned his head to look back at the lights of his home. He could still smell the perfume of Barsine's last embrace.

10

THE ARMY MOVED SOUTHWARDS with the wagon and
mule trains, in the direction of Mount Ida and the Gulf
of Adramyttion. There was no longer any reason to stay
in the north because the capital of the satrapy of Phrygia
had been occupied and was held by a Macedonian
garrison.

Parmenion had returned to assume deputy command
of the army while Alexander retained control of all
decisions regarding strategy.

'We will move south along the coast,' he announced
one evening during a war council. 'We have taken the
capital of Phrygia, now we will take the capital of Lydia.'

'Sardis,' Callisthenes said, 'the mythical capital of Midas
and Croesus.'

'It's difficult to believe,' said Leonnatus. 'Remember
the tales old Leonidas used to tell us? And now we're
going to see those very places.'

'Indeed,' confirmed Callisthenes, 'we'll see the Hermus,
on whose banks Croesus was defeated by the Persians
almost two hundred years ago. And we'll see the Pactolus
with its gold-laden sands, which gave birth to the legend
of Midas. And the tombs where the Kings of Lydia lie.'

'Do you think there will be any real money to be had
in those cities?' asked Eumenes.

'All you think about is money!' exclaimed Seleucus. 'Anyway, I suppose you're right.'

'Of course I'm right. Do you have any idea how much our Greek allies' fleet costs us? Any idea at all?'

'No,' replied Lysimachus, 'we have no idea, Mr Secretary General – you're here to know these things.'

'It costs us one hundred and sixty talents per day. That's one hundred and sixty. That means that our income from the Granicus and Dascylium will be enough for a couple of weeks if things go well.'

'Listen,' said Alexander, 'we're now heading for Sardis and I don't think we'll meet with much resistance. Then we will go on to occupy what's left of the coast as far as the border with Lycia, as far as Xanthus. At that stage we will have liberated all the Greek cities of Asia. And all this will be achieved before the end of the summer.'

'Magnificent!' said Ptolemy. 'And then?'

'We certainly won't be turning back home!' exclaimed Hephaestion. 'I'm just beginning to enjoy myself.'

'There is no guarantee it will be so simple,' replied Alexander. 'Up to now all we have done is dent slightly the Persian defences and it is almost certain that Memnon is still alive. And then we are not even sure that all of the Greek cities will open their gates to us.'

*

They marched for several days along promontories and bays of truly enchanting beauty – beaches shaded by gigantic pines and a succession of islands of all sizes that followed the coastline like a parade. Then they came to the banks of the Hermus, a large river with clear water that flowed over a bed of clean gravel.

The satrap of Lydia was a reasonable man by the name of Mitrites, and he knew he had no choice but to send emissaries to Alexander, offering him the city's submission. He then accompanied him personally to visit the stronghold with its triple walls, its buttresses and its trenches.

'It was from here that the "march of the ten thousand" set off,' said Alexander, as he looked out over the plain and the wind ruffled his hair and bent the willows and the ash trees.

Callisthenes accompanied him at a slight distance, taking notes on a slate. 'It's true,' he said. 'And it is here that Prince Cyrus the Younger lived, then satrap of Lydia.'

'And it is from here too, in a certain sense, that our expedition begins. Except that we will not take the same route. Tomorrow we go to Ephesus.'

And Ephesus also surrendered with no use of force. The garrison of Greek mercenaries had already left, and when Alexander established himself in the city the democrats who had been chased away came back and instigated a real manhunt. They led the people in attacks on the houses of the rich, on the nobles who up until that time had been allies of the Persian governor.

Some of these nobles sought refuge in the temples and they were dragged out and stoned to death – all Ephesus was in shock from the turmoil. Alexander sent the shieldsmen infantry out into the streets to re-establish order, guaranteed that democracy would be reintroduced and imposed a special tax on the rich for the reconstruction of the grand sanctuary of Artemis, which had been destroyed by fire years previously.

'Do you know what they say about the fire here?' Callisthenes asked him as they inspected the ruins of the enormous temple. 'They say that the goddess couldn't put the flames out because she was busy with your birth. Indeed, the fire took place twenty-one years ago, on the very day you were born.'

'I want it to rise again,' said Alexander. 'I want rows of gigantic columns, as thick as a wood, to support the ceiling and I want the best sculptors to embellish it and the best painters to decorate the interior.'

'It's a fine plan. You should start talking to Lysippus about it.'

'Has he arrived?' asked the King, his face lighting up.

'Yes, last night, and he cannot wait to see you.'

'Lysippus, gods in heaven! Those hands, that gaze . . . I have never seen such creative power burning in any man's eye. When he looks at you you can feel that he is in touch with your soul, that he is about to create another man . . . in clay, in bronze, in wax, it matters not – he is creating a man just as if he were god.'

'God?'

'Yes.'

'Which god?'

'The god that is in all the gods and in all men, but which only a few are able to see and to hear.'

The authorities of the city – the democratic leaders who years previously had taken up power under Philip's rule, had later been expelled by the Persians and were now returning with Alexander's arrival – could not wait to show Alexander the wonders of Ephesus.

The town stretched along a gentle incline towards the sea and towards the huge bay into which the Cayster river flowed. The port was teeming with vessels unloading all sorts of wares and loading up the cloth, spices and perfumes from the Asian interior destined to be sold in far-off places, in the depths of the Adriatic gulf, in the islands of the Tyrrhenian, in the land of the Etruscans and the Iberians. The buzz of all this feverish activity rose up to the city, mixed with the shouts of the slave merchants auctioning strong men and beautiful girls who had been led to this fate by a sad destiny.

The roads were flanked by porticoes on to which the richer and more sumptuous dwellings faced, while the sanctuaries of the gods were surrounded by the stalls of travelling merchants who offered passers-by amulets for good luck and for protection against curses, relics and pictures of Apollo and his virgin sister Artemis with her ivory countenance.

The blood from the tumults had already been washed from the roads and the grief of the relatives of the dead had been locked away in their homes. In the city there was only rejoicing and celebration – the people lined up to see Alexander and waved olive branches, while the young maids spread rose-petals as he passed by or threw them from the balconies of the houses, filling the air with a wild riot of colour and perfume.

Then they came to a magnificent palace, its atrium supported by marble columns capped with Ionian capitals, profiled in gold and painted blue, once the residence of one of the nobles who had paid in blood for his friendship with the Persians. It was now to be the dwelling of the young god who had descended from the slopes of Olympus to the edge of the immensity of Asia.

Lysippus was standing waiting for him in the antechamber. As soon as the sculptor saw Alexander, he came forward and embraced him, holding him close with those big, powerful hands.

'My good friend!' exclaimed Alexander as he returned Lysippus's embrace.

'My King!' replied Lysippus, his eyes brimming with tears.

'Have you washed? Have you eaten? Have they given you clean clothes?'

'I'm fine, please do not worry. My only wish is to look at you again – looking at your portraits isn't the same thing. Is it true that you will pose for me?'

'Yes, but I also have other plans. I want a monument such as no one has ever seen before. Sit down.'

'Tell me,' said Lysippus while the servants prepared more seats for dignitaries and for Alexander's friends.

'Are you hungry? Will you eat with us?'

'With pleasure,' replied the great sculptor.

The servants brought the tables and arranged them in front of each of the guests and brought the speciality of the city – grilled fish seasoned with rosemary and salted olives, pulses, greens and bread fresh from the oven.

'Well,' began the King while everyone helped themselves, 'I want a monument to commemorate the twenty-five *hetairoi* of my Vanguard who fell during the first attack against the Persian cavalry. I had their portraits drawn before putting them on the funeral pyre so that we can produce faithful likenesses. You must depict them in all the fury of the charge – as if we could almost hear the thunder of their galloping, the snorting of the horses. The only thing missing will be the breath of true life, a power which the gods as of yet have not granted you.'

He lowered his head, while a veil of sadness came down across his face in the midst of all that cheer, in the midst of the cups of wine and the plates full of wonderfully aromatic dishes.

'Lysippus, my friend . . . those lads are ashes now, but you must capture their living souls, gather them from the wind before they are lost completely and meld them into the bronze, render them eternal!'

He had stood up and he walked now towards a window that gave out over the bay, shimmering under the midday sun. Everyone was eating, drinking, joking, warmed by the weather and the wine. Lysippus followed him.

'Twenty-six equestrian statues . . . Alexander's troop at the Granicus. It will be a tangle of hooves and muscled backs, of gaping mouths shouting war cries, of arms brandishing swords and spears in anger. Do you understand, Lysippus? Do you understand what I'm trying to explain?

'The monument will stand in Macedonia and will remain for eternity to celebrate those young men who gave their lives for our country, rejecting a dull, ordinary existence, lacking in all glory.

'I want you to pour into the molten bronze your very own vital energy, I want your art to be a vehicle for the greatest miracle the world has ever witnessed. Those who pass in front of the monument must tremble with admiration and awe, as if the horsemen were actually about to attack, as if their mouths were about to utter the cry that goes beyond death, beyond the mists of Hades from which no one has ever returned.'

Lysippus looked at Alexander in silent astonishment, his huge, calloused sculptor's hands hanging motionless, apparently lifeless, by his side.

Alexander took them and held them tight. 'These hands can achieve this miracle, I know. There is no challenge that you cannot meet, as long as you want to. You are like me, Lysippus, and it is for this reason that no other sculptor will ever model my statue. Do you know what Aristotle said the day you finished my first statue in our retreat in Mieza? He said, "If god exists, he has Lysippus's hands." Will you cast my fallen companions in bronze? Will you do it?'

'I will do it, Alexander, and the result will astound the world. I promise you.'

Alexander nodded and stared at him with his eyes full of affection and admiration.

'Come with me now,' he said and took Lysippus by the arm. 'Have something to eat.'

11

APELLES ARRIVED THE FOLLOWING afternoon, accompanied by a grand entourage of slaves and fine-looking women and young men. He was extremely elegant, though slightly eccentric with the amber and lapis lazuli pendants he wore round his neck and his brightly coloured clothes. Rumour had it that Theophrastus had written a small satirical booklet with the title *Charakteres* and that Apelles had been the inspiration for the section on the exhibitionist.

Alexander received him in his private apartments together with the beautiful Pancaspe, who still dressed in a young girl's peplum, the only way for her to display her splendid shoulders and cleavage.

'You look in fine shape, Apelles, and I am glad that Pancaspe's splendour is still a fount of inspiration for you. Few are those artists who enjoy the privilege of having such a muse.'

Pancaspe blushed deep red and moved closer to kiss Alexander's hand, but he simply opened his arms and embraced her.

'Your arms are still as strong as ever, Sire,' she whispered in his ear, in a tone of voice that would have reawakened the sexual drive of an old man who had been given up as dead three days previously.

'And I have other things which are no less strong, in case you had forgotten,' he murmured in reply.

Apelles coughed in slight embarrassment and said, 'Sire, this painting must be a masterpiece that will last through the centuries. Or rather, these paintings, because I would like to paint two of them.'

'Two?' asked Alexander.

'If you agree, of course.'

'Let us hear about it.'

'The first will depict you standing, poised to let loose a lightning bolt, like Zeus. And next to you will be an eagle, one of the symbols of the Argead dynasty.'

The King looked doubtful and shook his head.

'Sire, I must emphasize that both Parmenion and Eumenes agree with me on the fact that you should appear in this pose, especially because of its possible effect on your Asian subjects.'

'If they say so . . . and the other painting?'

'The other one will depict you astride Bucephalas, spear in hand, about to charge. It will be a memorable work, I can assure you.'

Pancaspe giggled.

'What's wrong with you?' asked Apelles, evidently irritated.

'I've had an idea for a third painting,' she replied.

'And what might that be?' asked Alexander. 'Aren't two enough? I can't spend the rest of my life posing for Apelles.'

'But you wouldn't be alone in this one,' explained Pancaspe with an even cheekier giggle. 'I'd thought of a painting with two figures – King Alexander depicted as the god Ares resting after battle, his weapons spread around him on a fine meadow, and I might be Aphrodite, attending to his pleasures. You know, a bit like the one you did at that Greek general's house . . . what was his name?'

Apelles's face suddenly drained of colour as he furtively elbowed Pancaspe. 'We must go now, the King doesn't have time for all these paintings. Two are more than enough, is that not so, Sire?'

'Exactly, my friend, that's exactly right. And now I must go; Eumenes has organized a full day for me. I will pose for you before supper. You may choose the subject you wish to begin with. If it is to be the equestrian pose, have the wooden horse prepared – I doubt Bucephalas will have the necessary patience for the portrait, not even for the great Apelles.'

The painter exited with a bow, dragging his reluctant model behind him, telling her off as they went down the corridor.

Immediately afterwards Eumenes introduced some new visitors – ten or so tribal chiefs from the interior who had heard about the arrival of the new master and had come to pledge their allegiance.

Alexander stood and walked towards them, shaking hands warmly with all of them.

'What is their petition?' he asked the interpreter.

'They wish to know what they must do.'

'Nothing.'

'Nothing?' replied the interpreter in amazement.

'They may return to their homes and live in peace as they did before my arrival.'

The one who seemed to be the leader of the delegation murmured something in the interpreter's ear.

'What did he say?'

'He's asking about the taxes.'

'Oh, the taxes . . .' Eumenes piped up. '. . . Well, they will remain exactly as they were because we too have our expenditure and . . .'

'Eumenes, please,' Alexander interrupted him, 'there's really no need to go into detail.'

The tribal chiefs conferred and declared themselves very happy with the situation. They wished the powerful new chief all the best and thanked him for his benevolence.

'Ask them if they wish to stay for supper,' said Alexander.

The interpreter did his job and the chiefs again conferred.

'Well then?'

'They are honoured by the invitation, Sire, but they say that the road is long and they are needed at home to milk the livestock, to help the mares give birth and . . .'

'I see . . .' said Eumenes, cutting the interpreter short, 'urgent affairs of state.'

'Thank them for their visit,' concluded Alexander, 'and remember to give them tokens of our hospitality.'

'What kind of tokens?'

'I don't know . . . weapons, clothes . . . whatever you like, but don't send them away empty-handed. These are old-fashioned people who still appreciate good manners. And in their own homes they are kings . . . do not forget this fact.'

Supper was served after sunset, when Alexander had finished his first session posing for Apelles, astride the wooden horse. The grand master, obviously, had decided to begin with the most difficult subject.

'And tomorrow I will go to the stables and have Bucephalas brought out – he too must pose for me,' said the painter as he threw a contemptuous glance at the padded wooden mock-up which Eumenes had managed to have prepared in a rush with the help of a craftsman from the theatre.

'In that case I advise you to pay a visit to my cook and collect a few of his honey-flavoured biscuits,' said Alexander. 'Bucephalas is partial to them and they will certainly help you make friends with him.'

An orderly came to announce that supper was served. Apelles was just completing his preparatory sketch of the figure. Alexander dismounted and came closer to the painter. 'May I look?'

'I cannot say no, Sire, but no artist is ever keen on showing an unfinished work.'

The King took one glance at the large tableau and his mood changed suddenly. The master painter had used charcoal to trace the basic lines of the image, rapid, whirlwind strokes, slowing down only occasionally to refine a few details – eyes, some locks of hair, hands, Bucephalas's dilated nostrils, his hooves drumming on the ground . . .

Apelles furtively checked the King's reactions.

'Remember, it is as yet unfinished, Sire, it is only a sketch. It will flesh out when colour is added and . . .'

Alexander lifted his hand to interrupt. 'It is already a

masterpiece, Apelles. This is an example of your best work – anyone can imagine the rest.'

Together they went to the banquet room where the dignitaries of the city were waiting for them, with the heads of the sacerdotal colleges and the King's companions. Alexander had given orders not to overdo it with the banquet because he did not want the Ephesines to get the wrong idea about him and his friends. The 'companions' the Macedonians had brought with them limited their activities to playing musical instruments, and the wine was served in the Greek manner – one part wine and three parts water.

Apelles and Lysippus, whose expertise and fame were recognized by all, were at the centre of conversation.

'I heard a really good one recently!' said Callisthenes, turning to Apelles. 'The one about the portrait you made of King Philip.'

'You did?' replied Apelles. 'Do tell me about it because right now I cannot remember it at all.'

Everyone started laughing.

'Well,' Callisthenes said, 'I'll tell it just as it was told to me. Now then, King Philip sent for you because he wanted a portrait to hang in the sanctuary at Delphi, but he said, "Make me a bit more handsome . . . what I mean is, be sure to get me from my good side, without the missing eye, make me a bit taller, my hair a bit blacker, without pushing it too much of course, you understand." '

'It's as if he were back here with us,' laughed Eumenes, and then, imitating Philip's deep voice, he said, ' "I don't know, I call this great painter and then I have to tell him how to do everything?" '

'Ah! Now I remember,' said Apelles, laughing heartily. 'That's exactly what he said.'

'Tell the rest of the story then!' Callisthenes said.

'No, no,' the painter replied, 'I'm enjoying myself too much listening to you.'

'If you put it like that. Well then, the master painter finally completes his painting and he has it brought out into the courtyard in the full light so that his illustrious client can admire it. Whoever has been to Delphi will have seen it – beautiful, splendid! The King is depicted wearing his gold crown, his red cloak and sceptre, he almost seems to be the image of himself. "Do you like it, Sire?" Apelles asks him. Philip looks at it first from one side and then from the other – he doesn't seem to be sure. "Do you want to know what I think?" he asks. "Of course, Sire," says Apelles. "Well . . . in my opinion it doesn't really look like me."'

'That's right, that's it!' said Apelles, laughing ever more heartily. 'The fact is that by making his hair blacker, his beard neater, his complexion rosier, in the end it really didn't look like him at all.'

'So?' Eumenes asked.

'This is the good bit,' Callisthenes started again, 'if it's a true story. Anyway, because the portrait was in the courtyard so that it could be admired in full light, at that moment one of the stable boys passed by, leading the King's horse by the bridle. The animal, as it passed in front of the painting, began swishing its tail, shaking its head and neighing noisily, to the astonishment of all those present. Apelles looked first at the King, then at the horse, and then at the painting and in the end said, "Sire, may

I now tell you what I think?" "By Zeus, of course," the King replied. "I'm sorry to have to tell you, but I am afraid your horse knows more about painting than you do." '

'That's just what I told him,' laughed Apelles. 'That's exactly what happened.'

'And what did he do?' asked Hephaestion.

'The King? He shrugged his shoulders and said, 'Ah! You're always right. We'll pay you for it just the same. Now that you've done it, I might as well keep it.'

Everybody applauded, and Eumenes confirmed that Apelles had indeed been paid for the painting which everyone praised, even those who had never seen it.

Apelles now felt himself to be truly at the centre of everyone's attention and he continued to make the most of it, like a consummate theatrical actor.

Alexander made his excuses, saying that the early rise that awaited him the following morning meant he had to retire. He was due to inspect the marine fortifications and he left the others to continue the evening with more wine, less watered down now, and new 'companions', a trifle more daring than the previous ones.

When he entered his apartments he found Leptine waiting for him, holding a lamp burning with a warm light, but the girl herself was obviously annoyed about something. Alexander looked at her while she turned her back to lead him with the light through into the bedchamber and he simply couldn't understand why she was so sullen, but he asked no questions.

When the door of his bedchamber was opened, however, he understood everything. Pancaspe lay stretched out on his bed, naked and in a pose reminiscent of some mythical heroine – Danaë, perhaps, waiting for the golden rain, or Leda waiting for the swan, he was not really sure which.

The girl stood up, moved towards Alexander and proceeded to undress him, then she knelt down on the rug before him and started kissing his thighs and his belly.

'Your ancestor Achilles's weak point was his heel,' she whispered as she lifted her eyes, subtly made up, to his face. 'As for your weak point ... let's see if I still remember.'

Alexander caressed her hair and smiled – she had spent so much time with Apelles she found it impossible to speak of anything without making some reference to mythology.

12

ALEXANDER LEFT EPHESUS ROUGHLY halfway through spring, his plan being to move on to Miletus. Lysippus, the King's project vivid in his mind, set off towards Macedonia with written orders for the regent – Alexander asked Antipater to make sure the sculptor had everything he needed for the creation of the gigantic work.

His first port of call was Athens, where he met Aristotle, who now held regular lessons in his Academy. The philosopher received Lysippus in a private room and had chilled wine served.

'Our King has asked me to send his greetings and to pay homage to you, and to let you know that as soon as he is able, he will write you a long letter.'

'I thank you. Echoes of his feats have not been slow in reaching us here in Athens. The three hundred sets of armour he sent to the Acropolis have attracted thousands of sightseers and word of the dedicatory inscription with its gibe at the Spartans has sped like the wind to the Pillars of Hercules – Alexander certainly knows how to make people talk about him.'

'How are things here in Athens?'

'Demosthenes still exerts considerable influence, but the King's achievements have fired the people's imaginations. Indeed, many of them have relatives who are with the military in Asia – the army or the navy – and this makes them tend towards a prudent political leadership. But we must not delude ourselves – should the King fall in battle there will be an immediate uprising and all his friends will be sought out door-to-door and arrested, and there is no doubt I will be the first. But tell me, how has Alexander behaved up to now?'

'As far as I can say, with great equilibrium – he has been clement with his defeated enemies and in the cities he has gone no farther than re-establishing democracy, without demanding any change in organization.'

Aristotle nodded gravely and stroked his beard as a sign of approval – the pupil was evidently putting into practice the teachings of his master. Then the philosopher stood up. 'Would you care to see the Academy?'

'With great pleasure,' replied Lysippus as he followed.

They went out into the internal portico and walked around the central courtyard, in the shadow of an elegant colonnade of Pentelic marble with Ionic capitals. In the middle there was a well with a low brick wall around its edge in which there was a deep groove worn by years of friction from the rope. A servant was hauling up a bucketful of water at that moment.

'We have four slaves, two for cleaning and two for serving at table. We often have guests from other schools and some of our pupils stay here with us for a time.'

They then went through an arched doorway: 'This is the political science sector, where we already hold the constitutions of more than one hundred and sixty cities in Greece, Asia, Africa and Italy. And here,' he continued as they walked along a corridor on which there were other doors, 'we have the naturalistic sector with collections of minerals, plants and insects. Finally, in this other area,' he continued as he accompanied his guest into a large hall, 'we have the rare animals collection. I had a taxidermist come from Egypt; he is an expert in sacred cats and crocodiles, and he works extremely quickly.'

Lysippus looked around and was increasingly fascinated, not so much by the stuffed animals – snakes, crocodiles, vultures – as by the anatomical drawings, in which he recognized the skill of a consummate artist.

'Obviously we have to be very much on our guard against forgeries and scams of all kinds,' continued Aristotle. 'Since word has spread of our collection, we have received the most outlandish offers – Pharaoh's rats, basilisks and even centaurs and sirens.'

'Centaurs and sirens?' repeated Lysippus in amazement.

'Precisely. And we are even invited to inspect these wonders before we purchase them.'

'How can that be?'

'Elementary taxidermy. It is not by coincidence that the offers come for the most part from Egypt, where embalmers and taxidermists have thousands of years of experience. For these craftsmen sewing the torso of a man on to the body of a foal, ably concealing the stitches with skin and mane and then embalming everything is nothing at all. The end result of such masterful handiwork is really quite impressive, I assure you.'

'I can well believe it.'

Aristotle moved towards a window from which there was a view of Lycabettus, with its cover of pine trees, and in the background the Acropolis and the great mass of the Parthenon. 'What will he do now, in your opinion?'

Lysippus understood immediately that Aristotle had not stopped thinking about Alexander for even one instant.

'All I know is that he will head south now, but no one knows his true intentions.'

'He will go on,' said the philosopher, turning towards the artist. 'He will continue until he feels he can breathe freely and no one will be able to stop him.'

*

Apelles had stayed on alone at Ephesus, and was busy working on his big equestrian portrait of the King of Macedon. The King himself in the meantime had started off again on his march to Miletus.

The painter had concentrated above all else on the head of Bucephalas, depicting it so realistically that it was as if the animal were about to leap out of the painting. Apelles wanted to astound his client, and he had already organized transport to take him to Alexander's next camp together with the paintings, so that the King could admire the finished articles.

He had dedicated a long time and much work of precision to depicting the bloody foam around the bit in the horse's mouth, but he hadn't managed to reach quite the right depth of colour. Pancaspe, who never shut up, drove him wild with rage – the initial joys of their falling in love had long since passed.

'If you don't shut that mouth of yours,' shouted the exasperated painter, 'I'll never manage to finish this!'

'But, dear . . .' Pancaspe started again.

'Enough!' screamed Apelles, completely out of his mind as he threw a paint-sodden sponge at the painting. By some extraordinary miracle the sponge hit the painting just at the corner of Bucephalus's mouth before it fell to the floor.

'There you are,' she whinged. 'Happy now? You've ruined it! And I suppose it will all be my fault, won't it?'

But the painter was not listening. He walked incredulous towards his painting, his arms raised in a gesture of utter wonder. 'It cannot be true,' he murmured. 'By the gods, it is not possible.'

The mark of the sponge had rendered the bloody saliva on Bucephalas's mouth with a realistic effect that no human ability could ever have equalled.

'Oh, now . . .' chirped Pancaspe as she too became aware of the miracle.

Apelles turned towards her and lifted his index finger until it was almost touching her nose: 'If you ever tell anyone about how this particular detail was achieved,' and his finger moved slowly to point to the miraculous splash of colour, 'I will personally bite that pretty little nose of yours off your head. Understand?'

'Perfectly, my beloved,' nodded Pancaspe as she gradually retreated from his menacing gaze.

And she really did mean it at that precise moment, but discretion was certainly not the greatest of her virtues and within a day or two all the Ephesines came to know just how the great Apelles had painted the wonderful detail of the bloody foam around Bucephalas's mouth.

13

THE COMMANDER OF THE garrison at Miletus, a Greek by the name of Eghesikratos, sent a message to Alexander in which he declared he was ready to hand the city over. Although the King had the army advance with the intention of taking possession, as a precautionary measure he sent a squadron of cavalry on ahead as scouts, across the river Meander, under the command of Craterus and Perdiccas.

They forded the river and climbed up the slopes of Mount Latmus, but just as they went over the crest they stopped, dumbstruck at the incredible spectacle there before them – a fleet of warships was rounding the Miletus promontory, each of the vessels taking up position to close off the gulf.

Behind the first group came others and then yet more, until the entire gulf was teeming with hundreds of ships and the sea boiled with the foam of thousands of oars cutting through it. Muffled by the distance, yet still distinct, came the booming of the drums that beat the rhythm for the rowers.

'Oh, by the gods,' murmured Perdiccas. 'The Persian fleet!'

'How many ships do you think there are?' asked Craterus.

'Hundreds ... at least two, perhaps three hundred. And our fleet is on its way here – if they end up being taken by surprise in the gulf, they'll be annihilated. We must get back as soon as possible and signal to Nearchus to stop. They outnumber us by at least two to one!'

They turned their horses and went down the slope at a gallop, spurring them on towards the army on its march southwards.

They reached their companions on the left-hand bank of the Meander and immediately went to the King, who together with Ptolemy and Hephaestion was supervising the passage of the cavalry across the bridge of boats that had been constructed by his engineers near the estuary.

'Alexander!' cried Craterus. 'There are three hundred warships in the Gulf of Miletus. We have to stop Nearchus or they'll sink our fleet!'

'When did you see them?' asked the King with a frown.

'A short while ago ... we had just reached the top of Mount Latmus when the first ones appeared and then others came, and yet more ... there was no end to them. Enormous ships with four or five rows of oars.'

'I even saw some of the eight-row reinforced types,' added Perdiccas.

'Are you sure?'

'Of course I am! And they're equipped with bronze battering-rams at least one thousand pounds in weight.'

'You have to stop our fleet, Alexander! Nearchus knows nothing of this and he is still on the other side of the Mycale promontory ... he'll end up sailing straight into the Persians if we don't warn him.'

'Keep calm,' said the King, 'there is still time.' Then he

turned to Callisthenes, who was sitting not far away on a small stool. 'Give me a slate and a stylus.'

Callisthenes provided the writing equipment and Alexander quickly wrote a few words and gestured to a horseman of his guard. 'Take it immediately to the signalman on the Mycale promontory and tell him to send the message to our fleet straight away. Let's hope it reaches them in time.'

'I think it will,' said Hephaestion, 'the southerly wind that's blowing helps the Persians coming up from the south, but it's against our ships coming from the north.'

The horseman set off at a gallop across the bridge of boats in the opposite direction to the flow of soldiers, crying out for everyone to clear the way, then he gave the horse free rein and spurred it on up the slopes of the Mycale headland. Stationed up there was a group of surveyors who were observing Nearchus's fleet off to the north. They were equipped with a mirror-like polished shield for sending signals.

'The King sends orders for this message to be sent without delay,' he said, handing over the slate. 'The Persian fleet is in the Gulf of Miletus – three hundred warships.'

The signalman studied the sky and saw a cloud advancing from the south, driven forwards by the wind. 'I cannot send it just yet, we must wait for that cloud to pass by. Look, it's blocking out the sun as we speak.'

'Damnation!' swore the horseman. 'Why don't you try with flags?'

'They're too far away,' the signalman explained, 'they wouldn't be able to see us. We have to be patient – it won't take long.' Indeed, the shadow of the cloud now covered the headland, while the fleet proceeded in full sunlight, all lined up neatly behind Nearchus's flagship.

The cloud seemed to stop moving completely and the fleet approached the western point of the headland and began moving out towards starboard, ready to round it.

Finally the sun reappeared from behind the last fringe of cloud and the surveyors straightaway began signalling. The message was transmitted almost immediately, but the fleet continued forwards towards the headland.

'But have they seen us?' asked the horseman.

'I hope so,' replied the signalman.

'Then why don't they stop?'

'I don't know.'

'Signal again then, quickly!'

The surveyors tried again.

'By Zeus! Why don't they respond?'

'Because they can't – they are in the shadow of the cloud now.'

The horseman bit his lip as he strode backwards and forwards. Occasionally he looked down towards the army and imagined the King's humour at this moment.

'Message received!' exclaimed the signalman. 'The flagship is lowering its sail and they are steering with their oars. They'll reply soon.'

The flagship now continued at reduced speed and the foam generated by the oars could be seen clearly as the rowers guided the vessel to a sheltered area under the headland.

A light flashed from the bow and the signalman read out:

' "We . . . move landwards . . . landwards." Excellent! They've understood. Quickly, go and report to the King. The sun is not with us for signalling from here.'

The horseman galloped off down the hill and reached the King, who had called a full meeting of his high command on the beach. 'Sire! Nearchus has received the message and as I speak is manoeuvring the flagship,' he announced as he leapt to the ground. 'Any moment now you will see him round the headland.'

'Very well,' replied Alexander. 'From this position we can also keep check on the movement of the Persian fleet.'

By that time the Great King's enormous fleet had almost completely covered the area between the Miletus peninsula and the foothills of Mount Latmus, while on the other side Nearchus's flagship was rounding Cape Mycale and coasted towards the mouth of the Meander, soon followed by the other ships in the allied navy.

'Perhaps we have got away with it,' said the King. 'For the moment at least.'

'Indeed,' said Craterus, 'if we hadn't signalled the danger Nearchus would have ended up face to face with the Persians, obliged to engage with them from a situation of hopeless inferiority.'

'And what is your plan now?' asked Parmenion.

He had just finished speaking when one of the shields-men arrived with a dispatch. 'There is news from Miletus, Sire.'

Alexander opened the message and read it.

Philotas, son of Parmenion, to Alexander, Hail!

The commander of the Miletus garrison, Eghesikratos, has had a change of heart and is no longer willing to open the gates of the city to you.

He has now put his faith in the protection of the Great King's fleet.

Keep up your spirits and take good care.

'It was to be expected,' said Alexander. 'Now that the Persian ships are anchored in the bay, Eghesikratos feels invincible.'

'Sire,' announced one of the shieldsmen, 'a launch from our flagship is approaching the coast.'

'Good, our sailors will join us for our war council.'

Shortly afterwards Nearchus alighted on the beach and behind him was the Athenian commander of the allied fleet, Karilaos.

The King greeted them warmly and informed them of the situation, then he asked the opinions of all those present, in descending order of age, beginning with Parmenion.

'I am not an expert in matters regarding the sea,' began the old general, 'but I believe that if King Philip were here he would take the enemy fleet by surprise, counting on the greater speed and manoeuvrability of our ships.'

Alexander's mood changed abruptly, just as it did every time he was compared publicly with his father the King.

'My father always fought when the chances of achieving victory were good, otherwise he always played a game of cunning,' he replied brusquely.

'In my opinion it would be a mistake to engage in

battle,' said Nearchus. 'They outnumber us three to one and we are landlocked, we have little room for manoeuvre.'

Others expressed their points of view, but soon they all realized that Alexander was not concentrating on the meeting. Instead, he was watching an eagle on the lookout for fish, flying in wide circles above the beach. Suddenly the eagle dived down at high speed, grabbed a large fish in its claws and then, its wings beating wildly, gained height and flew off with its prey.

'Did you see that fish? It trusted in its mastery of the water and it came too close to the shore, where the eagle made the most of a situation that just then was favourable to her. And this is exactly what we will do now.'

'What do you mean?' asked Ptolemy. 'We have no wings.'

Alexander smiled. 'Remember the last time you reminded me of this fact? We were moving into Thessaly and we had the insurmountable wall of Mount Ossa there before us.'

'That's right,' admitted Ptolemy.

'Good,' the King began again. 'Well, my view is that we cannot risk a naval clash under these conditions – not only does our enemy have a crushing superiority in terms of numbers, but they have more powerful, more robust ships. If our fleet were to be wiped out, then my prestige would be destroyed with it. The Greeks would rise up and the alliance that I have worked so hard to create would fall apart, with disastrous consequences. These then are my orders – beach all of our ships, making sure that the first to be hauled out of the water are those carrying the pieces of the siege engines. We will assemble them and take them to the walls of Miletus.'

'You want to beach the entire fleet?' asked Nearchus incredulously.

'Precisely.'

'But, Sire . . .'

'Listen, Nearchus, do you think that the Persian infantry aboard their fleet is any match for my phalanx lined up on the shore?'

'No, I don't think so.'

'Of course it isn't,' said Leonnatus. 'They really are no match at all. And if they were to attempt it we would destroy them before they even reached dry land.'

'Right,' said Alexander, 'and therefore they will not attempt it.'

'Nevertheless,' continued Nearchus, who had now understood the King's intentions, 'they cannot remain at anchor for ever. To strengthen their ships they have increased the number of rowers, but in doing so they have left no room aboard for anything else. They cannot cook, they cannot keep sufficient stocks of water, they are almost completely dependent on supplies from land.'

'Which we will block using our cavalry,' concluded Alexander. 'We will patrol every corner of the coast, especially every river mouth and every stream, every spring. They are out there, at anchor, and soon they will have no food, no water, all they will have is the blazing sun and a burning thirst in their throats, a twisting hunger in their bellies, while we will have everything we need.

'Eumenes will direct the assembly of the siege engines, Perdiccas and Ptolemy will lead the attack on the eastern side of the walls of Miletus as soon as the engines have opened a breach. Craterus, assisted by Philotas, will set off with the cavalry along the coast to prevent any landings; Parmenion will move the heavy infantry to support the other operations and the Black will give him a hand. Isn't that so, Black?'

'Exactly, Sire,' replied Cleitus.

'Excellent. Nearchus and Karilaos will guard the beached ships with the infantry and their crews will be armed too. If necessary, they will dig trenches. Miletus must be made to regret its about-turn.'

14

IT WAS LATE SPRING by now, and the day was a fine one. The noonday sun was high in the skies and the sea was as still as a millpond.

From the summit of Mount Latmus, Alexander, Hephaestion and Callisthenes contemplated the splendid spectacle there before them. To the right the Mycale headland jutted out into the sea like a spur, and beyond it they could make out the profile of the large island of Samos.

To the left was the stout Miletus peninsula. The city, destroyed by the Persians two hundred years previously because it had dared to rebel against their power, had been magnificently rebuilt by its most illustrious son, the architect Hippodamus, who had planned it carefully on an orthogonal grid of wide main roads and narrower secondary roads for neighbourhood traffic.

On the highest point he rebuilt the temples of the acropolis, resplendent with marble work painted in brilliant colours, ornaments in bronze, gold and silver, and statuary groups that stood majestically and dominated the huge bay. In the centre he had opened up the great square, a point of confluence for all the roads and the heart of the city's political and economic life.

Not far off the coast was the small island of Lade, like

a sentry posted to watch over the entrance to the great gulf.

At the far north-eastern extremity, near the mouth of the Meander, Nearchus's ships could be seen, beached and protected by a ditch and a palisade against any possible attack from an infantry landing by the enemy.

Out in the middle of the bay the distance made the Great King's three hundred ships look like little toy boats ready for children to play with.

'It's incredible!' exclaimed Callisthenes. 'Here in these waters, in this very stretch of sea, the outcome of the Persian Wars was decided – that small island near the city is Lade, and it was there that the rebel Greeks were crushed by the Persians.'

'Callisthenes will now give us a history lesson, as if his uncle's lessons at Mieza weren't enough for us,' said Hephaestion.

'Quiet,' said Alexander. 'If you do not know the past, you cannot understand the present.'

'And down there, on the Mycale headland,' Callisthenes continued unfazed, 'our men paid them back in full some twenty-five years later. The fleet then was under the command of Leotychides, King of Sparta, and they struck while the Persian fleet was beached.'

'That's interesting,' said Hephaestion, 'today the roles are reversed.'

'Indeed,' said Alexander, 'and our men are sitting comfortably in the shade, eating fresh bread, while they have been out there roasting in the sun for three days now and if they have anything at all left to eat it can only be ship's biscuits. Their water must be rationed now to one or two dippers a day per head. They'll have to take a decision soon – attack or go on their way.'

'Look,' Hephaestion pointed out to him, 'our siege engines are setting off. By evening they will be under the walls of the city, and tomorrow we will start battering their fortifications.'

Just then an orderly from the Vanguard arrived on horseback with a dispatch, 'King! A message from Generals Parmenion and Cleitus,' he announced, handing over a slate.

The King read:

Parmenion and Cleitus to King Alexander, Hail!

The barbarians have made three attempts at landing to refresh their water supplies at various points along the coast, but on each occasion they have been repulsed.

May you be in good cheer.

'Magnificent!' exclaimed Alexander. 'Exactly as I had envisaged. Now we can move back down.'

He dug his heels into Bucephalas and started down at a walk towards the bay to meet up with the convoy of siege engines on its way towards Miletus.

Eumenes approached him, 'Well then? What's the view like from up there?'

'Splendid,' replied Hephaestion for Alexander. 'You can see the Persians roasting over a slow grill. They'll be cooked to perfection before long.'

'Can you guess who has just arrived?'

'No.'

'Apelles. He has finished his equestrian portrait and he wants to show it to you, Alexander.'

'Oh, by the Gods! I don't have time for paintings just now. I'm making war. Thank him, pay him and tell him we'll meet up just as soon as I find the time.'

'As you wish, but you'll give him an attack of spleen,' said Eumenes. 'Ah! I was forgetting – there is no news of Memnon. Absolutely nothing. It appears he has vanished into thin air.'

'I cannot believe that,' said the King. 'Memnon is too cunning. And it is certainly too dangerous for us not to know his whereabouts.'

'The fact is that none of us has ever seen him. We don't know what he looks like. They also say that he has never suffered any wound in battle that might distinguish him. He fights wearing a Corinthian sallet without any crest, which completely covers his face apart from the eyes. And it is difficult to recognize a man in the reel of battle from just one look.'

'That is true. But I am still not convinced by this disappearance. Have you found the Greek doctor who treated him? Parmenion says he is from Abydos, Ariston is his name.'

'He has disappeared as well.'

'And is his home at Zeleia still under surveillance?'

'There is no one left there now, only the servants.'

'Do not stop looking for him. He is the one we must fear more than anyone else. He is the most dangerous of our enemies.'

'We will do what we can,' replied Eumenes and he moved back into the convoy of siege engines.

'Wait!' Alexander called out.

'Here I am. What's wrong?'

'You said that Apelles is here?'

'Yes, but . . .'

'I have changed my mind. Where is he?'

'He is down at the naval camp. I have had them prepare a tent and a bath for him.'

'Well done. I'll see you later.'

'But what . . .' Eumenes didn't even manage to finish his sentence and Alexander was already at a gallop, heading in the direction of the camp.

Apelles was irritated by the fact that no one had been assigned to look after him and almost none of these military types recognized him as the greatest painter of his time. On the contrary, they were all crazy for Pancaspe, who went swimming in the sea naked and on dry land paraded about with the shortest military cloak that barely covered her modesty.

He was delighted when Alexander dismounted and came towards him, his arms wide open. 'Apelles – grand master of the brush! Welcome to my humble camp, but you really shouldn't have . . . I would have come to you as soon as possible. I am anxious to see the fruit of your genius.'

Apelles made a slight bow with his head. 'I had no wish to disturb you in the midst of such an important siege, but at the same time I simply could not wait to show you my work.'

'Where is it?' asked Alexander, sincerely anxious to see it.

'Here, in my tent. Come.'

The King noticed that Apelles had had a white tent pitched for himself, so that the light within was uniform and equally diffused, thus reducing interference with the colours of the painting.

The artist led the way inside and waited until the King's eyes had adjusted to the light. The work was covered by a curtain and a servant held a cord, waiting for a word from his master. In the meantime Pancaspe had come in and she now took up position near Alexander.

Apelles nodded and the servant pulled the curtain to one side, uncovering the painting.

Alexander was speechless, struck by the remarkable evocative power of the image there before him. The details which had fascinated him so much in Apelles's sketch and which had made him think the work was more or less complete at that stage had now acquired body and soul. All those particulars shone now with the moist vividness of real life, dense with atmosphere, and miraculously pulsing with vigorous movement.

The figure of Bucephalas was of such expressive power that the horse seemed to be alive and breathing fury from its nostrils. His hooves seemed to break out of the vertical plane of the painting and into real space, contending for space with the observer. The horseman was equally impressive, but also very different from the way Lysippus had depicted him in his sculptures up until that time. The infinite tonalities of the colours had allowed the painter to achieve a disturbing realism – on the one hand even more effective than bronze, on the other somehow almost a desecration of the figure of Alexander.

The King's face showed all the anguish and the ardour of the conqueror. There was nobility in the great sovereign's features, but there was also the fatigue and the sweat that stuck his hair to his temples in disorderly licks, his eyes too wide in a superhuman effort to dominate the situation, his forehead contracted in such a frown that it seemed almost painful, the tendons in his neck standing out and his veins turgid in the fury of battle. There was a man on that horse in all his greatness, but he was also mortally weary and heavily burdened with misery. This was not a god, as in Lysippus's works.

Apelles anxiously watched the King's reactions, fearing that he might explode into one of his now famous rages. But Alexander actually embraced him. 'It's wonderful! I look at this painting and I see myself at the height of battle. But how did you manage this? I posed for you astride a wooden horse and Bucephalas was standing outside his stable. How on earth . . .'

'I spoke with your men, Sire, with the companions who are by your side as you fight, with those who know you well. And I also spoke with . . .' and here Apelles lowered his head, '. . . Pancaspe.'

Alexander turned to the girl and she looked at him with a smile full of complicity. 'Would you be so kind as to leave us alone for a moment?' he asked her.

Pancaspe seemed surprised and almost resentful of the request, but she obeyed without any discussion. As soon as she left, Alexander began, 'Do you remember the day I posed for you at Ephesus?'

'Yes,' replied Apelles, trying to fathom what this was leading to.

'Pancaspe mentioned a painting for which she had posed as Aphrodite, a painting you had created for . . . she was just about to say the name of your client, but you had her keep quiet.'

'Nothing goes by you.'

'A King is very much like an artist – he has to dominate the scene and he cannot allow himself the luxury of distraction. If he is distracted, he is dead.'

'That is true,' said Apelles, and he timidly lifted his eyes to meet Alexander's, preparing himself for the difficult moment.

'Who commissioned that painting from you?'

'You see, Sire, I could never imagine that . . .'

'There is no need to apologize. An artist goes where he is required. That is the way things work. Speak freely, you have nothing to be afraid of, I assure you.'

'Memnon. It was Memnon.'

'I don't know why, but I had imagined it was him. Who else in this area could afford a painting of this type and of this size by the great Apelles?'

'But I assure you that . . .'

Alexander interrupted him. 'I told you there is nothing to explain. I simply want to ask you a favour.'

'Whatever you wish, Sire.'

'You obviously saw him?'

'Memnon? Why, yes, of course.'

'Well then . . . draw me a portrait of him. None of us knows what he looks like, and we need to be able to recognize him if we happen to find him there before us . . . understand?'

'I understand, Sire.'

'Then set to it.'

'Now?'

'Now.'

Apelles picked up a sheet of papyrus and some charcoal and began working.

15

BARSINE DISMOUNTED together with the boys and headed for the house, which was illuminated discreetly, with just one lamp burning under the portico. She entered the atrium and found her husband standing there before her, leaning on a crutch.

'My love!' she cried and ran forward, embracing him and kissing his lips. 'My life has not been worth living without you.'

'Father!' exclaimed the boys. Memnon held them fast, closing his eyes to savour the emotion.

'Come, follow me! I've had supper prepared. We must celebrate.'

They were in a fine house in the middle of an estate between Miletus and Halicarnassus, procured for them by the Persian satrap of Caria.

The tables were arranged in the Greek manner, with dining beds and craters brimming with Cypriot wine. Memnon invited his wife and his children to take their places and he lay down on his own bed.

'How are you?' asked Barsine.

'Very well, I am almost fully recovered. I still use the crutch because the doctor has advised me not to put any strain on the leg yet, but I feel good and I could easily walk without it.'

'And does the wound itself still hurt?'

'No, the Egyptian doctor's treatment was extremely effective – the wound closed and healed in a matter of days. But please eat . . . help yourselves.'

The Greek cook brought them fresh bread, various cheeses and hard-boiled duck's eggs, while his assistant served a soup of broad beans, chickpeas and peas.

'What will happen now?' asked Barsine.

'I had you brought here because I have many important things to tell you. The Great King in a personal decree has nominated me commander-in-chief of the Anatolian region. This means that I can even give orders to the satraps, enlist men and make use of any resources I deem necessary.'

The boys were fascinated by his every word and their eyes shone with pride.

'So this means you will start making war once again,' said Barsine, much less enthusiastically.

'Yes, as soon as possible. And so . . .' he continued, lowering his head, as if studying the colour of the wine in his cup.

'What is it, Memnon?'

'And so this is no place for you. It will be a fight to the bitter end, there will be no safe places for anyone . . .' and he hesitated as his wife shook her head. 'You must understand, Barsine, because this is also what the Great King himself wants. You will go to Susa, you and the boys, and you will live in court, respected and revered by everyone there.'

'The Great King wants us as hostages you mean?'

'No, I honestly don't think so, but it is certainly a

simple fact that I am not a Persian. I am a mercenary, a paid swordsman.'

'I will not leave you.'

'And neither will we,' said the boys.

Memnon sighed. 'There is no other way. You will set off tomorrow. A carriage will take you as far as Kelainai, and from there on you will be safe. You will travel along the King's Road, where there will be no danger, and you will reach Susa towards the end of next month.'

As he spoke, Barsine lowered her eyes and tears started to run down her cheeks.

'I will write to you,' Memnon began again. 'You will hear from me often because I will use the royal messengers, and you will be able to write to me by the same means. And when it is all over I will join you at Susa where the Great King will grant me the highest honours and he will repay me for services rendered. Finally we will be able to live in peace wherever you wish, my love, here in Caria, or in our palace in Zeleia, or on the coast in Pamphylia, and we will watch our children grow. Be strong now and don't make our parting more difficult than it already is.'

Barsine waited for the boys to finish eating and then she sent them off to bed.

They went to their father one at a time and embraced him, the wellspring of emotion making their eyes brim with tears.

'I want no tears in the eyes of my young soldiers,' said Memnon. And the boys kept their chins up and looked on proudly as their father stood to say goodbye: 'Good night, my sons. Sleep well, because you have a long journey ahead of you. You will see wonderful things – palaces gleaming in a thousand colours, lakes and gardens worthy of fantastic stories. You will taste the rarest fruit and foods. You will live like gods. Go now.'

The boys kissed his hand – a Persian custom – and went to bed.

Barsine dismissed the servants and accompanied her husband to his room. She had him sit in an armchair and for the first time in her life she did something she had never done because of the strong sense of modesty that had been part of her upbringing since childhood – she undressed before him and stood there naked in the warm red light of the lamps.

Memnon gazed upon her as only a Greek could gaze upon beauty in its highest manifestation. His eyes ran over her amber skin, over the smooth oval of her face, her shapely neck, her elegant shoulders, her ample and full bosom, her nipples dark and erect, her belly pliant, the velvet down between her legs shining.

He held out his arms to her, but she moved backwards until she lay down on the bed. While he gazed at her with fever in his eyes she opened her thighs, ever more audacious, stripping herself of the last veil of modesty to give her man all the excitement and pleasure she was capable of, before leaving him for what was perhaps to be the longest time.

'Look at me,' she said. 'Do not forget me. Even if you should take other women to your bed, even if they should offer you young eunuchs with shapely thighs, remember me, remember that no other can ever give herself to you with all the love that burns in my heart and in my flesh.'

She spoke in a voice that was both low and resonant, and the timbre of her words had the same warmth as the light from the lamps that flowed over her skin – dark and shining like bronze – transforming her body into an enchanted landscape.

'Barsine,' murmured Memnon as he in his turn took off his long *chlamys* and rose there before her naked and powerful. 'Barsine . . .'

His statuesque body, hardened by a hundred battles, was marked by scars and the most recent wound ran down his thigh in a long reddish ridge, but from his imposing muscles, from his solid gaze there came a formidable energy, unbowed and unflinching, a supreme vitality.

For a long moment she caressed him with her eyes alone, insistently, while he came towards her, his movements still slightly uncertain. When he lay down beside her, she used her hands to caress his mighty thighs, right up to the groin, and her mouth to awaken pleasure all over his body. Then she mounted him so that he would feel no pain in the ardour of their love. She crouched on top of him and sent her hips into the same incessant movements of the dance with which she had conquered him when he had first set eyes on her in her father's house.

By the time they fell back alongside each other, both of them exhausted, a slight glow was just beginning to spread over the sinuous profile of the hills of Caria.

16

THE CRASH OF the battering-rams working away cease-lessly on the walls of Miletus resounded like thunder as far as the slopes of Mount Latmus, and the rocks thrown by the big catapults could even be seen from the sea.

The Persian admiral called a meeting of his commanders on the quarterdeck of his ship to discuss what was to be done, but the reports from his officers were not encouraging – to throw men who were consumed by hunger and thirst into such a risky landing was tantamount to suicide.

'We must go to Samos,' proposed a Phoenician from Arados, 'take on supplies of food and water, and then return to attempt a landing from a position of strength against their naval camp. Then we will burn their ships, attack their army from behind as they are busy laying siege to Miletus and give the inhabitants of the city the possibility of breaking out – thus the Macedonians will have to defend themselves on two fronts and on difficult ground and we will have the best of it.'

'Yes, I agree,' said a Cypriot navarch. 'If we had attacked immediately, before they had dug in there in front of their ships, we would have had more chance of winning, but we can manage it this way too.'

'All right,' said the Persian admiral, since all those

present were of the same opinion. 'We will go to Samos to replenish our food and water. This is my plan – once the crews and soldiers on the ships have regained their strength, we will make use of the sea breeze to return during the night and attack their naval base. If the surprise succeeds then we will set them ablaze and attack the army from behind under the walls of Miletus.'

Shortly afterwards a standard hoisted on the flagship signalled to the fleet to ready its oars and to prepare to set off.

The ships lined up in an orderly fashion, in rows of ten, and when the drums started beating out the rhythm of their forward pace, they set off northwards, towards Samos.

Alexander, outside the walls on the northern side of Miletus, heard one of his men shout, 'They're off! The Persian fleet is going!'

'Magnificent,' said Seleucus, who at that moment was on duty as Alexander's field adjutant. 'The city will be forced to surrender. Their situation is hopeless now.'

'No, wait a moment,' said Ptolemy. 'The flagship is signalling something to the city.'

Indeed, they could see flashing signals from the stern of the great vessel as it headed offshore, and soon came the response – a long red standard flying from the highest tower in Miletus, followed by a blue one and then a green one.

'They confirm receipt of the message,' explained Ptolemy, 'but because the sun is not in a favourable position, they cannot do it with light signals.'

'And what do you think it all means?' asked Leonnatus.

'That they will come back,' replied Seleucus. 'I think they're going to Samos to get supplies of food and water.'

'But the commander on Samos is an Athenian – one of our allies,' replied Leonnatus.

Seleucus shrugged his shoulders. 'They'll get what they want, just wait and see. The Athenians are afraid of us, but they do not love us. All you have to do is take a look at the troops here. Have you ever seen them join in a party or any celebration with us? And their officers? They look down their noses at us as if we were lepers and they come to the war councils only if the invitation carries the signature of Alexander himself, otherwise they won't move a finger. I expect the Persian fleet to receive everything it needs at Samos.'

'Whatever happens, it makes no difference to us,' said Alexander. 'Even with their thirsts quenched and their bellies full, the Persians will have to decide whether or not to land because I have no intention of putting our fleet back in the water. And Nearchus agrees with me. The only thing we must do is to guard the entrance to the bay with our fast launches so as to avoid a surprise attack at night or at dawn. Let the navarch know.'

It was obvious now that the Persian fleet was heading towards Samos, and the King returned to the walls of the city to intensify their attack.

Lysimachus was there directing the siege engines and at that moment he had just called up an enormous battering-ram to work at a point where they had dug a pit the previous night with the aim of weakening the walls and causing a partial collapse.

'I want these walls battered constantly, day and night,

incessantly from now onwards. Bring up the Chaeronaea drum as well – it will be heard in the city and will drive them to panic. And it will not stop beating until the walls have collapsed with the force of the battering-rams.'

Two horsemen galloped down to the camp and informed the navarch of the King's orders.

The admiral sent some ten launches off into the sea with jars of oil on board, the intention being to burn it during the night if necessary. He also organized the transportation of the big drum to the walls of Miletus.

Before long the launches were already offshore, waiting for the Persian fleet to return. And the 'Thunder of Chaeronaea', as the soldiers now called it, made itself heard. It was a gloomy, booming noise, rhythmic and menacing, as it echoed off the surrounding mountains and headed out towards the coast. And this thunder was soon followed by the crashing of the battering-rams as they were driven against the walls by hundreds of pairs of arms, while the catapults let fly with rocks aimed up at the battlements to keep the defenders at a distance.

Whenever one team exhausted its strength, another took its place and when an engine broke down, it was immediately substituted by another one which worked – there was no rest or respite for the inhabitants of the besieged city.

As darkness fell, the Persian fleet, with the sea breeze in its favour, began manoeuvring into the bay at full sail, heading for Nearchus's camp. But the small groups of men on the launches were keeping vigilant lookout in the darkness. As soon as they saw the enormous silhouettes of the Persian vessels not far from them, they opened the jars of oil and poured them into the sea, one after another, so as to create a long slick. Then they set fire to it.

A snake of flames slithered over the dark surface of the waters, lighting up a huge area, and the trumpets of the land divisions immediately sounded the alarm. In an instant the shoreline was teeming with lights and resounding with calls and shouts. By torchlight they prepared to meet the danger.

The Persian fleet made no attempt to cross the line of flames and the admirals quickly gave orders to their crews to row backwards.

As the sun rose the bay was empty.

*

Nearchus was the first to give the news to Alexander:

'Sire, they have gone! The Persian ships have left the gulf.'

'Which way did they go?' asked the King, as his attendants laced up his breastplate and Leptine followed him around with his usual Nestor's Cup.

'We don't know, but a lookout up on the Mycale promontory says he saw the tail end of their fleet disappear towards the south. I think they've gone, never to return.'

'May the gods hear you, Admiral.'

Just then the Athenian commander Karilaos came in as well, fully armed.

'What do you think?' Alexander asked him.

'That we have been lucky,' replied Karilaos. 'In any case, I would have had no qualms about facing them out at sea.'

'But things have worked out well for us,' replied Alexander. 'This way we have saved men and ships.'

'And now?' asked Nearchus.

'Let us wait until the afternoon – if there is still no sign of them, launch the ships and keep them ready and at anchor.'

The two officers left to join their crews. Alexander mounted his horse and together with Seleucus, Ptolemy and Perdiccas headed for the siege line. The racket of the battering-rams and the 'Thunder of Chaeronaea' greeted them before Parmenion did.

The King looked up to the walls and saw the breach that was opening up wider at every blow. An assault tower was gradually being brought into position.

'We are about to launch the decisive attack, Sire!' shouted Parmenion above the noise.

'Have you passed my orders on to the men?'

'Yes. No massacres, no rapes, no sacking. All those who disobey to be executed on the spot.'

'Have the orders been translated for the barbarian auxiliaries?'

'Yes Sire.'

'Very well. You may begin.'

Parmenion nodded, then gestured to one of his men, who waved a yellow standard three times. The assault tower moved in once more, coming even closer to the walls. Then there came a great crash as a huge part of the wall collapsed under the blows of the battering-ram, lifting up a great cloud of dust in which it was impossible to distinguish enemies from allies.

From the top of the tower a bridge was lowered on to

the wall and a Macedonian patrol jumped out on to the battlement. Their orders were to drive back the defence troops waiting at the breach created by the battering-ram. The fight quickly became furious and more than a few Macedonians fell from the heights of the bastions and the edge of the walkway, but soon they managed to form a bridgehead up there. They cleared the way of Miletan defenders and sent down a rain of arrows and javelins on those on the other side.

As soon as the dust cleared, a division of shieldsmen rushed through the opening, followed by the Thracian and Triballian assault infantry.

The soldiers of Miletus were demoralized, exhausted by their ordeal, and they began to give way as Parmenion's troops penetrated the city beyond the walls.

A certain number of soldiers – those of more humble social origin – surrendered, and their lives were spared. But the Greek mercenaries and the élite troops made up of members of the aristocracy, fearing the worst, ran to the other end of the city, took off their armour and jumped into the sea. They swam in desperation towards the small island of Lade where there was a small fort they would use in their final defence.

Alexander entered the conquered city on horseback and immediately went to the western parapet of the walls. Off in the distance he could see the enemy fleeing – some of them, exhausted, were drowning, while others continued swimming steadily towards their destination.

The King turned back with Hephaestion and together they galloped to the naval camp at the foot of Mount

Latmus, where almost all of the ships had been launched now. He boarded the flagship and gave orders to head for Lade.

When they were close to the mooring, he saw that the survivors of the siege were already inside the fort. Armed only with their swords, completely drained of strength, still soaked through from their swim across – they looked like ghosts. He told Hephaestion to keep behind him and started moving forward.

'Why have you sought refuge here?' he shouted.

'Because this place is small enough to be defended by a few men.'

'How many of you are there?' Alexander shouted once more, under the walls now. Hephaestion and his body-guards gathered around him to protect him with their shields, but he sent them back.

'Enough of us to make the job of taking this place a difficult one.'

'Open the gates and no harm will come to you. I have great respect for valour and courage.'

'Who are you, boy?' asked the same voice.

'I am the King of Macedon.'

Hephaestion ordered the guards to move forward once more, but Alexander gestured to them to stay where they were. The Miletans conferred for some time and then the same man spoke again. 'Do I have your word as King?'

'You have my word as King.'

'Wait then, I am coming down.'

There came the noise of bolts being pulled before the gate of the fort opened and there stood the man whose voice they had all heard. He was about fifty, his beard long and unkempt, his hair encrusted with salt, his limbs lean, his skin wrinkled. He found the King standing there before him, alone.

'May I come in?' asked Alexander.

17

THE SOLDIERS OF MILETUS who had taken refuge on the island of Lade pledged their allegiance to Alexander after meeting him and speaking to him. Three hundred of them, the majority, signed up with his army to follow him in his campaign.

The city received the conquerors' full respect. No looting was tolerated and a motion was approved which called for the restoration of the walls. Eumenes summoned a meeting of the city council on Alexander's orders and had it ratify the re-establishment of all democratic institutions, together with the transfer of all taxes from the Great King to Alexander. He took the opportunity to call immediately for an advance on the taxes, but even then the situation remained critical because of the enormous war expenses.

The following day, at a meeting of the high command, the secretary illustrated the situation with a punctilious presentation of the expedition's accounts that left everyone present with a bad taste in their mouth, despite the great victories achieved up to that point.

'I don't understand,' said Leonnatus. 'All we have to do is help ourselves to whatever we need. This city is rolling in riches and we have asked for a derisory sum.'

'I'll explain it to you,' said Ptolemy patiently. 'You see,

Miletus is now part of our realm – to loot it would be like looting a Macedonian city such as Aegae or Drabescus.'

'But King Philip didn't see things that way when he took Olynthus and Potidaea,' replied the Black.

Alexander became visibly more tense, but he did not reply. Neither did anyone else say anything. It was Seleucus who broke the silence: 'Those were different times, Black. King Philip had to set an example, we instead are uniting all the Greek world into a single homeland.'

At this point Parmenion asked permission to speak: 'Men, we must not concern ourselves with such problems – all we must concentrate on now is the liberation of Halicarnassus. We have to garner our strength for this final effort and then our work will be complete.'

'Is that so?' asked Alexander with a certain tone of resentment. 'I have never said anything of the kind. I have not set any limits to our enterprise. But if you don't feel up to it, General, you may turn back whenever you wish.'

Parmenion lowered his head and bit his lip.

'My father had no wish to . . .' began Philotas.

'I understand perfectly what your father was trying to say,' replied Alexander, 'and I had no intention of humiliating a great soldier. But General Parmenion has been through many battles, many sieges, many sleepless nights and at his age he is no longer an eager new recruit. No one would blame him if he felt he wanted to return home for a well deserved rest.'

Parmenion lifted his head and looked around like an old lion surrounded by his cubs, all of whom had become too full of themselves.

'I have no need of rest,' he said, 'and I can still teach anyone here, apart from the King, a few things or two.' But it was quite clear that he really meant 'including the King'. 'How to hold a sword, for example. And if I may be allowed to make my own decisions regarding this matter, there is only one way to send me home before the end of this expedition is over, whatever its final destination may be, and that is as a handful of ashes inside a funeral urn.'

There then followed a long silence, broken in the end by Alexander himself: 'That is what I wanted to hear. General Parmenion will remain to support us with all his valour and all his experience, and we thank him from the depths of our heart. But now,' he continued, 'I must inform you of a serious decision I have made this very day after having considered the matter long and hard – we must do without the fleet now.'

The King's words provoked a buzz of comment throughout the royal tent.

'Do without the fleet?' Nearchus repeated incredulously.

'Exactly,' confirmed the King, impassible. 'Events over recent days have confirmed that we have no need of it. Twenty ships to transport the disassembled siege machines will be enough. We will move forward by land and take the coast and the ports – in this way the Persian fleet will find itself without moorings and without supplies.

'They can always land in Macedonia,' Nearchus pointed out.

'I have already sent a letter to Antipater asking him to keep guard. And in any case, I really don't think they would do that.'

'This would save us over one hundred and fifty talents a day – money we don't have,' said Eumenes, 'but far be it from me to bring it all down to a question of money.'

'Furthermore,' said the King, 'the fact that we no longer have an escape route by sea will motivate our men even more. Tomorrow I will inform Karilaos of my decision. You, Nearchus, will take command of the small fleet we will have left. It's not much, but it is very important.'

'As you wish, Sire,' the admiral said resignedly. 'And let us hope you are right.'

'He is most surely right,' said Hephaestion. 'I have never known him make a mistake. I am with Alexander.'

'Me too,' said Ptolemy. 'We do not need the Athenians. And then, I am sure they will soon present us with the bill for their collaboration and I am equally sure it will not come cheap.'

'Are we all agreed then?' asked the King.

They all assented, apart from Parmenion and the Black.

'Cleitus and I do not agree,' said Parmenion, 'but this matters not. Up to now the King has shown that he has no need of our advice. He knows that he can count on our devotion and our support just the same.'

'Support that is essential to our plans,' said Alexander. 'If the Black were not here with us, my adventure in Asia would already be over. At the Granicus he was the one who chopped off the arm that was about to decapitate me – let us not forget this. And now, let's eat because I am starving! Tomorrow I will assemble the army and give the men my news.'

Eumenes brought the meeting to an end and gave instructions for the invitation to dinner to be sent to the Athenian officers together with Callisthenes, Apelles and Pancaspe, all of whom accepted enthusiastically. He then sent for some fine-looking 'companions' – experts in keeping up the spirits of a group of young men. They were all from Miletus, elegant and refined, emanating the dark and mysterious beauty of oriental goddesses, daughters of men who came from across the sea and women who came down the rivers from the great highlands of the interior.

'Send one of them to General Parmenion!' shouted Leonnatus. 'I want to see if he can still give us lessons with his staff as well as with his sword!'

The joke had them all laughing and lightened the tension of what was a difficult moment. Although none of them were actually afraid, the imminent departure of the fleet signified a point of no return, almost a sort of foreboding of their leaving the homeland behind, perhaps for ever.

Evening had just begun when Alexander got up to leave – the Cypriot wine had left him a little fuzzy-headed and he was somewhat embarrassed by the ever-increasing audacity of Pancaspe, who ate with her left hand although she wasn't left-handed, her right hand being otherwise occupied elsewhere.

As soon as he was outside he had Bucephalas brought to him and set off at a gallop towards the interior. He wanted to savour the perfumed air of the spring and the light of the full moon which was rising just at that moment.

Ten men from his personal guard had set off to follow him, but their animals struggled to keep up with Bucephalas, who gave no sign of slowing down, not even on the uphill path on Mount Latmus.

Alexander rode for a long time, until he felt the horse drenched in sweat. Then he slowed to a walk and continued forward on the rolling plateau that opened out before him, small villages and isolated homes of peasants and shepherds spread here and there. The guards, expert at their job by now, kept their distance, but they also kept their eyes on him.

Occasionally he saw patrols of Macedonian cavalry at full gallop, accompanied by the barking of dogs on the farms, or by the sudden flight of flocks of birds, disturbed in their rest. His army was gradually taking possession of the Anatolian interior, the unchallenged realm of ancient tribal communities.

Suddenly he saw signs of a fuss along the road that led to the small city of Alinda – a group of horsemen galloping with torches, accompanied by shouting and insults.

He took his traditional wide-brimmed Macedonian hat, put it on his head, wrapped his cloak around him and moved closer at a walk.

The horsemen had stopped a carriage escorted by two armed guards who were offering resistance – spears in hand, they refused to have their passengers leave the vehicle.

Alexander approached the Macedonian officer who was

commanding the patrol and gestured to him. Initially the officer reacted with his own gesture of irritation, but for an instant the moonlight illuminated the white ox-skull mark on Bucephalas's forehead and the man recognized his King.

'Sire, but what . . .'

Alexander gestured for him to keep his voice down and asked, 'What is happening?'

'My soldiers stopped this carriage and we would like to know who is travelling in it and why they are travelling at night with an escort, but they offer resistance.'

'Tell your horsemen to move back and explain to the men of the escort that they need not be afraid, that no harm will come to the people on the carriage, so they should show themselves.'

The officer did as he was told, but the men protecting the vehicle failed to respond. At that moment, however, a woman's voice came from behind a curtain, 'Wait . . . they don't understand Greek . . .'

And immediately a woman wearing a veil slipped gracefully to the ground, her foot resting on the step. Alexander asked the officer to light his way with a torch and moved nearer.

'Who are you? Why are you travelling at night with armed men? Who is with you?'

The woman's countenance was of startling beauty – two large dark eyes with long lashes, full, well-drawn lips and above all else a proud yet dignified bearing, coloured by the slightest touch of apprehension.

'My name is . . . Mitrianes,' she replied with a slight

hesitation. 'Your soldiers have occupied my home and my property under Mount Latmus and I have therefore decided to join my husband in Prusa, in Bythnia.'

Alexander looked at the officer, who proceeded to ask the woman, 'Who else is in the carriage?'

'My sons,' she explained, and then she called out to them. Two fine-looking young men appeared. One looked like his mother; the other was very different – blue-green eyes and blond hair.

The King studied them closely. 'Do they understand Greek?'

'No,' replied the woman, but Alexander noticed the look she threw to her sons, as if to say, 'Let me do the talking.'

'Your husband cannot be Persian – this boy has blue eyes and blond hair,' said the King, and he realized that the woman was distinctly ill at ease. He took off his hat, uncovering his face, and moved even closer to her, fascinated by her beauty and by the aristocratic intensity of her gaze.

'My husband is Greek and he was . . . physician to the satrap of Phrygia. I have heard nothing from him for a long time and I am afraid that something may have happened to him. We are trying to reach him.'

'But not now – this moment is too dangerous for a woman and two boys. You will be my guests tonight and tomorrow you will continue on your way with more adequate protection.'

'Please, O powerful Lord, do not bother yourself. I am sure that nothing will befall us if you let us go. We have a long way to travel.'

'Do not worry. You have nothing to be afraid of, neither for yourself nor for your boys. No one will dare treat you badly.' Then he turned to his men: 'Take them to the camp!'

He leapt on to his horse and sped off, accompanied by his guards, who in all this had not lost sight of him for even an instant. Along the way they met Perdiccas, anxious because of Alexander's disappearance.

'I am responsible for your safety and if you could only bring yourself to let me know when you intend going off on your own, I . . .'

Alexander interrupted him. 'Nothing has happened, my friend, nothing at all. I know how to look after myself. How is supper going?'

'The usual thing, but the wine is too strong – our men aren't used to it.'

'They'll have to get used to all sorts. Come on, let's get back.'

The arrival of the carriage with the two foreign guards caused excitement and curiosity in the camp. Peritas started barking and even Leptine had questions to ask: 'Who's in there? Where did you find them?'

'Prepare a bath in that tent,' the King ordered her, 'and beds for two boys and a woman.'

'A woman? Who is this woman, my Lord?'

Alexander threw her a severe look and Leptine set to without another word.

Then he said, 'When she is ready, tell her I will receive her in my tent.'

The pavilion of the war council was not far off and from it now came drunken cries, the somewhat tuneless music of whistles and flutes, girlish giggles and the shouting of Leonnatus, louder than any other noise.

Alexander had them bring him some food – figs, honey and milk, then he picked up the portrait of Memnon that Apelles had left on his table and was struck by the expression of fathomless melancholy that the painter had captured.

He put it down on the table once more and started reading the correspondence which had reached him over previous days – a letter from the regent Antipater telling him that the situation at home was quiet on the whole, apart from the Queen's intemperate insistence on interfering in affairs of state, and a letter from Olympias herself in which she protested that the regent had deprived her of her liberty and of any possibility of acting in a manner befitting her rank and her role.

There was no mention of the fine gifts he had sent her following the victory on the Granicus. Perhaps she had not received them yet.

18

SHE WAS STANDING THERE before him when he lifted his eyes from the correspondence. She wore no veil now, her eyes slightly emphasized with a simple black line in the Egyptian manner, her body wrapped in a dress of green linen worked in the oriental style, her raven-black hair gathered to the top of her head after the Greek fashion. Although they were in his tent, Alexander's foreign guest seemed still to emanate the moonlight in which he had seen her for the first time.

The King moved towards her and she knelt to kiss his hand. 'I had no idea, my Lord . . . forgive me.'

Alexander took both her hands and guided her to her feet, the two of them so close as their eyes met that he could smell her hair – the perfume of violets.

He was stunned. Never before had he so suddenly desired a woman, to hold her tight in his arms. She was aware of this, yet in the same instant she felt in his gaze an almost irresistible force that attracted her . . . like the light of a lamp that attracts a moth.

She lowered her eyes and said, 'I have brought my sons to pay homage to you.' Then she moved back to the entrance of the tent and had the two boys come in.

Alexander moved towards a tray filled with food and fruit, 'Please have something to eat . . . help yourselves.'

But as he turned to speak to the boys he understood in the blink of an eye what had happened while his back was turned.

One of the young men had seen the portrait of Memnon on the table and had shown such surprise that his mother had thrown him an urgent look and put her hand on his shoulder.

The King pretended not to have noticed. He simply repeated, 'Don't you want to eat? Are you not hungry?'

'Thank you, my Lord,' replied the woman, 'but our journey has tired us out and we wish only to retire, with your permission.'

'Certainly. You may go. Leptine will carry this tray to your tent – if you are hungry or thirsty during the night you may help yourselves as you wish.'

He called the girl and had her accompany them, then he returned to his table and took the portrait of his adversary in his hands once more, studying it as if in an attempt to fathom Memnon's gaze and to discover the secret of his mysterious energy.

*

The night was half-way through and the camp was completely immersed in silence. A guard completed his tour and the officer in command made sure that the sentries at the entrances to the camp were all awake. When the echoes of the calling and the passwords had died away, a cloaked figure came out of the guests' tent furtively and headed towards the King's quarters.

Peritas was asleep in his kennel and the sea breeze brought him only the scent of salt water, carrying all other smells off towards the open country. The two sentinels at the royal pavilion were leaning on their spears, one to the right and one to the left of the only entrance.

The cloaked figure stopped for a moment before setting off with decision towards the soldiers, bearing a tray.

'It's Leptine,' said one of them.

'Hail, Leptine. Why don't you come to keep us company later? We're tired and we feel terribly alone.'

The woman shook her head as if used to jokes of this kind, offered them some of the food on the tray and entered.

In the light of two lamps the figure uncovered her head, revealing the proud countenance of the foreign guest. She gazed long on the portrait of Memnon, which still lay on the table, and brushed it with her fingertips. Then she slipped a long pin with an amber head from her hair and moved lightly towards the curtain which separated the King's bed from the rest of the tent. On the other side was the feeble light of a third lamp.

She moved the curtain to one side and went in. Alexander was sleeping on his back, covered only by his military *chlamys*. Alongside him was a stand bearing the armour he had taken from the temple of Athena at Troy.

At that very moment, far away in her bed in the palace at Pella, Queen Olympias turned in her sleep, tormented by a nightmare. All of a sudden she sat up and let forth with a sharp, bloodcurdling cry which resounded throughout the silent rooms of the building.

The Persian woman sought Alexander's heart, holding the hairpin in her left hand, then she raised her right hand to strike the amber head, but just then the King awoke with fire in his eyes. Perhaps it was only the shadow projected by the lamp, but his left eye, dark as the night itself, made him look like some alien and titanic creature, almost a mythological monster. The woman's hand hung in mid-air, suspended and incapable of unleashing the mortal blow.

Alexander raised himself slowly, pushing his chest against the bronze point so that a drop of blood appeared there. He continued staring at her without blinking at all.

'Who are you?' he asked when he was standing there before her. 'Why do you want to kill me?'

19

THE WOMAN LET THE HAIRPIN fall to the ground and covered her face with her hands as she burst into tears.

'Tell me your name,' said Alexander. 'I will not harm you. I saw your son's reaction on seeing Memnon's portrait on my desk. He is your husband, is that not so? He is, isn't he?' he repeated, raising his voice and grabbing her by the wrists.

'My name is Barsine,' replied the woman without lifting her face, her voice feeble now, 'and I am Memnon's wife. Please do not harm my sons, and if you fear the gods, do me no dishonour. My husband will pay the highest ransom – whatever you ask – as long as his family is returned to him.'

Alexander had her lift her face and as he looked into her eyes he felt himself burn with desire once more. He understood that if he kept this woman near him she would be able to do whatever she wished with him. And in her gaze, too, he saw a strange apprehension which was different from maternal anxiety or the fear of a woman alone being held as a prisoner. What he saw there were flashes of an atavistic and powerful emotion, controlled by a will that was strong, yes, yet bore signs of strain. He asked her:

'Where is Leptine?'

'In my tent, guarded by my sons.'

'And you took her cloak . . .'

'Yes.'

'Have you harmed her?'

'No.'

'I will let you go and these events will remain our secret. There is no need for a ransom, I do not make war with women and children – when I meet your husband I will fight him personally and I will win, if I know that the prize will be to share my bed with you. Go now, and send Leptine to me. Tomorrow I will have you escorted wherever you wish to go.'

Barsine kissed his hand as she murmured incomprehensible words in her native tongue, then she went off towards the door, but Alexander called her back:

'Wait.'

He moved towards her, towards those splendid, tearful and trembling eyes, took her face in his hands and kissed her lips.

'Farewell. Do not forget me.'

He led her out of the tent and stood watching her as the two *pezhetairoi* stood at attention, their spears held firmly, on seeing their King.

Leptine returned shortly afterwards, angry and upset at having been held prisoner by two boys, but Alexander calmed her down:

'There is nothing to fret about, Leptine – the woman was afraid for her own personal safety. I have reassured her. Go to sleep now, you must be tired.'

He kissed her and returned to his bed.

The following day he gave orders for Barsine to be

escorted as far as the banks of the Meander with her own guards and he himself followed the small convoy for some stadia.

When he stopped, Barsine turned to wave goodbye.

'Who is that man?' asked Phraates, the younger of her sons. 'Why did he have a portrait of our father on his desk?'

'He is a great soldier and a good man,' replied Barsine. 'I do not know why he had that portrait of your father – perhaps because Memnon is the only man in the world who can be compared to him.'

She turned once more and saw that Alexander was still there, motionless astride Bucephalas, atop a windswept hill. She would remember him this way.

*

Memnon remained for ten days on the hills around Halicarnassus, waiting for all his soldiers who had survived the Battle of the Granicus, about a thousand in total, to join him and re-form the ranks. Then one night he entered the city on horseback, alone, wrapped in his cloak and wearing a Persian turban that almost completely covered his face. He rode towards the council chamber.

The great assembly hall stood near the giant Mausoleum, the monumental tomb of the dynast of Caria, Mausolus, who had made the city the capital of his realm.

The moon was now high in the sky and it illuminated the great structure – a cube of stone crowned by a portico of Ionic columns, in turn surmounted by a stepped pyramid supporting the stately four-horse chariot in bronze which carried an image of the former sovereign.

The decorative sculptures, created by the greatest artists of the previous generation – Scopas, Bryaxis, Leochares – represented episodes from Greek mythology, a cultural heritage which had come to form part of the indigenous culture, particularly those stories which were traditionally set in Asia, such as the struggle between Greeks and Amazons.

Memnon stopped for a moment to look at a relief in which a Greek soldier held an Amazon by the hair as he pinned her back down with his foot. He had always wondered why Greek art, so sublime, depicted so many scenes of violence against women. And he had decided that it must simply have been fear, the same fear that made them keep their women segregated in the harems and meant that for social occasions they had to turn to the participation of the 'companions'.

He thought of Barsine, who was safely along the King's Road now, by the golden gates, and he felt a deep wave of regret wash over him. He remembered her gazelle-like legs, her dark complexion, the violet perfume of her hair, the sensual timbre of her voice, her aristocratic pride.

He struck the flanks of his horse with his heels and moved further on, trying to chase the melancholy away. But right at that moment the special powers granted him by the Great King himself were of no consolation whatsoever.

He went past the bronze statue of the most illustrious citizen of Halicarnassus, the great Herodotus, author of the monumental *History*, the first to narrate the titanic clash between Greeks and barbarians during the Persian wars and the only one to have understood its underlying causes, himself being the son of a Greek father and an Asian mother.

On reaching the council building he dismounted, walked up the steps, illuminated by two rows of tripods bearing gigantic lamps, and knocked repeatedly on the doors until someone came to open for him.

'I am Memnon,' he said, uncovering his head. 'I have just arrived.'

They led him into the chamber where all of the civil and military dignitaries of the city were gathered together – the Persian commanders of the garrison, the Athenian generals Ephialtes and Thrasybulus who led the mercenary troops, and Orontobates, the satrap of Caria, a corpulent character who immediately stood out because of his eye-catching clothes, his earrings, his precious ring and the shining solid gold *akinake* which hung from his belt.

The local dynastic ruler was also present – Pixodarus, the King of Caria, a man of about forty with a very black beard and hair just slightly streaked with grey around his temples. Two years previously he had offered his own daughter in marriage to one of the princes of Macedon, but the arrangement had fallen through and so he had compromised on the new Persian satrap of Caria, Orontobates, who was now his son-in-law.

Three seats had been prepared for chairmanship of the assembly – two were already occupied by Pixodarus and Orontobates, while Memnon took his place on the third, to the right of the Persian satrap. It was clear that everyone was expecting him to speak immediately.

'Men of Halicarnassus and men of Caria,' he began. 'The Great King has honoured me with a tremendous responsibility – to halt the invasion of the King of Macedon, and I have every intention of completing the task, no matter what the cost.

'I am the only one here who has seen Alexander face to face and who has taken on his army with spear and sword, and I can assure you he is a fearsome enemy. Not only is he valiant on the battlefield, to the point of fearlessness, but he is also skilful and unpredictable. The manner in which he took Miletus shows us what he is capable of, even in conditions of complete inferiority at sea.

'But I have no intention of being taken by surprise – Halicarnassus will not fall. We will force him to use up his strength and energies under these walls to the point of total exhaustion. We will continue to receive supplies by sea, where our fleet rules, and so we will resist for as long as it takes. When the right moment comes we will break out and crush his debilitated soldiers.

'This is my plan: the first thing is that we will not let them near us with their war engines – powerful and effective machines designed specifically for King Philip by the best Greek engineers. Then we will use his own tactics against him: the Macedonian prevented our fleet from taking on supplies of food and water by taking control of all moorings along the coast and we will do exactly the same thing, preventing him from unloading the machines from his ships anywhere near our city. We will send divisions of cavalry and assault troops to every bay which is less than thirty stadia from Halicarnassus.

'Furthermore, the only point where he can hope to attack us is the north-eastern sector of our walls. We will dig a trench there – forty feet long and eighteen feet wide – so that even if he should succeed in landing his machines, he will not be able to move them up to the city walls.

'That is all I have to say for now. Make sure that work begins tomorrow at dawn, and it must continue day and night without interruption.'

Everyone agreed with the plan, which indeed seemed infallible, and gradually they left the chamber and disappeared along the city roads, white under the light of the full moon. Only the two Athenians – Thrasybulus and Ephialtes – remained behind.

'Do you have anything to say to me?' asked Memnon.

'Yes,' replied Thrasybulus. 'Ephialtes and I would like to know to what extent we can count on you and your men.'

'I could ask you the same question,' said Memnon.

'What we mean is,' said Ephialtes, a large man at least six feet tall and as massive as Hercules himself, 'that we are motivated by a hatred for the Macedonians who have humiliated our homeland and have forced us to accept shameful peace conditions. We have become mercenaries because it was the only way to fight our enemy without damaging our city. But you? What drives you to do this? Who can guarantee that you will remain faithful to the cause even when it is no longer convenient for you? Ultimately you are a . . .'

'Professional mercenary?' Memnon interrupted him. 'Yes, it is so. Just as my men are, one and all. The most abundant commodity on the market today is mercenary swords. You claim that your hatred is a guarantee. Should

I believe that? I have often seen fear prevail over hatred, and it could easily happen to you too.

'I have no homeland other than my honour and my word, and you must trust that. Nothing is more important for me, together with my family.'

'Is it true that the Great King has invited your wife and your sons to Susa? And if this is true, does it not perhaps mean that not even he trusts you and he has taken your family hostage?'

Memnon looked at him with an ice-cold gaze. 'To defeat Alexander I need blind loyalty and obedience from you. If you put my word in doubt then I do not want you. Go now, I release you from your bond. Go now, while there is still time.'

The two Athenian generals seemed to confer simply by exchanging a look, and then Ephialtes spoke. 'We only wanted to know if what they say about you is true. Now we know. You may depend on us, to the bitter end.'

They walked out and Memnon was left standing alone in the great chamber.

20

ALEXANDER, AFTER CONSULTING his officers, left the camp outside the walls of Miletus as Nearchus's men were taking the siege machines apart before loading them on to the ships and transport barges anchored just offshore. They had decided that once this operation was completed, the admiral would round the Cape of Miletus to look for a suitable mooring as close as possible to Halicarnassus. With him he had two Athenian captains who were in charge of the two small battle fleets of triremes.

The beach was bustling with soldiers and resounded with shouts and noises of all sorts – hammer blows, calls, rhythmic chanting from the crews as they hauled the disassembled pieces on board.

The King took a last look at what remained of the allied fleet and at the city standing peaceful now on its promontory, before giving the signal to set off. Ahead of him opened up a gentle valley nestling between the olive-covered foothills of Mount Latmus to the north and Mount Grios to the south. Down below was the dusty, winding road that led towards the city of Mylasa.

It was a hot, fine day; the silver of the olive trees shone from the hillsides, while in the poppy-covered fields white-coloured cranes rooted along the streams searching for frogs and young fish. As Alexander's army passed, a moment's curiosity caused the birds to lift their heads and their long beaks and then they calmly set to rooting once more.

'Do you believe the story of the cranes and the pygmies?' Leonnatus asked Callisthenes as they rode alongside each other.

'Well . . . Homer mentions it and Homer is felt to be a reliable source,' replied Callisthenes, without seeming too sure of the matter.

'That's true . . . I remember old Leonidas's lessons when he spoke of the continuous battles between the cranes, who kept trying to carry off the pygmies' babies in their beaks, and the pygmies, who kept trying to break all the cranes' eggs. I think these are just children's tales, but if Alexander really intends to go as far as the edge of the Persian empire then we may well get to see the land of the pygmies.'

'Perhaps,' replied Callisthenes, shrugging his shoulders, 'but if I were you I wouldn't count on it. These are nothing more than folk tales. Apparently if one travels up the Nile one really does meet black-skinned dwarfs, but I doubt very much that they are no taller than my forearm, which is what their name means, and that they use their axes to cut grain. Stories become altered and deformed with the passage of time and as they pass from mouth to mouth. For example, if I were to start saying that cranes take pygmy babies to carry them off to couples who cannot have children then I will have added an imaginative new detail to a story that is already very imaginative, but there would still be a certain verisimilitude to it. Don't you think so?'

Leonnatus was a bit puzzled. He turned round to check his mules, which were loaded down with heavy sacks.

'What have you got in there?' asked Callisthenes.

'Sand.'

'Sand?'

'Yes.'

'But why?'

'I use it for training for wrestling. We might just find ourselves on rocky terrain up ahead and if I don't have my sand then I can't train properly.'

Callisthenes shook his head and dug his heels into his mule. Some time later he was overtaken by Seleucus, galloping on towards the head of the column. He drew rein alongside Alexander and pointed to something on the crest of Mount Latmus.

'Have you seen that up there?'

The King looked up in the direction Seleucus indicated.

'What is it?'

'I have sent a pair of scouts on ahead to take a look – it's an old lady; she has been following us, together with her entourage, since this morning.'

'By Zeus! I could have expected anything of this land, except to be followed at a distance by some elderly lady.'

'Perhaps she's out hunting for something!' laughed Lysimachus, who was riding nearby and had heard everything.

'Don't be stupid,' replied Seleucus. 'What shall we do, Alexander?'

'She certainly presents no danger to us. If she needs us, she will make the first approach. I don't think there's any reason to worry.'

They continued at a walk, protected by groups of horseback reconnaissance troops who cleared the way, until they reached a large open space just where the valley began to open up like a funnel in the direction of the city.

The signal to halt was given and the shieldsmen pitched canvas coverings to provide some shade for the King and his commanders.

Alexander leant on an elm tree and drank water from a flask. It was a very hot day now.

'We have visitors,' said Seleucus.

The King turned towards the hill and saw a man on foot approaching the camp. He was leading a white mule by the halter. Sitting on the animal was an elegantly dressed woman who was quite old despite her finery. Behind came another servant carrying a parasol, while a third chased away the flies with a horse-mane brush.

Bringing up the tail of the procession was a meagre division of not at all aggressive-looking soldiers, and at the very end an entourage of carts of various sizes together with beasts of burden.

When the caravan was about half a stadium away, it came to a halt. One of the men from the escort came forward to the place where Alexander was resting in the shade of the elm tree and asked to be taken to him.

'O Great King, my Lady, Ada, Queen of Caria, asks for an audience with you.'

Alexander nodded to Leptine to tidy up his cloak and his hair and to arrange his diadem, then he replied, 'Your Lady is most welcome whenever she wishes.'

'Even now?' asked the foreigner in Greek with a marked oriental accent.

'Even now. We have very little to offer, but we would be most honoured if she should care to sit at our table.'

Eumenes, understanding the nature of the situation, immediately gave orders for them to pitch at least the roof of the royal pavilion, so that the guests might sit in some shade. He had tables and chairs arranged so very quickly that as they saw the Queen approaching everything was ready.

A footman knelt on all fours and the great dame came down from her mule using his back as a step. She then approached Alexander, who welcomed her with demonstrations of profound respect.

'Welcome, great Lady,' he said in his most refined Greek. 'Do you speak my tongue?'

'I most certainly do,' replied the female dignitary, who was now being offered a carved wooden throne that had been unloaded from one of the carriages of her entourage. 'May I sit down?'

'Please do,' said the King as he invited her to sit with a gesture and he sat in his turn, surrounded by his companions. 'These here before you are my friends, closer to me than brothers, and all members of my personal guard – Hephaestion, Seleucus, Ptolemy, Perdiccas, Craterus, Leonnatus, Lysimachus, Philotas. This one here by my side, the one who looks most warlike,' and at this he couldn't help but give a half smile, 'is my secretary general, Eumenes of Cardia.'

'Hail, Secretary General.' The elderly woman greeted Eumenes with a gracious bow of her head.

Alexander studied her carefully: she was between fifty and sixty years old, closer to sixty. Her hair was not dyed and she made no attempt to hide the grey around her temples, but she must have been a woman of considerable charm once. Her woollen dress, Carian with a pattern of squares, each one embroidered with a scene from mythology, clung to her, revealing a figure that just a few years previously must have made her extremely attractive.

Her eyes were a fine amber colour, bright and serene, highlighted with delicate make-up, her nose straight, her cheekbones prominent, all of which granted her an expression of great dignity. Her hair was gathered into a bun, on top of which was a light golden crown decorated with lapis lazuli and turquoise, but both her clothing and her deportment carried something melancholic and in some way antiquated, as if her life no longer made any sense to her.

The pleasantries and the introductions took some considerable time. Alexander noticed that Eumenes was scribbling something on a sheet which he then placed on the table before him. Out of the corner of his eye Alexander read:

The person before you is Ada, Queen of Caria. She has been married to two of her own brothers, one of whom was twenty years younger, but they are both dead now. Her last brother is Pixodarus, who you will remember could have been your father-in-law and who has effectively ousted her from power. This could be a most interesting meeting. Make the most of it.

No sooner had he read those few lines than the woman sitting before him began her speech: 'I am Ada, Queen of Caria, and I now live an isolated life in my fortress at

Alinda. I am sure that my brother would chase me from there if he had the strength to do so. Life and destiny have failed to grant me any children and I am now approaching my old age with a certain amount of sadness in my heart, but above all else I am pained by the treatment I have received from the last and most wicked of my brothers, Pixodarus.'

'But how did you know all this?' whispered Alexander to Eumenes who was sitting next to him.

'It's my job to know these things,' his secretary general replied. 'And then, if you remember, haven't I already got you out of trouble with these people once before?'

Alexander indeed remembered his father's fury on the day he had ruined all prospect of marriage between his stepbrother Arrhidaeus and Pixodarus's daughter, and he smiled to himself, reflecting on the bizarre nature of fate – this lady, whose appearance and demeanour were so particular, a complete stranger to him, could have been a relative.

'May I ask you to sit at our humble table?'

Ada graciously bowed her head once more. 'I thank you and I accept with great pleasure. Nevertheless, being aware of the nature of army cooking, I have taken the liberty of bringing something from home which I hope you might appreciate.'

She clapped her hands and her servants brought loaves of warm bread from the carriages, cakes with raisins, tarts, puff pastries made with honey, rolls filled with beaten egg, flour, mulled wine and many other delicacies.

Hephaestion's mouth fell open and a line of saliva dribbled down off his chin on to his breastplate; Leonnatus was tempted to reach out immediately, but Eumenes promptly stood on his foot.

'Please,' said Ada encouragingly, 'help yourselves, there is plenty for everyone.'

They all attacked the food, which reminded them of their childhood – dishes prepared by the expert hands of their mothers and nannies. Alexander nibbled on a biscuit and then moved closer to the Queen, sitting down next to her on a stool.

'Why have you come to me, my lady, if I may ask?'

'As I explained, I am Queen of Caria, daughter of Mausolus, he who is entombed in the great monument at Halicarnassus. Pixodarus, my brother, has usurped the throne and now holds the city, after having become a relative of the Persian satrap Orontobates, to whom he gave his daughter in marriage. I have been stripped not only of power, but of my prerogatives, my incomes and most of my residences.

'All of this is unfair and those responsible must be punished. I have therefore come to you, young King of Macedon, to offer you the fortress and the city of Alinda. Whoever controls Alinda controls the entire interior of the country, territory without which Halicarnassus cannot survive.'

She made this speech in the most natural manner possible, as if she were talking of some sort of parlour game. Alexander stared at her in amazement, barely able to believe his ears.

Queen Ada nodded to a servant to come closer with a tray of sweetmeats, so that the King might help himself: 'Another biscuit, my boy?'

21

ALEXANDER WHISPERED TO EUMENES that he wished to be left alone with his guest and shortly afterwards his companions took their leave. They did so one by one, each mentioning some prior engagement out of respect for Queen Ada. Peritas on the other hand actually put in an appearance, attracted as he was by the scent of the delicacies.

'My lady,' Alexander began, 'I do not think I have understood fully – you want to offer me the fortress and the city of Alinda without asking anything in return?'

'Not exactly,' replied the Queen. 'There is something I would like in return.'

'Speak, and if I can, I will give you this thing. What do you wish?'

'A son,' replied Ada, as if this desire were the most natural thing in the world.

Alexander went pale and sat there motionless, biscuit in hand, staring at the Queen with his mouth open. Peritas barked as if to let his master know that he would gladly have the biscuit if it was not going to be eaten.

'My lady, I do not believe I am able . . .'

Ada smiled. 'Now *I* don't think you have understood, my boy.' The fact that she insisted on calling him 'my boy' when they had only just met seemed extremely significant of something. 'Unfortunately, I have never had the consolation of being a mother, and perhaps all things told it has been better this way, given the dynastic customs and requirements by which I had to marry my brothers – first one and then another. Each time I was widowed my grief was twofold for this reason.

'But if fate had granted me a normal husband and a child of my own then I would have wanted a son like you – handsome and kind and noble in bearing yet decided in character, courageous and audacious, but also affable and affectionate as they tell me you are, an opinion which I can now say I share, having met you. In other words, I am asking *you* to become my son.'

Alexander was dumbfounded, while Queen Ada looked at him with her amber eyes – gentle and melancholic.

'Well then? What do you say to that, my boy?'

'I . . . I don't know how we could manage . . .'

'It is very simple – an adoption.'

'And by what procedure would this adoption take place?'

'I am Queen: if you agree, all I need do is pronounce the words and you become my son.'

Alexander looked at her with increasing bewilderment in his eyes.

'Am I perhaps asking too much of you?' said Ada with a slightly worried expression.

'No, it's just that . . .'

'What?'

'I simply wasn't ready for such a request. On the other hand I can only be flattered and therefore . . .' Ada leaned forward slightly to listen better, as if to make sure she would not miss any of the words she was expecting, '. . . therefore I am delighted and honoured to accept your offer.'

The Queen was moved to tears, 'You really do accept?'

'Yes.'

'I must warn you, I will require that you call me "Mother".'

'As you wish . . . Mother.'

Ada dried her eyes with an embroidered handkerchief, then she lifted her head, straightened her shoulders, cleared her throat and declared, 'Then I, Ada, daughter of Mausolus, Queen of Caria, adopt you, Alexander, King of Macedon, as my son, and I name you sole heir of all my realm and all my goods.' She held out her hand and Alexander kissed it.

'I will await you tomorrow at Alinda, my boy. And now, my dearest, you may kiss me.'

Alexander stood up and kissed her on both cheeks, appreciating as he did so her oriental perfume of sandal-wood and wild rose. Peritas approached, wagging his tail and whining in the hope that perhaps this lady would give him a biscuit.

The Queen stroked him, 'This animal of yours is most amusing . . . even if he is a little on the large side.' She then departed with her entourage, leaving an abundance of food for her son and his friends, all strapping young men with remarkable appetites. Alexander stood watching her as she left on the white mule, one servant holding the large embroidered parasol, another swishing away the flies. When he turned round he found Eumenes looking at him and the secretary general didn't know whether to burst out laughing or keep a straight, solemn face befitting the gravity of the circumstances.

Alexander said, 'Let me tell you there will be real trouble if you ever let my mother know . . . Olympias is capable of having me poisoned.' Then he turned towards his dog, who had lost his patience with this pointless waiting and was barking wildly. 'And you can go straight to your kennel!' he shouted.

*

Early the following day Alexander ordered Parmenion to lead the army towards Mylasa and to accept, in his name, the surrender of all the cities – large and small – along the way. The King himself, together with Hephaestion and his personal guard, set off at a gallop towards Alinda.

They rode through enormous vineyards which emanated the delicate but intense perfume of their invisible blossom, green expanses of wheat fields, and then pastures dotted with infinite varieties of flowers of every colour, among which large red splashes of poppies dominated.

Alinda appeared before them in the heat of the midday sun, standing dominant at the top of a hill, surrounded by massive walls of grey stone above which towered the gigantic mass of the fortress, a grim rock with turrets from which flew the blue standards of the realm of Caria.

On the walkways the soldiers were lined up, armed with long lances and with bows and quivers worn across their backs, and before the main gate was a squadron of cavalry lined up in two rows – horsemen in their parade armour astride splendidly bedecked horses.

As they came closer the gates opened and there before

them was Queen Ada sitting on a canopied litter, shoul-
dered by sixteen semi-naked slaves and preceded by Carian
maids dressed in Greek-style peplums, all of them scat-
tering rose-petals on the ground.

Alexander dismounted and together with Hephaestion
continued on foot until they came to the gatehouse. Ada
made a gesture for the slaves to lower her, and she walked
towards her adoptive son and kissed him on the face and
on the head.

'How are you, Mother?'

'All the better for seeing you,' the Queen replied. Then
she had the litter taken away, took Alexander by the arm
and walked with him towards the city, where a cheering
crowd had gathered, anxious to see Ada's son.

Flowers and rose- and poppy-petals rained down from
the windows of the houses all around, gliding gently in
the spring breeze which bore with it the fragrance of cut
grass and fresh hay.

Then there came the music of flutes and harps to
accompany their walk – a sweet and vaguely infantile
music which reminded Alexander of the songs his wet
nurse used to sing him when he was an infant.

On the arm of his gentle, affectionate and essentially
unknown mother in the midst of all those celebrating
people, he felt moved. And this land, in which the other
side of every hill held a mystery that might just be a
violent ambush or the magic of an enchanted place, this
land was captivating him ever more, inciting him to keep
on looking for new wonders. What exactly was out there
beyond the mountains that rose above the towers of
Alinda?

They reached the entrance to the fortress, decorated with figures in relief of the gods and heroes of this ancient place, and before them stood a line of dignitaries dressed in the finest clothes, all woven with gold and silver. At the top of the stairway which led inside, two thrones had been prepared – a central, higher one and one to the right of it, a lower and more modest one.

Ada indicated the more imposing throne and took her own place alongside. The square in front of the fortress in the meantime had been filling up and when the entire space was full of people, of all social backgrounds and from all over the land, a herald brought them to silence. In a stentorian voice the same herald then recited the act of adoption in Carian and in Greek.

The applause seemed endless, and the Queen responded with the slightest wave of her hand while Alexander raised both his arms to the sky, just as he always did before his assembled troops.

Then the doors behind them opened and the two sovereigns, mother and son, disappeared inside.

22

ALEXANDER AND HEPHAESTION would have liked to leave that very same day, but it was simply impossible. Ada had prepared a fine banquet for the evening and had invited all the dignitaries of the city. Many of them had paid a considerable sum of money to be there and had brought precious gifts for the Queen, as if she were in fact a young mother with her firstborn child.

The following day the guests were taken to visit the fortress and the city, and although they insisted, it was quite out of the question for them to leave before the afternoon. Even then Alexander had a difficult time freeing himself from his new mother – he had to explain to her that all things told he was actually at war and that his army was waiting for him on the road to Halicarnassus.

'Unfortunately,' sighed Ada as she said goodbye to him, 'I cannot give you any soldiers. Those I have are barely enough to protect the stronghold here. But I can give you something perhaps more important than soldiers.'

She clapped her hands and immediately twelve or so men appeared with beasts of burden and carts full of hessian sacks and wicker baskets.

'Who . . . who are these men?' asked Alexander, somewhat alarmed.

'Cooks, my boy, cooks, bakers and confectioners . . .

the best there are this side of the Straits. You must eat properly, my dear, with all the ordeals you'll be facing . . . the war, the battles . . . unfortunately I can well imagine the poor quality of your victuals. I don't believe anyone has ever sung the praises of Macedonian cooks for the quality and refinement of their dishes. I imagine all you get is salted meat and unleavened bread, stuff that is difficult to digest, and so I thought I would . . .' and the Queen was set to go on for ever.

Alexander, however, interrupted her with a polite gesture. 'You are very kind, Mother, but in all sincerity this is not exactly what I need. A good night march is what's required for breakfast with an appetite, and after a day on horseback supper is always good, whatever has been prepared. And when I am truly thirsty, fresh water is better than the best of wines. In truth, Mother, these men would cause me more problems than they would solve. Thank you in any case, I am as grateful as I would be if I had accepted them.'

Ada lowered her head, 'I simply thought you would appreciate my looking after you.'

'I know,' replied Alexander as he took her by the hand. 'I know and I do . . . I am most grateful. But you must let me live as I am used to living. Whatever becomes of me I will always remember you with deep affection.'

He kissed her and then mounted Bucephalas and galloped off under the relieved gaze of the cooks, for whom the prospect of the military life had in truth not been so very attractive.

Ada watched until he disappeared, together with his friend, behind a hill. Then she turned towards her kitchen staff and said, 'What are you doing standing there? Come on, get to work. Tomorrow, before sunrise, I want you to have produced the best dishes you can manage and then we'll have them all sent to my boy and his friends wherever they may be. What sort of mother would I be if I did any less for him?'

The cooks set to their work – mixing, blending, baking – to create a series of delicacies for their Queen's new son.

The following morning and even the morning after that, the first thing Alexander saw outside his tent was a squadron of Carian cavalry delivering warm bread, fresh biscuits, and delicately filled cakes.

It was beginning to be rather embarrassing and both Alexander's companions and his soldiers started making jokes about it. He decided therefore to solve the problem at the source, even though with considerable regret. On the third day, when they were now near Halicarnassus, he sent the men and the food back to Alinda without having touched it at all, together with a letter he had written in his own hand:

Alexander to Ada, his most beloved mother, Hail!

I am sincerely grateful to you for the good things you send me every morning, but I regret I must beg you to suspend these consignments. I am not used to such rich food, but rather to a simple, rustic diet. And above all else I do not wish to enjoy privileges that my soldiers are denied. They must know that their king eats the same food and runs the same risks as they do.

Take good care.

From then on Ada's oppressive attentions ceased altogether and military operations began again at full pace. On leaving Mylasa, Alexander moved southwards and reached the coast once again, but here it was dotted with an infinity of small and large inlets, peninsulas and promontories. Along certain tracts the soldiers marched on in tandem with the fleet, which made the most of the deep waters near the coast, and at moments they were so close they could communicate by shouting across.

On the third day after Mylasa, just when the army was about to set up camp on the shore, a man approached the sentries and asked to be taken to the King. Alexander was sitting on a rock on the beach, together with Hephaestion and his companions.

'What do you want of us?' asked the King.

'My name is Euphranor and I come from Myndus. My fellow citizens have sent me to tell you that the city is ready to welcome you and that your fleet may moor safely in our harbour, a sheltered and well-defended port.'

'Luck is on our side,' said Ptolemy. 'A good port is exactly what we need to unload the ships and assemble the siege engines.'

Alexander turned towards Perdiccas. 'Go with your men to Myndus and prepare moorings for our fleet. Then send someone to report to me and I will inform our navarchs.'

'But Sire,' objected the messenger, 'the city hoped to see you in person, to prepare a welcome worthy of . . .'

'Not now, my good friend; now I must lead my army as close as possible to the walls of Halicarnassus and I want to oversee the operations myself. For the moment please thank your fellow citizens for the great honour they have bestowed upon me.'

The man took his leave and Alexander continued with his war council.

'I think you made a mistake in sending back all that food to Queen Ada,' laughed Lysimachus. 'It would have been very useful in facing up to this latest escapade.'

'That's enough,' said Ptolemy to shut him up. 'If I have understood what Alexander is thinking of doing then you soon won't have anything to joke about at all.'

'I think so too,' confirmed Alexander. He unsheathed his sword and began drawing in the sand. 'Now then – this is Halicarnassus. It spreads out around this gulf and has two fortresses – one to the right and one to the left of the harbour. From the sea, therefore, it is completely impregnable. Not only this, by sea they have a continuous supply line which means that we cannot lay siege to the city, we cannot effect a blockade.'

'Indeed not,' Ptolemy agreed.

'What would you suggest, General Parmenion?' Alexander asked.

'Given the situation we have no choice – our only possibility is to attack from the landward side, open up a breach and break into the city until we take the harbour. At that point the Persian fleet will have been ousted completely from the Aegean sea.'

'Exactly. This is precisely what we must do. Perdiccas, tomorrow you will go to Myndus and take possession. Then have the fleet moor in the harbour, unload the war machines, assemble them and have them move towards Halicarnassus from the west. We will be there waiting for you, having prepared the way for positioning the assault towers and the battering-rams.'

'That's fine,' said Perdiccas with a nod. 'If you have no other orders I will go to brief my men.'

'On you go, but come back to see me before you retire tonight. As for the rest of you,' he said as he turned towards his other companions, 'each one will be assigned his own position when we are within sight of the walls, that is tomorrow evening. Now go to your divisions and after supper, if possible, go to sleep early because these next few will be trying days.'

The council was brought to an end and Alexander took a walk, alone, along the shore, watching the sun as it descended, setting fire to the waves while the many islands offshore, large and small, slowly darkened.

At that hour of the evening, with the prospect of such a difficult ordeal before him, he felt a sharp sense of melancholy penetrate his soul and he recalled his childhood years when it was all a dream and a story and his future appeared before him as a long ride astride a winged charger.

He thought of his sister, Cleopatra, who perhaps was alone now in the palace at Buthrotum, on the cliffs above the sea. He thought of the promise he had made to think of her every day before nightfall and he hoped that she might feel his thoughts now, that the warm breeze might stroke her cheeks like a gentle kiss. Cleopatra . . .

When he returned to his tent, Leptine had already lit the lamps and was preparing his supper.

'I didn't know whether you had guests for supper, so I have set the table for you alone.'

'That's fine. I really don't feel like eating.'

He sat down and his meal was served. Peritas stretched out under the table to wait for the leftovers. Outside, the camp buzzed with the noise that accompanied every supper time and came before the quiet of the night and the silence of the first watch.

Eumenes came in with some sheets of papyrus in his hand.

'A message has arrived,' he said as he handed it to Alexander. 'It is from your sister, Queen Cleopatra of Epirus.'

'That's strange. Just now, as I was walking on the shore, I was thinking of her.'

'Do you miss her?' asked Eumenes.

'Very much. I miss her smile, the light of her eyes, the timbre of her voice, the warmth of her affection.'

'Perdiccas misses her even more – he would give an arm just to be able to embrace her with the other one. I'll leave you now.'

'No, stay. Have some wine.'

Eumenes poured himself some wine and sat on a stool while Alexander opened the letter and began to read:

Cleopatra to her most beloved Alexander, Hail!

I cannot begin to imagine where this missive will reach you – on a battlefield, during a moment of rest, or while you are besieging a fortress. I beg you, my dear brother, please take no unnecessary risks.

We have all heard word of your feats and we are proud of you. Indeed, my husband is almost jealous. He is impatient, he cannot wait to set off to find equal glory. On the contrary, I would rather he did not leave at all because I am afraid of solitude and because it is fine to have him near me here in this palace above the sea. At sunset we walk up to the highest tower to watch the sun descend to the waves until darkness obscures everything, until the evening star rises up into the sky.

I would so like to write poetry, but when I read the edition of Sappho that mother gave me as a keepsake and encouragement for my new life, I feel that I am too ambitious.

However, I sing and I make music. Alexander has given me a handmaiden who plays the flute and the lyre wonderfully and she is teaching me with great patience and dedication. Every day I make sacrifices to the gods and ask them to protect you.

When will I see you again? Keep your spirits up.

Alexander closed the letter and lowered his head.

'Bad news?' asked Eumenes.

'Oh no. It's just that my sister is like one of those little birds that is taken from the nest too early – sometimes she remembers that she is still a young girl and she misses the home and the parents she no longer has.'

Peritas whined and came nearer his master, rubbing his head against a leg, looking for a caress.

'Perdiccas has already left,' the secretary started again. 'Tomorrow he will be at Myndus and will take possession of the harbour for our fleet. All the other companions are with their divisions, except for Leonnatus who has taken a couple of girls to bed. Callisthenes is in his tent busy writing, but he is not the only one.'

'No?'

'No. Ptolemy keeps a diary too, a sort of memoir. And I've heard tale that Nearchus writes too. I don't know how he manages on that boat – it never stops bobbing up and down in the water. I myself was sick twice when we crossed the Straits.'

'He must be used to it.'

'Indeed. And Callisthenes? Has he let you read anything?'

'No, nothing at all. He is very protective of his work. He says I will be allowed to look at it when he has finished the final draft, and not before.'

'That means years.'

'I'm afraid so.'

'It will be no joke, you realize that.'

'What?'

'Taking Halicarnassus.'

Alexander nodded and scratched Peritas behind the ears, ruffling his coat.

'No, I am afraid it won't be.'

23

PERITAS'S GROWLING WOKE Alexander suddenly and the
King soon understood what had alarmed his dog –
the drumming gallop of a patrol of horsemen followed by
an agitated exchange of information among the men outside his tent. He threw a *chlamys* over his shoulders and
ran outside. It was still dark and the moon was only
just above the silhouette of the hills in a dark, milky sky,
veiled by low clouds.

One of the men from the patrol approached him and
said, breathless, 'Sire! It was an ambush . . . a trap!'

'What do you mean?' asked Alexander, grabbing him
by the shoulders.

'It was a trap, Sire. As we approached the gates of
Myndus, we were attacked from all directions – arrows
and javelins rained down on us like hail from the sky,
squadrons of light cavalry swooped on us from the
hills, striking quickly and retreating while others arrived
immediately afterwards. We defended ourselves, Sire,
we couldn't have put any more into it. If the fleet had
entered that harbour, they would have wiped it out
completely – there were catapults with fire-bombs everywhere.'

'Where is Perdiccas?'

'He is still down there. He managed to take a sheltered

area and gather his men. He needs reinforcements, as soon as possible.'

Alexander let the man go, but as he pulled his hands away he saw that they were red with blood: 'This man is wounded! Quickly, call a surgeon!'

Philip the physician, whose tent was not far off, came immediately with his assistant and led the soldier away to take care of him.

'Inform all your colleagues of the situation,' the King said to him. 'Have them prepare tables, warm water, bandages, vinegar . . . all the necessary equipment.'

In the meantime Hephaestion, Eumenes, Ptolemy, Craterus, Cleitus and Lysimachus had all arrived, all of them dressed and armed.

'Craterus!' cried the King as soon as he saw him.

'Sire!'

'Have two squadrons of cavalry assemble immediately and take them to Perdiccas – he is in trouble. Do not engage the enemy. Collect the dead and the wounded and come back.'

Then he turned. 'Ptolemy!'

'Sire!'

'Take a patrol of scouts and a group of light cavalry – Thracians and Triballians. Go along the coast and look for a mooring of whatever kind to unload the engines. As soon as you find one, signal to the fleet, have them moor as quickly as possible and help them unload.'

'Right away, Sire!'

'Black!'

'Sire!'

'Have all of our light catapults towed to the entrance

of the harbour at Myndus – no one must enter and no one must leave, not even the city's fishermen. If you find a good site, let fly with as many incendiary missiles as you can. Burn the city down if possible, right to the very last house.'

Alexander was furious and his rage was growing.

'Memnon,' he growled.

'What did you say?' asked Eumenes.

'Memnon. This is Memnon's doing. He is paying me back, blow for blow. I cut the Persian fleet off from the coast and he is doing the same to me, preventing my ships from mooring. It's him, I am sure of it. Hephaestion!'

'At your service, Sire!'

'Take the Thessalian cavalry out, together with a squadron of Companions, ride towards Halicarnassus and choose a suitable place for a camp on the eastern or northern side of the walls. Then find a site for the siege engines and have the labourers come to flatten and prepare it. Quickly!'

They were all awake by now – cavalry units were riding past in every direction, orders were being shouted everywhere, together with cries and shouts and the neighing of horses.

General Parmenion arrived, in full armour and weaponry and followed by two attendants.

'At your service, Sire!'

'We have been tricked, General. Perdiccas has fallen into a trap at Myndus and we still have no news of the outcome of it all.

'But I do know what we will do now. Give orders for

the men to have breakfast and then have the infantry and the cavalry lined up ready to march. At sunrise I want them already on their way. We are going to attack Halicarnassus!'

Parmenion nodded and turned to his attendants, 'You heard the King, didn't you? Get moving then!'

'General . . .'

'Is there anything else, Sire?'

'Send Philotas to Myndus with a group of horsemen – I need to know as soon as possible what is happening there.'

'Here he is now,' replied Parmenion, pointing to his son running towards them. 'I'll have him set off immediately.'

Hephaestion, in the meantime, was setting off from the camp with his squadrons, raising up an enormous cloud of dust, galloping off towards Halicarnassus.

They came within sight of the city at dawn and saw that the area under the walls was completely deserted. Hephaestion looked around and then spurred his steed onwards to take by surprise an open space that appeared suitable for their camp.

But the terrain between them and Halicarnassus was gently rolling countryside and it was difficult to see exactly what lay near the walls, so prudence demanded that they move forward at nothing more than a walk.

Everything seemed calm in the silence of sunrise, but suddenly Hephaestion heard a strange noise, sharp and rhythmical, like metal objects striking rock or soil. He continued up to the top of a low hill and was amazed at the spectacle that lay before him.

There was a huge trench down there, perhaps thirty-five feet wide and eighteen feet deep. Hundreds of men were busy working on it, carrying out the soil and broken rock and piling it up to form an equally enormous dyke.

'Damn!' exclaimed Hephaestion. 'We waited too long. You!' he shouted to one of his men, 'Turn back immediately and tell Alexander.'

'Of course,' replied the horseman as he turned and sped off back towards the camp. But at that precise moment one of the gates of Halicarnassus opened and a cavalry squadron came out at a gallop along the only passable route left between the trench and the walls.

'They're coming at us!' shouted the Thessalian commander. 'Over there . . . on that flank!'

Hephaestion ordered his division to make an about turn and then he rushed at the enemy as they spread out in file along the narrow passage in order to reach open ground as quickly as possible.

He arranged his men along a front line some two hundred feet long, four horses deep and directed the attack towards the head of the enemy column which was now beginning to gallop along the dyke to take up position in a sufficiently long line to bear the brunt of the imminent clash. Indeed, they met so close to the wall that the Persians had no time to build up speed and Hephaestion managed to drive them back.

The workers who had been down at the bottom of the ditch were terrified by the noise of the battle and abandoned their tools, climbing up the bank on the side nearest the city as quickly as possible and running for the gates.

But the defenders of Halicarnassus had already closed all the entrances to the city.

A group of Thessalians took the passageway between the trench and the walls and began attacking the labourers with a thick rain of javelins until they had all been wiped out. But before long another division of cavalry appeared from a side gate in the walls and attacked the Thessalians laterally, forcing them to gather together and respond.

The skirmishes continued with attacks and counterattacks, but Hephaestion finally got the upper hand by deploying the *hetairoi*, the Companions, still fresh, in front of the now exhausted Thessalians. He then chased what was left of the enemy right back to the gates, which this time were opened to let them in.

The Macedonian commander dared not follow them through the huge doors between the two massive bulwarks crawling with archers and javelin throwers. He decided it was enough to have taken the ground beneath the walls and he had his men start on digging another trench on the side of the passage while they waited for the labourers to come. Some horsemen instead were sent to scout for springs that might provide water for men and horses when the rest of the army arrived.

Suddenly one of the *hetairoi* pointed to something up on the walls: 'Look, Commander,' he said, indicating the highest tower. Hephaestion turned and moved closer to get a better view. He saw a soldier up there, encased in a shining iron breastplate, his face completely hidden by a Corinthian sallet helmet. He held a long, straight spear in his hand.

A cry rang out behind Hephaestion. 'Commander, the King!'

Alexander, at the head of the Vanguard, arrived at a gallop astride Bucephalas. Within moments he was alongside his friend and he lifted his eyes towards the tower, where the armour of the mysterious warrior shone brightly in the morning sun.

He stared in silence and knew that he too was being observed: 'It's him. It is him, I can feel it.'

At that moment in a far off place, beyond the city of Kelainai, along the road of the Great King, Barsine had stopped with her sons in a hostelry. She reached into her bag for a handkerchief to wipe her face and felt something unfamiliar there. She pulled it out and saw that it was a container with a sheet of papyrus inside. It was the sheet on which Apelles had drawn, with a few masterful strokes, a portrait of her husband, Memnon. Through her tears, Barsine read the few words which had been added at the bottom in a rushed and irregular hand:

Your own countenance is impressed with equal force
in the mind of *Aléxandre.*

24

THE ENTIRE CITY could be seen from the top of the hill and as Alexander dismounted all his Companions immediately did likewise. It was truly a stupendous sight. A huge natural bowl, verdant with olive trees and here and there dotted with the dark flames of cypresses, gently sloping like a theatre down towards the massive stone walls which enclosed the city towards the north and the east, interrupted only by the huge reddish gash of the trench Memnon had had dug at some two hundred feet from the base of the walls.

To the left was the acropolis with its sanctuaries and its statues. At that very moment smoke from a sacrificial rite rose from the altar up towards the clear sky, petitioning the gods' help in defeating the enemy.

'Our priests have offered a sacrifice as well,' said Craterus. 'I wonder who the gods will listen to.'

Alexander turned to him, 'To the strongest.'

'The engines will never manage to get anywhere near that ditch,' said Ptolemy. 'And at that distance we will never succeed in breaching the walls.'

'That's certainly true,' said Alexander. 'We're going to fill in the trench.'

'Fill in the trench?' asked Hephaestion. 'Do you have any idea how much . . .'

'You will start straight away,' continued Alexander, without batting an eyelid. 'Take all the men you require and fill it. We will cover you with catapult fire at the walls. Craterus will take care of that. What news is there of our war engines?'

'They have been unloaded in a small inlet some fifteen stadia from our camp. Assembly is almost complete and Perdiccas will transport them here.'

The sun was just beginning to descend towards the horizon above the sea, exactly midway between the two towers which watched over the entrance to the harbour. Its rays steeped the gigantic mausoleum that rose at the middle of the city in a bath of molten gold. Atop the great pyramid the four-horse chariot looked as though it was about to set off into the emptiness, to fly galloping through the violet clouds of sunset. Some fishing boats entered the port, sails fully open, like a flock of sheep returning to its pen before darkness. The fresh fish would soon be transferred into baskets and sent off to the houses where the families of Halicarnassus were preparing supper.

The sea breeze blew through the trunks of the age-old olive trees and along the paths that led up through the hills. The shepherds and the peasants were all returning peacefully to their homes, the birds to their nests. The world was about to nod off in the peacefulness of the evening.

'Hephaestion,' said Alexander.

'Here I am.'

'Have a night shift organized for the labourers. The work must be incessant, just as when we cut the stairway out of the rock face on Mount Ossa. Even if it rains or hails, you must keep on without any interruption. I want movable shelters set up for the labourers. And have the blacksmiths make tools if necessary; the engines must be in position within four days and nights at the latest.'

'Wouldn't it be better to begin tomorrow?'

'No. Right now. And when it is dark you will work by torchlight, or light bonfires. This work does not call for precision – all you have to do is to shovel the earth into the ditch. We will not eat supper this evening until we have put the ballistae in place and begun the shovelling.'

Hephaestion nodded and returned to the camp at a gallop. Shortly afterwards a long line of men with spades, shovels and picks, followed by carts drawn by oxen, headed towards the trench. Alongside them came the ballistae, pulled by pairs of mules. These were gigantic bows made of laminated oak and ash, capable of propelling iron bolts a distance of some five hundred feet. Craterus had them take up position and as soon as a group of enemy archers began to let fly with arrows from the tops of the city walls, he gave orders for a return sally and a volley of the heavy iron missiles cleared the battlements.

'You may start your work!' he shouted, while his men rushed to reload the ballistae.

The labourers jumped down into the trench and then clambered up on the other side, by the dyke, and started shovelling soil into the trench which lay gaping behind them. The dyke itself protected the workers, so that there was no need, at least during this stage of their work, to cover them with the mobile roofs. Craterus, seeing that his men were now safe, had the ballistae aim at what was known as the Mylasa Gate and the smaller side gate to the east, in case the besieged Halicarnassians attempted any sudden sorties against the labourers.

Hephaestion gave orders for other teams to move up towards the hills with saws and axes – wood for burning, for illuminating the site during the hours of darkness would soon be required. The huge enterprise was under way.

Only then did Alexander return to the camp and invite his companions to supper, but he had given orders for them to organize regular reports on the progress of the work and the development of the situation.

The night passed without incident and the work progressed according to the King's orders. The enemy could do nothing to prevent it.

By the fourth day sufficiently large areas of the trench had been filled and levelled, so that the siege engines could move forwards to the walls.

They were the same engines Philip had used at Perinthus – towers up to eighty feet high with suspended battering-rams at various levels, manoeuvred by hundreds of men safely sheltered inside the structure. Soon the great bowl of the Vale of Halicarnassus resounded with the rhythmic crash of the iron-headed rams beating ceaselessly against the walls, while the labourers continued to fill the trench below.

The defenders of the city had not envisaged the filling in of the trench in such a short time and they found it impossible to impede the work of the towers; within seven days a breach had been opened and much of the bastions flanking the Mylasa Gate had been reduced to rubble. Alexander sent his assault troops in over the piles of stone with orders to open up the road towards the centre of the city, but Memnon had already lined up his defence and he drove the Macedonians back without too much trouble.

The battering-rams continued their work over the following days, driving into the walls to widen the breach, while the ballistae and the catapults were brought up to keep the besieged troops under pressure. Victory seemed close at hand, and Alexander called his commanders to his tent to organize the final thrust.

Only those troops who were manning the assault towers and a certain number of forward sentries, arranged at regular intervals along the line of bastions, were left under the walls.

There was a new moon that night, and the sentries called to one another in the dark to maintain contact, but Memnon was listening to them as well. Wrapped in his cloak, he stood motionless on the battlements, looking down into the darkness and concentrating hard to try to catch what the sentries were saying to one another.

A few days previously some Macedonian nobles, friends of Attalus and the late Queen Eurydice, had come to offer their assistance to the inhabitants of Halicarnassus in their struggle with Alexander.

Memnon suddenly remembered this group and ordered his field adjutant, standing there with him in the darkness, to bring them to him immediately. It was a peaceful night – a light sea breeze was gradually refreshing the heat of the late spring day and Memnon occasionally lifted his eyes to the huge starry vault that curved away to the eastern horizon. He thought of Barsine and of the last time he had seen her naked on his bed, opening her arms and gazing at him with fire in her eyes. At that moment his feeling of loss was a sharp, physical pain.

He realized he wanted to face Alexander in a duel, convinced that his desire for Barsine would give him a devastating, indomitable power. The voice of his field adjutant woke him from this reverie: 'Commander, the men you asked me to call are here with me.'

Memnon turned and saw that the Macedonians had come armed and in battledress. He had them approach.

'Here we are, Memnon,' said one of them. 'We are ready, at your service.'

'Can you hear these men calling to one another?'

The men listened out. 'Of course. These are Alexander's sentries.'

'Good. Now, take off your armour and keep just your swords and your daggers – you will have to move with great agility out there in the dark, and in silence. This is what I want you to do: exit from the side gate and each one of you will seek out one of Alexander's guards, creep up behind him and take him out of action. But you must be ready to take his place immediately and to reply to the signals. You all have the same accent and the same pronunciation – no one will realize what has happened.

'As soon as you have taken control of a substantial tract of the guard line, you will give a signal – an owl call – and we will send an assault division with torches and incendiary arrows, to burn the towers. Understood?'

'Perfectly. You may count on us.'

The Macedonians set off and shortly afterwards they took off their armour and went down the stairs to the walkway which led to the side gate. When they found themselves out in the open they split up and crawled on all fours towards the sentries.

Memnon waited in silence on the battlement, looking out towards the big assault towers which loomed in the darkness like giants. Then he thought he recognized the voice of one of the sentries – perhaps part of the plan had already succeeded. Some more time went by and then he heard, quiet at first but then loud and clear, the call of an owl coming from a point along the wall at an equal distance between the two towers.

He went down the stairs quickly and approached the division which was getting ready for the sortie.

'Be careful. If you go out like that, with torches lit, you will be spotted straight away and part of our advantage will be wasted. Here's my plan: you must get as close as possible and as silently as possible to the point where our soldiers have replaced the Macedonian sentries – down there, between the two towers. Remain there hidden away until a second group brings you a covered brazier and amphorae full of bitumen; at that point blow the trumpets with all the breath you have and attack the Macedonian garrison, while the others set fire to the towers.

'The Macedonians believe they have virtually won the siege and they do not expect to be attacked now. Our sortie will be a success. Now, it is time, go now.'

The men headed for the side gate and, one by one, slipped out into the open, followed by the group carrying a jar full of embers and amphorae full of bitumen. Memnon watched on until the last of them had gone out and the iron gate had been closed, then he crossed the city on foot, towards his quarters. He did this almost every evening, strolling incognito among the people, listening to their talk, savouring their moods. The house he was staying in rose at the foot of the acropolis, and it was reached by first walking up a stairway and then along a narrow, steep path.

A servant was waiting for him with a lighted lamp. He opened the door that led in to the courtyard and accompanied his master towards the entrance portico. Memnon went to his bedchamber on the upper floor, where the handmaids had prepared a warm bath. He opened the window and listened: the sound of a trumpet had suddenly torn through the silence of the night, from the north-eastern side of the walls. The assault had begun.

A handmaid approached: 'Would you care to take your bath now, my Lord?'

Memnon did not reply and waited until he saw a reddish glow and then a column of smoke ascending and twirling its way into the dark sky.

Only then did he turn and unlace his armour. 'Yes,' he said.

25

THE ORDERLY WAS BREATHLESS as he rushed into the tent, but he managed to shout nevertheless: 'Sire! An attack! They have set fire to the assault towers!'

Alexander jumped to his feet and grabbed him by the shoulders. 'What do you mean? Are you out of your mind?'

'They took us by surprise, Sire ... they killed the sentries and managed to break through. They had amphorae full of bitumen and we simply couldn't put the flames out.'

Alexander pushed him to one side and ran outside: 'Quickly! Raise the alarm! Get all the men out! Craterus – the cavalry! Hephaestion, Perdiccas, Leonnatus – send out the Thracians and the Agrianians ... quickly!'

He leaped on to the first horse that came his way and set off at top speed towards the line beneath the wall. The fire was clearly visible now and two columns of flame and smoke stood out, rising and twisting in dense swirls into the black sky. When he reached the trench he heard the noise of fighting coming from each of the five assault towers.

In a matter of instants Craterus's heavy cavalry together with the Thracian and Agrianian light cavalry reached Alexander and rushed on ahead, engaging the attackers. The men from Halicarnassus were promptly forced to retreat to safety through the side gate. But two of the towers were completely lost – enveloped in smoke, they collapsed one after the other with a great crash, releasing a vortex of sparks and fresh flames which soon devoured what was left of their structure.

Alexander dismounted and walked towards the inferno. Many of his soldiers were dead, and it was clear that they had been taken by surprise in their sleep because they were not wearing their armour.

Hephaestion appeared soon afterwards: 'We've driven them back into the city. And now?'

'Gather up the dead,' replied the King, his expression as dark as the night around them, 'and set about rebuilding the towers. Tomorrow we will continue our attack with what we have left.'

The commander of the troops in service on the towers arrived, his head bowed, his spirits low: 'It was my fault. Punish me if you will, but do not punish my men because they did what they could.'

'The losses you have suffered are sufficient punishment for a commander,' replied Alexander. 'Now we must understand where the mistake was made: was there no one checking the sentries?'

'It seems impossible, Sire, but I had done the rounds just before the attack began and I heard the calls of the sentries. I had given orders to use only the thickest Macedonian dialect in order to avoid any problems . . .'

'And so?'

'With my own ears I heard all of them call out in

perfect Macedonian, but you must find this hard to believe.'

Alexander ran his hand over his forehead. 'I believe you, but from now on we must be continually aware that this opponent is the most cunning and the most dangerous we have had to face so far. As of tomorrow double the number of sentries and change the passwords at every change of guard. Now, gather up the dead and have the wounded taken back to the camp. Philip and his surgeons will take care of them.'

'I will do exactly as you have ordered and I promise that nothing like this will ever happen again, even if I have to stand guard myself.'

'That won't be necessary,' replied Alexander. 'What you should do instead is have our naval men teach you how to signal at night with a polished shield and the light of a fire.'

The commander nodded, but just then his attention was drawn by a figure walking around the embers of the burned towers, every now and then bending over as if inspecting something on the ground.

'Who is that?' he asked.

Alexander looked in the direction indicated and recognized the man as he turned and his face was illuminated for an instant in the flames.

'No need to worry – it's Callisthenes.' And as he spurred his horse on towards his official chronicler, he turned and shouted to the commander: 'Take care! If it happens again, then you'll pay for this time as well!'

Soon he was alongside Callisthenes, who was crouching down, observing one of their dead soldiers, definitely a sentry because he was dressed in full armour.

'What are you looking at?' asked the King as he leaped to the ground.

'Dagger,' replied Callisthenes. 'They used a dagger. A single stab wound to the back of the neck. And down there is another one – identical.'

'So the attackers were Macedonian.'

'What does this have to do with using a dagger?'

'The duty commander told me that all the sentries, right up to the very last moment, replied to all the calls in Macedonian dialect.'

'Does that surprise you? You certainly have no shortage of enemies back home – people who would be very pleased to see you humiliated and destroyed. And some of them will have come here to Halicarnassus – it's not such a long journey from Thermai.'

'What exactly are you doing here now?'

'I am a historian. The autopsy is essential procedure for anyone who aspires to being a true witness to events.'

'And so Thucydides is your model? I would never have guessed. Such unadulterated rigour does not become you – you enjoy living it up too much.'

'I take what I can wherever I find it, and in any case I have to know all there is to know: I decide what should not be told, what should be told and how to tell it. This is the historian's privilege.'

'And yet there are things happening right now which you cannot even guess at. While I can.'

'And what would these things be? If I may ask.'

'Memnon's plans. I realize now that he has studied everything I have done and perhaps everything my father Philip ever did. And this is what allows him to be one step ahead of us.'

'And in your opinion what is he thinking about now?'

'About the siege of Perinthus.'

Callisthenes would have liked to ask more, but he found himself alone with the corpse which lay at his feet as Alexander leaped on to the horse and rode off. The smouldering remains of the two towers collapsed, releasing a sheet of flame and a whirlwind of smoke which the wind soon dispersed.

The towers were rebuilt with some difficulty, using the hard, knotty trunks of olive trees, and the siege operations were slowed down. Memnon, who was receiving supplies regularly by sea, was in no rush to risk another sortie, and Alexander did not want to use the other machines without first checking them thoroughly because they too had been damaged by smaller fires.

What worried him most of all were the noises coming from inside the city – unmistakable noises, similar to those which his own carpenters were making as they reconstructed the towers.

When the new engines were finally in position and the rams started widening the breach, Alexander found himself faced with exactly what he had feared – a new semicircular bastion uniting the segments of the wall which were still intact.

'The same thing happened at Perinthus,' Parmenion recalled when he saw the improvised fortress appear behind the opening created by the battering-rams.

'And that's not all,' said Craterus. 'Just follow me please . . .'

They climbed to the top of one of the towers, the easternmost one, and from there they saw what the besieged citizens of Halicarnassus were busy preparing – a gigantic quadrangular structure made of wood with great square beams, connected lengthwise and crosswise.

'It has no wheels,' said Craterus. 'It is anchored to the ground.'

'They have no need of wheels,' said Alexander. 'They simply want to keep the breach in their sights. When we try to enter, they will let fly with showers of bolts and arrows – they will massacre us.'

'Memnon is a tough specimen,' commented Parmenion. 'I had warned you, Sire.'

Alexander turned sharply without making any attempt to conceal his annoyance. 'I will demolish the walls and even that damned wooden tower, General, whether Memnon likes it or not.' Then he turned to Craterus. 'Keep the tower under surveillance and let me know what they are up to.' He hurried down the steps, mounted his horse and returned to the camp.

*

The breach was widened even further, but each Macedonian assault met with a counterattack from Memnon, and his new bastion provided an excellent position for his archers, who easily picked off the attackers as they came through. The situation was virtually a stalemate, while the summer sun became warmer by the day and Alexander's reserves more and more depleted.

One night it was Perdiccas and his officers who led the garrison on the breach. Some wine had arrived from Ephesus, a gift from the city's administration for Alexander, and the King had had some of it distributed to his officers.

It had been some time since they had drunk anything as good as this and Perdiccas and his men were anything but moderate in their consumption. By midnight they were all under the influence. One of them started singing the praises of the beauty of the women of Halicarnassus, of which he had heard tale from a merchant at the camp, and the others became excited – bragging and challenging one another to sort out the siege once and for all with a surprise turnaround attack.

Perdiccas came out of the tent and looked at the accursed breach on which so many brave Macedonian soldiers had already died. At that moment the light sea breeze seemed to clear his mind and he had a vision of himself beneath the walls of Thebes, slipping in through the city gates with his men to resolve the stalemate.

He thought of Cleopatra and the warm, fragrant night in which she had welcomed him to her bed. A night just like this one.

After all, he felt, victory was always possible if determination was greater than the adversity faced, and like all drunks he believed he was invincible and believed he could give substance to his dreams. And in his dream he saw Alexander lining up the assembled army to honour him and to have the heralds declaim a solemn commendation for the conqueror of Halicarnassus.

He went back into the tent with a deeply troubled expression on his face and said quietly, so that only those nearest him could hear, 'Gather the men, we are going to attack the bastion.'

26

'DID YOU SAY we're going to attack the bastion? Is that really what you said?' asked one of his officers.

'That's exactly what I said,' replied Perdiccas. 'And this very night everyone will see whether you really have the guts you've been bragging so much about.'

Everyone started laughing. 'Are we ready then?' another one started shouting.

Perdiccas was incredibly serious in his drunkenness: 'Go to your divisions, there isn't much time. A lantern raised above my tent will be the signal. Bring up the ladders, the hooks and the ropes – we will attack in the old manner, in silence, without the assault towers and without catapults. Get a move on!'

His companions looked at him, their faces a mixture of amazement and incredulity, but then they obeyed because Perdiccas's tone left no room for negotiation, his expression even less so. Shortly afterwards the lantern was raised above his tent and they all approached the walls in a tight formation, silently, towards the breach through which they could see the improvised bastion built within the city, like a sort of unifying arch.

'Keep close to the walls which are still standing right up to the last moment,' ordered Perdiccas, 'and then, on my signal, start the attack. We have to surprise the sentries on their rounds before the support troops have time to reach us. As soon as we have taken the battlement, we will sound the alarm with the trumpets to call the King and the other commanders. And now . . . forward!'

The officers passed on the order and the troops advanced in the darkness up to the two edges of the breach, then they rushed towards the base of the bastion, a distance of about one hundred paces. But as they were just about to start climbing up, putting the ladders in position and swinging their grappling hooks, the silence of the night was torn by sharp trumpet blasts, by shouts and the clangour of weaponry.

The battlement was teeming with soldiers and other warriors in full armour came streaming out of the side gate and the Mylasa Gate, taking Perdiccas's divisions by surprise from behind and crushing them against the bastion, from which the bolts and arrows rained down in sheets.

'Oh, by the gods!' exclaimed one of the officers. 'We're in a trap. Sound the alarm, Perdiccas, sound the alarm! We need help from the King!'

'No!' shouted Perdiccas. 'We can still do it. Push back the attack on our flank, while we climb up the bastion.'

'You're out of your mind!' shouted the officer. 'They're all over us. Sound the alarm or I'll do it myself, damn you!'

Perdiccas looked around and the instinct of self-preservation injected a flush of fire into his veins. His mind suddenly reacted to the drunkenness and he realized that disaster was imminent.

'Follow me!' he ordered. 'Everyone behind me! We'll clear the way right up to the camp. The alarm! Sound the alarm!'.

The trumpet ripped into the still air of the summer's night, echoed against the walls of the huge natural bowl and bounced back to Alexander's camp as a long wailing noise.

'It's the alarm trumpet, Sire!' shouted one of the guards as he burst into the royal tent. 'It's coming from the bastion.'

Alexander leaped from his bed and grabbed his sword. 'Perdiccas ... that stupid bastard has got himself into trouble. I might have known it would happen!'

He ran outside shouting, 'To your horses! To your horses, men! Perdiccas is in danger!' and he himself set off at a gallop followed by the royal guard which was always ready for battle at any time, night and day.

In the meantime Perdiccas was leading his men in their retreat and was making ground, fighting furiously to open up a way out. But Halicarnassian troops had gathered on the battlements above the breach and they had an easy time of it, given the superior nature of their position, while the Macedonians had to clamber up through the rocks and the rubble of the ruin.

The trumpeter continued to blow his sharp, anguish-ridden calls, while Perdiccas, his hands and knees bloody, battled his way to the breach and sought to fight through the enemy lines with all the courage and the strength that comes with sheer despair.

When he heard the galloping of Alexander's cavalry, he had already opened up a passage and was leading his men behind him down to the other side towards the camp.

Memnon's troops closed ranks in a compact line, effected an about turn and stood with their backs to the bastion. The terrain before them was littered with the corpses of Macedonian soldiers, led to their deaths in a suicidal attack by the irresponsible enthusiasm of their commander.

Alexander appeared before his men suddenly, as if born out of the night – the glow of the torches illuminated his face with an intense bloodlike warmth and his hair curled on each side of his face like a lion's mane.

'What have you done, Perdiccas? What have you done? You led your men to slaughter!'

Perdiccas fell to his knees, exhausted by the battle and by his despair. Alexander's cavalry took up position to face a possible enemy attack. But Memnon's experienced men held firm on the breach, shoulder to shoulder, in close ranks, waiting for their opponent's next move.

'We will wait for dawn,' said Alexander. 'To make any move now would be too dangerous.'

'Give me more troops and let me attack . . . let me redeem myself, Alexander!' cried Perdiccas, completely out of his mind.

'No,' replied the King, his voice firm. 'We cannot afford to make any more mistakes. You will have your moment, Perdiccas.'

And so they waited in silence for the rest of the night. Every now and then the darkness was rent by a burning arrow fired to illuminate the space in front of the breach. The flaming missiles flew through the air like meteorites, quivering and sizzling as they stuck fast in the ground.

As the sun rose, the King ordered Perdiccas to conduct a roll-call of his men to see how many of them were dead or missing. Of the two thousand he had taken with him on the attack, only one thousand seven hundred men responded. The others had fallen in the ambush and their bodies lay unburied, between the breach and the bastion.

The King sent a herald to ask for a meeting with Memnon.

'I have to negotiate for the return of our soldiers' bodies,' he explained.

The herald listened to the conditions the King was proposing, then took a white drape, mounted his horse and set off towards the enemy lines, preceded by three blasts on the trumpet, the signal for a truce.

From the breach there came another three blasts and the man moved forward slowly, at a walk, to the base of the rubble.

Some time passed by and a second herald came down on foot from the top of the breach – he was a Greek from the colonies with a marked Doric accent, probably from Rhodes.

'King Alexander asks to negotiate the return of the bodies of his fallen soldiers,' said the Macedonian herald, 'and he wishes to hear the conditions imposed by your commander.'

'I have no authority to negotiate any conditions,' replied Memnon's herald. 'Nevertheless, Commander Memnon is prepared to meet your King in person, immediately after sunset today.'

'Where?'

'Down there,' and the Greek pointed to a wild fig tree growing near a monumental tomb along the road that led in the direction of Mylasa from the city gates. 'But you must move your army back by one stadium – the meeting will take place at exactly half-way between the two lines. Commander Memnon will have no escort with him, and he expects the same of Alexander.'

'I will report your words to the King, and if I do not return to you immediately then it means that the King accepts.'

He mounted his horse and started back towards Alexander. The Greek waited for a moment and then climbed back up the rubble and disappeared among the rows of soldiers on the battlement.

Alexander had his army move back the required distance; then he returned to the camp and waited for sunset in his tent. For the rest of the day he ate no food and drank no wine. He was taking the defeat personally, and Memnon's formidable ability to reply in kind and with awesome force humiliated him. For the first time in his life he felt a frustrating sense of impotence and profound solitude.

The triumphs he had enjoyed up until that moment now seemed remote and almost forgotten – Memnon of Rhodes was a millstone that blocked his way forwards, an obstacle which with the passing of time seemed ever more insurmountable.

He had given orders to the guards not to let anyone in and not even Leptine had dared approach during the day. By now she could read his expression, she could see the light and the shadow in the depths of his eyes, as if they were a sky carrying portents of a storm.

But as sunset approached and Alexander was getting ready for his meeting with his enemy, the noise of an argument reached him in his tent and then, immediately afterwards, Perdiccas burst in, brushing aside the King's guards.

Alexander nodded and his soldiers left them alone.

'I deserve to die!' exclaimed the distraught Perdiccas. 'I have cost so many brave soldiers their lives, I have brought dishonour on our army and I have forced you into a humiliating negotiation. Kill me!' he shouted, holding out his sword.

His face was haunted, his eyes red and troubled. Alexander had not seen him in this state since the siege of Thebes. He studied him without batting an eyelid, and then pointed to a chair: 'Sit down.'

Perdiccas continued to hold out the sword, his hands and arms trembling wildly.

'I told you to sit down,' Alexander ordered again with a slightly higher, even firmer tone of voice.

His friend collapsed into the chair and the sword fell from his hands.

'Why did you attack the bastion?' asked Alexander.

'I had been drinking, we had all been drinking . . . it seemed feasible to me . . . a dead certainty even.'

'It was because you were drunk. Any man in his right mind would have realized that it was tantamount to suicide – at night and on that terrain.'

'There was no one on the battlements. Total silence. There weren't even any sentries.'

'And you fell for it. Memnon is the most formidable opponent we will ever come across. Understand? Do you understand that?' he shouted.

Perdiccas nodded.

'Memnon is not only a valiant fighter – he is a man of extraordinary cunning and intelligence who watches us night and day, studying our every lapse in concentration, every false step, every unthinking move. Then he strikes with devastating force.

'Here we are not on a battlefield on which we can unleash the superior power of our cavalry or the phalanx. What we have before us is a rich and powerful city defended by a well-trained army which has a strategic advantage over us because of its location, a city which suffers none of the difficulties normally associated with a siege. Our only chance is to open a sufficiently wide breach in their walls to succeed in overwhelming Memnon's defences. And this can only take place in the full light of day.

'It is our strength against theirs, our intelligence against theirs, our prudence against theirs. Nothing else. Do you know what we will do now? We will remove the rubble, we will clear the stone from the breach until we free the terrain completely and then we will send in the towers against the semicircular bastion and we will destroy it. If they build another one, we will eliminate that, we will continue in this manner – methodically – until we have driven them all into the sea. Do you understand, Perdiccas?

'Until then you will obey my orders and my orders alone. The loss of your men is sufficient punishment. Now I will bring back their bodies. You, with your division, will pay the funeral respects, you will placate their tormented souls with sacrifices. The day will come when you will be able to repay your debt. For now, I order you to live.'

He picked up the sword and offered it to his friend.

Perdiccas accepted it, sheathed it and stood up to go. His eyes were full of tears.

27

THE FACE OF THE man who stood before him was hidden by a Corinthian helmet. His bronze breastplate was decorated in silver, and he carried his sword hanging from a chain-mail baldric. Over his shoulders was a cloak of blue linen which the evening breeze filled like a sail.

Alexander instead wore no helmet and had walked to the designated point leading Bucephalas by the bridle. He said, 'I am Alexander, King of Macedon, and I come to negotiate the ransom for my fallen soldiers.'

The man's gaze flashed for an instant through the shadow of his helmet and in that moment Alexander recognized the light of the eyes that Apelles had succeeded in capturing in his drawing. The voice was metallic as it rang out from the cavity of the sallet: 'I am Commander Memnon.'

'What do you require for the return of my soldiers?'

'The answer to a question.'

Alexander looked at him in amazement. 'Which question?'

Memnon seemed to hesitate for a moment and Alexander felt that he was about to ask for news of Barsine, because a man in his position must have informers everywhere and it was almost certain – having heard what had happened – that he was tormented by doubt.

But the question was another: 'Why have you brought war to these lands?'

'It was the Persians who first invaded Greece; I come now to avenge the destruction of our temples and our cities, to avenge our young soldiers who fell at Marathon, at Thermopylae, at Plataea.'

'You are lying,' replied Memnon. 'You feel nothing for the Greeks and they feel nothing for you. Tell me the truth. I will speak to no one of it.'

The wind grew stronger and enveloped the two warriors in a cloud of red dust.

'I have come to build the biggest realm that has ever been seen on earth. And I will not stop until I have reached the waves of the farthest ocean.'

'That is what I feared.'

'And you? You are not a king, you are not even a Persian. Why are you so obstinate?'

'Because I hate war. And I hate young, reckless madmen such as yourself who want to achieve glory by spilling blood all over the world. I will make you eat dust, Alexander. I will force you to return to Macedon, to die with a dagger in your back just like your father.'

The King did not react to this provocation: 'There will never be peace for as long as there are borders and barriers, different languages and customs, different gods and beliefs. You should join me.'

'It is not possible. I have only one word, and one conviction.'

'Then the best will win.'

'Not necessarily – fate is blind.'

'Will you return my dead to me?'

'You may take them.'

'How much of a truce will you allow us?'

'Until the end of the first watch.'

'That will be enough. I am grateful.'

The enemy commander lowered his head as a sign of agreement.

'Farewell, Commander Memnon.'

'Farewell, King Alexander.'

Memnon turned his back and walked towards the northern side of the walls. A side gate opened and his blue cloak disappeared into the darkness of the entrance. The heavy door, reinforced with iron, closed behind him with a long grating noise.

Alexander returned to the camp and told Perdiccas to go and collect his dead.

The bearers picked up the bodies one by one and consigned them to the priests and their attendants so that they might clean the bodies up and prepare them for the funeral.

Fifteen great pyres were constructed and on each of these the bodies of twenty men were placed, dressed in their armour, washed, combed and perfumed.

A guard of honour from Perdiccas's ranks shouted out the name of each fallen soldier as he was mentioned by their commander. At the end the ashes were gathered and placed in urns together with the swords of the dead, held over the pyres until red hot and then ritually bent. The urns were then sealed and marked with a scroll which carried the name, family and place of origin of each of the deceased.

The following day the urns were loaded on to a ship

and sent to Macedonia, to rest for eternity in the land of their ancestors.

That same day, under cover of the ballistae, the Macedonians began to remove the rubble from the breach so as to clear the way for their siege engines. From the top of the hill Alexander observed the operations and saw that inside the city Memnon's gigantic tower continued to rise.

Eumenes approached. As usual he was in full combat dress, even although up until that moment he had not taken part in even a single military exercise.

'When that tower is completed, it's going to be difficult getting anywhere near the bastion.'

'Yes,' said Alexander. 'Memnon will have catapults and ballistae installed up there and he'll have us kept under constant fire at close range.'

'All he'll have to do is aim into the crowd to cause a massacre.'

'And that is why I want to open up the breach before he has completed the tower.'

'It cannot be done.'

'Why?'

'I have calculated the progress rates of the work. You must have seen the clock I've had constructed on the hill.'

'Yes . . . I have seen it.'

'Well . . . their tower rises at approximately three cubits per day. You must have noticed the other instrument I've had constructed alongside the clock.'

'Of course . . .' replied Alexander, with the slightest trace of annoyance in his voice.

'If you are not interested, I'll just keep it all for myself,' rejoined Eumenes, resentfully.

'Don't be stupid. What is that instrument?'

'A little toy of my own invention – a viewfinder on a turntable which aligns a sighting pole with the object being observed. By means of a simple geometric calculation, I can establish how much per day the new construction rises.'

'Well?'

'Well . . . when we have removed less than half of the rubble around the breach, they will have completed their work . . . in other words they will then be able to tear us apart with a few shots from up there. I have calculated that they will have twelve catapults positioned on three platforms, one above the other.'

Alexander lowered his head and after a short while said, 'So . . . what do you suggest we do?'

'Do you really want my opinion? Well . . . I would forget about clearing the rubble and I would concentrate all our engines on the north-eastern sector, where it seems the walls are less thick. If you would care to take a look at my instruments . . .'

Alexander let himself be led to the site and put his eye to the sight.

'There . . . you have to aim first through the external side and then the internal side on the left-hand side of the breach. Can you see? And now turn to the right-hand side . . . like that.'

'It's true,' Alexander agreed as he stood up straight. 'The walls are less thick on the other side.'

'Exactly. Now . . . if you locate all the towers there, by tomorrow evening you could certainly open up a sufficiently wide breach to work around the semicircular bastion and take it from the side. The Agrianians are excellent climbers and if you send them in on that flank they will free up the way for the assault troops who can thus enter the city and take the defenders from behind.'

Alexander put his hands on Eumenes' shoulders, 'And to think that up to now I've had you working as my secretary. If we are victorious, you will take part in all the meetings of the high command with full permission to express your opinions. And now let us move those towers and start battering the walls immediately. I want continuous shifts, night and day. The good people of Halicarnassus won't be getting much sleep for as long as we are around.'

*

The King's orders were carried out without delay. Over the following days, with considerable effort and the use of hundreds of men and animals, the assault towers were moved to the north-eastern side of the walls and the work of the battering-rams began again. It was an obsessive, implacable hammering – a deafening noise that made not only the walls tremble, but also the ground beneath them. Eumenes, on orders from Alexander, personally inspected each of the assault machines, accompanied by a group of engineers who corrected the balance and added on platforms to increase their performance.

Conditions inside the towers were frightful – the heat and dust, the lack of space, the physical effort involved in pushing the gigantic iron-clad beams against the stone walls, the violent counterblows, the unbearable noise were all ordeals for the men involved in this undertaking.

Water-bearers were continually going up and down the stairs, to slake the thirst of the men suffering in their inhuman work.

But they all felt that the King was watching them closely, and indeed he had promised a generous prize for the first men to bring the defences of the enemy tumbling down. Alexander, however, was aware that the success of their mission was not entirely dependent on the engines and how they functioned – he felt sure that Memnon was planning some countermove.

He called Parmenion, Cleitus the Black and his companions – Hephaestion, Perdiccas, Leonnatus, Ptolemy, Lysimachus, Craterus, Philotas, Seleucus and Eumenes – to a meeting on the hill.

The secretary general was still covered in dirt and partially deaf from the noise, to the point where the others had to raise their voices in order to be heard. Behind them, the army had been put on alert and was lined up ready for action: in the front row the shieldsmen, armed with light weapons and playing the role of assault troops, together with the Thracian and Agrianian troops. Behind them, in the centre and on the left wing, was the Macedonian heavy infantry; to the right the hoplites of the Greek allies. Out on the flanks was the cavalry. Bringing up the rear were the reserves, under Parmenion's command – Philip's veterans, men of extraordinary experience and extremely tough in battle.

They all waited in silence, their arms at their feet, in the shade of the first row of olive trees.

In the meantime, on Perdiccas's orders, a row of ballistae had been positioned on a rise and aimed at the

Mylasa Gate, from which the Halicarnassians might easily launch a sortie.

'Eumenes has something to tell us,' announced Alexander.

The secretary took a look at his solar clock, at the shadow projected on to the wooden face by a pole standing at its centre.

'Very soon, the wall will begin to collapse on the north-eastern side. The upper layers of stone blocks are already giving way and the lower ones are shifting under the blows of the heavier battering-rams on the lower platforms. The collapse should be simultaneous over a width of at least one hundred and fifty feet.'

Alexander looked around – his generals and his companions all looked tired after the long battles, the sleepless nights, the continuous counterattacks, the ambushes, the ordeals and the fatigue of the months of siege.

'Today everything is at stake,' he said. 'If we win, our fame alone will open up every gate from here to Mount Amanus. If we are defeated, we will lose all we have conquered up to now. Remember one thing above all else – our opponent is certainly about to make his crucial move, and none of us can say exactly what it will be. But just look at that tower . . .' and he pointed to the gigantic trellis of wood which stood now, bristling with ballistae and catapults, over one hundred feet high, '. . . and you realize how formidable he is. And now our army will advance to the siege engines. We must be ready to move forwards as soon as the breach opens. Go!'

Perdiccas asked to speak: 'Alexander, I ask of you the privilege of leading the first assault. Give me the shieldsmen and the assault troops and I promise by the gods that tomorrow you will sit and dine in the palace of the Satrap of Halicarnassus.'

'Take all the men you need, Perdiccas, and do what you must.'

They all went to join their men and when the trumpet blew they set off on the march towards the towers. Only the veterans, under the watchful gaze of General Parmenion, waited motionless in the shade of the olive trees.

28

AT SUCH A CRUCIAL moment Alexander felt there was only one horse he could trust fully, and so he had Bucephalas brought to him. He stroked the stallion's muzzle and his neck and then, at a walk, rode him down towards the walls. At Alexander's request, Hephaestion and Seleucus rode alongside him on their own chargers.

A sharp whistling noise made them turn and they saw that the great tower behind the round bastion was in operation now and tight flurries of iron bolts were being fired at the right flank of the Macedonian army.

'Take cover!' shouted the Black. 'Get out of there or they'll run you through like stuck birds. Out of there ... move, I said!'

The right wing effected a rapid about-turn and took up position behind the centre while Cleitus ordered his own men to run for the cover of the walls, where the ballistae could not reach them. In the meantime, Lysimachus, who was commanding his own batteries of war-engines from the high ground, replied with a fierce counterattack in the direction of the tower. Some Halicarnassians took the full force of the direct hit and plummeted, screaming loudly, from the top of the construction.

There now came the noise of the great blocks of stone

as they fell from the eastern sector of the walls, hammered by the constant blows from the battering-rams.

Perdiccas set to with his shieldsmen and the Agriani-ans. He shouted like a madman as he rushed forward, his spear held tightly, but just then there came a trumpet blast, quickly followed by another – sharp, tense, lacer-ating. An orderly came galloping up to Alexander: 'Sire! King Alexander! Alarm on the eastern flank! Alarm!'

Hephaestion turned to Alexander, 'It's impossible. There are no gates on the eastern flank.'

'Yes there are,' said Seleucus. 'Near the coast.'

'But we would have seen them arriving at this dis-tance,' said Hephaestion.

Another orderly arrived: 'Sire! They have come down over the top of the walls – thousands of them. They used ropes and fishing nets! They're on us, Sire!'

'Don't spare the horses!' ordered Alexander. 'Quickly . . . quickly!' and he spurred Bucephalas on towards the rearguard of his men and saw there thousands of Persian soldiers attacking from the right, letting loose great showers of arrows and javelins. The trumpets rang out again, from the left this time.

'The Mylasa Gate!' shouted Seleucus. 'Alexander, look! It's another sortie!'

'Keep the side gate covered!' shouted the Black. 'Care-ful, damn you! Leonnatus! Leonnatus! Over on that side! Watch out for your flank!'

Leonnatus turned with his *pezhetairoi* and found himself facing the mercenary infantry, led by the giant Ephialtes, wielding a bronze shield with a fiery-eyed gorgon which had serpents for hair, shouting, 'Forward! Forward! Now is the time! Let's finish them all off!'

The King rode right up to the front line, where the Persian assault troops had joined forces with Ephialtes's Greek mercenaries and were attacking furiously, while the catapults on the bastion were now in action with long, arching shots.

Under a fearful rain of missiles, the Macedonians began to break up and the Greek mercenaries started moving forward, pushing them back with their shields. Alexander, who at that moment was off on the left flank, drove Bucephalas into the midst of the fighting; he brandished his double-bladed axe and shouted wildly to encourage his men. An enormous stone fell not far from him, crushing one of his men like an insect. Blood spurted all over Bucephalas's flanks and the horse reared up, neighing loudly.

The King tried in vain to push towards the centre, where his soldiers were taking the brunt of the enemy initiative, but the fighting there before him and the rain of stones from the catapults blocked his way and all his energies simply went into stemming the tide of enemy soldiers which flowed from the Mylasa Gate.

The Black saw Ephialtes come forward like a wild fury and wedge himself and his men into the Macedonian centre, which continued to lose ground. The young *pezhetairoi* gave way in front of the frighteningly compact drive of the mercenaries. Only Perdiccas, out on the extreme left of the line-up, held his ground. But the situation was deteriorating. From the top of the bastion tower the catapults began to fire unusual projectiles – amphorae full of pitch and bitumen which landed at the base of the Macedonian assault towers, spreading their contents over the ground. Immediately afterwards, up on the walls, the Persian archers appeared, letting loose a cluster of fire arrows. The fire roared as it spread and enveloped the engines, transforming them into colossal torches.

Perdiccas then turned command over to his lieutenant and climbed up through the flames to the first platform, where sheer terror had driven his men to abandon their battering-ram which swung freely in its supports.

'Back to your positions!' he shouted. 'Resume your positions! The walls are about to collapse. Come on, one last blow!' He threw his shield to the ground and grabbed a handle of the battering-ram himself, while tongues of flame licked threateningly through the cracks in the flooring.

Initially the men simply watched on in amazement, astonished by his superhuman courage and then, one by one, they returned to their positions and resumed their task of driving the battering-ram into the walls, shouting to overcome the terror and the unbearable heat of the flames. The great iron head, driven on by the desperation of hundreds of arms, regained impetus and crashed noisily against the walls. The enormous blocks, already loosened, started to move, then one or two actually fell down in a cloud of smoke and dust. Further blows opened up a wide breach and the enormous collapse that resulted helped to suffocate the fire.

At the centre of the Macedonian line, however, the

retreat of the *pezhetairoi* was about to become a rout under the unstoppable drive of Ephialtes. Then the Black shouted out: 'Leonnatus, stop him!' Hearing his words, Leonnatus cleared his way through the enemy ranks with a series of wild axe blows and found himself facing Ephialtes.

The two colossi stood there breathless, both of them unrecognizable in their ordeal. They were both bleeding from many wounds and their bodies glistened with sweat like statues in the rain.

Alexander turned around and saw his father's veterans motionless in the shadow of the olive trees, unfazed and rested under the impassive gaze of Parmenion. He shouted: 'Trumpet, call up the reserves!' It really was their last chance; the rough, rocky ground was littered with stones and made it impossible for the cavalry to charge.

Parmenion heard the trumpet blast, insistent and full of anguish, calling him to lead his men into battle: 'Veterans, for King Philip and for King Alexander, forward!' And suddenly the sound of thunder tore through the leaden air – the thunder of Chaeronaea!

The enormous drum, hidden among the olive trees, made itself heard and the powerful phalanx started moving forward, spears erect, like some frightful porcupine, in a rhythmic march, shouting at each step: '*Alalalài! Alalalài!*'

Alexander, who had struggled almost as far as the centre, ordered Leonnatus's *pezhetairoi* to open up on the flanks to let the veterans through, and indeed they rushed in like an avalanche against Memnon's mercenaries, who were exhausted by now. Leonnatus in the meantime was fighting like a lion against his gigantic adversary and the deafening clangs of their blows travelled out over the plain, echoes of a titanic clash.

Leonnatus had plenty of experience as a wrestler and he pulled a feint on Ephialtes, immediately forcing him down on to one knee. In an instant the Macedonian drew himself up with both feet planted firmly and let fly with a tremendous backhand blow from his axe into the giant's back, bringing him firmly to the ground.

As the sun set the soldiers continued fighting, crazed with fatigue and fury in the reel of battle. The Greek mercenaries, already exhausted, had lost their commander now and the unstoppable force of Parmenion's veterans began to have its effect – they retreated with dignity at first and then started fleeing with no sense of order, simply trying to reach the Mylasa Gate or the side gate on the northern sector, near the sea. But the defenders of the city were frightened by what they had seen and they closed all the gates so that many of their soldiers were left to perish beneath the walls, run through by the *sarissae* of Parmenion's men.

When Alexander had the order to cease combat sounded, Perdiccas was firmly installed on the breach in the eastern sector, a division of Agrianians had scaled the round bastion and had cleared it of defenders, yet others had scaled the wooden tower and aimed the ballistae and the catapults towards the centre of the city.

Many torches and fires were lit, to protect them against counterattacks by the enemy during the night.

Halicarnassus was now at the mercy of its conqueror.

29

ALEXANDER DID NOT SLEEP that night. The outcome of his battle with Memnon had been so uncertain right up to the last moment. More than once he had felt himself to be on the verge of defeat and humiliation; it was impossible to sleep with all that on his mind.

His men had lit a bonfire on the battlement and he waited for the light of day completely unable to relax, almost as though all his senses were clenched tight in spasm. It was a moonless night, and the whole city was immersed in darkness and silence – the only fires burning were those on the huge breach guarded by his soldiers, on the brick bastion occupied by the Agrianians and at the base of the great wooden tower. The Macedonians were clearly visible, while their enemy remained hidden away.

How many of them were left? How many armed men were concealed out there in the shadows? Perhaps they were preparing an ambush, or perhaps Memnon was waiting for sea-borne reinforcements.

When his triumph was at hand, the King felt that fate might be about to trick him once again; right up to the very last moment the enemy commander might invent some new tactic. Memnon was older and more experienced, he had managed so far to contain Alexander, to respond to each blow in kind, or even to pre-empt his moves.

That evening Alexander gave orders that anyone found drinking even a drop of wine was to be executed, whether the offender was a humble soldier or the most famous general. He also ordered that everyone should remain in full battledress.

Groups of his men patrolled door to door with lighted torches, right up to the side gate, maintaining contact with one another by means of shouted signals. Of all the commanders, Perdiccas was the most vigilant. After a long day of continuous and exhausting fighting, after having guided through the flames the battering-ram that had inflicted the decisive blow on the walls of Halicarnassus, he had not conceded himself even a moment's respite. He went from one guard post to another, shaking his men as they succumbed to sleep. He goaded the younger men, exhorting them to make up for their poor performance in comparison with the veterans who, despite their age, had succeeded in grabbing victory from the jaws of defeat.

Alexander looked at him and then looked at Leonnatus, a giant in the darkness as he leaned on his spear, and Ptolemy, who just then was patrolling on horseback out on the plain with the other horsemen of the guard corps to avert a possible attack from outside. And Lysimachus, standing upright there near the catapults, and farther off the grey hair of Parmenion, who like an old lion had kept out of the way initially, preserving his own strength and that of his men, waiting for the moment when the fatal blow was required to annihilate the enemy. These men were the backbone of his army.

At other moments he searched for other thoughts to provide distraction, to lighten his heart, thoughts other than the war and the fatigue of battle – he thought of Mieza and the deer grazing along the flower-covered banks of the river, or of naked Diogenes, who was certainly happily asleep now in his churn by the seashore, together with the dog who shared his food and his bed. The dreams of Diogenes the philosopher were lulled by the sound of the waves breaking on the pebble-covered shore. What were the dreams of the old wise man? What were his mysterious visions?

And he thought, too, of his own mother, and when he imagined her sitting in her solitary room reading the poetry of Sappho, he felt that deep down in himself there was still a little boy, an insecure child who instinctively starts in the night, frightened by the cry of a nocturnal bird echoing in the empty sky.

The time passed in these reveries seemed endless. He jumped suddenly when someone put a hand on his shoulder.

'Hephaestion, is that you?'

His friend handed him a bowl of warm soup. 'Eat something. Leptine made it for you and had it sent down here with an orderly.'

'What is it?'

'Broad bean soup. It's good – I've tasted a spoonful.'

Alexander started eating, 'It's not bad at all. Shall I leave you some?'

Hephaestion nodded, 'Just like the old times, when we were up in the mountains, in exile.'

'That's true. But there was never any warm soup back then.'

'You're right.'

'Do you miss those days?'

'No . . . no, certainly not. But it's nice to think back on them. Just you and me against the world.' He put a hand on Alexander's head and ruffled his hair. 'Things are different now. Sometimes I wonder if it'll ever happen again.'

'What?'

'Just you and me alone, together on a journey.'

'Who knows, my friend?'

Hephaestion leaned forward to poke the fire with the point of his sword and Alexander noticed something hanging from his friend's neck, something small that glinted in the light of the flames: it was a milk tooth, a tiny incisor mounted in gold, and he recalled the day when, as a child, he had given it to Hephaestion as a token of eternal friendship.

'Until death?' Hephaestion had asked him.

'Until death,' he had replied.

At that moment came the call of a sentry, signalling to his companions to the right and left of him. Hephaestion moved off to continue his rounds. Alexander saw him disappear into the darkness and had the feeling, very strong and clear, that if there was a journey being made ready for the pair of them in the future, it was in the direction of some mysterious region, wrapped in darkness for now.

More time passed and they heard the calls of the

second watch. It must have been around midnight. Then Alexander heard footsteps approaching and rubbed his tired eyes. It was Eumenes.

The secretary general sat down nearby and seemed to stare into the fire.

'What are you looking at?' asked the King.

'The fire,' replied Eumenes. 'I don't like this fire.'

The King turned towards him with an expression of surprise on his face. 'What's wrong with the fire?'

'The flames are turning in our direction, the wind has changed direction. It's blowing from the sea now.'

'Just as it does every night about this time.'

'Exactly. But tonight it's different.'

Alexander stared at him and suddenly a frightful thought leapt into his mind. Almost immediately a cry of alarm off to the right confirmed the vision that had come to him so suddenly – a fire was raging at the base of one of the great wooden towers.

'There's another one!' shouted Eumenes, pointing to a house just in front of them, a hundred feet or so away.

From the left came the voice of Perdiccas: 'Fire! Fire! Alarm!'

Lysimachus arrived breathless from running: 'They're out to roast us alive!' he said. 'They're burning all the houses next to the breach and the brick wall. The wooden tower is going up like a torch . . . look!'

Memnon was playing the last card in his hand, counting on the favourable wind. Alexander jumped to his feet: 'Quickly! We have to stop them lighting other fires – send out the assault troops, the shieldsmen, the Thracians and the Agrianians. Kill all those you find setting fires.'

In the meantime all the companions were running to him to receive their orders. Seleucus, Philotas, Leonnatus and Ptolemy were all present.

'Listen to me!' shouted Alexander above the roar of the flames which the wind was driving ever higher and in their direction. 'You, Seleucus, and you, Leonnatus, take half of the *pezhetairoi*, cross through the quarter they have set fire to and line up on the other side – your job is to block any counter-attack. It is clear they aim to regain control of the breach.

'Ptolemy and Philotas – line up the rest of the troops behind the breach and station guards on all the gates! I want no surprises from behind. Lysimachus, get the ballistae and the catapults out of here or they'll end up being destroyed when the tower collapses! Go now! Move!'

The wooden tower was now completely enveloped in fire and the rising wind brought tongues of flame that licked the eastern sector of the breach. The heat was almost unbearable and the glow of the huge torch spread light over an immense area around the walls, so that the Agrianian archers were easily able to sight the Halicarnassians setting the fires and pick them off with their arrows. The beams of the base were soon consumed by the flames and the enormous trellis fell with a terrible crash, raising a column of smoke some three hundred feet high, higher than any tower, higher than any building in the whole city.

Alexander was forced to abandon his observation point because of the heat, but he installed himself on the next tower, near the side gate, where he still had a good view.

From there he sent his orderlies off to the various sectors and received news from them on the situation as it developed.

He ordered Lysimachus to use the catapults to destroy the houses near the buildings which were already alight and to contain the fire – the rain of huge stones launched from the war-engines immediately increased the din and the confusion of that infernal night.

But the King's countermoves proved to be the right ones. The assault troops' and the Agrianians' operations put an end to the fires, while the heavy infantry lined up on the other side of the burned quarter dissuaded the Persians and the mercenaries from making any attempt to surprise the Macedonian army, all of whom were dazed and rattled by the violence of the flames.

Eumenes called up many labourers from the camp and had them shovel dust, sand and rubble on to the fires which were still burning. Gradually they were brought under control. The wooden tower that had involved so much work was reduced to a great pile of ash and embers, out of which jutted massive beams, carbonized and smouldering.

As dawn broke, the first rays of the sun struck the golden four-horse carriage on the top of the Mausoleum, while the rest of the city was still in darkness. Then, slowly, as the disc of the sun gradually appeared above the mountains, the cone of light descended the great stepped pyramid and shone on the multicoloured frieze by Scopas and Bryaxis, illuminating the fine Corinthian colonnade, the golden volutes, the fluted shafts, profiled in gold on a background of purple.

In that riot of colour, in that triumph of crystalline light, the spectral silence which enveloped Halicarnassus was truly unsettling. Could it be that not even the mothers of the city cried for their sons who had fallen in battle?

'Can it be?' Alexander asked Eumenes, who had approached just then.

'It is possible,' replied the secretary. 'No one cries for a mercenary. The mercenary has no mother, no father, and not even any friends. All he has is his spear, the tool with which he earns his daily bread – the stalest and most bitter of all breads.'

30

PTOLEMY RAN TO HIS SIDE: 'Alexander, we await your orders.'

'Take Perdiccas and Lysimachus, divide the assault troops and the shieldsmen between you and search the entire city. The Greek hoplites and our *pezhetairoi* will follow you as reinforcements. You must flush out all the armed men who are left alive, and above all else you must look for Memnon. I do not want him to come to any harm – if you find him, bring him to me.'

'We will do as you say,' said Ptolemy, and off he went to inform his companions.

The King waited, together with Eumenes, under the roof of a blockhouse on the walls, from which he had a reasonable view of Halicarnassus. Not long afterwards Ptolemy sent him an orderly with this message:

The satrap Orontobates, the tyrant Pixodarus and the Persian garrison have all taken refuge in the two fortresses in the port. They are both impregnable, there being no room for us to bring up the siege engines. For the moment there is no sign of Memnon. I await your orders.

Alexander had Bucephalas brought to him and set off on horseback through the city streets. All doors and windows were closed tight – the people of the city were terrified and had locked themselves indoors. When he came in sight of the two fortresses which protected the entrance to the harbour, he went immediately to Perdiccas.

'What shall we do, Alexander?'

The King studied the fortifications, then he turned back and looked in the direction of the walls.

'Demolish all the houses on the left-hand side of the road that leads here and then destroy all those in the area of the harbour – in this way we will be able to bring up the engines and position them next to the fortresses. The Persians must understand that there are no walls or bastions in all this region behind which they can find refuge. They have to understand that they must leave now, and never return.'

Perdiccas nodded, leaped on to his horse and galloped to the quarter which had been razed the night before to collect groups of labourers and saboteurs, those who were still in a fit state to work. He had to have them woken with trumpet calls because they had fallen asleep where they were when the exhausting night's work had ended.

The chief engineer, a Thessalian by the name of Diades, had the two upper platforms of one of the siege towers taken apart to use them as supports for a ram with which they would demolish the houses near the harbour. Eumenes called some heralds and sent them off to organize the evacuation of the houses.

When the people understood that there had been no massacres, nor rapes nor looting, they started coming out of their homes. The children first – curious to understand what all the movement in the city was about – then the women and last of all the men.

The demolition work, however, proved to be much more extensive than envisaged because many of the houses were built one on top of another and when one wall was brought down, many others were ruined too. Indeed, because of this it was later said that Alexander had in fact razed all Halicarnassus to the ground.

Within four days a sufficiently large area had been cleared to allow the siege machines to be brought up and they set to work battering the fortresses. But that very night, Memnon, Orontobates and Pixodarus, together with a certain number of soldiers, all embarked on some ships in the harbour and sailed offshore to join the greater part of the Persian fleet to the north, in the waters of Chios.

The surviving Greek mercenaries, however, installed themselves in the acropolis, which because of its dominant position was truly impregnable.

Alexander had no desire to waste more time chasing them out of there, given that in any case they were completely surrounded by his own troops. He had a trench dug around the citadel and left some officers of minor rank in charge, waiting for the mercenaries' surrender.

Then Alexander called a meeting of his high command in the city's assembly rooms. Callisthenes was there too, his request to attend having been accepted. While they began deliberating on what was to be done, a Halicarnassian delegation was announced – dignitaries who wanted to meet the King.

'I don't want to receive them,' said Alexander. 'I don't trust them.'

'But there are decisions to be made regarding the political make-up of a most important city,' Parmenion pointed out.

'You could introduce a democratic system like the one in Ephesus,' said Callisthenes.

'Right,' said Ptolemy ironically. 'That way you'll keep Uncle Aristotle happy, don't you think?'

'And what's wrong with that?' asked Callisthenes, somewhat irritated. 'Democracy is the fairest and most balanced system for governing a city, it is the system which provides the greatest guarantee of . . .'

Ptolemy interrupted him before he could finish the sentence, 'But this lot have really put us through it. We have lost more men on these walls than we did on the Granicus. If it was up to me . . .'

'Ptolemy is right!' shouted Leonnatus. 'They must realize who is giving the orders now and that they have to pay for the damage they have caused us.'

The discussion would certainly have degenerated into a riot, but just then Eumenes heard movement outside the door and went to take a look. When he realized what was happening, he returned to Alexander and whispered something in his ear. The King smiled and stood up.

'Would anyone care for a biscuit?' he asked, raising his voice. Not only was the question enough to quieten them all, but they stood looking at one another in bewilderment.

'Are you joking?' said Leonnatus, suddenly breaking the silence. 'I'd eat a whole side of beef, never mind the biscuits. But I do find myself wondering who on earth could have had such a bizarre idea as to bring us biscuits at this moment and . . .'

The door opened and Alexander's adoptive mother, Queen Ada, entered, dressed in full regalia and followed by a train of cooks with great trays filled with warm biscuits. Leonnatus's jaw dropped at the sight and Eumenes took a biscuit and pushed it into his mouth.

'Eat up, and shut up!'

'Mother dearest, how are you?' asked Alexander, standing up and moving forward to greet her. 'Quickly, a chair for the Queen. But what a pleasant surprise! I would never have expected to see you at this moment.'

'I thought that after all these terrible ordeals then you might just appreciate a good biscuit or two,' replied Ada, half-way between being serious and facetious. 'And I've also come to make sure that you don't treat my city too cruelly.'

The King took a biscuit and began crunching on it. 'They are excellent, Mother, and it was stupid of me to send them back last time. As for your city, that is exactly what we are discussing right now, but now that you are here I think I know exactly what we must do.'

'And what might that be?' asked Ada. Callisthenes was about to ask the same question but his jaw dropped as well, leaving him completely speechless.

'That we nominate you satrap of Caria in place of Orontobates, with full powers over Halicarnassus and all its surrounding lands. My generals will make sure they are all brought under control.'

Callisthenes managed to shake his head, as if to say

'madness', but the Queen was moved by Alexander's words: 'But my son, I don't know if . . .'

'I do know,' said Alexander interrupting her. 'I know that you will be an excellent leader and I know that I will be able to trust you completely.'

He had her sit down on his own throne and turned to Eumenes. 'Now you may bring in the delegation from the city. It is only right that they should know who will be governing them from tomorrow onwards.'

*

The search operations were still under way when Apelles's arrival was announced. The master of the brushes hurried to pay homage to the young King and make a proposal.

'Sire, I believe that the time has come for you to be represented as you truly deserve; that is to say, as a god.'

Alexander had to work hard not to burst out laughing. 'You really think so?'

'But there is no doubt of it. Indeed, I was so sure of your victory here that I had already prepared a small sketch which I would ask your permission to show to you. Of course, you must understand that the completed work will look quite different on a tableau of ten by twenty feet.'

'Ten feet by twenty feet?' repeated Leonnatus, to whom in all sincerity the use of all that wood and that paint for a not so very tall youngster like Alexander seemed like a waste.

Apelles threw him a disdainful look – in his eyes

Leonnatus was nothing but an uncultivated barbarian, and what was more he had red hair and a freckled complexion. The great painter turned back to Alexander: 'Sire, my proposal also makes considerable sense if you bear in mind that your Asiatic subjects are used to being governed by superior beings, by sovereigns who are like gods and who have themselves represented as gods. For this reason I feel I should depict you with all the attributes of Zeus – the eagle at your feet and a lightning bolt in your right hand.'

'Apelles is right,' said Eumenes, who had come in together with Leonnatus and was standing looking at the artist's sketch. 'The Asians are used to thinking of their rulers as superhuman beings. And that is how they should see you.'

'How much would this deification cost me?' asked Alexander.

The painter shrugged his shoulders. 'I imagine that with a couple of talents . . .'

'Two talents? But my friend, with two talents I pay for bread, olives, and salted fish for my men for almost one month.'

'Sire, I do not believe that such considerations should concern a great king.'

'A great king, no,' interrupted Eumenes, 'but a secretary, yes, since the soldiers take it out on me if there's not enough food or if it isn't good enough.'

Alexander looked first at Apelles, then at Eumenes, then at the sketch and once again at Apelles. 'I must admit, however, . . .'

'Isn't it beautiful? Imagine it full size, with its captivating colours, the blinding lightning bolt flashing from your hand. Who would ever dare challenge a young god such as that?'

At that moment Pancaspe entered and walked straight to Alexander, embraced him and kissed him on the mouth. 'My Lord,' she greeted him, staring into his eyes. She held herself so close that he could feel her firm breasts digging into his chest, not unlike the heads of the battering-rams on a siege engine against the wall of a city. The expression on her face clearly indicated that she was ready for anything and was completely free of any possible inhibition.

'My dearest girl . . .' replied Alexander without giving away any hostage to fortune, '. . . it is always a pleasure to see you again.'

'A pleasure which is yours whenever you wish,' she whispered close to his ear, sufficiently close to touch it slightly with the moist point of her tongue.

The King turned once again to Apelles to put an end to this embarrassing situation: 'I must consider it further. It is a large sum of money. In any case I look forward to seeing you both at supper.'

The painter and his uninhibited companion left the room just as Ptolemy, Philotas, Perdiccas and Seleucus entered, all of them keen on knowing what Alexander intended to do now.

The King had them sit around a table on which he had unfolded his map. 'Here we are . . . this is my plan: the engines will be dismantled and transported on carts to Tralles because Parmenion, who will march towards the interior to secure the submission of all the lands along the Meander and the Hermus valleys, will have need of them if some city should decide to resist.'

'And us?' asked Ptolemy.

'You will come with me. We will move down the coast through Lycia, as far as Pamphylia.' And as he spoke he traced with a pointer the route he intended to follow.

Eumenes looked at him and then studied the faces of his companions and realized that none of them had understood the nature of this undertaking.

'You really want to take that route?'

'Yes,' replied Alexander.

'But there is no way through there. No army has ever attempted to travel along those rocks, those cliffs above the sea. And they have certainly never attempted it in autumn, or in winter.'

'I know,' replied Alexander.

31

In the end Apelles was given the commission to paint Alexander's portrait, but for only half the sum he had originally requested. This was due to some tough bargaining by Eumenes, who actually wanted to pay him even less. In any case, the artist set to work immediately in a studio Queen Ada had set up for him, not far from the city's agora, its assembly place. But because the King had no time to spare for posing, Apelles had to make do with a series of charcoal drawings he managed to make at mealtimes and during the entertainment following the banquet – a recital by Thessalus, Alexander's favourite actor, together with some musical performances. Apelles hung the drawings on the walls of the studio, dressed a model up to look like the King, and set to work.

Alexander had no opportunity to admire the finished work because he was far away by the time Apelles completed it, but those who did see it were all agreed on its beauty, even though the King's complexion was felt to be a trifle too dark. It almost seemed, however, that the artist had done this deliberately to create greater contrast with the blinding white of the lightning bolt.

Before leaving the King spoke with Parmenion privately in one of the rooms in Ada's palace.

Alexander welcomed the old general with a cup of wine as he entered and Parmenion kissed his King on both cheeks before sitting down.

'How are you, General?' the King asked him.

'I am fine, Sire. And are you well?'

'Much better now that we have taken Halicarnassus, and much of the credit goes to you and your veterans. Your support was crucial.'

'You honour me too much. I did no more than carry out your orders.'

'And now I must ask you to carry out another order.'

'At your service, Sire.'

'Take the Thessalian cavalry together with Amyntas, a squadron of the *hetairoi*, and the heavy infantry of our Greek allies, and move back towards Sardis.'

Parmenion's face lit up, 'Are we going back home, Sire?'

Alexander shook his head, disappointed by Parmenion's reaction, and the old general lowered his head, humiliated by his own rash misinterpretation of his King's words.

'No, Parmenion, we are not going back home. We are consolidating our conquests before moving forward. Come, look at this map – you will travel back up the valley of the Hermus and take complete control of Phrygia. You will also take the siege engines, in case any city should decide to offer resistance.

'As for me, I will continue along the coast as far as Termessus. In this way I will cut off the Persian fleet from all the harbours in the Aegean Sea.'

'You really think so?' and Alexander could hear a

certain tension in the general's voice. 'I have received information according to which Memnon is enlisting more men at Chios and is preparing to sail to Euboea and from there Attica and then central Greece to encourage them all to rise up against us.'

'I am aware of this.'

'And do you not think we should return home to face this challenge? What's more, winter is approaching and . . .'

'Antipater is quite capable of dealing with the situation. He is a wise ruler and an excellent general.'

'Of course, Sire, there is no doubt about that. So my job is to occupy all of Phrygia.'

'Precisely.'

'And then?'

'As I told you, in the meantime I will move along the coast, to Termessus, and then I will turn northwards, towards Ancyra, where you will meet up with me.'

'You plan to travel along the coast to Termessus? Are you aware that for many stadia the road turns into an extremely narrow and dangerous path across the cliffs – no army has ever dared pass through there.'

Alexander poured some wine and took a few sips.

'I know. I have already been informed.'

'What's more, Ancyra is in the mountains, at the very heart of the plateau, and when we arrive there it will be midwinter.'

'Yes, midwinter.'

Parmenion sighed, 'Well, if that's the way it is . . . I'll go to get ready. I imagine I don't have much time.'

'No, indeed you don't,' replied Alexander.

Parmenion emptied his cup, stood up, took his leave with a slight bow of his head and started walking towards the door.

'General.'

Parmenion stopped and turned, 'Yes, Sire.'

'Take good care of yourself.'

'I will try.'

'I will miss your advice and your experience.'

'I will miss you too, Sire.'

He left and closed the door behind him.

Alexander returned to his map to study the route he planned to follow, but not long afterwards he heard agitated voices behind the door and the sentry shouting, 'I cannot disturb the King with this nonsense.'

The King opened the door and asked, 'What are you talking about?'

A young man from the *pezhetairoi* infantry stood there, clearly an ordinary soldier because he wore no insignia indicating any rank.

'What do you want?' he asked.

'Sire,' interrupted the sentry, 'do not waste your time with this one. His problem is he's feeling a bit randy and he's dying to give his little wifey one.'

'Seems perfectly reasonable to me,' said Alexander with a smile. 'Who are you?' he then asked the soldier.

'My name is Eudemus, Sire, and I am from Drabescus.'

'Are you married?'

'Sire, I was married shortly before we set off from Macedonia – I spent two weeks with my wife and I haven't seen her since. Now I've heard that not only are we not going back to Macedonia, but we're pushing on eastwards. Is it true?'

Alexander thought to himself for a moment about just how powerful the information systems operating among his troops were, but quickly decided it was not so surprising after all. 'Yes, it is true,' he replied.

The young soldier lowered his head in resignation.

'You don't seem so keen on following your King and your companions.'

'That's not it, Sire, it's just that . . .'

'You want to sleep with your wife.'

'The truth is . . . yes. And there are many others who feel the same way. Our families wanted us to marry because we had all been called up and they wanted us to leave an heir in case . . . you never know when you're at war.'

Alexander smiled. 'There is no need to say any more. They wanted me to marry as well, but one of the few advantages of being king is that one gets married only if one wants to. How many of you are there?'

'Six hundred and ninety-three.'

'By the gods, right down to the last detail!' exclaimed the King.

'Well yes . . . we thought that since winter was coming there wouldn't be any fighting and so we wanted to ask you . . .'

'For permission to return to your wives.'

'That's exactly how it is, Sire,' admitted the soldier, encouraged by Alexander's openness.

'Did your companions choose you to represent them?'

'Yes.'

'Why?'

'Because . . .'

'Please speak frankly.'

'Because I was the first through the breach when the wall collapsed and I jumped from the burning siege tower only after the battering-ram had brought the wall down.'

'Perdiccas mentioned a soldier who carried out this deed, but he didn't tell me his name. I am proud to meet you in person, Eudemus, and I am happy to grant your wish and that of your companions. You will each be given one hundred Cyzicus staters and two months' leave.'

The soldier was so moved his eyes filled with tears. 'Sire, I . . . really . . .' he stammered.

'But there is one condition.'

'Whatever you say, Sire.'

'When you return, you must bring me more warriors. One hundred for every one of you – foot-soldiers or horsemen, it matters not.'

'I give you my word. You can count them as already being in the ranks.'

'And now you may go.'

The soldier didn't know how to thank Alexander and stood there motionless.

'Well? Weren't you dying to run back home to your wife?'

'Yes, but I just wanted to tell you . . . I just wanted to say that . . .'

Alexander smiled and gestured to him to wait. He went over to a casket, took from it a gold necklace with a small cameo depicting the goddess Artemis and gave it to him.

'She is the protectress of brides and mothers. Give it to your wife and tell her it is a gift from me.'

The soldier wanted to speak, but the lump in his throat prevented him. All he managed, with a tremor in his voice, was, 'Thank you, Sire.'

32

THE SIX HUNDRED AND ninety-three young men who had expressed their desire to join their wives left at the beginning of autumn for the journey back to Macedonia, where they would spend the winter. Shortly afterwards Parmenion also set off with part of the army and the Thessalian cavalry. The King, after having consulted the old general, gave command of this last to his cousin Amyntas, who had always displayed great valour and loyalty. The Black, Philotas and Craterus were part of this group too.

Alexander then held a restricted council meeting with Seleucus, Ptolemy and Eumenes, inviting them to supper.

So as to avoid problems of jealousy arising, he had arranged for his other companions, including Hephaestion, to be busy with duties in the surrounding area, and the chosen three were left feeling that they were in the camp and had been invited by chance. But the subject which Alexander broached left them in no doubt that at that moment the King was calling upon their intelligence rather than their physical prowess.

Not even the servants were admitted – only Leptine brought the food to them as they sat around a table, just like the days when they used to attend Aristotle's lessons at Mieza.

'Our informers tell me that Memnon has had an enormous sum of money sent to him from the Great King. It was transported by sea – an extremely risky operation. He intends to use it to enlist over one hundred thousand men, an army with which he will invade Greece. But perhaps more important is the fact that he has apparently already begun distributing gifts among many influential figures in all the Greek cities. General Parmenion has already expressed his opinion . . .'

'That we should return home?' Seleucus guessed.

'Indeed,' replied Alexander.

Leptine began serving their supper: grilled fish with beans and wine cut with water. It was a light meal, a sign that the King wanted them all to remain clear-headed.

'And what are your plans?' asked Ptolemy.

'I have already made a decision, but I want to know your view. Seleucus?'

'I say we should push on. Even if Memnon should succeed in taking Greece, what will he have achieved? He will never manage to enter Macedonia because Antipater simply will not allow it. And if we continue to occupy all the ports along the Asian coast, the Great King will eventually lose contact with him. In the end he will have to capitulate.'

'Ptolemy?'

'I see things as Seleucus does – let's continue. If we could find some way of killing Memnon, though, that would be a good thing. It would save us no end of problems and would be like the Great King having his right arm amputated.'

Alexander seemed shocked and surprised by this proposal, but he continued his consultation: 'Eumenes?'

'Ptolemy is right. We must continue, but if we can we must also eliminate Memnon – he is too dangerous and too intelligent. He is unpredictable.'

Alexander was silent for a short while, chewing his fish without much enthusiasm, then he took a sip of wine.

'Let us continue onwards then. I have already asked Hephaestion to go on ahead to the pass which they say is very difficult terrain, between Lycia and Pamphylia. In a few days we will know if it really is as bad as they say. Parmenion will go back up the Hermus valley as far as the highlands, where we will meet with him in spring. Our route will be the one which leads from the coast to the centre of Anatolia.'

He stood up and went over to the map which he had had set up on an easel. 'Our rendezvous is here. At Gordium.'

'Gordium? Do you know what Gordium is famous for?' asked Ptolemy.

'He knows, he knows,' said Eumenes. 'King Midas's chariot, tied to its yoke by means of an inextricable knot. An ancient oracle of the Great Mother of the gods says that whoever undoes that knot will be lord of all Asia.'

'And is this why we are going to Gordium?' asked Seleucus suspiciously.

'We digress,' said Alexander, cutting him short. 'We are not here to speak of oracles, but to establish a plan of action for the coming months. I am glad you all agree on the fact that we must push forwards. Indeed, we will not stop during the autumn, nor during the winter. Our men are used to the cold – they are men of the mountains, the Thracian and Agrianian auxiliaries even more so, and Parmenion knows that he must not stop until he reaches his destination.'

'And Memnon?' asked Eumenes, bringing the most burning question back on to the table.

'No one will ever lead me to kill him in an act of treachery,' replied the King, hard-faced. 'He is a valiant man and he deserves to die with his sword in his hand, not poisoned in his bed or stabbed in the back as he crosses through the shadows.'

'Alexander, listen,' said Ptolemy, trying to have him see reason. 'These are no longer the days of Homer, the armour you keep near your bed never really did belong to Achilles – at the most it's two or three hundred years old – and the truth is that you yourself are aware of these facts. Think of your soldiers – Memnon is still capable of causing the deaths of thousands of them. Is this what you want, just to keep faith with your ideals of heroism?'

The King shook his head.

'All this without considering,' said Eumenes, 'that Memnon might easily plan the same fate for you – pay an assassin to kill you, corrupt your physician and give him instructions to poison you . . . have you ever considered that? Memnon has access to enormous sums of money.'

'Has it ever occurred to you,' continued Seleucus, 'that he might lend support to your cousin Amyntas, to whom you have given control of the Thessalian cavalry?'

The King shook his head. 'Amyntas is a good man and

he has always displayed loyalty. I have no reason to doubt him.'

'I am still convinced that the risks are too great,' repeated Seleucus.

'Me too,' agreed Eumenes.

Alexander hesitated for a moment – he had a vision of his adversary there before him under the walls of Halicarnassus, his face hidden by the burnished helmet on which the silver rose of Rhodes stood out, and he heard his voice once again: 'I am Commander Memnon.'

He shook his head a third time, yet more decided now, 'No, I will never give orders for such a thing. Even in war a man remains a man and my father used to tell me that the son of a lion is a lion . . .' and then he paused before adding, '. . . and not a poisonous snake.'

'There is no point in insisting,' Seleucus surrendered. 'If the King has made his mind up, then that's the way it must be.'

Ptolemy and Eumenes nodded, but without too much conviction.

'I am glad you all agree,' said Alexander. 'Now then, let's take a look at this map and try to organize our march along the coast.'

The meeting continued until they were too tired to go on. Eumenes retired first, followed shortly by Ptolemy and Seleucus. But as soon as they were all outside the secretary signalled and asked them to come to his tent. He had them sit down and sent an orderly to call Callisthenes, who by that time was certainly fast asleep on the other side of the camp.

'What do you think?' began Eumenes.

'About what?' asked Ptolemy.

'But it's obvious, isn't it? About the King's refusal to have Memnon eliminated,' replied Seleucus.

'I understand Alexander,' Eumenes said, 'and you must understand him as well. Indeed, our enemy inspires nothing but admiration – he is an exceptional man, able in mind and with his sword, but it is precisely for this reason that he represents a mortal danger. Imagine he succeeds in causing an uprising among the Greeks, imagine that Athens, Sparta and Corinth join him. The allied armies would march northwards to invade Macedonia, the Persian fleet would effect a pincer move from the sea . . . are we really so sure that Antipater would manage to fend them off? And if Antipater should fail? And if Memnon should reawaken the ambitions of some survivor of the Lyncestian dynastic branch, for example the commander of our Thessalian cavalry, thus unleashing a civil war or bringing about military rule? If Memnon were to win, he could block the Straits and prevent our return, for ever. Is that a risk we wish to take?'

'But neither can we go against Alexander's wishes,' said Seleucus.

'I say that we can, as long as he knows nothing of it. I will not take the responsibility alone, however. If we all agree then we proceed, otherwise we let things be as they are and face the risks as they come.'

'Let's say we are all in agreement,' replied Ptolemy, 'what exactly would your plan be?'

'And why have you sent for Callisthenes?' asked Seleucus.

Eumenes took a look outside the tent to see if the historian was on his way, but there was no sign of him.

'Listen: as far as we know, Memnon is now on Chios, ready to sail northwards, presumably to Lesbos. There he will wait for a favourable wind to cross the sea to Greece. He will have to wait some time, however, because he has to gather and load all the necessary supplies for the expedition. This is the moment to act and eliminate him once and for all.'

'And how?' asked Ptolemy. 'An assassin, or poison?'

'Neither one, nor the other. An assassin would never get close enough to him – he is always surrounded by four men who are blindly loyal and who would automatically kill anyone who approached closer than the authorized distance. As for poison, I imagine that he has his food and drink tasted, he has been in contact with the Persian world for many years and he will certainly have learned these things.'

'There are poisons which have a delayed effect,' Ptolemy offered.

'That is true, but they are still poisons. The effects and the symptoms are well known. If in the end it comes to be known that Memnon was poisoned then suspicion would immediately fall on Alexander and we cannot allow that to happen.'

'And so?' asked Seleucus.

'There is a third possibility.' As he spoke, the secretary lowered his eyes as though almost ashamed of what was going through his mind.

'What would that be?'

'An illness, an incurable illness.'

'But that's impossible!' exclaimed Seleucus. 'Illnesses come when they come and go when they go.'

'Apparently things are not that simple,' said Eumenes. 'It seems that some illnesses are caused by very small creatures, invisible to the human eye, which pass from one body to another. I know that Aristotle carried out secret experiments before he went to Athens, based on his inquiries into spontaneous generation.'

'In other words?'

'In other words it seems that in certain situations these creatures are not spontaneously generated at all – but rather they spread. And anyway Callisthenes knows about this. He knows about the experiments and could write to his uncle. At the beginning nothing would happen – that way no one would suspect his cook or his doctor. Memnon would act and move normally. It would be days before any effects were visible.'

They all looked at one another – amazed and at the same time troubled by the plan and this new knowledge.

'It seems to me it will be an extremely difficult plan to put into action, it calls for a series of complex circumstances to be engineered,' said Ptolemy.

'That is true, but it is also the only possible approach, in my view. There is one fact which is in our favour, however, and that is that Memnon's physician comes from the school of Theophrastus and . . .'

Seleucus looked at Eumenes in surprise, 'I had no idea your duties involved spying.'

'Obviously I have been doing a good job, since this very fact itself is secret information. Anyway, King Philip in his day had already put me in touch with all his Greek and barbarian informers.'

At that moment Callisthenes appeared in the tent, 'What do you want of me at this hour?' he asked, his voice still full of sleep.

*

Alexander was having difficulty sleeping as well. The idea that Memnon was planning an attack on Greece, or on Macedonia even, worried him greatly. Would old Antipater be up to the job? Wouldn't it be better to send Parmenion back home?

While Leptine busied herself with her work, he left the tent and walked along the seashore.

It was a warm, peaceful night and his pace assumed the rhythm of the noise of the waves on the pebbles. An almost full moon spread a diaphanous clarity over the many islands which dotted the surface of the water, and it illuminated the white houses dotting the hillsides, down to the bays and the small harbours.

The beach was suddenly interrupted by a rocky promontory, but instead of turning back, Alexander climbed up to the summit, from where the view was even more beautiful.

As he was climbing, the addition of the physical effort to the great mental fatigue which had been weighing for some time on his soul suddenly made him feel mortally tired and in need of help. Without any apparent reason his father came to mind. Indeed, he almost seemed to see him, standing there erect on the headland. He wished it were true, he wished he could run towards him just as he used to do at Mieza and shout out, 'Father!' And he would have liked to sit down beside him and ask his advice.

He was lost in these thoughts as he approached the summit and the view of the next section of the coastline opened up before him. What he saw there amazed him. On the other side of the promontory there was a sort of necropolis – many monumental tombs dug into the rock and others standing solitary and proud on the shore, spectral in the whiteness diffused by the moonlight, some of them partially submerged by the waves of the sea.

And there was a man standing there, in silence, with a lantern hanging from a stick he had placed in the sand. His back was turned to him.

He was of the same build as his father and was wrapped in a white cloak fringed with a golden frieze, like the one Philip had been wearing on the day he was assassinated. Alexander stopped and stood there speechless, almost unable to believe his eyes, almost expecting the man to turn and speak to him with Philip's voice and with Philip's gaze. But the man stood there motionless – only the white cloak moved, fluttering in the wind with a slight rustling, like the wings of a bird.

The King approached, stepping lightly, and saw that there was a spring gurgling from a rock, a crystalline flow which reflected the light from the man's lantern. A small stream, the overflow, ran from the spring across the sand of the beach to the salty waves of the sea. The man, who must have heard him, did not turn – he seemed to be looking at something within the spring. Alexander approached even closer, but in the darkness his scabbard struck against a rock. The man turned suddenly in the darkness and his eyes shone strong in the light of the lantern – Philip's eyes!

Alexander jumped, a shiver ran over him and he was about to cry out, 'Father!'

But in just an instant he recognized the differences in the man's features and the darker colour of his beard. A stranger he had never seen before until this moment.

'Who are you?' he asked. 'What are you doing here?'

The man stared at him with a strange expression and again Alexander perceived something familiar – he somehow felt his father's gaze in those burning eyes.

'I am observing this fount,' replied the man.

'Why?'

'Because I am a seer.'

'And what do you see there? It is dark, and the light of your lantern is feeble.'

'For the first time in living memory, the surface of the water has fallen by almost one cubit and has revealed a message.'

'Of what do you speak?'

The man lifted up the lantern and held it close to the rock from which the spring gurgled. The glow of the light illuminated an inscription in some unknown alphabet.

'I speak of this,' he explained, pointing to the inscription.

'And can you read it?'

The seer's voice became strange, as if someone else was speaking with his larynx:

'The Lord of Asia approaches, he who in his eyes has both the day and the night.'

Then he lifted the lantern and held it near Alexander's face: 'Your right eye is as blue as a clear sky and the left one is as dark as the night. For how long had you been watching me?'

'Not for long. But you have not answered my question: who are you?'

'My name is Aristander. And who are you, with your eyes of light and of darkness?'

'Do you not know me?'

'Not sufficiently.'

'I am the King of Macedon.'

The man studied him again, intensely, the lantern still held near his face: 'You will reign over Asia.'

'And you will follow me, if you are not afraid of the unknown.'

The man lowered his head, 'I am afraid of just one thing, a vision which has haunted me for ages without my being able to understand its meaning – a naked man being burned alive on his funeral pyre.'

Alexander said nothing, he seemed to be listening to the constant, rhythmic breaking of the waves. When he turned towards the summit of the headland he saw his guards up there, watching over this impromptu meeting. He took his leave. 'I have a very difficult day ahead of me, I must go back. I hope to see you in the camp tomorrow.'

'I hope so too,' replied the man. And he set off in the opposite direction.

33

THE FLAGSHIP ROCKED GENTLY at anchor in the harbour at Chios and a launch approached slowly. The royal standard, bearing an image of Ahura Mazda, flapped slightly with each gust of the night breeze and from the stern deck came the faint glow of a lantern.

All around was the Great King's war fleet – more than three hundred vessels equipped with rostrums, battle triremes and quinqueremes, all lined up along the docks, held fast by large mooring ropes.

The launch drew up alongside and a sailor beat on the hull with his oar: 'Message for Commander Memnon.'

'Wait,' replied the watch officer, 'I'll have a ladder lowered down to you.'

Shortly afterwards the sailor climbed up the rope ladder which had been lowered from the bulwark and asked to see the supreme commander.

The watch officer searched him and then led him aft, where Memnon was still awake, writing letters and reading the reports sent to him by the governors and commanders of the Persian garrisons still loyal to the Great King, and by the informers he had throughout Greece.

'A message for you, Commander,' announced the sailor as he handed over a roll of papyrus.

Memnon took it and saw immediately that the seal was his wife's – the first letter he had received from her since their parting.

'Is there anything else?' he asked.

'No, Commander. But if there is a reply, I will wait.'

'Good. Go to the galley and have them give you something to drink and eat if you are hungry. I will call for you as soon as I have finished.' Once alone, Memnon's hands shook as he unrolled the missive.

Barsine to Memnon, her beloved husband, Hail!

My love, after a long journey we reached Susa safe and sound and King Darius has welcomed both myself and your sons, paying us great honour. We have been assigned a wing of the palace with servants and hand-maids and a wonderfully beautiful garden, a *pairidaeza* with flowers of every imaginable colour, fragrant roses and cyclamens, ponds and fountains with coloured fish, and birds from every part of the world, peacocks and pheasants from India and the Caucasus, and tamed leopards from far off Ethiopia.

Our situation would be enviable were it not for the fact that you are so far away. My bedchamber is desolate, too big and too cold without you.

A few nights ago I picked up the edition of Euripi-des's tragedies which you gave me as a present and I read *Alcestis*, with tears in my eyes. I cried, my dear husband, thinking of that heroic love so intensely described by the poet, and I was particularly struck by the passage in which the woman goes to her death and her husband promises that no other woman will ever take her place. He says that he will have a great sculptor create an image of her and will have it placed in his bed, to lie beside him.

Oh, if only I could do the same! If only I had called some great artist, one of the great *yauna* masters, Lysippus or Apelles, and had had him sculpt your image, or had your portrait painted to adorn my rooms, to embellish the most intimate sanctums of my bedchamber.

Only now, my beloved husband, only now that you are far away do I understand the meaning of your people's art, the stirring power with which you *yauna* represent the nudity of the gods and the heroes.

I would like to be able to look upon your naked body, even if only a statue or a painting, and then I would close my eyes and imagine that by divine will your image might acquire life and come out of the painting or down from its pedestal, and come to me like that night before our parting when we made such love, and you would caress me with your hands, kiss me with your lips.

But war keeps you far from me, war which brings only mourning and grief and destruction. Come back to me, Memnon; let someone else lead Darius's army. You have already done more than enough, no one can find fault with you and everyone tells of your valiant feats in defending Halicarnassus. Come back to me, my dear husband, my shining hero. Return to me because all the riches in Susa, all the riches in the world are nothing compared to an instant spent in your arms.

Memnon rolled up the letter, got to his feet, and walked towards the gunwale. The lights of the city glowed faintly in the peace of the evening, and from the dark streets and squares came the shouts of children playing hide-and-seek, making the most of the last warm days of autumn. From farther away came a song, a young man's serenade for his loved one who perhaps was listening, blushing in some nearby shadow.

He felt oppressed by an endless melancholy, by a mortal tiredness, but at the same time there was the awareness that his shoulders bore the destiny of a limitless empire, the hopes of a great sovereign and the esteem of his soldiers. All these things combined meant that he could not give in to those feelings of melancholy.

He had received news of the last of his diehard warriors; blocked in the acropolis at Halicarnassus, they were resisting to the bitter end, struggling against hunger and thirst. He could not bring himself to accept the fact that he had been unable to free them. Oh, if only the great Daedalus had really existed – father of Icarus, the inventor capable of making wings for man! He would fly to his wife by night to make her happy and then return to his place of duty before sunrise.

But the Great King's orders were quite different – he was to sail for the island of Lesbos, from where he was to prepare for the landing in Euboea: the first Persian invasion in over one hundred and fifty years.

He had recently received a letter from the Spartans, who declared themselves ready to ally with King Darius and to lead a general uprising of the Greeks against Macedonia.

He returned to his table and began writing:

Memnon to Barsine, his dearest wife, Hail!

Your letter has stirred in me the most beautiful and moving memories – those moments we spent together at Zeleia and in Caria before our final separation. You cannot imagine the pain I feel in missing you and how the image of your beauty recurs every night in my dreams. I will desire no woman and I will have no peace until I succeed in embracing you once more.

I must make this final effort – this will be the definitive battle – and then I will return to live in peace alongside my sons and in your arms, for as long as the gods grant me life and breath.

Kiss our boys for me and take good care.

As he rolled the letter he thought how this inert material would receive the touch of Barsine's fingers, light as petals and just as perfumed. He sighed, then he called the messenger and handed it to him.

'When will it reach her?' he asked.

'Soon, in less than twenty days.'

'Good. May your journey be a safe one, may the gods protect you.'

'And may they protect you too, Commander Memnon.'

He watched the sailor disappear on his launch before returning aft and calling for the captain of the ship.

'We sail now, Captain. Signal the other ships.'

'Now? But would it not be better to wait for dawn? Visibility would be better and . . .'

'No. I want our movements to remain secret. What we are about to do is of the utmost importance. Signal to the other ships that I also want all the commanders of battle units to come to a meeting, here on the flagship.'

The captain, a Greek from Patara, bowed and set about his orders. Shortly afterwards, several launches approached Memnon's ship and their occupants climbed on board.

One after another they saluted the commander and took up their positions on the benches arranged to the sides of the poop deck. Memnon sat at the stern, on the navarch's throne. He wore his blue cloak and his armour. His Corinthian helmet was placed before him on a stool – polished and with the silver rose of Rhodes set into the forehead.

'Commanders, at this moment fate offers us our last chance to redeem our honour as soldiers and to earn the money we receive from the Great King. There are no longer any harbours in which we can seek refuge, except for the remote ports of Cilicia or Phoenicia, many days' sail away. We therefore have no choice, we must move forwards and cut off at the root the source of our enemy's strength.

'I have received a *skytale* with a secret message from the Spartans. If we invade the mainland they and their army are willing to join with us against Alexander. I have therefore decided to sail to Lesbos and from there towards Skyros and Euboea, where we will meet up with those Athenian patriots who will give us their support. I have sent a messenger to Demosthenes and I believe that his response will certainly be positive. That is all for now. Return to your ships and prepare for departure.'

The flagship slipped slowly out of the harbour with its

stern lamps burning, and all the other vessels followed. It was a clear, starry night and Memnon's helmsman was firm with the rudder. On the second day the weather changed and the sea swelled up under a strong southerly wind. Some of the ships suffered damage and the fleet had to proceed under oars for almost two full days.

They reached their destination on the fifth day and entered the great western roadstead, waiting for the weather to improve. Memnon gave orders for all the damaged vessels to be repaired and sent his officers to recruit mercenaries to join them. In the meantime he visited the island and was much charmed by it and asked to be shown the homes of the poets Sappho and Alcaeus, both natives of Lesbos.

In front of the house said to be Sappho's, there were several itinerant scribes copying her lyrics to order on wooden tablets or on rolls of papyrus, which were much more expensive.

'Could you copy one for me in Persian?' Memnon asked a more oriental-looking scribe.

'Yes, of course, my Lord.'

'Well then . . . copy me the one which begins:

> I see he who sits beside you
> As an equal of the gods
> For he may listen to you
> As you speak sweetly
> And smile so desirably.'*

---

* Sappho, fragment 31.

'I know it, Lord,' said the scribe as he dipped his straw into his inkwell. 'It is a song of jealousy.'

'Yes, it is,' nodded Memnon, apparently impassive. And he sat on the wall waiting for the scribe to finish his translation.

He had heard that Barsine had been for a while in Alexander's hands and there were moments when this fact left him full of dread.

34

On leaving Halicarnassus Alexander advanced eastwards with his army along the coast, even though everyone had tried to dissuade him. Indeed, there was a passage through Lycia, but no one would ever have attempted it in winter. The route was little more than a path along the cliffs which towered above the boiling, rocky seas below – all of it exposed to the western winds, which always brought rough weather.

As the waves broke on the rocks they exploded into great globules of foam, churning angrily against the rock before flowing back to rush and crash once more against the promontory, desolate and at the complete mercy of the elements.

Hephaestion had ridden as far as this headland and brought back with him vivid impressions of the place: 'It is truly frightful,' he told Alexander. 'Imagine a mountain higher than Athos and more massive than Pangaeos, its surface smooth and black as burnished iron descending vertically to the sea. Its summit, perpetually enveloped in cloud, resounds with the rumble of thunder. I watched the lightning bolts flit between the sky and the top, and sometimes they fell to the sea below in blinding flashes. The pathway is a very old one, cut by the Lycians out of the rock, but it is always slippery because of the spray from the waves and the seaweed that grows in abundance during the winter season. Falling into the sea down there means instant death – the waves would immediately drive any man, no matter how strong a swimmer, on to the sharp rocks which form a sort of crown at the base of the steep slope and they would cut him to shreds in no time.'

'Did you cross through to the other side?' asked Alexander.

'Yes.'

'And how?'

'I used the Agrianians. They fixed bolts in the cracks in the rock and tied ropes to them, so that we were able to hold on when the waves came.'

'That seems an excellent idea,' said the King. 'That's how we'll get through the pass.'

'But there were only fifty of us,' said Hephaestion, 'you plan to send twenty-five thousand men and five thousand horses by this route. How will you manage with the horses?'

Alexander was quiet for a moment as he gathered his thoughts, then he said, 'We have no choice. We'll attempt this pathway and take control of all the Lycian ports – we will cut off the Great King's fleet from our sea. If necessary I will go on ahead with only the infantry, but I will go, come what may.'

'As you wish. We are not afraid of anything, but I wanted you to be fully aware anyway of the risks involved.'

They left the following day and soon reached the city of Xanthus, perched up on its rock above the river of the same name. In the surrounding area, carved into the rock, were many tombs with monumental façades in the shape of buildings or colonnaded temples. It was said that one of these contained the body of the Lycian hero Sarpedon, cut down by the sword of Patroclus during the Trojan War.

Alexander wanted to see it and he stood there enrapt before the ancient sepulchre, consumed by time and by the elements. The marks of an ancient inscription, completely illegible now, could barely be made out. Callisthenes, who was standing nearby, heard him murmuring verses from Homer – the speech made by the Lycian hero to his men immediately before the final clash in which he lost his life:

> Ah, could we but survive this war
> to live forever deathless, without age,
> I would not ever go again to battle,
> nor would I send you there for honour's sake!
> But now a thousand shapes of death surround us,
> and no man can escape them, or be safe.
> Let us attack – whether to give some fellow
> glory or to win it from him.*

Then, turning to Callisthenes, he asked, 'Do you think he would repeat these words if he were still able to speak today?' And in his voice there was some inkling of a deep sadness.

'Who can tell? No one has ever succeeded in returning from Hades.'

Alexander approached the tomb and put his hands and

---

* Homer, *Iliad* XII, 322–8, translated by Robert Fitzgerald.

his forehead on it, as though trying to hear a voice made weak by centuries of distance. Then he turned and set off once more to lead his army on its way.

They proceeded down the river to the estuary, where the port of Patara opened up – the most important harbour in all Lycia. The city had some fine buildings in the Greek style and the inhabitants dressed in the Greek manner, but their language was very old and completely incomprehensible without the aid of interpreters. The King made sure his army was billeted properly and ordered a halt of several days. He hoped to receive news from Parmenion, who at that point should have been up on the interior highlands, but no word came from the general. A ship from Macedonia did arrive, however, the last one before the winter.

The commander had taken a difficult and little used route, so as not to risk any contact with Memnon's fleet. He brought with him a report from Antipater on the situation in the homeland and on the bitter conflicts he was enduring with the Queen Mother, Olympias.

Alexander was upset and profoundly saddened by this, but he brightened up when he saw on another roll of papyrus the royal seal of the Molossians and the hand-writing of his sister Cleopatra. He opened the missive with a certain apprehension and began reading:

Cleopatra, Queen of the Molossians, to her brother Alexander, King of Macedon, Hail!

My beloved brother, more than a year has gone by since I embraced you for the last time and not a day goes by that I do not think of you and miss you.

Echoes of your achievements have reached the palace here in Buthrotum and this makes me most proud, but pride is no compensation for your absence.

My husband and your brother-in-law, Alexander, King of the Molossians, is about to leave for Italy. He has gathered a great army of almost twenty thousand men, valiant warriors well trained in the Macedonian manner and schooled after the principles of our father, Philip.

He dreams of conquering a great empire to the west and of freeing all Greeks from the threat of the barbarians in those lands – Carthaginians, Brutians, and Lucanians. But I am left here alone.

Our mother is increasingly bizarre, irritable and moody, and I avoid visiting her when I can. From what I hear, she thinks of you day and night and offers sacrifices to the gods so that Fortune might smile upon you. I can only curse war which keeps the people I most love in this world far from me.

Take good care.

So the western enterprise was about to begin. Another Alexander, almost his mirror image, bound to him by such deep ties of blood and of friendship, was ready to march in the direction of the Pillars of Hercules to conquer all the lands as far as the river Ocean. And one day they would meet up again – in Greece perhaps, or in Egypt, or in Italy – and that day the world would live the beginning of a new era.

He made the most of their break to have Eumenes read the 'Journal', the daily report the secretary general drew up with news of what was happening on the expedition, the distances covered on the march, the visits made and the visits received, the minutes of the high command meetings, and even the accounts.

'It's not bad,' he said after listening to a few pages. 'The descriptive passages have a certain literary elegance – they might even be reworked for a true and proper history of our expedition.'

'I don't exclude that possibility at all,' replied Eumenes, 'but for the moment I am doing no more than recording the facts, within the limits of the time I have available. Callisthenes is looking after the real history.'

'Quite.'

'But not only Callisthenes. You know that Ptolemy is also writing about the expedition. Has he let you read any of it?'

'Not yet, but I am curious to see it.'

'And the work of your admiral, Nearchus, also proceeds.'

'It seems everyone on this expedition is a writer. I wonder who will be given most credit. Anyway, I continue to envy Achilles, who had Homer to recount his deeds.'

'Days of old, my friend. To make up for it we have Nearchus, who is carrying out excellent work in establishing relations with the various communities which inhabit these lands. He knows many people here and is much esteemed. He recently explained his mariner's view of the situation to me.'

'Which is?'

'He is convinced that you cannot do without a fleet and that you should assemble one immediately. To leave Memnon with total domination of the seas is too dangerous.'

'And what do you think? It will be a financial question, if I'm not mistaken.'

'Perhaps we could afford it now with the income from Sardis and Halicarnassus.'

'Make arrangements then. Speak to Nearchus, negotiate with the Athenians, have the shipyards of the seaports we have conquered reopened. We can afford to take some risks now.'

'I will meet Nearchus on his ship and we will work out a few sums together. I really don't have the faintest idea how much a warship costs and how many we would need to make life difficult for that damned Memnon. But I also need to know what your intentions are for this coming winter.'

Alexander looked out of the window of the house he had chosen for his quarters and gazed at the snow-capped mountains, 'We will push on until we find the road that leads towards the interior – I must meet up with Parmenion as soon as possible and reunite our forces. I am worried, Eumenes. If one of our two contingents should be wiped out, there will be no hope left for the other.'

The secretary nodded, gathered his papers and left.

Alexander sat at his table, took a sheet, dipped his pen in the ink and began writing:

Alexander to Cleopatra, his dearest sister, Hail!

My beloved, do not be saddened by your husband's departure. There are men who are born to fulfil a destiny and he is among these. Alexander and I have made a pact and he leaves his land, his home and his bride in respect of our pledge. I do not believe that you would rather be the wife of a nobody, of a man without hope and without ambitions. Life would have been even more hateful. You were born of Olympias and Philip, as I was, and I know that you can understand. Your joy will be even greater after your separation, and I am certain that soon your husband will send for you to go and see the sun set on the divine and mysterious waters of the far Ocean on which no ship has ever sailed.

Aristotle says that the Greeks in their cities look over this sea like frogs on the banks of a pond, and he is right. But we are born to know different lands and different seas, to cross borders that no one has ever dared cross. And we will not stop before we have seen the extreme limit granted to human kind by the gods.

This, however, is not enough to salve the pain of missing you, and I would give anything, right now, to sit at your feet and to rest my head in your lap and listen to your sweet voice.

Remember me, as we agreed in our pact, every time you see the sun set over the sea, every time the wind brings you voices from far away.

35

SOME TEN DAYS AFTER the arrival of Alexander's army in the city, a visitor was announced – a man by the name of Eumolpus of Soloi.

'Do you know who he is?' Alexander asked Eumenes.

'Of course I know. He is the best informer you have east of the Taurus mountains.'

'If he is my best informer, why on earth don't I know him?'

'Because he always dealt with your father and . . . with me.'

'I hope you don't mind then if I actually deal with him personally now,' said Alexander ironically.

'Not at all,' Eumenes responded promptly. 'All I ever hope to do is save you from some of your more boring duties. In fact, if you prefer I'll make myself scarce . . .'

'Don't be stupid, and have him come in.'

Eumolpus had not changed much since the last time Eumenes had seen him at Pella; the informer still felt the cold terribly and because the sea had been too rough he'd had to travel on a mule over the snow-covered mountains of the interior. Peritas growled as soon as he saw him with his fox-fur cap on his head.

'What a nice little dog,' said Eumolpus with a rather worried expression. 'Does he bite?'

'No, as long as you take that fox off your head,' replied Eumenes.

The informer placed his cap on a stool and Peritas immediately bit into it and continued to chew it throughout the interview.

'What news do you bring?'

Eumolpus began with a series of niceties and compliments regarding the young King's glorious feats and then came to the point.

'Sire, your deeds have caused considerable panic at court in Susa. The magi say that you are the incarnation of Ahriman.'

'Their god of evil,' explained Eumenes, somewhat embarrassed. 'Similar to our Hades, lord of the underworld.'

'You see, this god of theirs is always represented as a lion and since you wear a helmet in the shape of a lion's head, the resemblance really is striking.'

'And apart from this?'

'The Great King places great store in Memnon's abilities – apparently he has sent him two thousand talents.'

'An enormous sum of money.'

'Exactly.'

'Do you know what the money is for?'

'For everything, I believe – enlisting new men, bribes, financing possible allies. But I have heard of more funds, another two thousand talents, which are apparently travelling overland towards the interior of Anatolia.'

'And what is this money for?'

Eumolpus shook his head, 'I really have no idea. Isn't

one of your generals in that area? Perhaps he will be able to give you more precise information . . .'

An ugly prospect suddenly flashed through Alexander's mind – what if the Great King attempted to corrupt Parmenion? He immediately chased away what he considered to be a shameful thought.

'Does Memnon have the Great King's unconditional support?'

'Completely. Nevertheless, there are more than a few nobles at court who harbour a terrible envy of this foreigner, this Greek to whom the King has entrusted supreme command of his troops and who has also been granted powers over all the Persian governors. After King Darius, Memnon is the most powerful man in the Persian empire. However, if you ask me whether by any chance there are, or there might be any conspiracies against him . . .'

'I am not asking you anything of the kind,' Alexander cut him short.

'Forgive me,' replied the informer, 'I had no wish to offend you. Ah! There is one other thing.'

'Speak.'

'Memnon's wife, Barsine, a woman of most striking beauty, has arrived at court.'

Alexander reacted with a barely perceptible start, which the expert eye of Eumolpus did not fail to catch: 'Do you know her?'

The King did not reply and Eumenes gestured to Eumolpus to abandon the subject and to pick up again where they had left off.

'As I was saying, a woman of most striking beauty – shapely legs, the breasts of a goddess, the darkest of eyes – I don't dare imagine what a rose of Pieria she must have between her thighs . . .' Eumenes again signalled to move on. 'And she has brought with her their two sons, two fine young men, one of them with a Greek name who looks like his mother, and one with a Persian name who looks like his father. Is that not extraordinary? There are those who say that the Great King wanted them at court as hostages because he does not trust Memnon.'

'And is that true, in your opinion?'

'Do you really want to know what I think?'

'That's a stupid question.'

'Quite right. Well . . . I don't believe it. In my opinion King Darius trusts Memnon blindly, precisely because he is a mercenary leader. Memnon has never signed a contract, but he has never gone back on his word. He is a man of iron.'

'I know,' said Alexander.

'There is also another thing which you should bear in mind.'

'And what is that?'

'Memnon rules the waves.'

'For the moment.'

'Quite. Now, as you well know, Athens receives all its grain from the Black Sea through the Bosphorus. If Memnon were to block this trade, the city would be struck by famine and this could force them to change allegiance together with their entire fleet, resulting in the most powerful military armada of all time.'

Alexander lowered his head. 'I know.'

'And does this prospect not frighten you?'

'I am never frightened by things that have not yet come to pass.'

Eumolpus was speechless for a moment, then he continued. 'There is certainly no doubt that you are your father's son. Anyway, for now it seems that the Great King has decided not to make any move and to leave Memnon as much room as possible. The duel is between you two. But if Memnon should falter, then the Great King will join the battle, and with him will come all of Asia.'

He pronounced these last words in a sombre tone that surprised his listeners.

'I thank you,' said Alexander, 'my secretary general will pay you for your services.'

A wry smile came over Eumolpus's face: 'With regard to this, Sire, I wanted to ask you for a slight increase in the payment your father used to give me, long may his glory last. My work, under the circumstances, becomes increasingly difficult and risky, and for some time now a vision of yours truly impaled on a stake has been haunting my dreams, dreams which I can assure you were once much sweeter.'

Alexander nodded and exchanged a look with Eumenes.

'I'll take care of it,' said the secretary general as he accompanied Eumolpus to the door. The man took a disconsolate look at what remained of his warm fox-fur hat, saluted the King with a bow, and left.

Alexander watched them walking along the corridor together and could still hear the informer continuing with his lament: 'Because if I really have to have something rammed up me, I'd rather it be some strapping young lad's prick than the sharpened rods those barbarians use.'

And Eumenes replied, 'Well, you'd be spoiled for choice here ... we've got over twenty-five thousand of them.'

The King shook his head and closed the door.

Because he had received no news from Parmenion, Alexander decided the following day to set off on their march along the risky coastal pass which Hephaestion had described so effectively and so frighteningly.

He sent the Agrianians on ahead to fix bolts and ropes in the rock face for his soldiers to hold on to, but all this complex equipment proved unnecessary. The weather changed all of a sudden – the wet, gusty wind from the west fell and the sea became as calm and smooth as a bowl of oil.

Hephaestion, who had accompanied the Agrianians and the Thracians, turned back to report that the sun was drying out the pass and that it was no longer dangerous.

'It seems the gods are with you.'

'So it seems,' replied Alexander. 'Let's take it as a good omen.'

Ptolemy, riding immediately behind them, and commanding the King's guard, turned to Perdiccas. 'I can just imagine what Callisthenes will write.'

'I had never really thought about this undertaking from the point of view of the chronicler's problems.'

'He'll have it that the sea parted before Alexander because it recognized his regal and almost divine power.'

'What about you? What will you write?'

Ptolemy shook his head. 'Let's just forget it and keep going – we've still got a long way to go.'

Once beyond the pass, Alexander led the army towards the interior, climbing up steep pathways until they reached the summit of the snow-capped cliffs. The villages were left in peace for the most part, unless their inhabitants attacked the soldiers or refused to provide whatever supplies were needed. Then, on the other side of the mountains, they descended into the valley of the river Eurymedon, from which they were able to climb back up towards the interior and the highlands.

It was a relatively narrow valley, with steep sides of red rock which contrasted with the deep blue of the water of the river. Light brown stubble extended on both sides and over the few places where the land stretched away flat from the banks.

They continued for a whole day until, at sunset, they found themselves before a bottleneck, protected on both sides by twin fortresses which rose up from two rocky outcrops. Behind them, on a rocky mound, a fortified city could be made out.

'Termessus,' said Ptolemy as he drew up alongside Alexander on his horse, pointing to the stronghold, red in the last rays of the sun.

Perdiccas approached the King from the other side: 'It's not going to be an easy job, turfing out that eagle's nest,' he said worriedly. 'From the bottom of the valley to the top of the walls must be at least four hundred feet. Not even if we mounted all our siege engines one on top of the other could we ever reach that height.'

Seleucus arrived with two officers from the *hetairoi*

cavalry. 'I think we should set up camp. If we go on they might attack, and we have nothing to respond with.'

'All right, Seleucus,' agreed the King. 'Tomorrow, with daylight, we will see what can be done. I am sure there must be a pass somewhere. It's just a question of finding it.'

At that moment, behind him, came a voice: 'It is my city. A city of magi and seers. Let me go on alone.'

The King turned and saw that the voice belonged to Aristander, the man he had met at the spring by the sea, the man who had read the unreadable inscription.

'Hail, Seer!' he greeted him. 'Come to me and tell me what you intend doing.'

'It is my city,' repeated Aristander. 'A magic city in a magic place. A city where even the children know how to read the signs in the sky and the guts of the disembowelled. Let me go on ahead, before the army moves.'

'Very well, you may go. No one will make any move until you return.'

Aristander turned with a nod and started walking briskly along the slope below the twin fortresses. Some time later, dark by now, his cloak shone white like a solitary ghost as he made his way up the steep sides of the rock of Termessus.

36

ARISTANDER STOOD THERE BEFORE HIM like a vision and the only lamp burning in the tent added an even more haunted look to his face. Alexander leapt to his feet, as if he had been stung by a scorpion.

'When did you return?' he asked. 'And who let you in?'

'I've told you – I know much of magic and I can move through the night wherever I like.'

Alexander stood up and took a look at his dog. Peritas was sleeping peacefully, as if he were alone in the tent.

'How did you do this?' the King asked again.

'That is of no importance.'

'What is of importance then?'

'The news I am about to give you. My fellow citizens have left only the sentries who guard over the pass up there on the rock, all the others have retired for the night inside Termessus. Take them by surprise and lead your army through. On the other side you will see a pathway to the left of the mountain; it leads to the gates of the city. Tomorrow, your trumpets will awaken the people of Termessus.'

Alexander went outside and saw that the camp was immersed in silence – everyone was sleeping peacefully while the sentries kept themselves warm near their fires. He turned towards Aristander and the seer pointed to the sky: 'Look! An eagle flies in widening circles above the walls. This means that the city will be at your mercy after this night attack. Eagles do not fly at night, it is most certainly a sign from the gods.'

Alexander gave orders for everyone to be woken up without the blast of the trumpets, then he called for Lysimachus and the Agrianian commander. 'This is a job for you. I know that there are only groups of sentries up there on the rock. You must take them by surprise and eliminate them in silence, after which we will lead the army through the pass. If your mission is successful, signal to us by throwing stones down.'

The Agrianians were given instructions in their own language and Alexander promised them rewards if they pulled it off. They were pleased to accept the challenge. Across their shoulders they put their hemp ropes and satchels containing hammers and bolts and other equipment, while they slipped their daggers under their belts. When the moon appeared for a short while from behind the clouds, Alexander saw them climbing up the face with their incredible mountaineers' agility. The more reckless of them climbed bare-handed and free as far as they could, before tying their ropes to some protruding stone or to an iron bolt inserted into a crack and then lowering them so that their companions would have an easier ascent.

The moon returned behind the clouds and the Agrianians disappeared altogether. Alexander moved forward, followed by Ptolemy and his personal guard, to the entrance of the pass. They waited there hidden from view.

Shortly afterwards they heard a loud thump, followed

by another and then another – the Agrianians were throwing down the bodies of the sentries.

'They've done their job,' said Ptolemy as he took a quick look at the smashed bodies. 'You can send the army forward now.'

But Alexander gestured to him to be patient. Soon came several repetitions of the same noise, followed by the sharp sound of stones falling from on high and ricocheting off the rocky walls.

'What did I tell you?' repeated Ptolemy. 'They've done their job. These people are very quick and in these sorts of situations they are unbeatable.'

Alexander asked him to pass instructions on to the army divisions to move forward in silence along the pass and the long column set off, while the Agrianians, their mission accomplished, lowered themselves down the rock face, recovering their ropes along the way.

The guides and the scouts who went on ahead soon found the pathway on the left-hand side of the gorge which led up to the city. Before dawn the army was lined up beneath the walls, but the terrain was so rough there was not even enough room to pitch camp.

As soon as his tent was ready on one of the few spaces available between the rocks, Alexander called a meeting of his companions. And while the herald was moving around looking for them, Hephaestion announced another visitor for Alexander – a man by the name of Sisines, an Egyptian, who asked to speak to the King as soon as possible.

'An Egyptian?' asked Alexander in his surprise. 'But who is he? Have you ever come across him before?'

Hephaestion shook his head. 'To tell you the truth, no. But he claims to know both of us, to have worked in his day for King Philip, your father, and to have seen us both running and playing in the courtyard at Pella. He looks as though he has travelled a long way to reach us.'

'And what does he want?'

'He says he wants to speak to you alone.'

The herald arrived just then: 'Sire, the commanders are here and are waiting outside.'

'Show them in,' ordered Alexander. And then he turned to Hephaestion and said, 'Have him fed and find him some shelter until there's a tent ready. Then come back here – I want you to be present for the council.'

Hephaestion set about his orders and immediately afterwards the King's friends entered the tent – Eumenes, Seleucus, Ptolemy, Perdiccas, Lysimachus and Leonnatus. Philotas was with his father in the Phrygian interior, together with Craterus and the Black. They all kissed Alexander on the cheeks and sat down.

'You have seen the city,' began Alexander, 'and you have seen the terrain – rocky, inhospitable. Even if we were to build assault towers with wood from the forests, we would never manage to drag them into position, and a tunnel is out of the question because it would mean cutting through bare rock with mallets and chisels. Impossible! The only solution is to effect a blockade of Termessus, but without any idea of when the city will fall – it could be days, it could be months . . .'

'At Halicarnassus we didn't worry ourselves with such considerations,' said Perdiccas. 'We simply took the time required.'

'Let's build a mountain of wood against the walls, set fire to it and roast them out,' said Leonnatus.

Alexander shook his head, 'Have you seen how far away the woods are? And how many men would we lose sending them to carry wood under the walls without protective covering and without any barrage fire? I will not send my men to their deaths, unless I run the same risks, and you with me. What's more, time is against us. It is vital we meet up with Parmenion's troops as soon as possible.'

'I have an idea,' said Eumenes. 'These barbarians are exactly like the Greeks – they are always busy with internecine fighting. The inhabitants of Termessus will certainly have enemies somewhere, and all we need to do is strike an agreement with them. After that we can start off again towards the north.'

'That's not a bad idea,' said Seleucus.

'Not at all,' said Ptolemy. 'Assuming we manage to find them, these enemies.'

'Will you take care of it?' Alexander asked his secretary.

Eumenes shrugged his shoulders, 'Of course, if no one else is going to deal with it.'

'So we're all agreed then. In the meantime, however, while we are here we will apply the blockade – no one is to enter and no one is to leave the city. Now you may go and see to your men.'

The companions dispersed to their units and shortly afterwards Hephaestion returned: 'I see you have already finished. What have you decided?'

'That we have no time to go into combat with this city. We're trying to find someone who might do the job for us. Where is our guest?'

'He's waiting outside.'

'Bring him in then.'

Hephaestion went out and returned immediately with a rather elderly man, nearer seventy than fifty years old, his hair and his beard grey, dressed like a native of the mountains.

'Come,' Alexander invited him. 'I know that you have asked to speak to me. Who are you?'

'My name is Sisines and I come with a message from General Parmenion.'

Alexander looked into his dark, flighty eyes. 'I have never seen you before. If Parmenion has sent you then you will certainly have a letter bearing his seal.'

'I have no letter – it would have been too dangerous if I were captured. I have orders to transmit to you in person the things I have been told.'

'Speak then.'

'With Parmenion there is a relative of yours, he leads the cavalry.'

'He is my cousin, Amyntas of Lyncestis. He is an excellent soldier and for this reason I gave him the Thessalian cavalry.'

'And do you trust him?'

'When my father was assassinated, he immediately came to my side and since then he has always been loyal.'

'Are you sure of this?' the man asked again.

Alexander began to lose his patience. 'If you have something to tell me, spit it out instead of beating around the bush.'

'Parmenion has intercepted a Persian messenger who was carrying a letter from the Great King to your cousin.'

'May I see it?' asked Alexander, stretching out his hand.

Sisines shook his head with a slight smile. 'It is a most delicate document that we certainly could not risk losing, if I were captured. General Parmenion, however, has authorized me to transmit orally the content of the letter to you.'

Alexander gestured for him to continue.

'The Great King's letter offers your cousin Amyntas of Lyncestis the throne of Macedon and two thousand talents in gold in return for your life.'

The King was speechless. He thought immediately of what Eumolpus of Soloi had said regarding a large sum of money having left the palace at Susa for Anatolia and he thought of the valour and loyalty his cousin had demonstrated up until that moment. He suddenly felt he was being caught up in a web of conspiracies in which valour, strength and courage were worthless, a situation which was a thousand times more suited to his mother's talents than his own. In any case it was a situation that required an immediate solution.

'If this proves to be untrue I will have you cut to pieces and thrown to the dogs,' he said.

Peritas, dozing in a corner, lifted his head and licked his chops, as if suddenly interested in this new twist to the conversation. But Sisines did not seem to be perturbed in the slightest. 'If I am lying, it will not be difficult for you to establish the fact once you meet up with Parmenion.'

'But what proof do you have that my cousin intends to accept the money and the Great King's proposal?'

'In theory I have no proof. But consider the facts, Sire

– would Darius have made such a proposal and risked a sum of money of that size if he had not been sure of the answer? And do you know of any man who can resist indefinitely the attractions of power and riches? If I were in your place, Sire, I would not take any risks. With all that money your cousin could employ a thousand assassins, he could pay off an entire army.'

'Are you suggesting what my next move should be?'

'By the gods, no, Sire. I am a faithful servant who has done his duty crossing snow-covered mountains, suffering hunger and cold, risking his life more than once in lands which are still in the hands of the soldiers and the spies of the Great King.'

Alexander did not reply, but he understood that at this point he had no choice, that a decision in any case had to be made. Sisines interpreted the silence in the most logical manner.

'General Parmenion gave me orders to return as soon as possible with your instructions. And these cannot be written either – I must report to him in person. Indeed, the general honours me with his complete trust.'

Alexander turned his back because he did not want Sisines to read his thoughts in his face. Then, after reflecting on and considering everything, he turned and said, 'This is my message for General Parmenion:

I have received your communication and I thank you for having brought to light a conspiracy that could have resulted in grave setbacks to our enterprise, or even my own death.

We have no proof, however, on the basis of what

I have been told, that my cousin had any intention of accepting the money and the proposal.

I would therefore ask you to keep him under arrest until my arrival and until I have an opportunity to question him personally. But I want him to be treated in a manner befitting his rank and his station. I hope you are well. Take good care.

Repeat it now,' ordered Alexander.

Sisines looked him straight in the eye and repeated the message verbatim, without any hesitation whatsoever.

'Fine,' replied the King, hiding his amazement. 'Now go and eat and sleep. You will have a bed for the night. When you feel sufficiently rested and ready, you will set off again.'

'I will ask for a satchel of food and a skin of water and I will leave straight away.'

'Wait.'

Sisines, who at that moment was bent over, bowing to take his leave, immediately straightened up, 'At your service, Sire.'

'How many days did it take you to reach us from the general's position?'

'Eleven days on the mule.'

'Tell Parmenion that I will leave Termessus in five days' time at the most and that I will join him in Gordium in the same time it took you to come here.'

'Do you want me to repeat this message as well?'

'That will not be necessary,' said Alexander. 'I thank you for the information you have brought to me and I will tell Eumenes to reward you for your troubles.'

Sisines responded, 'That will not be necessary, Sire. My reward is to have contributed towards safeguarding your person. I ask no more than this.' He gave the King a last look which could have meant anything, then he bowed respectfully and left. Alexander sat heavily on a stool and put his face in his hands.

He sat there motionless for a long time – his thoughts returning to the days, back in Pella, when as a child he played with his companions and his cousins at hide-and-seek or with a ball and he felt like shouting or crying.

He had no idea how much time passed before Leptine came to him and put her hand on his shoulder, 'Bad news, my Lord?' she asked softly.

'Yes,' replied Alexander, without turning.

Leptine put her cheek to his shoulder. 'I have managed to find some wood for burning and to warm some water. Would you care to take a bath?'

The King nodded and followed the girl into the private section of the tent where a tub full of steaming water awaited him. Leptine undressed him in the lamplight, darkness having fallen some time previously.

37

With Aristander's help, Eumenes managed to draw up an agreement with a nearby people, the Selghaeans, sworn enemies of the Termessians even though they spoke the same language and worshipped the same deities. He gave them money and had Alexander grant their leader a high-flown title such as 'Supreme Dynast and Autocrat of Pisidia'. The Selghaeans immediately took up position around the city, ready for the siege.

'I told you that Termessus would soon be at your mercy,' Aristander reminded the King, interpreting the situation in his own, highly original manner.

The King made sure of the surrender of some nearby cities along the coast, Side and Aspendos for example, beautiful places built partly in the Greek style with squares, colonnades and temples adorned with statues. He had these cities pay him the taxes they previously paid to the Persians. Finally, before setting off northwards he left a group of officers from the *hetairoi* and a division of assault troops from the shieldsmen together with his barbarian allies under the walls of Termessus.

The Taurus mountains were covered with snow, but the weather was reasonably good, the sky clear and deep blue in colour. Here and there isolated clumps of beech and oak still bore their ochre and reddish leaves, standing out from the blinding whiteness like jewels on a silver tray. As the army advanced the Thracians and the Agrianians, led by Lysimachus, were sent on ahead to occupy the passes and to avoid surprise attacks; in this way the march proceeded without any serious danger cropping up.

Eumenes bought plenty of supplies in the villages so as not to irritate the local population and to ensure the quietest possible passage of the army across the ridges of the great mountain chain.

Alexander rode alone and in silence, ahead of everyone and astride Bucephalas. It was clear to them all he was preoccupied with some problem. He wore a Macedonian hat, with its typically wide brim and over his shoulders was a military *chlamys* of heavy wool. Peritas trotted along almost seeming to run in and out among the hooves of the great stallion. The two animals had established a friendly understanding some time previously and when the dog was not asleep at the foot of Alexander's bed, he would settle down in the straw near Bucephalas.

After three days of march over the mountains, they came within sight of the interior highlands – a flat, burned plain, swept by a bitter cold wind. Far off in the distance a body of water could be seen shining, clear and dark, surrounded by an extent of blinding whiteness.

'More snow,' grumbled Eumenes, who once again was feeling the cold and had definitively abandoned his short military *chiton* for a pair of warmer Phrygian trousers.

'No . . . it is salt,' said Aristander, riding alongside him. 'That is Lake Ascania, saltier than the sea. In the summer much of it evaporates and the layer of salt extends outwards. The locals sell it throughout the valley.'

As the army passed over the salt, the sun was just beginning to descend behind the mountains and the shining sun refracted by millions of salt crystals created a fantastic effect – an unreal, magic atmosphere. The soldiers looked on in silence at this marvel without managing to take their eyes from the continuous changes in colour, from the rays of light refracted by the infinite crystalline facets into triumphs of fire-like sparks.

'Gods of Olympus!' said Seleucus. 'What splendour! Now we really can say that we are far from home.'

'Yes,' agreed Ptolemy. 'I have never seen anything like this in all my life.'

'And this is not all that awaits you,' continued Aristander. 'Farther on is Mount Argaeus, which spits fire and flames from its summit and covers whole regions with ash. It is said that the giant Typhon is chained up within it.'

Ptolemy made a gesture to Seleucus to follow him and spurred his horse forward as though off to inspect the column. He continued for half a stadium before drawing rein and slowing to a walk.

'What's wrong with Alexander?' he asked.

Seleucus drew up alongside, 'I don't know. He has been this way ever since the Egyptian visitor came to see him.'

'I don't like Egyptians,' Ptolemy declared. 'Who knows what nonsense he has put into Alexander's head? This seer was bad enough, this Aristander.'

'I think Hephaestion knows something, but he won't give anything away.'

'I'm sure. He always does exactly what Alexander wants him to do.'

'Right. What can it be about? It certainly must be bad news. And then all this haste to move onwards ... do you think something might have happened to Parmenion?'

Ptolemy looked briefly at Alexander, riding ahead but not very far off.

'He surely would have said something. And then Parmenion is with the Black, Philotas, Craterus and even Alexander's cousin, Amyntas, who has command of the Thessalian cavalry. Is it possible that no one survived?'

'Who knows? Perhaps an ambush ... or perhaps Alexander is thinking about Memnon. That man is capable of anything – as we speak he might well have landed in Macedonia, or at Piraeus.'

'What shall we do? If he invites us to supper this evening then perhaps we could ask him.'

'It depends on what sort of mood he's in. Perhaps it would be better to speak with Hephaestion.'

'Yes, that's it. Let's do that.'

In the meantime the sun had disappeared below the horizon and the two friends' thoughts turned to the young women they had left behind in Pieria or in Eordaea and who perhaps at that melancholy time of day were thinking of them.

'Have you ever thought of getting married?' Ptolemy suddenly asked.

'No. And you?'

'Me neither. But I wouldn't have minded marrying Cleopatra.'

'Oh yes!'

'Perdiccas wouldn't have minded either, if it comes to that.'

'Right. Perdiccas too.'

A great shout came from the head of the column. The scouts were returning at a gallop from a reconnaissance mission, the last before dark: 'Kelainai! Kelainai!'

'Where?' asked Eumenes.

'Five stadia in that direction,' replied one of the scouts, pointing to a hill in the distance on which myriad lights twinkled. It was a wonderful sight, like a giant anthill illuminated by thousands of fireflies.

Alexander seemed to liven up and he lifted his arm to stop the column: 'We will camp here,' he ordered. 'Tomorrow we will approach the city. It is the capital of Phrygia and the seat of the Persian satrap of the province. If Parmenion has not already taken it, we will do the job; there must be a lot of money locked away in that fortress.'

'His mood seems to have changed,' said Ptolemy.

'Indeed,' said Seleucus. 'He must have remembered what Aristotle used to say: "There is either a solution to the problem and therefore it is pointless to worry about it, or there is no solution and it is pointless to worry about it." Perhaps he will invite us to supper after all.'

38

WINTER WAS WELL ON its way, and Aristotle arrived in Methone on one of the last ships to leave Piraeus. The captain had decided to make the most of a strong and constant southerly wind to deliver a consignment of olive oil, wine and beeswax which otherwise would have had to wait in the warehouses until the arrival of spring, and lower prices.

On landing he climbed up on to a carriage drawn by a pair of mules and asked the driver take him to Mieza. He had the keys to all of the buildings with him and was authorized to come and go and make use of the facilities whenever he wished. He was perfectly aware that he would meet someone whom he very much wanted to speak to, someone who would perhaps be able to give him first-hand news of Alexander – Lysippus.

The sculptor was busy working in the foundry when Aristotle arrived, creating the clay model for the great statuary complex of Alexander's troop on the Granicus, which would then be cast in its final proportions for the monument itself. It was almost evening and lamps were already burning inside the laboratory, the refectory, and in some of the guests' rooms.

'Welcome, Aristotle!' Lysippus greeted him. 'I am sorry, but I cannot even shake hands with you – I'm all dirty. If you wait just one moment, I will be with you.'

Aristotle moved closer to look at the model. It was a sculpture of twenty-six characters on a platform some eight to ten feet in length. The effect was amazing – the churning of the water and the furious rhythm of the charging horses could almost be felt physically. And in it all Alexander stood out proud in his armour, the wind in his hair, astride a rampant Bucephalas.

Lysippus rinsed his hands in a basin of water and came closer.

'What do you think of it?'

'Superb. What strikes one most in your works is the quivering energy within the forms, like a body in the midst of some all-consuming orgasm.'

'The visitor will see them all of a sudden,' Lysippus explained, with inspiration written all over his face as he lifted his enormous hands to describe the scene, 'on coming over the top of a small rise. The impression will be of having the troop charging towards the observer, of being crushed by them. Alexander asked me to make them immortal and I am expending all of my energies in satisfying him and to repay, at least in part, their parents for their sad losses.'

'And at the same time you are granting him the status of a living legend,' said Aristotle.

'I think that will happen without my help, won't it?'

Lysippus took off his leather apron and hung it on a nail. 'Supper is almost ready, will you have something to eat with us?'

'I'd be delighted,' replied Aristotle, 'Who else is here?'

'Chares, my assistant,' replied the sculptor, pointing to the young man with thin hair who was over in the corner, working away with a gouge on a piece of wood and who greeted the philosopher with a respectful bow of his head. 'And then there is an envoy from the city of Tarant, Evemerus of Kallipolis, a good man who perhaps will have news for us of King Alexander of Epirus.'

They left the foundry and walked along the internal portico towards the refectory. Aristotle thought sadly of the last time he had eaten there with King Philip.

'Will you stay long?' Lysippus asked.

'Not very long. I have given instructions to Callisthenes, with my most recent letter to him, to reply to me here at Mieza and I am anxious to read what he has to say. Then I will go on to Aegae.'

'Are you going to the old palace?'

'I will make an offering at the King's tomb and I must see a few people.'

Lysippus hesitated for a moment. 'I have heard a tale that you are investigating the assassination of King Philip, but perhaps these are just rumours.'

'They are not rumours,' Aristotle stated, apparently impassible.

'Does Alexander know?'

'I believe so, even though initially he had given the job to my nephew Callisthenes.'

'And the Queen Mother?'

'I have not communicated the fact to her, but Olympias has ears and eyes everywhere. It is most likely that she knows.'

'And are you not afraid?'

'I am confident that the regent, Antipater, will make sure that nothing untoward happens to me. Can you see that carriage driver over there?' he said, pointing to the man who had brought him to Mieza and who that moment was tending to his mules in the stables. 'In his bag he carries a Macedonian sword of the type issued to the palace guards.'

Lysippus took a look at the character – a mountain of muscles who moved as stealthily as a fox. He could see, even at this distance, that he was a soldier of the royal guard. 'By the gods! He could pose for a statue of Hercules.'

They made their way to the dining room.

'No dining beds,' said the artist. 'Things are still as they were, everyone eats sitting at table.'

'I prefer it. I'm no longer used to eating stretched out. Well then, what news do you have of Alexander?'

'I imagine that Callisthenes keeps you informed.'

'Of course. But I am keen to know your own impressions. Have you seen him recently?'

'Yes, once, to show him the plan for the sculpture.'

'And how was he?'

'He is completely immersed in his dream. Nothing will stop him until he reaches his goal.'

'And in your opinion, what is that goal?'

Lysippus was silent for some time, he seemed to be watching a servant poke the fire in the grate. Then he said, without turning, 'To change the world.'

Aristotle sighed. 'I think you have understood. The thing is, will he change it for the better or for the worse?'

At that moment the foreign guest, Evemerus of Kallipolis, entered, and introduced himself while supper was being served – chicken soup with beans, bread, cheese and hard-boiled eggs with oil and salt. And wine from Thasos.

'What news do you have of Alexander of Epirus?' asked Lysippus.

'Important news,' replied the guest. 'The King leads his own and our armies together and moves on from victory to victory. He has defeated the Messapians and the Iapyges and all of Apulia is in his hands, a land almost as big as his own realm.'

'And where is he now?'

'He must be in his winter quarters now, waiting to continue his campaign next spring against the Samnites, a barbarian people to the north, in the mountains. He has made an alliance with other barbarians, called Romans, who will attack from the north while he will march from the south.'

'And how do the people of Tarant see him?'

'I am not a politician, but as far as I can understand, they view him positively . . . at least for the moment.'

'What do you mean?'

'My fellow citizens are strange people – their main passions are trade and living the good life. For these reasons they have no taste for combat and when they find themselves in trouble they call on someone to help them. This is exactly what they have done with Alexander of Epirus. But I am sure there will be those who are already saying that he is helping them too much and too well.'

Aristotle smiled sarcastically, 'Do they think that Alexander has left his land and his young bride, that he is facing dangers and difficulties, sleepless nights, endless marches and bloody battles just to let them concentrate on trade and the good life?'

Evemerus continued. 'A group of wealthy citizens has had the idea of collecting money for a grand project which will spread the city's fame throughout the world.'

Lysippus, who had finished eating, rinsed his mouth with a cupful of red wine and leaned against the backrest of his chair. 'Carry on,' he said.

'They would like to build a gigantic statue of Zeus, not in a temple or in a sanctuary, however, but in full light, in the open air, at the centre of the agora.'

At this point young Chares' eyes widened. More than once the young assistant had spoken to his master of the dreams and the fantasies he nourished.

Lysippus smiled, imagining his assistant's thoughts, then he said, 'The point is, just how gigantic?'

Evemerus seemed to hesitate for a moment, then all of a sudden said, 'Let's say forty cubits.'

Chares started, Lysippus gripped the arms of his chair and sat up straight.

'Forty cubits? Gods in heaven, man! Do you realize you're talking about a statue as tall as the Parthenon in Athens?'

'Indeed. We Greeks in the colonies think big.'

The sculptor turned to his young assistant. 'What do you think, Chares? Forty cubits is some size, no? Unfortunately there is no one in the world, at the moment, capable of erecting a giant of that size.'

'The remuneration would be most generous.'

'It's not a question of remuneration,' replied Lysippus. 'It's a matter of techniques – we simply don't have the necessary techniques to keep the bronze liquid long enough to cover such distances and the temperature of the external casting block cannot be increased accordingly without risking the fracture of the mould. I'm not saying it's completely out of the question; you might ask other artists . . . why not Chares here, for example?' he said, ruffling the hair of his timid pupil. 'He says that one day he will create the largest statue in the world.'

Evemerus shook his head. 'If the great Lysippus doesn't feel up to it then who else would dare undertake the job?'

Lysippus smiled and put a hand on his assistant's shoulder, 'Chares perhaps. Who knows . . .?'

Aristotle was struck by the imaginative expression on the young man's face. 'Where are you from, lad?'

'Lindos, on the island of Rhodes.'

'You're from Rhodes . . .' repeated the philosopher, as if the name reminded him of something which had recently become familiar to him. Then he returned to the topic at hand. 'Down there they call statues "colossi", isn't that so?'

A servant began clearing the table and poured some more wine. Lysippus took a sip and then said, 'Your idea is in any case a fascinating one, Evemerus, even if unrealizable in my opinion. I am anyway very busy now and I will be for some years to come, so I will not have time to study and plan a work of this kind. But you may tell your fellow citizens that from this moment onwards there is an image of Zeus in Lysippus's mind and it might just take real shape, sooner or later – perhaps in a year, in ten years, perhaps in twenty . . . who knows?'

Evemerus stood up. 'Farewell then, Lysippus. If you

should change your mind then please know that we are ready to welcome you in Tarant.'

'Farewell, Evemerus. I must return to my studio, where a troop of horsemen in clay await the life-giving qualities of cast bronze – Alexander's troop.'

39

ARISTOTLE ENTERED his old rooms, lit the lamps and opened his personal chest, taking from it the letter he had been expecting from Callisthenes – a sealed roll of papyrus tied with a leather string. It was written entirely in a secret and unique code, to which only he, his nephew and Theophrastus held the key. The philosopher held the template over the document, isolating the important words from the completely random text surrounding them, and began to read the message.

When he had finished he took the sheet over to the lamp and watched it curl right to the very last corner as the flames consumed it and its secret, leaving only myriad tiny fragments. He then went down to the stables and woke the carriage driver who had brought him to Mieza. He gave him a sealed package together with a letter and explained how important it was that he followed these orders to the letter: 'Take the best horse and set off immediately for Methone. The captain on whose ship I came from Piraeus should still be there. Tell him to take you to Theophrastus at the location indicated in the letter. Give him the package. If for any reason you do not reach Theophrastus, seek out my nephew Callisthenes and deliver the package to him.'

'I doubt the captain will want to sail – the bad weather is very nearly on us now.'

Aristotle pulled a bag of money from his cloak. 'This might help persuade him. Now go, quickly.'

The man chose a charger from the stables, took out his sword and hung it on his belt while the package took the place of the weapon in his bag. He set off immediately at a gallop.

Although it was late at night, Lysippus was still at work and he went over to the window of the studio when he heard a noise, but it was only Aristotle moving quickly along the portico of the internal courtyard. The following morning, while he was shaving in front of the mirror, he saw the philosopher again, fully dressed and with his travelling satchel over his shoulder, walking towards the stables where the mules were being yoked up to a carriage. He dried his face quickly, intending to go down and say goodbye, but a servant knocked at that very moment and handed him a note which read:

Aristotle to Lysippus, Hail!

Important business means that I must leave immediately. I hope we will meet again soon. I wish you all the very best in your work.

Take good care.

When he looked out of the window once more Aristotle was already disappearing atop the small carriage as it moved along the north road. The sky was grey and the day cold, it might even have snowed. The sculptor closed the window and finished shaving before going down to have breakfast.

*

The philosopher travelled all day, stopping only to eat a light meal in a hostelry at Kition, the half-way point of his journey. When he reached Aegae it was already dark and he went straight to King Philip's tomb, in front of which two tripod lamps were burning on either side of an altar. He poured a phial of a fine oriental perfume into the tripods and collected himself in meditation before the great stone portal, surmounted by beautiful hunting scenes that decorated the architrave. At that moment it was as if he could see the King once again, dismounting from his horse in the courtyard at Mieza, swearing because of his crippled leg, and shouting, 'Where is Alexander?'

Aristotle repeated to himself, quietly, 'Where is Alexander?'

Then he turned his back on the great tomb and moved away. He slept in a small house he still owned at the edge of the city and stayed there through all of the following day, reading and putting some of his notes in order. The weather continued to worsen and dark clouds gathered on the peaks of Mount Bermion which were already dusted with snow. He waited for darkness to fall, put on a cloak, covered his head with its hood and started walking through the almost deserted streets.

He passed in front of the theatre where the King had been assassinated in a cloud of dust and a pool of blood at the height of his glory; then he carried on along a path that led to the fields. He was looking for a solitary tomb.

Before him rose a group of age-old oak trees in the midst of an open space and Aristotle hid among the great rough trunks, blending in with the evening shadows. Not far away a modest tumulus could be made out, with a simple rock placed on top of it as a marker. The philosopher waited, motionless and lost in thought.

Every now and then he raised his eyes to the leaden sky and drew his cloak about his shoulders, to protect himself from the cold wind that had begun to blow down from the mountains with nightfall.

Finally the noise of footsteps along the path and the flickering light of a lantern made him turn to the left and he saw the figure of a small woman advancing briskly. She passed by him and stopped in front of the tumulus, not far away.

He watched her kneel down and deposit something on the burial mound, then she placed her hand and her head on the rock, covering it with her cloak, almost as if seeking to warm it. White crystals of sleet began to streak the darkness as they fell.

Aristotle sought more warmth, wrapping himself even more tightly in his cloak, but just then a gust of freezing wind caused him to cough suddenly. The woman stood up and turned in a flash towards the small oak wood.

'Who's there?' she asked, her voice trembling.

'One who searches for the truth.'

'Then show yourself,' replied the woman.

Aristotle came out of his hide and moved towards her. 'I am Aristotle of Stagira.'

'The great wise man,' nodded the woman. 'What brings you to this sad place?'

'I told you . . . I am looking for the truth.'

'Which truth?'

'The truth of King Philip's death.'

The woman, young and with large dark eyes, lowered her head and stooped, as though her shoulders bore a weight that was too much for her.

'I don't think I can help you in any way.'

'Why do you come out here in the dark to pay homage to this burial mound? This is the tumulus where Pausanias, the King's assassin, was buried.'

'Because he was my man and I loved him. He had already offered me nuptial gifts and we were to be married.'

'I have heard tale of this. This is why I have come here. Is it true that he was Philip's lover?'

The woman shook her head. 'I . . . I don't know.'

'They say that when Philip married his last wife, young Eurydice, Pausanias was consumed by jealousy and his behaviour drove the bride's father, the noble Attalus, wild with rage.' Aristotle did not miss a single expression on the woman's face and as he recounted the tale he saw tears running down her colourless cheeks. 'Rumour also has it that Attalus invited him to his hunting lodge where the huntsmen beat and raped him for a whole night.'

The woman was crying now, disconsolate, no longer able to contain her grief, but the philosopher continued, impervious. 'Pausanias then asked Philip to avenge this humiliation and because he failed to do so, he killed him. Is this really what happened?'

The woman sought to dry her tears with the hem of her cloak.

'Is this the truth?'

'Yes,' she said, sobbing.

'The whole truth?'

The woman did not reply.

'I know that the episode in Attalus's hunting lodge is true – I have my informers. But what was the cause of it all? Was it simply a dark affair of male love?'

The young woman made to leave, as though wishing to cut the conversation short there and then. The shawl over her head was already white with snowflakes and the ground at their feet was also covered with a thin white layer. Aristotle took her by the arm. 'Well?' he insisted, staring into her face with his grey eagle eyes.

She shook her head.

'Come,' said the philosopher with a suddenly more conciliatory tone. 'I have a house nearby and the fire should still be burning.'

The young woman followed him meekly, holding the lamp, and Aristotle led her to his home, had her sit next to the grate and poked the fire.

'All I can offer you is a warm infusion of herbs. I am only passing through.'

He took a jug from the fireplace and poured its steaming contents into two pottery cups.

'Well then, what do you know that I do not?'

'Pausanias never was the King's lover and he never had any affairs with men. He was a simple boy, of humble origins, and he liked women. As for King Philip, there was much talk about relations with men, but no one ever saw anything.'

'You seem to be very well informed . . . how?'

'I work in the palace kitchens.'

'This does not exclude, however, the possibility of there having been some episode of the kind, even an isolated one.'

'I don't think so.'

'Why?'

'Because Pausanias told me that by chance he had surprised Attalus in the midst of a secret, dangerous conversation.'

'Perhaps Pausanias was eavesdropping?'

'It is possible.'

'And did he tell you what the conversation was about?'

'No, but what they did to him, in my opinion, was designed to terrorize him, to crush him without actually killing him – the assassination of a member of the King's guard would have raised too many suspicions.'

'So, let's hypothesize – Pausanias surprises Attalus while he is engaged in some reckless conversation, let's say a conspiracy, and he threatens to reveal everything. Attalus invites him to an isolated place pretending to want to negotiate and then, to teach him a lesson, he leaves him to the violence of his huntsmen. But why then should Pausanias kill King Philip? It makes no sense.'

'And what sense is there in the rumour that Pausanias killed the King because he had refused to avenge the humiliation Attalus inflicted on him? Pausanias was a bodyguard – strong, skilled in weaponry – he could have easily sought revenge on his own.'

'That is true,' said Aristotle, thinking of the formidable build of his carriage driver. 'So how do you explain it all? If Pausanias was the loyal young man you describe, why did he assassinate his King?'

'I do not know, but if he had wanted to do so, don't you think there would have been better opportunities for a bodyguard? He could have killed Philip in his sleep, in his bed.'

'I have always thought so. But at this point it seems to me that neither of us can provide answers to our questions. Do you know of anyone else who might have more information? They say he had accomplices, or some sort of cover in any case – there were men waiting for him with a horse near the oak wood where we met a short time ago.'

'They also say that one of them has been identified,' said the young woman, suddenly staring directly into Aristotle's eyes.

'And where would he be now?'

'In a hostelry in Beroea, on the banks of the Haliakmon; he calls himself Nicander, but it's certainly a false name.'

'And what is his real name?'

'I do not know. If I did then perhaps I would be nearer knowing the reason why Pausanias did what he did and why he suffered so.'

Aristotle picked up the jug from the fire once again and was about to pour some more of the infusion into the young woman's bowl, but she stopped him with a gesture and stood up.

'I should go now, otherwise someone will come looking for me.'

'How can I thank you for the things . . .' began Aristotle, but she interrupted him:

'Find the real culprit behind all this and let me know.'

She opened the door and walked quickly along the deserted road. Aristotle called out to her, 'Wait . . . you haven't even told me your name!' But the young woman had already disappeared into the swirling cloud of white flakes, along the silent alleyways of the sleeping city.

40

THE REGENT ANTIPATER received him in the old throne room. Aristotle was all bundled up in a rough woollen cloak over a pair of Thracian felt trousers. A big fire roared in a hearth at the centre of the room, but much of the heat it generated disappeared together with the smoke out of the open hole in the middle of the ceiling.

'How are you, General?' asked the philosopher.

'Fine, when I am away from Pella. Even the very sight of the Queen gives me a headache. And how are you, Aristotle?'

'I too am well, but the years are beginning to take their toll. And then I have never been able to bear the cold.'

'What brings you to these parts?'

'I wanted to make an offering at the tomb of the King before returning to Athens.'

'Such devotion does you great honour, but such actions are also very dangerous. If you continue to shake off the guards I send to look after you, how can I protect you? Be careful, Aristotle, the Queen is a real tigress.'

'I have always been on good terms with Olympias.'

'But being on good terms with her is not enough,' said Antipater as he got to his feet and stood before the fire, his hands held out to gather its heat. 'I assure you it is not enough.' He took a silver jug that was standing at the edge of the hearth and a pair of cups of good Attic pottery. 'Some warm wine?'

Aristotle nodded.

'What news is there of Alexander?'

'Parmenion's latest message says he is marching across Lycia.'

'So everything is proceeding according to plan.'

'Unfortunately not everything.'

'What is the problem?'

'Alexander awaits reinforcements. The youngsters to whom he had granted compassionate leave are already on the Straits together with the new recruits, but they cannot pass because Memnon's fleet is operating a blockade. If my calculations are correct, at this moment he should be in Greater Phrygia, near Sagalassus or Kelainai, and he will certainly be worried now that no one has arrived.'

'And is there nothing to be done?'

'Memnon's naval superiority is overwhelming – if I were to send my fleet out he would sink it before it even got offshore. We are in trouble, Aristotle. My only hope is that Memnon might attempt a landing on Macedonian territory, in which case we might hope to nail him. But the man is extremely astute and he rarely makes mistakes.'

'What do you intend doing then?'

'Nothing, for the time being. I will wait until he decides on his next move – he cannot rest at anchor for ever. And you, Aristotle? Have you really come all this way just to make an offering at the altar of King Philip? If you do not tell me what you are really up to, I will find it even more difficult to protect you.'

'I came to speak to someone.'

'Does it have anything to do with the death of the King?'

'Yes.'

Antipater nodded as though he had been expecting this reply.

'And will you remain here for long?'

'I leave tomorrow. I am returning to Athens, if I can find a ship from Methone. Otherwise I will travel overland.'

'And how are things going in Athens?'

'Fine, as long as Alexander is victorious.'

'Exactly,' sighed Antipater.

'Exactly,' repeated Aristotle.

*

Alexander quartered his army at Kelainai, not far from the source of the Meander river and the official seat of the satrapy of Greater Phrygia. He encountered no resistance because the Persian soldiers had all taken refuge in a fortress at the highest point of the city – a rocky outcrop that descended steeply over a small lake of clear water from the river Marsyas, a tributary of the Meander. There could not have been many of them because they made no attempt to defend the city walls, which were rather dilapidated here and there.

Lysimachus went to reconnoitre the fortress and returned in a bad mood. 'It is impregnable,' he reported. 'The only access is through a postern half-way along, on the eastern side, but the steps leading to it are wide enough for just one man to pass at a time and it is in full view of the twin bastions. We should apply a blockade, and hope they don't have enough provisions to survive for any length of time. As for water, they'll have plenty of that since there must certainly be a well connected to the lake.'

'And if we were to ask them what their plans are?' proposed Leonnatus.

'This is no time to joke,' replied Lysimachus. 'We have no idea where Parmenion is and what sort of state his men are in – if we waste too much time on a blockade then we risk not meeting up with him at all.'

Alexander took a look at the ramparts of the fortress. The Persian soldiers certainly did not appear very warlike and they seemed more curious than alarmed by the Macedonian presence. They crowded on to the battlements and looked down, elbows leaning on the parapet.

'Perhaps Leonnatus's idea isn't such a bizarre one after all,' he said. Then he turned to Eumenes. 'Prepare a delegation with an interpreter and get as close as you can to the postern. They do not know our plans, but they will certainly know that nothing has stopped us as yet – it may well be that they have no desire to fight us.'

'That's right,' said Leonnatus, proud of the fact that the King had given credit to his proposal. 'If they had wanted to stop us, they could have attacked a hundred times while we climbed up here from Termessus.'

'It is pointless to waste our energies in such hypothesizing,' Alexander cut him short. 'We will await Eumenes's return and then we will know exactly what lies before us.'

'In the meantime I would like to take a look at the city, if anyone cares to accompany me,' said Callisthenes. 'They say that on the other side of the lake is the cave where the satyr Marsyas was skinned alive by Apollo for having challenged him to a musical competition, and for having lost, of course.'

Lysimachus assigned ten or so shieldsmen to escort Callisthenes on his tour of Kelainai. The expedition's historian had to be able to see the places he was to describe in his writings.

In the meantime Eumenes assembled his delegation. He made sure he had a herald and an interpreter and then set off for the postern, asking to speak with the commander of the garrison.

The response was not long in coming. The postern opened with a creaking noise and the commander came out, accompanied by a small group of armed men. Eumenes immediately realized that he was not Persian, but Phrygian, almost certainly a local. The Persian satrap must have left the city some time previously.

The secretary greeted the commander and then had the interpreter translate his words: 'King Alexander says that if you surrender then no harm will come to you and your men, and the city will suffer no damage whatsoever. If instead you resist, we will blockade the fortress and we will not allow anyone to leave it alive. What am I to tell the King?'

The commander must have made his decision already because he replied without any hesitation whatsoever: 'You may tell the King that we have no intention of surrendering, for the moment. We will wait two days, and if no reinforcements arrive from our governor, then we will surrender.'

Eumenes was amazed at the commander's ingenuous

sincerity, saluted him most cordially and went back to report.

'It's absurd!' exclaimed Lysimachus. 'If anyone else had told me this, I wouldn't have believed it.'

'And why not?' replied Eumenes. 'To me it seems to be the most sensible decision. The man has worked it all out – if the Persian governor sets up a counterattack and defeats us, then he will have to explain why he surrendered without fighting and he'll probably end up on the stake. If the governor fails to show up in the next two days, then that means he won't be coming at all and so he might as well surrender so as to avoid any more trouble from us.'

'It's the best solution,' said Alexander. 'The commanders may arrange their quarters in the city, requisitioning the necessary homes; officers of lower rank will stay with their troops in the camp. Have a battalion of the *pezhetairoi* stationed around the citadel and sentries at the bottom of the rock – no one must go in or come out of there. And I want a squadron of light cavalry – Thracian and Thessalian – on all the access roads to the city so as to avoid surprises. We'll see if this two days business is for real or if it's a joke. I await you all for supper in the governor's palace, where I have established my quarters – a fine, sumptuous residence. I hope you will enjoy the evening.'

At the appointed time Callisthenes also came to the governor's palace, having completed his tour of the city. A servant brought him some water for washing and then had him stretch out on one of the dining beds arranged in a semicircle around Alexander's. The King had also invited

Thessalus, his favourite actor, the seer Aristander and his personal physician, Philip.

'So, what have you seen then?' asked the King while the cooks began serving the supper.

'It is as I was telling you,' replied Callisthenes. 'In the cave where the source of the river Marsyas is located there hangs a hide which they say belonged to the satyr, skinned by Apollo. You know the story – Marsyas challenged the god Apollo to a musical competition. He was to play the cane flute, while the god was to play the lyre. Apollo accepted the challenge, but on one condition: if Marsyas lost then he would let himself be skinned alive. And that is what happened, understandably perhaps, because the judges were the nine Muses, and they certainly wouldn't have done anything to anger their god.'

Ptolemy smiled. 'It is difficult to believe that the skin in the cave is really the satyr's.'

'It would seem so,' replied Callisthenes. 'The upper part looks very much like a human skin, even though mummified, while the lower part is like a goat's.'

'That's not so difficult to achieve,' said Philip the physician. 'A good surgeon can cut and sew whatever he wants. There are some taxidermists who manage to create the most imaginative creatures – Aristotle once told me he saw an embalmed centaur in a sanctuary on Mount Pelion, in Thessaly, but explained that it was in fact a human torso skilfully joined to a foal's body.'

The King then turned to Aristander, 'What do you think? Has Callisthenes really seen the skin of a satyr or is it just a deft trick by the priests to attract pilgrims and collect rich offerings for their sanctuary?'

Many of the guests started laughing, but the seer sent a gaze of fire around the room and the laughter was soon extinguished, even the laughter which came from the strongest and most confident of the men.

'It is easy to laugh at these shoddy expedients,' he said, 'but I wonder if you are also laughing at the deeper meanings which lie behind such manifestations. Are there any among you, O valiant warriors, who have ever explored the regions that lie beyond the limits of our perception? Do any of you feel up to accompanying me on a journey towards the shadows of the night? You all know how to face death on the battlefield, but do you know how to face the unknown? Would you know how to do combat with immaterial monsters – invincible and evanescent monsters which our deepest nature keeps hidden from our very conscience?

'Have you ever wanted to kill your own fathers? Have you ever wanted to sleep with your own mothers or your own sisters? What do you see inside yourselves when you are drunk or when you rape some youngster, enjoying the act doubly because of his or her suffering? This is the nature of the satyr or the centaur, the ancestral beast with the cloven hoof and the wildly thrashing tail that lives in all of us and brings us all suddenly to the same level as the beasts! Laugh at these things, if you can!'

'No one was seeking to make fun of religion and the gods, Aristander,' the King said, trying to calm him down. 'If anything they were making fun of the shabbiness of some confidence tricksters who exploit people's credulity.

Come now, let us drink together and be hearty. We still have many ordeals to face before we discover what our destiny will be.'

They all started drinking and eating once more and the conversation soon livened up again, but from that moment onwards none of them ever forgot the expression on Aristander's face and the words that came from his mouth.

41

THE COMMANDER OF THE Kelainai garrison let the two days stipulated pass by and then duly surrendered. Thus much of the governor's treasure went into the coffers of the Macedonian army. Alexander let the commander keep his position and left some of his own officers together with a small contingent of soldiers to hold the fortress. Then he set off again on the north road.

When he reached Gordium, after five days' march across the highland and its light cover of snow, he found Parmenion already there waiting for him. The general had positioned lookouts on the hills around the ancient Phrygian city and so had received word as soon as the red standard with the golden Argead star appeared on the blinding white snow.

The old general went to meet Alexander with an escort of honour led by his son Philotas. When he was not far off, he had the guard line up and proceeded alone on foot, leading his horse by its halter. The King also dismounted and walked towards Parmenion, while the soldiers shouted their salute and their joy for the meeting of the two contingents.

Parmenion embraced the King and kissed him on both cheeks. 'Sire, you cannot imagine how happy I am to see you. I was most worried because we cannot fathom out the Persians' strategy.'

'I too am most happy to see you, General. Is your son Philotas well? And your men?'

'They are all well, Sire. And they have prepared a celebration for your arrival. There will be much drinking and merry-making.' As he spoke he walked alongside Alexander and every now and then Bucephalas gave his master a little push with his muzzle to attract his attention. The whole army proceeded behind them and all the cavalry, given the wide expanse they found themselves on, advanced in one long line just three rows deep, so that the sight of the two men walking calmly in the midst of that endless plateau was most striking. Behind them came the massed army and the rumble of tens of thousands of hooves at a walk.

'Have our reinforcements arrived?' the King asked.

'Unfortunately no.'

'Do you know whether they are at least on their way?'

'Not yet.'

Alexander walked on in silence because his next question was a particularly difficult one. Parmenion kept quiet so as not to make the situation any more awkward than it already was.

'Where is he?' Alexander suddenly said as if asking for information on some topic of minor importance.

'Sisines returned with your verbal message and I simply carried out your orders. Amyntas is in custody in his quarters and I have put Philotas in temporary command of the Thessalian cavalry.'

'How did he take it?'

'Badly, but that was to be expected.'

'I cannot believe it. He has always been loyal to me – I have seen him risk his life on more than one occasion.'

Parmenion shook his head. 'Power corrupts many men,' he said. But to himself he thought: Power corrupts all men. 'Still, we have no proof that he had actually accepted the deal.'

'The Persian messenger who brought the letter?'

'I am holding him prisoner. And I can let you see the letter.'

'Is it in Greek or in Persian?'

'It is in Greek, but that is no surprise. The Great King has many Greeks at court, including many Athenians, and he has no difficulty in drawing up documents of this kind.'

'And the promised payment?'

'No trace of it at all . . . for the moment at least.'

Parmenion's camp came into view now. It consisted for the most part of tents, but there were also some small wooden constructions, a sign that they had been there for some time.

At that moment there came a series of trumpet blasts and soon the entire contingent came out on to the open field to pay homage to their returning King.

Alexander and Parmenion mounted their horses and inspected the troops, who beat their swords on their shields creating a tremendous din and shouting rhythmically: 'Aléxandre! Aléxandre! Aléxandre!' The King was much moved as he saluted them, waving and gazing over the sea of rejoicing soldiers.

'We are in control of almost half of Anatolia,' said Parmenion. 'No Greek has ever conquered such vast lands, not even Agamemnon. What worries me, however, is the lack of movement from the Persians. At the Granicus it was the governors of Phrygia and Bithynia who did battle with us, of their own initiative. Back then there wasn't even enough time to consult the Great King. But at this stage Darius has certainly taken his decisions and I simply cannot understand this calm – no attacks, no ambushes . . . and not even a request for negotiation.'

'That's fine,' replied Alexander, 'because I have no intention of sitting down at the table with him.'

Parmenion was silent. By now he knew the King's temperament very well. There was only one enemy Alexander respected – Memnon, but for some time now there had been no news of him. It was only the delay of the reinforcements due from Macedonia which left them thinking that their most feared opponent was still very much alive and kicking.

The conversation continued in the old general's quarters and they joined up with their other companions – the Black, Philotas and Craterus – but it was clear they all wanted to savour the joy of the reunion rather than discuss military matters and soon the topics were wine and women rather than strategy and tactics. And there were women in abundance now, some of them managed by intermediaries, others who had spontaneously latched on to the troops attracted by gifts and promises, while others again had been bought as slaves from one of the many merchants who followed the army in the same way that fleas follow dogs.

Alexander stayed for supper, but as soon as the party began and a certain number of girls and young men had started dancing naked among the tables, he got up from his dining bed and moved away. There was a fine moon outside and the evening was pleasant and calm. He approached one of Parmenion's officers, who was inspecting the guard, and asked him, 'Where is Prince Amyntas being kept prisoner?'

The officer was immediately somewhat alarmed, seeing that the King was wandering around the camp alone at that time of night, and accompanied him personally to one of the wooden dwellings which had been built here and there. The guards opened the bolts and let him enter.

Amyntas was still awake, sitting by lamplight in a bare room, its walls of bare tree-trunks. He was reading a papyrus scroll, which was held open on top of a rough wooden table with two stones that he must have gathered from the ground. He lifted his head as soon as he realized there was someone in the doorway and rubbed his eyes to see better. When he understood who it was who stood there before him, he got to his feet and moved back towards the wall, an expression of pain and unease on his face: 'Was it you who had me arrested?' he asked.

Alexander nodded, 'Yes.'

'Why?'

'Didn't Parmenion tell you?'

'No. He simply had me arrested in front of my men in the full light of day and marched me off to this rathole.'

'In that case he misinterpreted my orders and has certainly been excessively prudent in carrying them out.'

'And what were your orders exactly?'

'To keep you under arrest until I arrived, not to dishonour you before your men.'

'And the reason why?' Amyntas asked again. He looked terrible – he certainly had not combed his hair for some time, neither had he shaved or changed his clothes.

'A messenger from the Great King was intercepted. He was carrying a letter for you promising two thousand talents and the throne of Macedon if you had me eliminated.'

'I have never seen such a letter, and had I wanted to kill you I could have done so a hundred times since the day they killed your father.'

'I couldn't take any risks.'

Amyntas shook his head. 'Who advised you to do this?'

'No one. It was my decision.'

Amyntas lowered his head and leaned against the wooden wall. The lamplight illuminated only the lower part of his face, so that his eyes remained in the shadow. At that moment he thought of the day Philip had been assassinated and how he had chosen to support Alexander so as not to unleash a dynastic war. He had been among those who had accompanied the young King, weapons drawn, to the palace and since then had always fought alongside him.

'You had me arrested without even seeing the evidence . . .' he murmured, his voice trembling. 'And I have risked my life many times for you in battle.'

'A king has no choice,' replied Alexander, 'especially at moments like this.' And he had a vision of his father falling to his knees in a pool of blood, the mortal pallor spreading over his face. 'Perhaps you are right, this affair probably makes no sense, but I cannot pretend that it hasn't happened. You would do the same thing if you were in my place. I can only seek to make your humiliation as brief as possible. But first I must know. I will send you a servant to wash you and a barber to wash your hair and shave you. You look terrible.'

He gave orders to the sentries to make sure that someone took care of Prince Amyntas, then he headed back to Parmenion's tent where the banquet had taken place. There came the noise of shouting and laughter, of crockery, of moans and grunting and the somewhat tuneless music of flutes and other barbarian instruments he did not recognize.

He went in and crossed the tent, climbing over several knots of naked, gasping bodies, coupled in every possible way on the mats which covered the floor. He went to stretch out alongside Hephaestion, embraced him and started drinking from his friend's cup. And he drank all through the night, first to the point of dejection and then to senselessness.

42

CALLISTHENES ARRIVED shortly before midday and entered accompanied by a member of the King's guard. Alexander was sitting at his work table and his face carried the signs of the previous night's binge, but he was sober now and alert. He had a sheet of papyrus unfolded before him and a steaming cup in his hand, probably an infusion prescribed by the physician Philip to help clear his hangover.

'Come in,' he said, 'I'd like you to take a look at this document.'

'What is it?' asked Callisthenes as he approached the table.

'It's a letter which was being carried by a messenger from the Great King, addressed to my cousin Amyntas. I'd like you to take a good look at it and tell me what you think.'

Callisthenes studied the text without showing any visible signs of surprise, then asked, 'What exactly would you like to know?'

'I'm not sure . . . who might have written it, for example.'

Callisthenes took another look, more carefully this time. 'Whoever it was has a good hand, without a doubt a cultivated, refined person. What's more, the papyrus is of excellent quality and the ink too. In fact . . .'

Alexander was surprised to see him moisten the tip of his finger with some saliva, run it across the writing and then bring it to his mouth.

'I can tell you that this type of ink is made in Greece using juice from elderberries and soot . . .'

'In Greece?' the King interrupted him.

'Yes, but that in itself does not mean much. People travel all over carrying their own ink with them. I use it too, perhaps even some of your companions . . .'

'Is there any other information you can glean from the document?'

Callisthenes shook his head. 'I don't think so.'

'If anything should come to mind, let me know immediately,' Alexander said. Then he thanked him and let him go.

As soon as Callisthenes left, the King called for Eumenes. While waiting for him he picked up a phial of his own ink, dipped the tip of his finger in it and tasted it, then did the same thing he had seen the historian do and noted that the taste of the two inks was identical.

Eumenes arrived almost immediately. 'You called for me?'

'Have you seen the Egyptian around the camp by any chance?' asked Alexander.

'Parmenion said that after having delivered your answer, he set off again.'

'This is strange too – try to find out more, if possible.'

'I will do what I can,' replied Eumenes. 'Is there any news of our reinforcements?' he asked before leaving.

Alexander shook his head. 'Nothing yet, unfortunately.'

When the secretary opened the curtain of the pavilion

to leave, a gust of cold wind entered, making the papers on the King's table fly. Leptine added some coal to the brazier which provided some meagre heat, while Alexander took a sheet and began writing:

Alexander, King of Macedon, to Antipater, Regent to the Throne and Custodian of the Royal Palace, Hail!

My congratulations on the wisdom with which you manage the government of the homeland while we fight in far off lands against the barbarians.

Recently Parmenion has taken prisoner a messenger of the Great King who was carrying a letter for my cousin Amyntas in which he promises him the throne of Macedon and a sum of two thousand talents in gold in exchange for my life.

This thing came to light thanks to an Egyptian by the name of Sisines who claims to have been a friend of my father Philip. This man has disappeared, however. He is about sixty years old with very little hair, an aquiline nose, dark, darting eyes, and a mole on his left cheek. I would like you to investigate him and to keep me informed if he should appear in the city or the palace.

Take good care.

Alexander sealed the letter and had it sent off immediately with a personal messenger, then went to Parmenion's tent. The general was stretched out on his camp-bed and a servant was massaging his left shoulder with olive oil and nettle juice; an old wound there, collected while fighting as a young man in Thrace, was giving him problems now that the bad weather had set in. He stood up immediately and put an overgown on. 'Sire, I was not expecting you. What can I give you? Some warm wine?'

'General, I would like to interrogate the Persian prisoner. Can you arrange an interpreter for me?'

'Of course. Now?'

'Yes. As soon as possible.'

Parmenion dressed quickly, gave orders to the servant to go and look for an interpreter, and led Alexander to the quarters where the captured messenger was being kept in strict custody.

'You have already interrogated him, I suppose,' said the King as they walked.

'Yes,' replied Parmenion.

'And what did he tell you?'

'Simply what we already know. That the Great King had given him a personal message for a *yauna* leader by the name of Amyntas.'

'And nothing else?'

'Nothing else. I had thought of torturing him, but then it seemed pointless – no one would ever entrust a simple courier with any information of any importance.'

'And how did you manage to intercept him?'

'It was all thanks to Sisines.'

'The Egyptian?'

'Yes. One day he arrived telling us he had seen a suspicious type in the merchants' and women's camp.'

'So you knew Sisines already?'

'Of course. He had worked for us as an informer during the first invasion of Asia, under your father's orders, but I hadn't seen him since then.'

'And did this not seem suspicious to you?'

'No, there was no reason for me to be suspicious – he had always been a reliable informer and had always been paid accordingly, as he was this time.'

'You should have kept him,' replied Alexander, obviously angered. 'At least until I arrived.'

'I am sorry,' said Parmenion, lowering his head. 'I did not feel it was necessary, and then he had told me he was on the trail of another Persian spy and so . . . but if I have made a mistake I beg forgiveness, Sire, I . . .'

'It matters not. You acted as you felt you had to. Now let's see this prisoner.'

In the meantime they had reached the shed where the Persian messenger was being held in custody and Parmenion ordered the guard to open the bolts.

The soldier obeyed and entered first, to ensure that everything was in order. But he came back out immediately, looking shocked.

'What's wrong?' asked the general.

'He . . . he's dead,' stammered the soldier, pointing inside the shed.

Alexander entered and knelt down by the body: 'Call my physician straight away,' he ordered. Then, turning to Parmenion, 'Evidently this man knew more than he told you, otherwise they would not have killed him.'

'I am sorry, Sire,' replied the general, embarrassed. 'I . . . I am a soldier. My place is on the battlefield; give me a task, even the hardest of tasks on the battlefield and I will always know exactly what to do, but in these intrigues I find myself out of my element. I am sorry . . .'

'Never mind,' said the King. 'We will see what Philip thinks.'

The physician arrived and set to examining the messenger's body.

'Are there any clues?' Alexander asked him after some time.

'He has almost certainly been poisoned, and almost certainly it was with last night's meal.'

'Can you tell what type of poison was used?'

Philip stood up and had some water brought to wash his hands. 'I think so, but I'll have to open him up . . .'

'Do what has to be done,' ordered the King, 'and when you have finished arrange for his funeral with the Persian rites.'

Philip looked around. 'But there are no towers of silence hereabouts.'

'Well, have one built then,' ordered the King, turning to Parmenion. 'There's no shortage of stone and there's no shortage of labour.'

'As you wish, Sire,' said the general, nodding. 'Any other orders, Sire?'

Alexander thought for a moment and then said, 'Yes, have Amyntas freed and reinstated to his rank. Only . . . be careful.'

'Of course, Sire.'

'Good. And now you may return to your massage, Parmenion. You must take good care of that shoulder. The weather is about to change again.' And then he added, looking at the sky, 'And it won't be for the better.'

43

ONE EVENING, ROUGHLY HALF-WAY through the winter, Commander Memnon suddenly felt unwell. There came a deep sense of nausea, strong pains in his joints and kidneys and his temperature soared. He took refuge in his cabin – his body shaking, his teeth chattering – and he refused all the food that was brought to him.

He managed only to take a little warm broth every now and then, but he did not always keep it down. His physician administered medicines for the pain and had him drink as much as possible to replace the liquids he lost continually in perspiration, but he could find nothing that would cure him.

Memnon's illness threw the entire crew into deep dismay, and many of them noticed the indifference of the new second-in-command, a Persian by the name of Tigranes, who up until then had led the Red Sea fleet. He was an ambitious, politicking man, who at court had never made any mystery of his disapproval of King Darius's decision to entrust general command to a *yauna* mercenary.

Tigranes took Memnon's place when it became clear that the Greek was no longer able to fulfil his responsibilities. The new commander's first order was to raise the anchor and to set a course southwards, abandoning the blockade of the Straits.

At that point Memnon asked to disembark on dry land immediately and Tigranes did not oppose the request. He also asked to be able to take five of his mercenaries with him, his most loyal soldiers, so that they might help him in the journey he was about to undertake. The new commander looked upon him with a certain amount of commiseration, convinced that the invalid would certainly never manage to travel very far, given the state he was in. In any case Tigranes wished him all the best in Persian and took his leave.

And so it was that a launch was lowered in the deep of the night. Six men were on board and the boat slipped through the water, driven by vigorous strokes of the oars, until they came to a small deserted inlet on the eastern coast of the Hellespont. That same night the six men began their journey – Memnon wanted to be taken to his wife and children.

'I want to see them before I die,' he said, as soon as they landed.

'You won't die, Commander,' said one of his mercenaries. 'You've been through much worse than this. But you just give the orders and we'll take you wherever you wish, even if it's to the ends of the earth, even if it's to hell itself. We'll carry you on our shoulders, if need be.'

Memnon gave a tired smile, but the thought of seeing his family once again seemed to restore some mysterious energy, a hidden force in him. One of his men went to look for some means of transport because their leader in any case was not fit enough to ride, and he returned the following day with a cart drawn by two mules, and four horses which he had bought on a farm.

The mercenaries held a meeting along the way and decided that one of them should go on ahead to the Great King's Road to send a message to Barsine, so that she might start travelling towards them. In truth there was no hope that their commander would last the journey to the palace at Susa, almost a month away.

For some days the illness seemed to have granted a truce and Memnon began eating again, but come evening the fever would rise once more, burning his temples and his very mind. He became delirious then and from his lips came the cries of a whole life spent in combat, in clashes, in frightful pains inflicted and received, the moans and the tears of lost hopes and vanished dreams.

The most senior of his soldiers, a man from Tegea who had always fought alongside him, looked upon him then in anguish and worry as he wiped his brow with a damp cloth and grumbled, 'It's nothing, Commander, it's nothing at all. It won't be a stupid fever that brings down Memnon of Rhodes, it won't . . .' And it was almost as though he was trying to convince himself.

The man who had been sent on ahead reached the road of the Great King at the bridge on the river Halys, which was said to have been built by Croesus of Lydia, and there he learned that they would not have to go all the way to Susa. King Darius had finally decided to give the insolent young *yauna* who had invaded his western provinces a lesson, and he was advancing now towards the Syrian Gates with half a million men behind him, hundreds of war chariots and tens of thousands of horsemen. The entire court was with him too, and Barsine was certainly among them. Thus Memnon's call travelled as quickly as the light of the fires and the reflections of the bronze mirrors from mountainside to mountainside, as fast as the headlong gallop of the Nysaean steeds until it reached the Great King under his marquee of purple and gold. And the Great King called for Barsine.

'Your husband is gravely ill,' he announced, 'and he has asked for you. He is coming along our Royal Road and hopes to see you one last time. We do not know if you can reach him before he dies, but if you wish to try then we will give you ten Immortals from our guard, as your escort.'

Barsine felt her heart shrivel in her breast, but she remained impassible, not even shedding a single tear. 'Great King, I thank you for having given me this sad news and for giving me permission to leave. I will go to my husband immediately and I will have no peace, I will neither sleep nor rest until I reach him and embrace him.'

She returned to her tent, changed into a felt bodice and leather trousers which made her look like an Amazon, took the best horse she could find and set off at a gallop, followed by the guards the Great King had assigned to her, who struggled to keep up with her.

She travelled for days and nights, resting only for a few hours every now and then while horses were changed or when she could no longer feel her limbs due to the fatigue. And then one evening, at sunset, she saw a small convoy advancing jerkily in the distance along the semi-deserted road – a covered cart drawn by two mules, escorted by four armed men on horseback.

She spurred her mount on until she was level with the

cart, leapt to the ground and looked inside – Memnon lay dying on a pile of sheepskins. His beard was long and his lips were cracked, his hair unkempt and ruffled. The man who until a short time previously had been the most powerful in the world after the Great King had been reduced to nothing more than a wretch.

But he was still alive.

Barsine caressed him and kissed him tenderly on the lips and on his eyes without knowing whether or not he recognized her, then she looked around, anguish-stricken, searching for some shelter. In the distance, up on a hill, she saw a stone house, perhaps some landowner's home, and she asked the men of her escort to go and ask for hospitality for some days, or some hours . . . she knew not for how long.

'I want a bed for my husband, I want to wash him and change his clothes, I want him to die like a man and not like an animal,' she said.

The chief of the guards obeyed and shortly afterwards Memnon was transported to the house, where the Persian owner welcomed him with full honours. A bath was soon warmed and Barsine undressed her husband, washed him and dressed him in clean clothes. The servants cut his hair, Barsine perfumed it and applied a refreshing compress to his forehead before putting him to bed and sitting alongside him, holding his hand.

It was late now and the owner came to ask if the fine lady might care to come down to supper to eat with the men who had accompanied her, but Barsine courteously declined.

'I have ridden day and night to be with him and I will not leave him now even for an instant for as long as he lives.'

The man left, closing the door behind him, and Barsine returned to her position alongside Memnon, touching him and moistening his lips every now and then. It was shortly after midnight when, exhausted by the fatigue, she dozed off on a chair and remained there, falling in and out of sleep for some time.

Suddenly she thought she heard her husband's voice in her dreams, but the voice continued to repeat her name, insistently: 'Bar . . . si . . . ne . . .' She sat up with a start and opened her eyes – Memnon had woken from his torpor and was looking at her with his big, blue, feverish eyes.

'My love,' she murmured as she put out her hand to caress his face.

Memnon stared at her with a wild intensity and seemed to want to say something.

'What do you want? Please speak.'

Memnon opened his lips again. It was as though some vitality had suddenly flowed into his limbs and his face seemed to have re-acquired the virile handsomeness it once had. Barsine moved her ear as close as possible to his mouth so as not to miss a single word.

'I want . . .'

'What do you want, my love? Whatever . . . anything, my beloved.'

'I want . . . to see you.'

And Barsine recalled the last night they had spent together and she understood. She stood up purposefully, moved backwards slightly so that her body was illuminated as much as possible by the light of the two lamps that hung from the ceiling of the room and began to undress. She took off her bodice, undid the laces that held the Scythian leather trousers in place. And in doing so she also undid all of her innate modesty, so that she stood there naked and proud before him.

She saw his eyes moisten, and two large tears ran down his sunken cheeks, and she knew that she had interpreted his wish correctly. She felt his gaze caress her face and her body slowly, sweetly, and she felt that this was his way of making love with her one last time.

Memnon said, with what was left of his voice, 'My boys . . .' and he sought her eyes to pass on to her in one last burning and desperate look all that was left of his life and his passion for her, then he let his head fall to the pillow and took his last breath.

Barsine wrapped a cloak around herself and fell on to her husband's inert body, covering him with kisses and caresses. The only sound in the house was her inconsolable crying, and the Greek mercenaries who were still awake outside, gathered around a fire, understood what had happened. They stood up and presented arms in silence to the honour of Commander Memnon of Rhodes, who had been denied a soldier's death – sword in hand – by some cruel fate.

They waited until dawn before going up to the room to collect his body for the funeral.

'We will burn him on the pyre, as is our custom,' said the eldest of them, the one who came from Tegea. 'For us the idea of abandoning a body to the dogs and the birds would be an unbearable shame – and this tells you just how different we are.'

And Barsine understood. She understood that at this final moment she had to step aside and let Memnon return among his people to receive his funeral honours according to the Greek rite.

They built a pyre in the midst of a meadow white with frost and placed their commander's body on top of it, dressed in his armour and with his helmet, adorned with the silver rose of Rhodes.

And they set it alight.

The wind blowing over the highlands fed the flames and they crackled as they voraciously consumed the mortal remains of the great warrior. His soldiers, lined up with their spears in their hands, shouted his name ten times to the cold, leaden sky and when the last echo of their shouts faded away, they realized they were completely alone in the world – fatherless, motherless, without brothers, without homes, with no place to come to.

'I swore I would follow him everywhere,' said the eldest, 'even to hell.' He knelt down, unsheathed his sword, put its point to his heart and threw himself forward with all his weight.

'So did I,' repeated his companion as he pulled his weapon out.

'As did we,' said the other two. They fell one after another in pools of their own blood, while the first call of the cockerel tore through the spectral silence of the dawn like a trumpet blast.

44

ALEXANDER'S DOCTOR, PHILIP, reported the results of his autopsy on the body of the Persian messenger who had carried the Great King's letter for Prince Amyntas.

'He was most certainly poisoned, but it is a type of poison I have never come across before. For this reason I think it is pointless to interrogate the cook – a good lad who does not have the necessary knowledge to prepare such a thing. I couldn't do it, let alone him.'

'Is it possible that the prisoner took the poison himself?' asked Alexander.

'It is possible. There are men in the Great King's guard who take an oath to serve him until death. I am afraid that for the moment it is going to be difficult to gather further information on this matter.'

Several days passed without any news of the reinforcements that were due from Macedonia and the morale of the soldiers began to wane in the lack of activity and the boredom of waiting. One morning Alexander decided to climb up to the sanctuary of the Great Mother of the gods at Gordium, which was said to have been founded by King Midas.

His friends and his priests accompanied him, these last having decided to dress for the occasion in their ceremonial gowns.

The temple was an ancient local sanctuary which housed a simulacrum of the goddess sculpted in wood and suffering much from woodworm. It was adorned with an incredible quantity of jewels and talismans, offerings from the faithful over the centuries. From the walls hung relics and votive gifts of all kinds and many representations of human limbs in terracotta and wood which testified to cures achieved or petitions for such cures.

There were feet and hands with marks of scabies represented in bright colours – eyes, noses and ears and barren uteruses which called for fertility and penises which in the same way were incapable of fulfilling their procreative function.

Each one of these objects represented numerous miseries, illnesses and pains which since time immemorial had afflicted the human race, ever since the halfwit Epimetheus had opened Pandora's box, freeing all the bad things which had invaded the world.

'All that was left at the bottom was hope,' recalled Eumenes, looking around him. 'And what are these things if not an expression of hope that is almost always disappointed and is yet such a close, even indispensable companion of mankind?'

Seleucus, who was standing alongside, was somewhat puzzled by this sudden manifestation of philosophic pedantry, and he looked Eumenes up and down. But there was no time for discussion because the priests were now leading them into a side chamber where the most precious relic of all was kept – King Midas's chariot.

It was a strange, four-wheeled vehicle of very primitive construction with a semicircular parapet on its upper part.

The steering gear consisted of a rudder which terminated with a bar connected to the axle of the rear bogey, while the yoke was fixed to the rudder by means of a hemp rope in a knot that was most complex and indeed was held to be impossible to untie.

An ancient legend said that whoever did untie that knot would one day reign over all Asia, and Alexander had decided to attempt a solution to the problem. Both Eumenes and Ptolemy, together with Seleucus, had insisted that he try.

'You cannot not attempt it,' Eumenes had pointed out to him. 'Everyone knows of this legend – if you choose to ignore it then they will all think that you have no faith in yourself, that you do not believe you can defeat the Great King.'

'Eumenes is right,' Seleucus had said. 'The knot is a symbol – it represents the junction of many roads and caravan trails in the city of Gordium, roads which lead to the ends of the earth. The fact is that you are already in control of that knot because you have conquered it by force of arms, but you must also undo the symbol, otherwise your efforts may not be sufficient.'

Alexander had then turned to Aristander. 'And you, seer, what do you have to say?'

Aristander had few words to offer, 'That knot is the sign of an absolute perfection, an established harmony, the binding of primeval energies which created life on this earth. You will undo the knot and you will dominate Asia and the entire world.'

This response comforted everyone, but Eumenes did not want to run any risks and had called for one of

Admiral Nearchus's officers, a man who knew every single type of knot used on war and merchant ships to teach the King his secrets, so that Alexander might feel confident about being able to solve the problem.

Furthermore, it was clear that the priests of the sanctuary would do all they could to simplify things for the new master and would never expose him to the ridicule of a failure.

'Here is the chariot of King Midas,' said one of them, pointing to the ancient woodwormed vehicle. Then with a smile he added, for Alexander's benefit, 'And here is the knot.' The smile was such that all those present, especially Eumenes, Seleucus and Ptolemy, were sure that everything would go well. They even called the lower-ranking officers to come and witness the King's feat.

But when Alexander bent down and started fiddling with the knot, he realized that he had been too optimistic. The hemp was pulled incredibly tight, and he could find no end to it – neither above nor below, nor on either side – with which to start undoing the tangle. The crowd in the meantime had increased in number and there was no space left at all inside the room – even the priests, wearing their ceremonial gowns, were standing crushed against one another, dripping with sweat.

The King felt himself suffocating and his anger and impatience were growing – he began to feel that in just a matter of instants his personal prestige, won so dearly on the battlefield with his spear and his sword, was about to be ruined by this situation, which offered no apparent way out.

He looked at Eumenes, who shrugged his shoulders

slightly to indicate that this time he had no ready-made solution, and then at the mask of stone of Aristander of Termessus, the seer who had spoken once and would clearly not speak a second time.

He looked at Seleucus and Ptolemy, Craterus and Perdiccas, and saw only consternation and embarrassment in their eyes. While he knelt down again at the inextricable knot, he felt the hilt of his sword pressing against his side and he knew that this was a sign from the gods. At that very same moment, a ray of sun penetrated the room through the skylight above, making his hair shine like a golden cloud and making the drops of sweat on his forehead sparkle like pearls.

In the deep silence which had fallen in the room, there came the metallic swish of the King's sword being pulled from its scabbard; the blade flashed like a lightning bolt in the strip of sunlight before it struck the Gordian knot with immeasurable force.

The hemp was cut clean through and released its hold on the yoke, which fell to the ground with a dry thump.

The priests looked at one another in amazement and then at Alexander, standing straight and firm on his legs and putting the sword back into its scabbard. When he lifted his head, they all saw that his left eye had darkened, it shone now between the light and the shadow of the ray that came down from above, black as the night.

Ptolemy cried, 'The King has undone the Gordian knot! Our King is Lord of Asia!'

All the companions shouted loud and the ovation was heard outside as well, by all the soldiers of the army who had gathered around the temple. They too started rejoicing, freeing all the joy which up until then had been repressed by fear and superstition, and they accompanied their shouts by beating their weapons against their shields to the point where the very walls of the ancient sanctuary shook.

When the King appeared, resplendent in his silver armour, they lifted him on to their shoulders and carried him around the camp in triumph, like the statue of a god. No one looked at Aristander, who moved off on his own, an expression of unease and discomfort written on his face.

45

A FEW DAYS LATER the long-awaited reinforcements arrived – both the new recruits and the young husbands who had left from Halicarnassus to spend the winter with their wives. These last were welcomed with whistles, hissing and booing from their comrades, who instead had faced all the rigours of the war and the winter and now were intent on shouting all sorts of obscenities. Some of them, waving enormous wooden phalluses, shouted at the tops of their voices: 'Did you enjoy the pussy? Now you have to pay for it!'

The officer leading them was one of Antipater's men, a battalion commander originally from Orestis by the name of Thrasyllus. He went straight to the King to make his report.

'Why did it take you so long to reach us?' asked Alexander.

'Because of the Persian fleet's blockade of the Straits; the regent Antipater had no intention of risking our forces in an open clash with Memnon. Then, one day, the enemy's ships suddenly raised their anchors and sailed southwards, making the most of a northerly wind, and we crossed the Straits.'

'A very strange event,' said Alexander, 'which certainly does not bode well. Memnon would never have loosened his grip unless it was to strike in some other place yet more vulnerable. I hope that Antipater . . .'

'Rumour has it that Memnon is dead, Sire,' the officer interrupted him.

'What?'

'This is what we have heard from our informers in Bithynia.'

'And how is he supposed to have died?'

'No one knows exactly. They say of some strange illness . . .'

'An illness. That's difficult to credit.'

'It is not confirmed, Sire. As I have already said, they are rumours which have yet to be substantiated.'

'Yes, of course. But go now and sort yourself and your men out, because we will be leaving as soon as possible. You will have one day's rest at the most, we have already waited too long.'

The officer saluted and Alexander was left alone in his tent to meditate on this unexpected news, which gave him neither relief nor satisfaction. In his mind and in his soul he had decided that Memnon was the only opponent worthy of himself, like the only Hector capable of fighting the new Achilles, and for some time he had been readying himself to face him in a duel, like a Homeric champion. Not even the idea of a personal clash with the Great King had the same resonant meaning for him.

He remembered perfectly the commander's imposing figure, the helmet covering his face, the timbre of his voice and the sense of dark oppression he felt knowing that he was always watching and was always ready to strike – indefatigable, elusive. An illness . . . that was not what he wanted, this was not a fitting coda to the epic clash he had set his mind on.

He called Parmenion and Cleitus the Black to arrange their departure within two days and communicated to them the news he had received. 'The commander of the reinforcements has told me that there are rumours to the effect that Memnon is dead.'

'That would be a great advantage for us,' replied the old general, without concealing his surprise. 'His fleet controlling the sea between us and Macedon was a most serious threat. The gods are on your side, Sire.'

'The gods have deprived me of fair combat with the only enemy worthy of me,' replied Alexander, his face as dark as thunder. But at that moment, all of a sudden, he thought of Barsine, of her dark and sensual beauty and he thought that fate perhaps had worked in such a way, with Memnon dying because of an illness, that Barsine would not hate him. He was ready at that moment to deal with any obstacle that might appear between himself and her, if only he knew where she was.

'Apparently somewhere between Damascus and the Syrian Gates,' came Black's voice, waking him up from his reverie.

Alexander turned suddenly towards him, as if the officer had read his thoughts. The Black returned his gaze in amazement, shocked by the reaction.

'What are you talking about, Black?' asked the King.

'I was talking about the dispatch that Eumolpus of Soloi has sent us.'

'That's right,' said Parmenion. 'He sent us a messenger with an oral report.'

'When?'

'Around mid-morning. He asked to speak with you, but you were out with Hephaestion and the rest of the guard inspecting the new recruits and so I received him.'

'You did the right thing, General,' replied Alexander, 'but are we sure he comes from Eumolpus?'

'The messenger communicated the password, which you know well enough.'

Alexander shook his head, ' "Sheep's brains!" Have you ever heard such an absurd password?'

'It's his favourite dish,' said the Black, raising his arms in resignation.

'As I was saying,' Parmenion continued, 'it seems that the Great King is on the march with his army towards the ford at Thapsacus.'

'The ford at Thapsacus . . .' the King repeated. 'So it is just as I imagined. Darius is out to block the pass at the Syrian Gates.'

'I think you are right,' said the Black.

'And how many of them are there?' asked Alexander.

'A lot,' replied Parmenion.

'How many?' asked the King impatiently.

'About half a million, if our information is correct.'

'Ten to one. That is a lot indeed.'

'What shall we do?'

'Continue forwards – we have no choice. Prepare to leave.'

The two officers saluted and headed for the door, but Alexander called Parmenion back.

'What is wrong, Sire?' asked the general.

'We too should establish a password for the exchange of oral messages, don't you think?'

Parmenion lowered his head, 'I had no choice when I sent Sisines to you – I had not envisaged such a situation before our splitting up.'

'That is true, but now we need a password for our messages. A similar situation might develop in the future.'

Parmenion smiled.

'Why are you smiling?'

'Because you have brought to mind the rhyme you always used to sing as a child. Old Artemisia taught you it, your mother's wet nurse, remember?

> The silly old soldier's off to the war
> And falls to the floor, falls to the floor!

'And then you would fall to the ground.'

'Why not?' said Alexander. 'It is certainly not a password anyone is going to guess.'

'And there is no need for us to memorize it. I will leave you now.'

'General,' Alexander stopped him once more.

'Sire?'

'What is Amyntas doing?'

'His duty.'

'Good. But keep him under surveillance, without his realizing it. And try to find out if Memnon really is dead and how it happened.'

'I will do what I can, Sire. Eumolpus of Soloi's messenger is still in the camp, I'll give him orders to investigate.'

*

The messenger left the following day and the army prepared to strike camp at dawn. Everything was prepared in advance – the animals were loaded up, the carts filled with provisions and weapons, while the route officers arranged the various stages which would take the army in seven days' march to the Cilician Gates, a pass through the Taurus mountains, so narrow that the beasts of burden had to travel in single file.

That same evening one of the soldiers who had arrived with the reinforcements appeared at Callisthenes's tent to deliver a package. The historian, busy writing, stood up to give the soldier some payment, and then, as soon as he was alone, he opened the package and saw that it contained an ordinary text – an essay on beekeeping that he had not ordered and so it most certainly was to be read in code. The decoded message read:

> I have sent Theophrastus the medicine and asked him to give it to the physician on Lesbos, but the weather is bad and it is unsure whether any ships will leave in the next few days. Everything is uncertain in this situation.

There then followed a letter which was not written in code:

> Aristotle to his nephew Callisthenes, Hail!
>
> I have met someone who knew Pausanias, the man who killed King Philip. The story we were told about him and his relationship with the king now proves difficult to believe because almost nothing in it appears to be true. I have identified one of the surviving accomplices and I met him in a hostelry in Beroea. He

was extremely diffident and continued to deny everything while I tried in every way possible to reassure him. I had no success. The only thing I was able to discover – by paying a slave, a woman who is also his concubine – is this man's true identity. Now I know that he has a young daughter whom he loves and keeps hidden away with the virgins in a temple to Artemis on the border with Thrace.

I must leave for Athens, but I will continue my investigations and I will keep you informed. Take good care and keep in good health.

Callisthenes placed the documents in a small chest and went to bed so as to be ready, the following day, to leave at dawn.

When Eumenes and Ptolemy woke him up it was still dark.

'Have you heard the news?' Eumenes asked.

'What news?' asked Callisthenes, rubbing his eyes.

'It appears that Memnon is dead. Of some sudden illness.'

'A sudden, incurable illness,' added Ptolemy.

Callisthenes sat up on the edge of his bed and poured some olive oil into the dim lamp.

'Dead? But when?'

'The news came with one of the officers who was leading the reinforcements. Calculating the time they took to reach us, I would guess that it perhaps happened fifteen days or a month back. Things have worked out just as we planned.'

Callisthenes recalled the date of Aristotle's letter and he too made a rapid mental calculation, coming to the

conclusion that there was no certainty that the event had
been caused by their actions, but neither could it be
excluded. He simply replied, 'Good . . . that's good.' Then,
as he finished getting dressed, he called a slave and told
her, 'Serve something warm for Mr Secretary General and
Commander Ptolemy.'

46

'SHEEP'S BRAINS,' ANNOUNCED the Persian cook, placing a plate of golden fritters on the table before Eumolpus of Soloi. And as he pronounced those words a not-at-all-reassuring smile revealed all thirty-two of his whiter than white teeth beneath his big black moustache.

The governor of Syria, the satrap Ariobarzanes, stretched out on a dining bed before him, smiled in an even more disconcerting manner. 'Isn't it your favourite dish?'

'Oh, yes, of course, O Light of the Aryans and Indomitable Leader. May the future bring you the honour of wearing the rigid tiara if the worst should ever come to pass – and Ahura Mazda most certainly does not augur it – that the Great King should climb the tower of silence to join his glorious ancestors.'

'The Great King is in perfect health,' replied Ariobarzanes. 'But please eat. How are these sheep's brains?'

'Mmm . . .' moaned Eumolpus, rolling his eyes to simulate the most intense enjoyment.

'And "sheep's brains" is also the password you use when you exchange secret messages with our enemies, is that not so?' asked Ariobarzanes without interrupting his smile.

Eumolpus coughed convulsively because a mouthful of sheep's brains had just gone down the wrong way.

'Some water?' asked the cook with overly dramatic concern in his voice as he poured some from a silver jug, but Eumolpus, crimson-faced, made a gesture to say that no, there was no need.

When he had recovered, his imperturbable air and his most charming smile both restored, he said, 'I'm afraid I haven't understood your little joke.'

'But it's no joke at all,' the satrap graciously informed him, ripping the wing from a roast songthrush and stripping it of meat with his teeth. 'It is quite simply the truth.'

Eumolpus managed to control the panic that was churning in his bowels, took another fritter and successfully improvised a display of savouring every morsel before observing, with a meek look on his face, 'Come along now, my illustrious host, you cannot seriously give credence to rumours which are doubtless most amusing, but which must not be allowed to cast aspersions on the reputation of a gentleman who has always . . .'

Ariobarzanes stopped him with a polite gesture, dried his hands on the cook's apron, put his feet on the floor, stood up and walked towards the window, signalling to Eumolpus to join him there.

'Please, my good friend.'

Eumolpus had no choice but to follow and to look down below. The few mouthfuls he had managed to swallow seemed to turn into poison in his belly and his face took on an ashen pallor. His messenger was hanging naked by his arms from a pole and long strips of skin had been peeled and were hanging now from various parts of his body, exposing the bloody mass of muscles underneath. In some places the skin had been stripped so deeply that the bones were exposed, while his testicles had been removed and hung around his neck like some sort of grotesque necklace. There was no sign of life.

'He told us,' Ariobarzanes explained, impassively.

Not far off a Hyrcanian slave was sharpening the tip of an acacia pole with an extremely sharp knife, occasionally rubbing the instrument on a piece of pumice so that the blade was kept smooth and almost luminescent.

Ariobarzanes looked at the stake and stared into Eumolpus's eyes as he made a most eloquent gesture with his hands.

The poor man gulped and shook his head convulsively.

The satrap smiled. 'I felt sure we would understand each other, old friend.'

'How . . . how can I help you?' the informer stammered without managing to take his gaze from the sharp end of the stake. At the same time his anus contracted instinctively in an unconscious and spasmodic attempt to bar access to such a frightful intruder.

Ariobarzanes returned to the table and stretched out on the dining bed, inviting Eumolpus to make himself comfortable. In fact he did manage to relax somewhat, hoping that the worst was perhaps over.

'What reply was the little *yauna* expecting?' asked the satrap, using the derogatory name to indicate the invader who had taken all of Anatolia.

'King Alexander . . . I mean the little *yauna*,' Eumolpus immediately corrected himself, 'wanted to know where the Great King would be waiting for him with his army.'

'Excellent! In that case I think we will send one of your messengers – not this one, whom I fear is no longer operational – to tell the little *yauna* that the Great King is waiting for him at the foot of the Syrian Gates with one half of his army, while the other half has been left to garrison the ford at Thapsacus. This should encourage him to attack.'

'Oh, yes, of course,' the informer nodded quickly. 'That foolish and presumptuous boy, who, please believe me, I have always disliked, will lower his horns and set off at a gallop, confident of victory and will get himself stuck in the narrow alley between Mount Amanus and the sea, while you instead . . .'

'We instead . . . *we* don't concern *you*,' Ariobarzanes cut him short. 'You will do what I told you this very day. You will call your man to the room next door, where we are able to see you and listen to you, and you will send him immediately to your little *yauna*. Following our victory, we will decide what to do with you. Certainly, if we find that you have contributed decisively then the stake you have just seen in the courtyard might be put to some other use. But should anything go wrong . . . whoops!' And, still smiling, he slipped the index finger of his right hand through the ring formed by the index finger of his left hand.

Eumolpus prepared to do what he had been told, while several pairs of eyes and ears would doubtless be watching him from a series of well-concealed spyholes all around the room, in the highly decorated, frescoed walls.

He explained everything to the new messenger: 'You will tell them that your colleague is ill and that for this reason I have sent you. And when they ask you for the password you will say . . .' and he coughed at this point, '. . . sheep's brains.'

' "Sheep's brains", my Lord?' the messenger asked in amazement.

'Yes, "sheep's brains". Why? Is there anything wrong?'

'No . . . no, not at all, everything's fine. So I will leave straight away.'

'Fine, good, off you go.'

Eumolpus of Soloi then left through a small door which led to the other room, where Ariobarzanes was waiting for him.

'May I go now?' he asked, not without a certain anxiety.

'You may,' replied the satrap, 'for now.'

*

From Gordium Alexander crossed Greater Phrygia until he reached the city of Ancyra, nestling at the bottom of a misty bowl formed by a group of hills. He reconfirmed the resident Persian satrap in his position, and added some Macedonian officers to the garrison.

Then he set off again on the march eastwards and came to the banks of the Halys, the great river that flows into the Black Sea and which for centuries had constituted the border between the Aegean and Anatolian worlds and the Asian interior, the extreme frontier beyond which it was unthinkable for the Greeks to go. The army marched along it to the southern meander, after which they proceeded along the banks of two big salt lakes surrounded by vast white areas.

Alexander accepted an oath of loyalty from the Persian satrap of Cappadocia and reconfirmed him in his position. Then he headed south with decision, without meeting any resistance, and set off over the enormous plateau, dominated by Mount Argaeus, a dormant volcano perpetually white with snow which rose every morning from the mists of dawn like a ghost. The landscape was often covered with white frost in the early hours of the day, but then, gradually, as the sun rose above the horizon, it would take on a reddish-brown colour.

Many fields had been ploughed and seeded, while here and there, in those places the plough had failed to reach, there was yellow stubble, grazing material for small flocks of sheep and goats. After two days' march the imposing ridges of the Taurus range came into view, their white peaks shining under the sun and turning red at sunset.

It seemed impossible that this immense territory should open up before them almost spontaneously and that so many tribes, villages and cities should succumb without offering any resistance.

The fame of the young leader had spread everywhere now, as had the news of the death of Commander Memnon, the only one, apart from the Great King himself, capable of bringing Alexander's advance to a halt.

After five days on the highland plateau, the path began to rise ever more steeply towards the pass that led on to the coastal plain of Cilicia. Every time they stopped in the evening, Alexander sat in his tent alone or with Hephaestion and his other friends to read Xenophon's *Anabasis*, the diary of the expedition of the ten thousand who seventy years previously had passed through that very same spot. The Athenian historian described the pass as extremely narrow, difficult to cross if defended.

Alexander opted to lead the column personally. The guards at the pass saw him and recognized him immediately in the rays of the rising sun, thanks to the red standard with the golden Argead star, the gigantic black horse he was riding and his silver armour, which flashed light with his every movement.

The guards also saw the interminable snake of men and horses which was climbing up slowly but inexorably, and they decided immediately that there were not enough of them to take the invaders on and chose to beat a hasty retreat. Thus the pass was left free and negotiable without any difficulty.

On the left-hand rock face, Seleucus recognized some inscriptions which could have been made by some of Xenophon's ten thousand and he showed them to Alexander, who was most interested in the discovery. Then they set off again and looked out over the vale of the Cydnus and the great green plain of Cilicia.

'We are in Syria,' said Eumenes. 'Anatolia is behind us now.'

'It's another world!' exclaimed Hephaestion, sending his gaze out as far as the thin blue line which hemmed the plain. 'And that's the sea over there!'

'Where will Nearchus be with our ships?' asked Perdiccas.

'He'll be somewhere down there,' replied Leonnatus. 'He might even be looking up at these mountains and grumbling to himself, 'Where on earth have that lot got to? Why don't they make contact?'

'It couldn't be easier,' replied Alexander. 'For this reason it is a good idea if we rush to occupy the ports along the coast. That way if Nearchus wants to come he can quite happily anchor anywhere, without any fear of ambushes.'

He spurred on Bucephalas and began moving downhill.

Lysimachus said to Leonnatus, who was now riding alongside him, 'If they had tightened down their garrison over the pass from those peaks up there, not even a fly would have been able to come through.'

'They're scared,' replied his friend. 'We've got them running like rabbits. No one can stop us now.'

Lysimachus shook his head. 'That's what you think. I don't like this quiet at all. What I think is that we are marching straight into the lion's jaws and the beast is patiently waiting for us with his mouth open.'

Leonnatus grumbled, 'And I will tear his tongue out.' Then he moved back to check the rearguard of the column.

In a relatively short distance the weather had changed completely, from fresh and dry as it had been up on the highlands, to warm and humid, and they all sweated profusely inside their armour.

With just one stop they reached Tarsus, not far from the sea. The city opened its gates to them because the Satrap of Cilicia had fled, preferring to join the Great King's army, which was continuing its inexorable march. Alexander had his army set up camp on the plain, while he himself, the crack troops and the higher-ranking officers found quarters in the best residences in the city. It was while he was in these lodgings that a visit was announced.

'There is a messenger who insists upon speaking to you personally, Sire,' said one of the guards who had been posted to the entrance.

'Who does he come from?'

'He claims to have been sent by a certain Eumolpus of Soloi.'

'In that case he must have a password.'

The guard left and shortly afterwards Alexander heard him laughing. It was certainly Eumolpus's messenger.

'The password is . . .' began the guard, barely stifling his laughter.

'I don't find it all that amusing,' the King said, cutting him short.

'The password is, "sheep's brains".'

'That's it. That's him . . . let him in.'

The guard moved off laughing once more and showed the messenger in.

'Sire, Eumolpus of Soloi has sent me.'

'I know . . . he does have such an absurd password. Why didn't he send the other messenger? I've never seen you before.'

'The other messenger had an accident, he fell from his horse.'

'What news do you have for me?'

'Important news, my Lord. The Great King is now not far from you and Eumolpus has succeeded in bribing a field adjutant of Darius himself to discover where the battle will take place, the battle in which he intends to wipe you out.'

'Where?'

The messenger looked around and saw the map which

Alexander always had with him arranged on an easel. He pointed his finger to a point between Mount Carmel and Mount Amanus.

'Here,' he said, 'at the Syrian Gates.'

47

THE NEWS FLEW THROUGH the camp like lightning, by word of mouth, spreading panic everywhere: 'The King is dead! The King is dead!'

'How did it happen?'

'He drowned!'

'No . . . he's been poisoned.'

'It was a Persian spy.'

'And where is he?'

'No one knows. He's disappeared already.'

'Let's look for him. Which way did he go?'

'Wait a moment, here's Hephaestion and Ptolemy!'

'And Philip's with them, the King's physician.'

'So he's not dead then!'

'How do I know? All I heard was that the King was dead.'

The soldiers immediately crowded round the three who sought to clear their way through to the camp entrance.

A group of shieldsmen set up a line to let them move more quickly between Philip's tent and the entrance.

'How did it happen?' the physician asked.

'We had just eaten,' began Hephaestion.

'And it was unbearably hot,' continued Ptolemy.

'And doubtless you had also been drinking?' asked Philip.

'The King was in a good mood and he'd had some Hercules' Cup.'

'Half an amphora of wine,' grumbled Philip.

'Yes,' said Ptolemy. 'Then he said that he couldn't bear the heat any more and when he looked out of the window and saw the Cydnus flowing, he shouted, 'I'm off to have a swim!'

'On a full stomach and on such a hot day?' Philip shouted, losing his temper now.

In the meantime the horses had arrived. All three of them mounted quickly and rode off at full tilt towards the river which was a couple of stadia away.

The King lay on the ground in the shade of a fig tree. He had been stretched out and covered with a cloak. His complexion was deathly grey, while his eyes were ringed black and his nails a bluish colour.

'Damnation!' shouted Philip as he leaped to the ground. 'Why didn't you stop him? He's more dead than alive. Out of my way! Clear off!'

'But we . . .' stammered Hephaestion, but he didn't manage to finish the sentence. He turned to face the trunk of the tree to hide his tears.

The doctor undressed Alexander and put his ear to the royal chest. He could hear a faint beating of the King's heart, but it was very weak and faltering. He covered him again immediately. 'Quickly!' he cried to one of the shieldsmen. 'Run to the King's quarters and have Leptine prepare a very hot bath and tell her to put more water on to warm and have her make a decoction of these herbs which I will give you now in these exact proportions.' He took a tablet from his bag together with a stylus and rapidly wrote out a prescription. 'Go now! Run like the wind!'

Hephaestion moved forward, 'What can we do to help?'

'Prepare a grid of canes and attach it to the harnesses of a pair of pack horses. We have to carry him back to his quarters.'

The soldiers unsheathed their swords, cut a bundle of canes from the riverbank and did as they had been told. Then they lifted the King delicately and placed him on the grid, covering him with a cloak.

The small convoy set off with Hephaestion up front, leading the two horses by their halters to regulate the pace.

Leptine met them at the door, her big eyes wide with worry and anxiety, her fear so great she asked no one what had happened – one look at the King was enough for her to realize the gravity of the situation. She hurried off quickly towards the bathchamber followed by the bearers, biting her bottom lip to stop her tears.

The King gave almost no signs of life now – his lips were blue, and his nails almost black.

Hephaestion kneeled down and lifted him up – his head and his arms fell backwards, like a corpse's.

Philip came nearer. 'Put him in the tub slowly. Lower him in gradually.'

Hephaestion murmured something quietly, a formula against misfortune, or a curse of some kind.

'I told him not to jump into the water with him being

so hot and so full of food, but he didn't listen to me,' whispered Leonnatus to Perdiccas. 'He said that he'd done it a thousand times and that nothing had ever happened to him.'

'There's always a first time,' said Philip, looking at them over his shoulder. 'You are a bunch of irresponsible idiots. Can't you understand that you are adults now? You bear responsibility for an entire nation on your shoulders. Why didn't you stop him? Why?'

'But we did try . . .' Lysimachus sought to justify their actions.

'My foot you tried! To hell with the lot of you!' Philip swore as he began massaging the King's body. 'You realize why it happened, don't you? Don't you? No, perhaps you really don't.' And the young men stood there, heads bowed, like children before an angry teacher. 'The waters of this river flow fast and full from the snows of the Taurus mountain range as they melt during the summer, but the course of the river is so short and its bed so steep that the water has no time to warm up and it arrives ice-cold when it flows into the sea. It's as though he had buried himself naked in the snow!'

Leptine in the meantime had knelt down by the side of the tub and was waiting for the physician to tell her what to do.

'Good, well done. You can help me too. Massage him like this – from the stomach upwards, gently. Let's try to get his digestion moving.'

Hephaestion approached aggressively, pointing his finger at Philip. 'Listen, Alexander is our King, he does what he wants and none of us has any right to interfere.

You are a doctor and your job is to make him better. Understand? You have to make him better and that's it!'

Philip looked him straight in the eye. 'Don't speak to me in that tone, because I am not your servant. I will do what has to be done and I will do it as I deem right and proper, is that clear? And now get out of my way . . . move!' Then, as they were all leaving the room, he added, 'Except for one of you. I need someone to help me.'

Hephaestion turned. 'May I stay?'

'Yes,' grumbled Philip, 'but sit in that chair and don't bother me.'

The King had regained some colour, but he was still unconscious and his eyes were closed.

'We have to empty his stomach,' said Philip. 'Quickly. Otherwise he won't make it. Leptine, have you prepared that decoction?'

'Yes.'

'Go and fetch it then. I'll continue with the massage.'

Leptine arrived with a phial full of an intense green liquid.

'Right, now give me a hand here,' ordered Philip. 'You, Hephaestion, hold his mouth open, he must drink this.'

Hephaestion did as he was told and the physician administered the liquid, pouring it into Alexander's mouth.

For a while there was no sign of reaction but then there came a spasm and a violent retching as the King brought up the contents of his stomach.

'What is that mixture?' Leptine asked, even more frightened now.

'An emetic which is now working as we can see, together with a medicine which will force his body to react.'

Alexander continued to vomit for a long time, while Leptine held his forehead and the servants cleaned the floor below the bath tub. Then there came a series of violent convulsions which wracked his body and were accompanied by terrible rattling noises from his throat as he struggled to breathe.

Philip's medicine was a powerful one, which provoked this violent reaction in the King's body, and it also debilitated him considerably. He came through it, but the convalescence seemed interminable and involved frequent relapses, accompanied by persistent and insidious fevers which slowly consumed him for days and days at a time.

It took months for there to be any sign of improvement and during this period the morale of the army suffered greatly. Rumours of his death continued to spread among the men, elaborated and seemingly confirmed by the parallel rumour that no one in command dared communicate the news officially. Finally, as summer moved into autumn, Alexander was able to get up and appear before the troops to give them heart, but he had to return to bed immediately afterwards.

He would stay in his room for hours, pacing back and forth, as Leptine followed him around with a cup of broth, begging him, 'Drink, my Lord, drink this and it will make you better.'

Philip came by every evening for his daily visit. The rest of his working day was spent out in the camp because many soldiers had fallen ill with the change in climate and food. Many of them had diarrhoea, others fever, nausea and vomiting.

One evening Alexander was sitting at his table, where he had begun again to deal with the correspondence which arrived from Macedonia and the conquered provinces, when a courier came in and handed him a sealed, secret message from General Parmenion. The King opened it, but just at that very moment Philip arrived.

'How are we today, Sire?' he asked, immediately setting about the preparation of the medicine he intended to administer.

Alexander looked quickly at the old general's note and read:

Parmenion to King Alexander, Hail!

According to information which has just reached me, your physician, Philip, has been corrupted by the Persians and is poisoning you.

Take care.

He replied, 'Quite well,' to Philip as he stretched out one hand to take the cup and with the other gave his doctor the letter. Alexander drank while Philip read.

The doctor showed no reaction whatsoever, and when the King had finished he poured what remained of the mixture he had prepared into a pot and said, 'Take another dose tonight before going to bed. Tomorrow you may start eating solids and I will leave instructions with Leptine regarding your diet – instructions which you must respect faithfully.'

'I will,' the King assured him.

'I will return to the camp then. Many of our men are unwell, did you know that?'

'I know,' replied Alexander. 'And it's a real problem. Darius is approaching, I can feel it. I really must get back on my feet.' Then, as Philip was about to leave, he asked, 'Who do you think it was?'

Philip shrugged his shoulders. 'I have no idea. But there are plenty of young, very able and very ambitious surgeons who might be capable of plotting their rise to the position of royal physician. If anything were to happen to me, one of them might take my place.'

'Just let me know who they are and I . . .'

'I don't think so, Sire. Soon we will need all the surgeons we have and even then I'm not sure there will be enough of us. Thank you in any case for your trust,' he added, closing the door behind him.

48

NEARCHUS'S FLEET dropped anchor off Tarsus about half-way through autumn and the admiral disembarked to greet and embrace Alexander, who had now completely recovered.

'Have you heard that Darius intends to prevent us from passing through the Syrian Gates?' the King said.

'Perdiccas has informed me. Unfortunately your illness will have given them all the time they needed to consolidate their positions.'

'Yes, but listen to my plan – we will move down along the coast, climb up towards the pass and then we will send out scouts to discover exactly where Darius is. We will dislodge his garrison with a surprise attack and then come down with the entire army to attack his forces on the plain. In any case they have a crushing superiority in terms of numbers – ten to one.'

'Ten to one?'

'This is what we have heard. I will leave our infirm and convalescent soldiers at Issus and then begin the march towards the pass. We set off tomorrow. You will follow us with the fleet and from now on we will keep close enough to ensure direct signalling between us.'

Nearchus returned to his ship and raised anchor the

following day, setting course southwards, while the army proceeded along the coast in the same direction.

They reached Issus, a city which stood at the foot of the mountains and which was laid out like the terraces of a theatre, and orders were given for all those men who were not battle-fit to be billeted there. Then he set off once more on the march towards the Syrian Gates.

The following evening he sent out an advance party of scouts, while Nearchus's flagship signalled that there was a swell on the way and that a storm was brewing.

'This is all we needed!' complained Perdiccas. His men sought to pitch camp in the rising wind, the tents flapping and flying like ships' sails in the midst of a squall.

When the camp was finally ready, around nightfall, the storm broke in earnest with a downpour, blinding lightning and thunder that resounded across the foothills of the mountains.

Nearchus had only just moored in time and his crews had to use sledgehammers to secure the harpoons which held the stern ropes thrown to them from the ships.

Finally it seemed the situation was under control and the entire chiefs of staff met together in Alexander's tent to eat a light supper and to discuss plans for the following day. It was almost time for them all to retire when a messenger arrived from Issus; soaked to the skin, breathless and covered in mud, he was immediately led before the King.

'What has happened?' Alexander asked.

'Sire,' the man began, still struggling for breath, 'Darius's army is directly behind us, at Issus.'

'What did you say? Have you been drinking?' shouted the King.

'No, unfortunately, I am sober, Sire. They arrived suddenly, towards sunset, taking the sentries outside the city by surprise and taking all the invalid and convalescent soldiers you left with us prisoner.'

Alexander thumped his fist on the table, 'Damn! Now I will have to negotiate with Darius for their release.'

'We have no choice,' said Parmenion.

'But how can they possibly be behind us all of a sudden?' asked Perdiccas.

'They couldn't have come through this way because we're here,' said Seleucus with an almost detached air, as though seeking to calm everyone. 'Neither by a sea-borne route because Nearchus would have seen them.'

Ptolemy moved towards the messenger. 'And if this were a trick to have us move away from the pass and give the Great King the time to move up and then attack us from the high ground? I do not know this man. Do you know him?'

Everyone moved nearer and studied the messenger, who sidled towards the door in fear.

'I have never set eyes on him,' said Parmenion.

'Neither have I,' said Craterus, looking at him suspiciously.

'But, Sire . . .' pleaded the messenger.

'Do you have a password?' asked Alexander.

'But I . . . there was no time, Sire. My commander told me to fly, so I climbed on my horse and flew.'

'And who is your commander?'

'Amyntas of Lyncestis.'

Alexander was speechless and exchanged a brief knowing look with Parmenion. At that same moment there came a flash of lightning so intense that it penetrated the tent and illuminated the faces of all those present in ghostly glare. Immediately afterwards came the crash of a deafening thunderclap.

'There is only one way of finding out what is going on,' said Nearchus as soon as the rumble had faded away, out towards the sea.

'And that is?' asked the King.

'I will go back to take a look. With my ship.'

'But you are mad!' exclaimed Ptolemy. 'You will sink like a stone in this storm.'

'Not necessarily. The wind is turning northwards – with a bit of luck I might manage it. Don't move from here until I come back, or until I send someone. The password is "Poseidon".'

He pulled his cloak around his head and ran out under the beating rain.

Alexander and his companions followed, carrying lanterns with them. Nearchus hauled himself up on to his flagship and gave orders for the moorings to be freed and for the oars to be put in the water. Soon the ship turned, pointing northwards, and as it moved away from the beach the white ghost of a sail opened up over its bow.

'He is a madman,' said Ptolemy, trying to shield his eyes from the lashing rain, 'he has even hoisted a sail.'

'He is not a madman,' replied Eumenes. 'He is the best mariner who has ever sailed the seas between here and the Pillars of Hercules, and he knows it.'

The whitish mark of the bow-sail was soon swallowed

up by the darkness and everyone returned to the King's tent to warm themselves around a brazier before going to sleep. Alexander was too shocked to rest and he remained outside, by the entrance, watching the fury of the storm, every now and then taking a look at Peritas, who whined in complaint at every thunderclap. Suddenly he saw a lightning bolt strike an oak up on the top of a hill and split it in two. The huge trunk burst into flames and in the light the fire produced he saw for a moment the white cloak and the silhouette of Aristander the seer, standing motionless in the wind and the rain, his hands raised towards the sky. Alexander felt a long shiver run down his back and he thought he heard the cries of many dying men, the desolate lament of many souls joining the ranks of the dead before their time, but then his mind seemed to plunge into some sort of dark oblivion.

*

The storm raged for the rest of the night and only towards morning did the clouds begin to clear, revealing some patches of blue in the sky. When the sun finally rose above the peaks of the Taurus range, the air had cleared and down on the beach the waves were breaking rhythmically, edged with long lips of white foam.

The scouts who had been sent south towards the Syrian Gates returned before midday and came before the King with their report: 'Sire, there is no one up there, and neither is there anyone down on the plain.'

'I do not understand,' said the King. 'I do not understand. Even the "ten thousand" passed through here. There is no other way . . .'

The answer arrived with Nearchus's ship as evening fell. His men had broken their backs rowing against the wind and close to the coast to bring the news that Alexander was waiting for. As soon as the flagship was sighted, the King rushed to the beach to meet the admiral, who was approaching aboard a launch.

'Well then?' he asked as soon as he stepped ashore.

'Unfortunately the messenger has told you the truth. They are behind us and there are hundreds of thousands of them – horses, war chariots, archers, slingsmen, lancers . . .'

'But how . . .'

'There is another pass – the Amanus Gates, fifty stadia to the north.'

'Eumolpus has betrayed us!' Alexander swore. 'He has sent us into this trap between the mountains and the sea while Darius came down behind us, cutting us off from Macedon.'

'He may not have done it deliberately,' said Parmenion. 'Perhaps they found out what he was up to and forced him into it. Or perhaps Darius was hoping to surprise you at Tarsus while you were still unwell.'

'None of this changes our current situation,' commented Ptolemy.

'Quite,' agreed Seleucus. 'We are in trouble.'

'What shall we do?' asked Leonnatus as he lifted his freckled face which he had kept bowed up until that moment.

Alexander stood in silence as he thought to himself, and then he said, 'Darius now knows exactly where we are. If we stay here he will come and wipe us out.'

49

ALEXANDER SUMMONED THE COUNCIL in his tent before sunrise. He had slept very little, but he seemed to be mentally alert and in perfect physical shape.

He outlined his plan briefly. 'Friends, the Persian army is far superior to us in number and so we must move out of this position, we are too exposed here. Behind us lies a vast plain, before us, the mountains. If we stay Darius will surround and then annihilate us. Therefore we must turn back and face him at some narrow spot where he will not be able to make use of his numerical superiority.

'He will not be expecting us to turn back and so we will take him by surprise. Remember the place where the Pinarus river flows into the sea? Well, that might be the right spot for us. The marching officers tell me that the space between the hills and the sea there is at the most ten or twelve stadia, but the terrain free of obstacles is no more than three stadia and is therefore good for our purposes. Our formation will be the most solid one we have – at the centre the *pezhetairoi* phalanx battalions and the Greek allies; to the right, off towards the hills, I will take up position with the Vanguard at the head of the *hetairoi* cavalry; out on the left flank General Parmenion will cover us from the seaward side with the remainder of the heavy infantry and the Thessalian cavalry. The

Thracians and the Agrianians will line up behind me as reserves.

'The phalanx will attack frontally and the cavalry laterally, just as they did at Chaeronaea, just as they did at the Granicus.

'I have nothing else to say. Many the gods be with us! Now go to your units and line them up in battle formation so that I may inspect them.'

It was still dark when the King, astride Bucephalas and dressed in his battle armour, his iron breastplate adorned with silver friezes and with an embossed bronze gorgon over his heart, addressed his troops. To his left and right were his bodyguards and his companions – Hephaestion, Lysimachus, Seleucus, Leonnatus, Perdiccas, Ptolemy and Craterus, all bedecked in iron and bronze from head to foot, their helmets adorned with high crests that waved in the cold wind of the autumn morning.

'Men!' he shouted. 'For the first time since we set foot in Asia, we must face the Persian army led by the Great King himself. He has come at us from behind and his army has cut off our escape route. He is certainly planning to advance along the coast and pin us down against these mountains, placing all of his faith in his own numerical superiority. But we will not simply sit and wait for him to come, we instead will go to him, we will take him by surprise in a narrow place and we will beat him. We have no alternative, men! We can only win, otherwise we will be annihilated. Remember! The Great King is always at the centre of his front line; if we succeed in killing him or in taking him prisoner then we will have won the war and conquered his empire in a single instant. And now, let me hear your voices, men! Let me hear the noise of your weapons!'

The army responded with a deafening roar, then all the officers and the soldiers together unsheathed their swords and began beating rhythmically against their shields, flooding the plain with a deafening clangour. Alexander lifted his spear and spurred Bucephalas forward so that the stallion advanced with his majestic stride, flanked by the other horsemen enclosed in their armour. Behind them there soon came the heavy, regular steps of the phalanx, which blended with the noise of thousands of hooves.

They proceeded northwards for some hours without anything particular happening, but about half-way through the morning a group of scouts who had gone on ahead returned at a gallop.

'Sire!' shouted their commander with an expression of horror on his face. 'The barbarians have sent us back the men we had left at Issus.'

Alexander looked at him, unable to understand what was happening.

'They have all been mutilated, Sire. They have cut off their hands. Many of them are already dead from loss of blood, others are dragging themselves along the road moaning and crying out in pain. It is a frightful sight.'

The King immediately set off at a gallop to see his men, and when he came to them they held out their bloody arms, the stumps bandaged up with filthy rags as well as could be managed under the circumstances.

The King's face broke into a grimace of horror; he leaped from Bucephalas and cried and shouted as though out of his mind as he began embracing his soldiers one by one.

One veteran dragged himself to Alexander's feet to tell him something, but he had used up all his strength and collapsed, dying there in the mud.

Alexander started shouting. 'Call Philip, call the physicians, quickly! Quickly! They must help these men.' Then he turned to his troops and said, 'Look at what they have done to our companions! Now you know what awaits you if we lose this battle. Not one of us must rest until this outrage is avenged.'

Philip arranged medical help for the wounded, having them put on carts that would take them back to the camp before meeting up with the army once more. He was well aware that before sunset his skills would again be required.

Darius's army came into sight around midday, spread out along a huge line on the northern bank of the Pinarus. It was an amazing spectacle – at least two hundred thousand soldiers lined up in battle formation, arranged in several rows and preceded by war chariots equipped with scythes which protruded menacingly from the hubs of the wheels. On the flanks were the Median, Cyssaean, Saka and Hyrcanian horsemen; at the centre, behind the chariots, was the infantry of the Immortals, Darius's guard, with their silver quivers, their golden-tipped spears and the long double-curved bows across their shoulders.

'Gods of Olympus, there are so many of them!' exclaimed Lysimachus.

Alexander said nothing as he continued staring at the

centre of the enemy line, searching for the Great King's chariot. Ptolemy interrupted him:

'Look! The Persians are manoeuvring out to the right!'

The King looked towards the hills and saw that a squadron of cavalry was setting off up towards the high ground in a move designed to surround his army.

'We cannot engage them at this distance. Send the Thracians and the Agrianians to stop them. They must not pass at any cost. Give the signal, we are about to attack!'

Ptolemy galloped off towards the Thracian and Agrianian contingents and sent them off towards the hills. Hephaestion gave a signal to the trumpeters and they sounded their instruments. More trumpet blasts came in response from the left-hand flank and the army set off, infantry and cavalry at a walk.

'And look over there!' said Hephaestion. 'Greek heavy infantry! They have lined them up at the centre.'

'And down there,' said Perdiccas, 'they're putting sharpened stakes into the ground.'

'And the river is swollen,' added Lysimachus, 'because of the rain last night.'

Alexander stood in silence watching the Agrianians and the Thracians, who had engaged the Persians and were driving them back. By now they were very close to the bank of the Pinarus. The river itself was not deep, but it was flowing fast and full of brown water between its two muddy banks. The King raised his hand again and the trumpets sounded the attack signal.

The phalanx lowered their *sarissae* and charged, the

Thessalian cavalry on the left set off at a gallop and Alexander spurred on Bucephalas, leading his *hetairoi*. He veered as much as possible towards the right, driving his horse into the river at the narrowest point, followed by the entire squadron, before the Persians managed to stop him, then he turned and set off with his spear in his hand to attack the flank of the enemy line-up.

At that same instant the phalanx entered the Pinarus, crossed it and began climbing up the right-hand bank. Facing them, however, they found the Greek mercenary infantry in perfectly compact formation. The terrain was rough and slippery, there were rocks on the riverbed and on the bank which broke up the Macedonian ranks and the Greeks made the most of these gaps, engaging the *pezhetairoi* in furious hand-to-hand combat.

Craterus, who was fighting on foot on the right of the phalanx, saw the danger and had the trumpets sound to call up the shieldsmen in support. Indeed, many of the *pezhetairoi* had been forced to abandon their *sarissae* and to unsheath their short swords to defend themselves from the furious assault of the Greek mercenaries, but they were in serious trouble now.

Off to the left, in the meantime, Parmenion had sent his Thessalian horsemen against the Persian right flank in waves, squadron after squadron. Each wave let loose a cloud of javelins and then turned back, while the second and third wave moved forwards at brief intervals. The Hyrcanians and the Saka in their turn contributed with furious charges, covered by dense sallies of arrows from the Cyssaean archers. Even a squadron of chariots was used in this area, but the rough ground did not help matters – many of the chariots overturned and the horses fled in terror, dragging behind them their drivers, tied to the reins at their wrists, tearing them to shreds on the rocks.

The battle raged on at length, with the Persians continually pushing forward fresh troops from their inexhaustible reserves. At a certain point one single brigade of the shieldsmen, led by Craterus, managed to break through behind the lines of the Greek mercenary foot-soldiers, isolating them from the rest of the Persian line-up and breaking up their formation.

These mercenaries were exhausted now by the fatigue, oppressed by the weight of their heavy armour, and, on finding themselves trapped between two lines of enemy troops, they began to lose ground and disperse and were finished off by the Thessalian cavalry. The shieldsmen then took up position on the two flanks while the *pezhetairoi* phalanx re-formed, lowered their *sarissae* and advanced towards the huge front presented by Darius's ten thousand Immortals, who moved forward forcefully, shield against shield, their spears lowered in readiness. A sharp trumpet blast came suddenly from the rearguard and then the noise of thunder broke through to dominate the infernal shouting and neighing and clangour of arms – the thunder of Chaeronaea!

The giant drum had been transported disassembled but now, reassembled and drawn by eight horses, it had reached the front line to add its powerful voice to the shouts of the soldiers.

The *pezhetairoi* shouted, '*Alalalài!*' and they rushed forward, heedless of their tiredness and the pain their wounds were causing them. Filthy all over with mud and with blood, they looked like wild furies straight from hell, but the Great King's Immortals were not frightened by them and in their turn they attacked with still compact energy. The two lines wavered slightly at the initial clash and more than once the front line moved forward and then backwards in response to the wild charges.

Out on the right wing Alexander, still on the front line, preceded by his standard-bearer with the red flag and the Argead star with its sixteen points, launched attack after attack, but the squadrons of Arabian and Assyrian horsemen counterattacked each time with unyielding valour, supported by the continuous, dense flights of arrows from the Median and Armenian archers.

When the sun began to dip towards the sea, the Thracians and the Agrianians had finally defeated the Persian cavalry they had been sent to engage with and they regrouped and went to the infantry units involved in the bitter hand-to-hand combat. Their arrival gave the tired *pezhetairoi* new vigour and new hope in the midst of the interminable battle, and Alexander renewed the Vanguard's attacks with a wild cry as he spurred Bucephalas on again. The ever-willing animal felt his rider's resolve, rose up on to his hind legs as he neighed loudly and then set off forwards on his powerful legs, clearing the enemy crowds out of the way with tremendous force.

All of a sudden, almost delirious with the effort, the Macedonian leader found himself face to face with his adversary and for an instant the two Kings' eyes met. Just then, however, Alexander felt a searing pain in his thigh and on looking down saw that an arrow had penetrated, just above his knee. He clenched his teeth and pulled it out, struggling to control himself, but when he looked up once more Darius had disappeared – his driver had turned the horses and was whipping them wildly in the direction of the hills, along the road that led to the Amanus Gates.

Perdiccas, Ptolemy and Leonnatus surrounded the wounded King and cleared some space around him, while Alexander shouted, 'Darius is escaping! Follow him! Follow him!'

The Persians were now feeling the full pressure of the concentric attacks of the enemy squadrons and they began to waver and to disperse. Only the Immortals maintained their positions, forming a square formation and continuing to repulse the Macedonian attacks blow for blow.

Alexander ripped a strip of cloth from his cloak, tied it around his thigh and set off once more on the chase. A horseman from the royal guard appeared before him with an unsheathed sabre, but the King instantly took his double-bladed axe from its holder and let loose such a blow that it snapped the sword in two. Just as the King was lifting the axe once more to finish off the guard, a strange play of light from the dying sun helped him recognize his opponent.

He recognized the brown face and the black beard of the giant archer who so many years before, with one single arrow, had struck down the lioness which had been about to drag him to the floor. That day was far off now, a day of hunting and celebration on the flower-filled plain of Eordaea.

The Persian recognized Alexander as well and stared at him speechless, as though struck by lightning.

'No one must touch this man!' shouted Alexander, and he set off at a gallop behind his companions.

The chase for Darius lasted until nightfall. The fleeing King would appear in the distance in the half-light only to disappear once again along new hidden roads in the thick vegetation which covered the hilltops. Suddenly, on coming round a bend, Alexander and his friends found themselves before Darius's abandoned chariot, the royal gown hanging there, together with the Great King's golden quiver, his spear and his bow.

'There is no point going on,' said Ptolemy. 'It is dark and Darius is on a fresh horse now – we'll never catch him. And you are wounded,' he added, looking at Alexander's bleeding thigh. 'Let's go back – the gods have been most generous to us this day.'

50

ALEXANDER RETURNED TO the camp in the middle of the night, soiled with blood and mud after crossing the plain, where fires were still burning and corpses and carcasses lay everywhere. Even Bucephalas was covered with a flaking layer of blood and dirt that gave him a spectral, nightmarish colour.

His companions rode alongside and, attached to the harnesses of their horses, towed behind them the Great King's war chariot.

The Persian camp had been completely ransacked and looted by the Macedonian soldiers, but the royal pavilions had been left untouched because they belonged to Alexander by right.

Darius's tent was gigantic, made entirely of decorated leather, with drapes of purple and gold. The supporting poles were of carved cedar, laminated in pure gold. The ground was covered with the most precious carpets imaginable. Inside, heavy curtains of white, red and blue byssus divided the various rooms, as though it were a true and proper headquarters, with the throne room for audiences, the dining room, the sleeping chamber with a canopy over the bed, and the bathchamber.

Alexander looked around without really taking in the fact that all these riches and such luxury were now at his complete disposal. The bathtub, the amphorae, the finger-bowls were all in solid gold and Darius's handmaids and his young eunuchs, all stunningly beautiful, had prepared a bath for their new master and were ready, trembling with fear, to obey his every command.

Still astounded, he continued to send his gaze into every luxurious corner as he murmured, almost to him-self, 'So this is what it means to be a king.' For one used to the austere simplicity of the palace at Pella, this tent was like a god's home.

He moved towards the bath, limping because of the pain from his wound, and immediately the women hur-ried about him, undressing him and preparing to wash him. In the meantime, however, Philip arrived to examine and treat his King. Indeed, Philip showed the handmaids how to wash Alexander without causing any more bleed-ing. Then he had the King lie down on a table and with the help of his assistants he operated, cleaning and drain-ing the wound then carefully sewing and bandaging. Alexander did not murmur even a single complaint, but the terrible effort, together with the superhuman feats of the battle, left him completely exhausted and as soon as Philip had finished he fell into a leaden sleep.

Leptine sent everyone away, made sure he was comfortable, and stretched out next to him, to keep him warm in the cold autumn evening.

He was awoken the following day by the sound of desperate crying coming from a nearby tent. Instinctively he put his foot to the ground and immediately his face contracted in a grimace of pain. The leg was painful, but the drainage Philip had effected with a silver cannula had minimized the swelling. Alexander was weak, but he was still able to move and to ignore the orders of his doctor, who had told him not to move for seven days.

He had himself dressed quickly and without even eating a thing he went out, limping, to discover the source of the crying. Hephaestion, who had slept in the entrance with Peritas, came close and offered him his arm, which Alexander declined. 'What has happened?' he asked. 'What is all this crying?'

'In that tent over there is the Queen Mother, Darius's wife and some of his three hundred and sixty-five concubines. The others are all at Damascus. They have seen Darius's war chariot, his gown and his quiver and they all think he's dead.'

'We must go to put their minds at rest then.'

He had himself announced by one of the eunuchs so as not to create too much embarrassment and they entered together. The Queen Mother, whose face was wet with tears and dirty with streaks of bistre make-up, had a moment of panic and threw herself at Hephaestion's feet, thinking he was the King, he being the taller and more imposing of the two. The eunuch, who had understood the situation, went pale and murmured to her in Persian that the King was in fact the other one.

The Queen shook her head in confusion and prostrated herself before Alexander, wailing even more loudly now and begging him to excuse her, but the King bent over and helped her up on to her feet and, while the eunuch translated into her language, said, 'It matters not, my Lady, for he, too, is Alexander.' And, seeing that she was beginning to feel somewhat less disconsolate, added,

'Please do not cry and do not despair. Darius is alive. He abandoned the chariot and the royal cloak and fled on horseback to be lighter and faster. He is certainly safe now.'

The Queen Mother bowed once more to take his hand and would not stop kissing it. The Great King's wife approached to pay the same homage and Alexander was struck by her incredible beauty. But then, looking around, he realized that all the other women were stupendous, so much so that he whispered in Hephaestion's ear, 'By Zeus, these women really are a sight for sore eyes!' But it was clear that he was looking for one woman in particular.

'Are there no other women in the camp?' he asked.

'No,' replied Hephaestion.

'Are you sure?'

'Absolutely certain.' And then, believing he had detected a slight air of disappointment from his friend, he added, 'But the Great King's full entourage is at Damascus. Perhaps you will find whoever you are looking for there.'

'I am not looking for anyone,' replied Alexander brusquely. Then he turned to the eunuch. 'Tell the Queen Mother, Darius's wife and all the others that they will be treated with every respect and that they have nothing to fear. They may ask us whatever they require and, if we can, we will provide it.'

'The Queen and the Queen Mother thank you, Sire,' the eunuch translated, 'and for your clemency and your good heart they ask for you a blessing from Ahura Mazda.'

Alexander nodded and then left, followed by Hephaestion. Outside he gave orders for those who had fallen in battle to be gathered up and for their funeral rites to be celebrated.

That evening Callisthenes wrote in his work that only three hundred and nine Macedonians had perished, but the real figure was much more bitter, and the King limped his way among the horribly mutilated and ravaged corpses and realized that there were in fact thousands of them. The greatest number of losses had been at the centre, at the point where the Macedonians had come face-to-face with the Greek mercenaries.

Many trees were cut down from the surrounding hills and giant funeral pyres were built. The bodies were burned before the assembled army. And when the funerals had been completed, Alexander inspected his soldiers with a red standard paraded before him, the bandage on his thigh clearly visible, the stains on it of the same bright colour as the flag. He had words of praise and encouragement for all the units, and also for the men who had fought with valour alongside him. He gave personal gifts to many of them, objects which they might keep as souvenirs.

At the end he shouted, 'I am proud of you, men! You have defeated the most powerful army on earth. No Greek or Macedonian has ever conquered such vast territory! You are the best, you are invincible – there is no power in the world which can withstand your force!'

The soldiers responded with a chorus of frenetic shouting, while the wind dispersed the ashes of their fallen companions and carried myriad sparks up towards the grey autumn sky.

When evening came Alexander had someone lead him to the Persian prisoner whose life he had spared on the battlefield. As soon as Alexander saw him sitting on the ground, bound hand and foot, he kneeled down alongside and undid the ropes. Then he asked him, using gestures as well, 'Do you remember me?'

The man understood and nodded.

'You saved my life.'

The soldier smiled and explained that he remembered there being another young man with Alexander on the lion hunt.

'Hephaestion,' said Alexander. 'He is around here somewhere. He is still alive.'

The man smiled again.

'You are free,' said Alexander, accompanying his words with an eloquent gesture. 'You may return to your people and to your King.'

The soldier seemed not to have understood, so the King had a horse brought and put the reins in his hands. 'You may go. There must be someone waiting for you at home. Children perhaps?' he asked, indicating with his hand, palm downwards, the height of the supposed child.

The man lifted the hand to an adult height and Alexander smiled, 'Yes. Of course, time passes.'

The Persian looked into Alexander's eyes with a grave and intense look and his black eyes shone with emotion as he brought his hand to his heart and then touched Alexander's chest.

'Go now,' said the King, 'before it is pitch dark.'

The soldier murmured something in his own tongue,

then leaped on to the horse and disappeared into the distance.

That same night the Egyptian Sisines was found in the camp, the man who the year previously had had Prince Amyntas of Lyncestis imprisoned, leading everyone to think that he had perhaps been bribed by Darius to kill Alexander and take his place on the throne. Ptolemy organized a brief trial and identified him beyond any doubt as a Persian spy, but before having him executed he sent for Callisthenes, because he was sure the historian would like to ask him some questions.

As soon as the Egyptian saw him he threw himself at his feet, 'Please have mercy on me! The Persians took me prisoner to make me give them information regarding your army, but I didn't tell them a thing, I have no . . .'

Callisthenes stopped him with a simple gesture. 'Undoubtedly the Persians treat their prisoners remarkably well, since you had a most luxurious tent, two slaves and three handmaids. And where are the signs of the torture they inflicted upon you? You look most healthy to me. A trifle pale perhaps.'

'But I . . .'

'Your only chance of saving your hide is to speak,' the historian threatened. 'I want to know everything, especially all about that business with Prince Amyntas – Darius's letter, the money he had promised for killing Alexander and so on.'

Some colour came back into Sisines's face, 'My most illustrious friend,' he began. 'I had no intention of revealing the most secret and most delicate facets of my work, but since my life is at stake, I nevertheless am forced most reluctantly to . . .' Callisthenes gestured to let him know that he had no time to waste. 'Anyway, as I was saying, I can demonstrate to you that I have done no more and no less than serve faithfully the Macedonian throne: the whole story was invented on orders from Olympias, the Queen Mother.'

Callisthenes immediately thought of the taste of the ink he had found on that letter, a most familiar taste. 'Continue,' he said.

'Well, Olympias was concerned that Amyntas might become a threat to her son Alexander sooner or later. Her boy, who is so far away, in foreign lands, exposed to all sorts of risks. What would happen if Alexander suffered a defeat? The troops might proclaim Amyntas King, obtaining in exchange an end to the campaign and their immediate return to the homeland with the prospect of a much easier life. She therefore had the letter written by a Persian slave that Philip had given her as a gift, and in order to achieve a convincing reproduction of the formulas of Persian diplomacy, she had the barbarian seals copied perfectly from examples in the palace archives and honoured me by entrusting me with the job of . . .'

'I understand,' Callisthenes cut him short, 'but what about the Persian messenger?'

Sisines cleared his throat. 'My delicate role has often necessarily led me into Persian circles where I have many influential friends. It was not so difficult for me to persuade the governor of Nisibis to lend me a Persian orderly and to give him the job of delivering a document.'

'Neither was it difficult to eliminate the messenger with poison when you were afraid he might speak.'

'It is always best to be sure of everything,' replied the Egyptian impassibly. 'Even though that poor man did not really have very much to say.'

Callisthenes thought to himself: This way, you are the only one holding the truth, but what exactly is that truth? And he said immediately, 'All of this explains many things, but it does not explain your presence here, surrounded by luxuries and diversions of all kinds. In truth there is nothing to stop us from believing the letter to be authentic.'

'I agree with you that this might just be a possibility worth evaluating.'

The historian was silent again as he thought to himself about the possibility that the Great King really had sought to bribe Amyntas, but there was no proof that the prince had accepted, apart from Sisines's insinuations. At that moment he decided it was time for him to take the responsibility for a decisive move in this matter. He lifted his eyes and looked Sisines straight in the face. 'The best thing for all concerned is for you to tell me the truth. You are a Macedonian informer found in a Persian camp in a compromising situation. Ptolemy has no doubts that you are a spy.'

'My noble Lord,' replied the Egyptian, 'I thank the gods that they have sent such an intelligent and reasonable man with whom it is possible to discuss matters in a realistic manner. I have a considerable quantity of money deposited at Sidon, and, if we can reach some agreement,

I will provide you with a version of the facts with which you might be able to convince Commander Ptolemy.'

'The best thing for everyone is if you tell me the truth,' repeated Callisthenes without taking the bait.

'Let's just say that I decided to go self-employed and, given my contacts, the Great King thought I might be able to return to Anatolia and convince the governors of a few cities to reopen their harbours to the Persian fleet and . . .'

'And cut us off from Macedon.'

'Would fifteen talents be enough to persuade you of my innocence?'

The historian stared at him with an inscrutable look on his face.

'And another twenty for Commander Ptolemy?'

Callisthenes hesitated slightly before replying, 'I think that will do fine.' Then he left the tent and went straight to Ptolemy.

'The quicker you do it, the better for all concerned,' Callisthenes said. 'Apart from being a spy, he also holds a certain number of rather embarrassing secrets regarding the Queen Mother and . . .'

'That's enough,' said Ptolemy. 'Not another word. What's more, I've never really liked Egyptians.'

'You might have to rethink that one,' replied Callisthenes. 'Before long you'll be meeting lots of them. Rumour has it that Alexander wants to take Egypt.'

51

FROM DAMASCUS, WHERE HE had been ordered to march as quickly as possible, Parmenion sent a message saying he had occupied the royal quarters and taken possession of the Great King's monetary reserves and his entourage:

Two thousand six hundred silver talents in coin and five hundred *minae* in ingots, more than three hundred and fifty concubines, three hundred and twenty-nine flute and harp players, three hundred cooks, seventy wine-tasters, thirteen confectioners and forty perfume makers.

'By Zeus!' exclaimed Alexander when he had finished reading. 'That is what I call living!'

'I also have a personal message to relay to you orally,' added the messenger after the King had rolled up the letter.

'Speak. What is it?'

'General Parmenion wants you to know that there is a noblewoman in Damascus who will come back with him together with her two children. Her name is Barsine.'

Alexander shook his head as though unable to believe what he had just been told. 'It's not possible,' he murmured.

'Oh yes,' replied the messenger. 'The general told me

that an old soldier will bring you the password, if you don't . . .'

'I see,' Alexander interrupted. 'I see now. You may go.'

*

Eight days went by before he saw her, a period which passed as slowly as an eternity. His head spun as he watched her ride by on horseback in the midst of the soldiers, in the procession of the royal entourage, surrounded by two rows of *hetairoi* from Parmenion's guard. She was wearing Scythian trousers made of leather and a grey felt jacket, her hair was gathered up at the back of her neck, held in place with two pins, and she was, although it seemed impossible, yet more beautiful than she had been when they first met.

Her face had acquired a slight pallor and her features were sharper now, so that those great dark eyes stood out even more and shone with an intense, vibrant light, as bright as the stars.

He went to her much later on, when the camp was already steeped in the silence of the first watch. He wore only a short military *chiton*, on his shoulders he carried a cloak of grey wool, and he had his arrival announced by a handmaid.

She had taken a bath and had changed her clothes – now she wore a long Persian gown which reached her feet and which clung lightly to her figure. Her tent smelled of lavender.

'My Lord,' she murmured, lowering her head.

'Barsine . . .'

Alexander moved a few steps closer. 'I have been waiting for this moment since the last time I saw you.'

'My soul is full of grief.'

'I know – you have lost your husband.'

'The best of men, the most affectionate father, the sweetest husband.'

'He was the only enemy I have ever respected, and perhaps the only one I have ever feared.'

Barsine kept her eyes low because she well knew that she was Alexander's prey now, she knew that the enemy's woman was the most prized reward for the victor who had fought through the pain and the wounds, the fatigue and the horror of the blood, the shouting, the massacre. But she had also been told that this young man had displayed pity and respect for the old Queen Mother, for Darius's wife and his children.

Alexander put out his hand and gently touched her chin, lifting her head so that he looked into her gaze and the changing colours of her eyes. He saw the intense blue of a clear sky, the blue that had been there in Memnon's eyes. He also saw the dark colour of death and the night and he felt himself being drawn in, as though into a dizzying vortex, as though he had looked upon a god or some creature of fantasy.

'Barsine . . .' Alexander repeated her name, and the sound of his voice vibrated with the deepest passion, a burning desire.

'You may do with me what you will, you are the victor, but I will always have the image of Memnon before my eyes.'

'The dead live with the dead,' replied the King. 'I am before your eyes now and this time I will not let you go because I have seen in your eyes that you want to forget death. And this time I am life for you. Look at me. Look at me, Barsine, and tell me that I am wrong.'

Barsine did not reply, but she looked him straight in the eyes with an expression that was both despair and confusion at one and the same time. Two enormous tears shone in her eyelashes like the purest springwater; slowly they ran down her cheeks and stopped to moisten her lips. Alexander moved closer until he could feel her breath on his face, until he felt her breasts against his chest.

'You will be mine,' he whispered. Then he turned suddenly and left. A moment later there came the sound of Bucephalas neighing, an excited drumming of hooves and then the hammering of a reckless gallop that tore through the silence of the night.

*

The following day Callisthenes received another letter in code from his uncle. It arrived with the messenger who brought mail from Antipater in Macedonia.

I have discovered the whereabouts of the daughter of the man who calls himself Nicander, Pausanias's accomplice in the assassination of Philip. The child is under the protection of the priests in the temple of Artemis on the border with Thrace. But the priest is of Persian origin, a relative of the Satrap of Bithynia, who in the past has sent money and fine gifts for the sanctuary. This makes me think that Darius himself is connected with the killing of Philip and, unbeknownst to anyone, I have been able to read a letter which is kept in the temple and which would seem to suggest that this hypothesis is most likely.

Callisthenes went to see Alexander.

'The investigations into your father's death are continuing and there is important news – it would seem that the Persians are directly involved and that they are still protecting someone who took part in the conspiracy.'

'This would explain many things,' said the King. 'And to think that Darius dares to send me a letter of this kind!'

He handed Callisthenes the message from the Great King which an envoy had just brought.

Darius, King of Kings, Lord of the Four Corners of the Earth, Light of the Aryans, to Alexander, King of Macedon, Hail!

Your father Philip was the first to offend the Persians back in the time of Arses, although he himself had suffered no affront at our hands. When I became king, you sent no embassy to confirm the old friendship and alliance, and then you invaded Asia, inflicting great damage. I therefore was obliged to face you in battle, to defend my land and to reconquer my ancient dominions. The outcome was that which the gods decided, but I write to you now as one king to his peer and ask you to free my children, my mother and my wife. I am willing to sign a pact of friendship and alliance – please send an envoy together with my messenger in order that we may draw up terms for the treaty.

Callisthenes closed the letter. 'In essence he blames it all on you, justifies his right to defend himself, while admitting the defeat, and states he is now willing to become your friend and ally as long as you release his family. What will you do?'

At that moment Eumenes came in with a copy of the reply that he had prepared for the King; Alexander asked him to read it. The secretary cleared his voice and began:

'Alexander, King of Macedon, to Darius, King of Persia, Hail!

Your ancestors invaded Macedon and the rest of Greece, bringing us great harm with no apparent reason. I have been elected supreme commander of the Greeks and I have invaded Asia to avenge your aggression. You assisted Perinthus against my father and you invaded Thrace, a territory which is ours.'

Alexander stopped him at this point. 'Add the following now:

King Philip was assassinated as the result of a conspiracy which you supported and the proof exists in letters you have written.'

Eumenes looked at both Alexander and Callisthenes in surprise and the historian said, 'I'll explain later.'

So Eumenes continued:

'Furthermore, you took the throne fraudulently, you bribed the Greeks to make war and you have done everything to destroy the peace I struggled so hard to construct. I defeated your generals and I defeated you on the open battlefield with the help of the gods and I therefore am now responsible for those of your soldiers who have come over to my side and those other persons who are still with me. It is you, therefore, who must address me as Lord of Asia. Ask whatever you deem right, either in person or sending your envoys. Ask for your wife, your children and your mother, and you will have them, if you convince me I should give them to you. In the future, if you wish to address me, you will address the King of Asia, not your peer, and you will have to ask for whatever you desire from he who is now in possession of everything that was previously yours. If you fail to do this, I will take measures in your regard, measures against someone who has violated the rules and the laws of the nations. If, however, you continue to claim your right to the throne, then do battle, fight to defend your throne and do not flee, because I will follow you everywhere.'

'You don't leave him much choice,' said Callisthenes.

'No, none at all,' replied Alexander. 'And if he is a man and a king, then he will have to do something about it.'

52

THE ARMY SET OFF southwards at the beginning of the winter, towards the Phoenician coast. Alexander indeed had decided to complete a total conquest of all the ports that were still accessible to the Persians, so as to prevent any enemy action in the Aegean and in Greece as well.

The people of Aradus greeted him with full honours and Sidon even promised to withdraw its fifty ships from the imperial fleet and turn them over to him. Excitement in the Macedonian camp was at fever pitch – it was as though the gods themselves were clearing the way before the young leader and the expedition seemed to have become a journey of adventure to discover new worlds, new peoples, and magnificent places.

The rest of the Great King's entourage which Parmenion had captured at Damascus arrived at Sidon – an incredible assembly of slaves, musicians, cooks, food-tasters, eunuchs, masters of ceremonies, dancers, flautists, magicians, seers, conjurers, all of whom were most bizarre for Alexander's soldiers and his officers. The King, however, gave them all a very warm and understanding welcome, concerning himself with what was to become of them, asking about their personal affairs, and making sure they were treated with respect.

Just when it seemed that the entire court had paraded before the King and his companions, another small group arrived, escorted by a division of Agrianians.

'We found this lot in the headquarters of the Satrap of Syria,' explained the officer in charge.

'But I know this one here,' said Seleucus, pointing to a stout figure with a crown of grey hair around his bald head.

'Eumolpus of Soloi!' exclaimed Ptolemy. 'But what a surprise!'

'My Lords! Sire!' the informer greeted them as he prostrated himself before them.

'Well, well, well . . . it's a strange thing indeed, but I'm beginning to suspect something,' said Perdiccas ironically.

'Me too,' added Seleucus. 'So this is how Darius managed to take us by surprise at Issus. Tell us, Eumolpus, how much did he pay you to betray us?'

The man was as white as a sheet and struggling to bring his facial muscles into something approaching a smile. 'But Sire, my Lords, you cannot truly believe that I could ever have . . .'

'Oh . . . most certainly,' said the officer, turning to Alexander. 'The Satrap of Syria, who is on his way now to pledge his allegiance to you, told me all about it.'

'Bring him in here!' ordered the King as he entered his tent. 'He will be judged immediately.'

Alexander sat surrounded by his companions and asked the informer, 'Is there anything you would like to say before you die?'

Eumolpus lowered his gaze and said nothing. His silence granted him an unexpected dignity, making him somehow very different from the jolly man – always ready with a joke – that they all knew.

'Do you have nothing to say?' repeated Eumenes. 'How could you do that? They had every opportunity to cut us all to pieces. That message from your courier drew us into a blind trap.'

'You're a swine!' swore Leonnatus. 'If it were up to me, you wouldn't get away with a quick death. I'd rip out all of your nails first, and then I'd . . .'

Eumolpus lifted his moist eyes to look into his judges' faces.

'Well?' Alexander asked the question one last time.

'Sire . . .' began the informer, 'I have always been a spy. As a child I earned my living spying on unfaithful wives for cuckolded husbands. I know no other trade. And I have always sought money, selling my services for the best offer. However . . .'

'However?' Eumenes pressed him, having assumed the role of principal interrogator.

'However, from the day I first entered King Philip's, your father's, service, I have spied for him alone, I swear. And do you know why, my Lord? Because your father was an extraordinary man. Oh, of course he paid me well, but it was not only a question of money. When I used to meet him to make my reports, he would have me sit down like an old friend, he himself would pour something for me to drink, he would ask after my health and that sort of thing . . . do you understand?'

'Why, have I perhaps not behaved as he did?' asked Alexander. 'Have I not always treated you as an old friend rather than a mercenary spy?'

'That is true,' said Eumolpus, 'and I have been loyal to you for this very reason. But I would have been so anyway, if only for the simple fact that you are your father's son.'

'Then why did you betray me? There has to be a reason for betraying a friend!'

'Fear, my Lord. The satrap who is now on his way to pledge loyalty to you, betraying as he does so the loyalty he has expressed previously to the Great King, frightened me to death by looking me in the eyes as he stripped a skewered thrush with his teeth as if to say, 'This is what's in store for you – you'll be torn to pieces like this thrush.' And then he took me to the window overlooking the courtyard.

'My messenger was down there, that fine lad I always used to send you – they had skinned him alive, castrated him and tied his balls around his neck.' Eumolpus's voice was trembling now, and the watery eyes of the old man were brimming with real tears. 'They had stripped his skin down to the bone . . . and that's not the end of it. There was a barbarian there sharpening a stake of acacia wood, smoothing it with pumice stone. He was preparing it for me, if I refused to do what they asked me to do. Have you ever seen them impale a man, my Lord? I have. They put a stake up into his body, but without killing him, and that man simply suffers all that a man can possibly suffer for hours, sometimes for days. I betrayed you because I was afraid, because in my life no one has ever required such an act of courage from me.

'And now, if you wish, have me killed . . . I deserve it, but please let it be a quick death. I know you have lost many men and that you had to face a bitter battle, but I knew that you would win, I knew it. And what satisfaction would it give you to torture an old man like me? An old man who would never have done you any harm if it had been up to him and who suffered so much in betraying you, much more than you can ever imagine, my boy.'

He said nothing else and sniffed loudly.

Alexander and his companions looked at one another and realized that none of them had the courage to find Eumolpus of Soloi guilty.

'I should have you killed,' said the King, 'but you are right – what is there to gain from it? And what's more . . .'

Eumolpus lifted his head, '. . . what's more I know that courage is a quality the gods grant to few people. You have not received this gift, but you have others – wit, intelligence, and perhaps even loyalty.'

'Does this mean I am not going to die?' asked Eumolpus.

'No.'

'No?' repeated the informer incredulously.

'No,' repeated Alexander, unable to prevent his face breaking into a half-smile.

'And will I be able to work for you once more?'

'What do you think?' the King asked his companions.

'I would give him a chance,' proposed Ptolemy.

'Why not?' Seleucus approved. 'When it comes down to it, he has always been an excellent spy. And after all, we are the victors now.'

'So we are all agreed then,' decided the King. 'But you really will have to change that damn password, since the enemy have got hold of it.'

'Oh, yes, of course,' said Eumolpus, visibly relieved.

'What password was that exactly?' asked Seleucus.

'Sheep's brains,' replied Alexander impassively.

'I would have changed it in any case,' said Seleucus. 'It strikes me as the most bizarre password I have heard in my life.'

'Indeed,' said Alexander. He gestured to Eumolpus to move closer. 'Now, tell me the new password.'

The informer whispered in his ear, 'Skewered thrush.'

Then he bowed and saluted all present most respectfully. 'I thank you, my Lords, my King, for your kind heart.' And he left, his legs still slightly unsteady due to the fright he had had.

'What's the new password like?' asked Seleucus as soon as Eumolpus had left.

Alexander shook his head. 'Crazy.'

53

THE INHABITANTS OF SIDON, who only a few years before had suffered terribly at the hands of the Persian garrison there, were enthusiastic about the arrival of Alexander and his promise to restore their institutions. But there were no survivors now of the reigning dynasty and a new King had to be chosen.

'Why don't you take care of it?' Alexander asked Hephaestion.

'Me? But I don't know anyone, I wouldn't even know where to start looking and then . . .'

'So we're agreed then,' the King cut him short. 'You will take care of it. I have to negotiate with the other Greek cities along the coast.'

So Hephaestion sought out an interpreter and began wandering around Sidon incognito, looking in the markets, eating in all the taverns and making sure he was invited to all the official dinners in the most prestigious residences. But he could find no one worthy of the role.

'No success yet?' Alexander asked him when they met at war councils. And Hephaestion would shake his head.

One day, still accompanied by his interpreter, he passed close by a small dry stone wall that wound its way up towards the far off hills and above which the canopies of all sorts of trees appeared – majestic cedars of Lebanon, cascades of pistachios and sweet clovers, and ancient fig trees spreading their rough, grey branches. He looked through the gate and was astounded at the wonders there before his eyes – fruit trees of every imaginable type, wonderfully composed and pruned bushes, fountains and streams, rocks from which succulent, spiny plants grew, plants he had never seen before in his life.

'They come from a city in Libya by the name of Lixus,' explained the interpreter.

Just then a man appeared leading a small donkey pulling a cart full of manure. He began spreading the fertilizer on the plants one by one, carrying out the job most diligently and lovingly.

'When the uprising against the Persian governor took place, the rebels decided to torch this garden,' the interpreter recounted, 'but that man stood before the gate and said that anyone who wished to commit such a crime would have first to dirty their hands with his own blood.'

'He is the King,' said Hephaestion.

'A gardener?' asked the interpreter in amazement.

'Yes. A man who is prepared to die to save the plants in a garden that is not even his, what would that man not do to protect his people and to make sure his city grows and thrives?'

And so it was. One day the humble gardener saw a procession of dignitaries arrive, escorted by Alexander's guard. They led him in full pomp and circumstance to the royal palace for his investiture. The man wore a peaceful, serene smile and his great calloused hands brought

Lysippus to the King's mind. His name was Abdalonymus and he was the best king in living memory.

*

From Sidon the army continued advancing southwards towards Tyre, where there was a grand temple to Melkarth, the Phoenicians' Hercules. There were two parts to the city – an old quarter on dry land and a new city on an island one stadium from the coast. It had been built recently and was most impressive due to its size and its imposing buildings. It had two fortified harbours and a wall one hundred and fifty feet high, the highest ever constructed by human hands.

'Let us hope they welcome us as they did at Byblos, Aradus and Sidon,' said Seleucus. 'That fortress is impregnable.'

'What are you thinking of doing?' Hephaestion asked him, looking at the reflection of the formidable wall in the blue waters of the gulf.

'Aristander has advised me to offer a sacrifice in the temple of my ancestor Hercules, whom the inhabitants of Tyre call Melkarth,' replied Alexander. 'There is our delegation setting off now,' he added, pointing to a launch that was slowly crossing the narrow channel which separated the city from dry land.

The answer came that afternoon and it infuriated the King.

'They say that if you wish to make a sacrifice to Hercules, then there is a temple in the old quarter here on the mainland.'

'I knew it,' said Hephaestion. 'That lot are over there

in their stone nest on that little island and they think they can ridicule whoever they like.'

'They cannot ridicule me,' said Alexander. 'Get another delegation ready. This time I will be more explicit.'

The new envoys set out the following day with a message which read: 'If you wish, you may enter into a pact of peace and alliance with Alexander. Otherwise, the King will do battle with you because you are allies of the Persians.'

The response, unfortunately, was equally unequivocal – the members of the delegation were thrown from the heights of the walls, dying horrendously and bloodily on the rocks below. Among them were friends and childhood companions of the King and this gruesome event dragged him down into a state of dark confusion which slowly simmered into the blindest fury. For two days he stayed in his quarters without receiving anyone; only Hephaestion dared enter on the evening of the second day and found him strangely calm.

Alexander was sitting reading by lamplight.

'Is it Xenophon as usual?' Hephaestion asked.

'Xenophon no longer has anything to teach us, and he has not had anything to teach us since we left the Syrian Gates. I am reading Philistus.'

'Isn't he a Sicilian writer?'

'He is the historian of Dionysius of Syracuse who seventy years ago conquered a Phoenician city on an island, just like Tyre – Motya.'

'And how?'

'Sit down and look,' Alexander took a straw and some ink and began sketching out a drawing on a sheet. 'This is the island and this is the mainland. Dionysius built a causeway to the island and had his siege machines transported along it, then he lined up his newly devised harpoon catapults, and sank many ships by puncturing their hulls and burned all the others by launching fireballs.'

'You want to build a causeway to Tyre? But that's a distance of at least two stadia.'

'Just like Motya. If Dionysius managed it, I can manage it too. Tomorrow we will start demolishing the old city and we will use the material for the causeway. They have to realize that I am not joking.'

Hephaestion gulped, 'Demolish the old city?'

'That's it exactly – demolish the old city and throw it into the sea.'

'As you wish, Alexander.'

Hephaestion left to pass the orders on to his companions while the King returned to his reading.

The next day he summoned all the engineers and mechanics who were on the expedition. They came with their instruments and with material for drawing and taking notes. Diades of Larissa, a pupil of Phayllus, who had been Philip's chief engineer, was their leader; he was the man who had built the assault towers which had demolished the walls of Perinthus.

'My illustrious engineers,' said the King, 'this is a battle which cannot be won without you. We will defeat the enemy on your drawing boards rather than on the battlefield. Indeed there will be no battlefield here at Tyre.'

From the window they could see reflections from the water around the high bastions of the city and the engineers understood exactly what the King meant.

'Well, this is my plan,' Alexander continued. 'We will build a causeway to the island, while you will design and build towers which are higher than the walls.'

'Sire,' Diades pointed out, 'that means towers higher than one hundred and fifty feet.'

'I imagine it does mean that,' replied the King unperturbed. 'These machines will have to be invulnerable and equipped with battering-rams and completely new catapults. I need machines capable of throwing rocks two hundred pounds in weight a distance of some eight hundred feet.'

The illustrious engineers looked one another in the face, all of them with an expression of helplessness. Diades remained silent, tracing apparently meaningless lines on a sheet of papyrus while Alexander stared at him. Everyone felt the King's gaze weighing more than the rocks their catapults were supposed to throw. Finally the expert lifted his head and said, 'It can be done.'

'Good. So you can start working on it straight away.'

In the meantime, outside, the old city resounded to the cries and shouts of the people who were being chased from their homes, together with the crashing and rumbling as roofs and walls came tumbling down. Hephaestion had had small suspended battering-rams mounted to help with the demolition. Over the following days teams of woodcutters, escorted by Agrianian shock troops, went up into the mountains to cut Lebanon cedars to be sliced into planks for constructing the machines.

Work on the causeway continued day and night, in shifts. Carts drawn by oxen and mules were used to transport the material to be thrown into the sea. From their high walls the inhabitants of Tyre laughed and mocked the Macedonians, making fun of their efforts. But by the end of the fourth month of work they had stopped laughing.

One morning, at daybreak, the sentries on duty on the battlements were shocked to see two colossal machines, each over one hundred and fifty feet high, coming towards them, creaking and groaning their way along the new dyke. These were the largest siege machines ever to have been built and as soon as they reached the end of the causeway they were put into action. Enormous rocks and crackling fireballs hissed through the air and crashed on to the battlements, spreading destruction and terror through the city.

The inhabitants of Tyre responded almost immediately by setting up catapults on the walls and aiming them at the Macedonians, who were still working on the causeway and the siege machines.

Alexander then had the wooden shelters and mobile roofs brought into action, all of them protected by animal skins which had not been tanned and which therefore could not catch fire. Work on the causeway continued almost undisturbed. The machines were pushed even further forward and their aim became ever more precise and deadly. If things had continued that way the walls would have been under close threat in a short time.

In the meantime the Sidon and Byblos fleets had arrived, together with ships from Cyprus and Rhodes which had been put under Nearchus's command, but the Tyre fleet, moored up in its inaccessible harbours, refused to do battle. In fact they were preparing a devastating surprise counterattack.

One moonless evening, after a day of incessant battering, two triremes came out of the port towing a fire-ship – an enormous vessel, completely hollow and filled with incendiary material. From its bow there protruded two long wooden beams from which two containers hung, each full of pitch and naphtha. When they were close to the causeway, the triremes increased the rhythm of the rowing to the maximum possible before releasing the fire-ship after having set it and the forward beams alight.

The vessel, at the centre of a roaring vortex of flames, moved forwards under its impetus, while the two triremes veered to each side. The burning mass ran aground on the edge of the causeway, not far from the assault towers. The two beams on the bow had been consumed now by the flames and they snapped, dropping the two incendiary containers, which exploded, spreading fire everywhere, attacking the bases of the two towers.

Macedonian counterattack teams ran immediately from the guard posts to put out the blaze, but from the triremes there now came armed assault troops who engaged them in battle. The fighting was fierce and frightful against the warm red of the fire, in the smoke and the whirling of the sparks, in the air which was unbreathable now because of the thick fumes from the naphtha and pitch. The fire-ship disintegrated in one last final flash and the two towers were completely enveloped in flames.

The very height of the constructions increased the internal draught of the fire so that the flames and the sparks rose more than one hundred feet above the tops of the enormous trellises, lighting up the entire gulf as though it were daylight and throwing a blood-coloured reflection against the bastions of the city.

From the top of the walls came the jubilant cries of the inhabitants of Tyre, and the massacre of the troops who had landed on the causeway – cut to pieces in a furious counter-attack – together with the destruction of the two triremes, was cold comfort to the Macedonians. Months and months of work, the construction genius of the best engineers in the world, had gone up in smoke in no time.

Alexander, astride Bucephalas, arrived at a gallop along the causeway, rushing through the fires like some fury from hell. He stopped just a short distance from the towers at the very moment in which they collapsed noisily in an explosion of flames, smoke and sparks.

His companions immediately rushed up to him, followed by the engineers and the technicians who had built those wondrous machines. The chief engineer, Diades of Larissa, looked on stone-faced, his eyes full of helpless anger, but his expression itself betrayed not the slightest sign of emotion.

Alexander dismounted, looked long and hard at the city walls and then at the destroyed machines and finally at his engineers, who seemed to be paralysed before the spectacle, and ordered: 'Rebuild them.'

54

A FEW DAYS LATER, while Alexander's engineers sought to find a way of rebuilding the machines as quickly as possible, a violent storm irreparably damaged the causeway they had worked so hard to build. It was as though the gods had suddenly turned their backs on their chosen one, and morale among the Macedonian men was sorely tested by this series of reverses.

The King became intractable and unapproachable, often riding alone along the seashore, looking out to the walled island whose inhabitants had dared mock him, or sitting on a rock contemplating the breaking of the waves on the shore.

Barsine was also in the habit of riding along the shore at dawn, before closing herself away in her tent with her handmaids, and one day she met him. He was walking, followed by Bucephalas, and his thigh still bore the scar of the wound received at Issus. His long hair was blown here and there by the wind and almost covered his face. Once more, just like the last time she had seen him, Barsine found herself shivering, almost as though the man there before her were some unreal being.

He looked at her, but said nothing, and she dismounted so as not to tower over him. She lowered her head and murmured, 'Sire.'

Alexander approached, touched her cheek lightly with the palm of his hand and looked into her eyes, tilting his head slightly towards his right shoulder as he always did when moved by deep, intense feelings. She closed her eyes because she was unable to bear the strength of his gaze, which shone through his hair as it blew in the wind.

The King surprised her with a sudden, passionate kiss, then he leaped on to Bucephalas and galloped off along the sand and the foam of the breaking waves. When Barsine turned to look at him, he was already far off, wrapped in clouds of iridescent spray raised by the stallion's hooves.

She returned to her tent and gave her emotions free rein as she fell, crying, on to her bed.

*

His anger assuaged, Alexander took the situation in hand once again and summoned an extended war council consisting of his generals, his architects, his engineers, together with Nearchus and the captains of the fleet.

'Events here are not the result of the wrath of the gods, but rather the result of our own stupidity. We will remedy this and Tyre will have no escape. Firstly, the causeway: our captains will study the winds and the currents in this channel and will instruct the architects accordingly, so that they may design a new structure which makes use of the strength and direction of the natural elements rather than countering them.

'Secondly, the siege engines,' he said, turning to Diades and his engineers. 'If we wait for completion of the causeway we will waste too much time. We have to make sure that the inhabitants of Tyre feel themselves to be under constant threat. They must realize that they will have no peace, neither by day nor by night. We will have two teams working at the same time – one will design and build the siege engines, which will advance along the causeway as soon as it is ready, the other will design floating assault engines.'

'Floating, Sire?' asked Diades, his eyes wide open.

'Exactly. I don't know how, but I am sure you will manage to do it, and soon. My companions have the job of quashing the tribes which inhabit the mountains of Lebanon so that our woodcutters may work undisturbed. When spring comes round once more we will take Tyre. I am sure of this, and I will explain why: I had a dream last night – I dreamed that Hercules appeared before me up on the walls of the city and with a gesture he invited me to join him up there.

'I recounted the dream to Aristander and he interpreted it immediately – I will enter Tyre and offer a sacrifice to the hero in his temple within the walls. I want this news to be spread among our men, so that they too are certain of our victory.'

'It will be done, Alexander,' said Eumenes, and he thought to himself that the coming of this dream was most convenient.

Work began again immediately. The causeway was to be rebuilt following instructions from the mariners of Cyprus and Rhodes who knew those waters well, while Diades, who had the most demanding task, designed assault towers each mounted on a platform fixed across the main decks of two warships bound side by side. In the space of a month two such structures were completed, and as soon as a calm day came along, the crews began to row them into position under the walls of Tyre. When they were close enough, the vessels were anchored and the battering-rams began crashing incessantly into the stone blocks.

The inhabitants of Tyre soon reacted and sent out divers in the night to cut the ropes anchoring the vessels, sending them adrift out towards the rocks. Nearchus, who was on watch in command of the royal quinquereme, immediately sounded the alarm and set off with ten or so ships towards the floating platforms which were struggling to manoeuvre because of the wind. He came alongside them, threw lines with hooks over the gunwales, and then towed them back into position, his crew breaking their backs as they rowed. The anchor ropes were replaced with iron chains, and the battering began once again. The Tyrians, however, in the meantime had lined the outside of the walls with sacks full of seaweed to soften the blows of the battering-rams. Tyre's stubborn resistance seemed to have no limits.

One day, while Alexander was up in the mountains engaged in operations against the increasingly aggressive Lebanese tribes, a ship from Macedonia moored at the new causeway. It brought supplies and messages and a rather special visitor, who was announced to General Parmenion. It was the King's old tutor, Leonidas, in his eighties now, who, having heard of his pupil's great enterprise, had decided to set off to meet him and congratulate him before dying. When the news spread all his other pupils wanted to see him – Seleucus, Leonnatus,

Craterus, Perdiccas, Philotas, Ptolemy, Hephaestion and Lysimachus; they all arrived shouting like children and crying out in chorus the old rhyme that used to drive him into a rage:

> 'Ek korì korì koróne!
> Ek korì korì koróne!

'Here comes the old crow!'

Then they started clapping their hands in rhythm, as they shouted: *'Didáskale! Didáskale! Didáskale!'*

On hearing them calling 'Teacher! Teacher! Teacher!' just as they used to do in greeting him every morning as they sat in the classroom with their slates on their knees, old Leonidas felt moved, but he kept his emotions well hidden and immediately sorted them out.

'Silence!' exclaimed the toothless old man. 'You're just the usual unruly lot! And I bet you haven't read a single book since you left home.'

'Hey, teacher!' shouted Leonnatus. 'You can't start with lessons now, can't you see we're busy here?'

'You really shouldn't have set out on such a voyage,' said Ptolemy. 'The weather's so bad, it's wintertime now. Why have you come?'

'Because I heard a tale of my boy's achievements and I wanted to see him before giving up the ghost.'

'And us?' asked Hephaestion. 'We're not bad either, you know.'

'As for giving up the ghost, Teacher, there's plenty of time for that,' said Perdiccas. 'You could have waited for the fine weather, for example.'

'Ah!' replied Leonidas, 'I know what I am doing, I have no need of advice from you children. Where is Alexander?'

'The King is up in the mountains,' explained Hephaestion. 'He is sorting out the Lebanese tribes who are still loyal to Darius.'

'Take me to the mountains then.'

'But really . . .' Ptolemy began.

'There's snow up there, Teacher,' Leonnatus grinned. 'You'll catch a chill.'

Leonidas, however, was resolute. 'This ship sets sail on its return voyage in five days' time and if I don't see Alexander then I will have come all this way for nothing. I want to see him again. And that is an order.'

Leonnatus shook his ruffled head and shrugged his shoulders, 'He's still our old teacher,' he grumbled. 'He hasn't changed one bit.'

'I'll have silence from you, you idiot! I remember, you know, I remember the frogs in my soup,' croaked the old man.

'Well then, who's going to take him up there?' asked Leonnatus.

Lysimachus stepped forward. 'I'll take him and that way I can deliver the messages as well.'

They set off the following day with an escort of *hetairoi* and reached Alexander towards evening. The King was amazed and much moved by the most unexpected visit. He took the old man into his care and dismissed Lysimachus, who returned to the camp down by the shore.

'You have been most reckless, *Didáskale*, to come all the way up here. It is dangerous – we must go up even higher to reach our auxiliary troops, the Agrianians, who are guarding the pass.'

'I am not afraid of anything. And tonight we will chat a little, you must have many things to tell me.'

They set off, but Leonidas's mule could not keep up with the soldiers' horses and so Alexander let them go ahead while he remained behind with his old teacher. At one point, after darkness had fallen, they found themselves before a fork in the road: the ground in both directions showed signs of horses' hooves and Alexander intuitively chose one of the paths, but he was soon in isolated, deserted country that he had never seen before.

The darkness had thickened and with it had come a cold wind from the north. Leonidas was numb now and he gathered his woollen cloak around his shoulders as best he could. Alexander looked at him, saw how much he was feeling the cold, his watery eyes full of exhaustion, and he felt a deep sympathy well up inside him. This old man, who had crossed the sea to be with him, would not see the night through in this wind. It was clear that Alexander had taken the wrong road, but it was too late now to go back and reach the others and, what was more, they could see almost nothing now. He had to light a fire somehow, but how exactly? He had no embers, nor could he see any dry wood nearby – all of the branches were sodden and covered with snow and the weather was worsening rapidly.

Suddenly he saw a fire glowing in the darkness, not far off, and then another. He said, 'Teacher, don't move from this position, I'll be back straight away. I'll leave Bucephalas with you.'

The horse protested with a snort, but Alexander reassured him and he stayed with Leonidas while Alexander slipped through the darkness towards the fires. They were enemy soldiers getting ready for the night and the fires had been lit to warm themselves and to cook by.

Alexander approached one of the cooks, who was putting some meat on a skewer. As soon as the man moved away to do something else, Alexander crawled over to the fire, grabbed a thick stick with glowing embers on one end, covered it with his cloak and turned back towards Leonidas. But just then the noise of a snapping twig gave him away. One of the enemy soldiers shouted out, 'Who goes there?' and approached the edge of the darkness, his sword unsheathed. Alexander hid behind a tree, his eyes watering because of the smoke, his breath held to stop himself coughing or sneezing. Fortunately for him, just at that moment another soldier, who had moved off to relieve himself in the woods, returned towards the camp.

'Ah, it's you,' said the soldier as he sheathed his sword just a few steps away from Alexander. 'Come on, supper's almost ready.'

The King slipped away again, careful this time not to make any noise, still keeping the smoking ember well hidden. It began to snow and the wind became even icier, as sharp as a blade – the old man must have been at the very limit of his endurance.

He reached him soon after, 'I am here, *Didáskale*. I have brought you a present,' he said, showing him the glowing stick. He then found a sheltered spot under a hidden rock and began blowing on the embers until the flames took hold. He added twigs and then branches until there were more flames than smoke and plenty of warmth.

Leonidas regained colour and some life. Alexander went to the pannier that was strapped to Bucephalas and took out some bread, which he crumbled for his toothless teacher, then he sat alongside him, near the fire.

Leonidas began chewing on the bread. 'Well then, my boy, is it true that you have taken Achilles's weapons, and his shield, the one Homer describes? And Halicarnassus? They say the Mausoleum is as high as the Parthenon and the temple of Hera at Argos put one on top of the other – is such a thing possible? And the Halys? You have seen it, my boy. I find it difficult to believe that it can be three times as wide as our Haliakmon, but you have seen it and you will know the truth. And the Amazons? Is it true that the tomb of the Amazon Penthesilea is near the Halys? And then I was wondering if the Cilician Gates are really as narrow as they say they are and . . .'

'*Didáskale*,' Alexander stopped him, 'you want to know many things. It is best if I answer one question at a time. As far as Achilles's weapons are concerned, things went more or less like this . . .'

And he talked with his teacher all night long and he shared his cloak with him, after having risked his life to defend him from the cold of the mountain. Safe and sound, they met up with the others the following day and because Alexander did not want him to run the risk of another winter crossing, he asked Leonidas to stay on at Tyre. He would set off again when the good weather returned.

55

THE NEW CAUSEWAY was ready towards the end of winter and its upper surface was levelled with beaten-down soil, to facilitate the passage of the new assault towers, which Diades had constructed incredibly quickly. On the floors corresponding to the level of the battlements, he had located batteries of catapults with torsion springs which launched heavy iron bolts horizontally, and on the top, dominating everything, were the ballistae. These devices threw not only rocks in an arching trajectory, but fireballs as well – incendiary devices steeped in pitch, oil and naphtha.

The Tyrians' reaction was fierce and the battlements seethed with soldiers, like the top of an anthill after a child has poked it with a stick. They too had mounted tens of catapults on the parapets and when they saw the invaders trying to burn the city gates, they poured down white-hot sand which they had heated in bronze shields over a blazing fire.

The sand penetrated the Macedonians' clothes and entered under their armour. The pain was terrible and it drove them to throw themselves into the sea as they sought relief from it. Others took off their breastplates, immediately presenting sitting targets for the archers, while others again were run through by harpoons and hooks launched from above by strange new machines and then dragged upwards to be left hanging and shouting until death put them out of their misery. The blood-curdling cries of these poor souls were a torment for the King, who could find no rest, neither by day nor by night. He prowled around at all hours like a hungry lion outside a sheep-pen. And his soldiers too became progressively more brutalized at the sight of such horrors.

Alexander, however, was reluctant to lead the final attack which would inevitably finish in a massacre and he tried to think of other, less drastic solutions that might save his honour and leave some way out for the Tyrians, whose great valour and extraordinary tenacity he greatly admired.

He took advice from Nearchus, of all his men the one with most chance of understanding the situation and the mentality of a city of seafaring people.

'Listen,' the admiral said to him, 'we have already wasted almost seven months here and we have suffered considerable losses. I think you should move on with the army and leave me to continue the blockade. I have one hundred warships now and others will arrive from Macedonia. No one will enter or exit from Tyre until they surrender, and then I will offer them honourable peace terms.

'Tyre is a wonderful city from every possible point of view – its mariners have sailed to the Pillars of Hercules and beyond. It is said that they have visited lands no other human being has ever seen and that they even know the course that leads to the Isles of the Blessed, which lie beyond the Ocean. Consider things carefully, Alexander, when this city forms part of your empire, is it not better that it should be preserved as it is rather than destroyed altogether?'

The King reflected long and hard on these words, but then he recalled some other news he had received recently. 'Eumolpus of Soloi informs me that the Carthaginians have offered assistance to Tyre and that the arrival of their fleet may well be imminent. And let us not forget that the Persians are still navigating in the Aegean and they might suddenly swoop on us here if I were to leave. No, the Tyrians must surrender. But I will leave them one last way out.'

So he decided to send another embassy to the city and chose the oldest and wisest of his councillors to participate in it. Leonidas came to hear of the initiative and asked to see the King.

'My boy, let me go as well. You won't remember, but your father Philip entrusted me with several secret missions, extremely delicate matters, and I was always successful, if I may say so, in a most accomplished manner.'

Alexander shook his head, 'It's out of the question, Didáskale. This affair is extremely risky and I have no wish to expose you pointlessly to . . .'

Leonidas put his hands on his hips. 'Pointlessly?' he asked. 'You have no idea what you are saying, my boy. This mission has no chance of success without your old Leonidas. I am the most expert and capable man you have available to you, and let me add that you were still wetting the bed when I first led a delegation on your father's orders, may his name live on for eternity. It was a mission to deal with the ferocious and barbarian Triballians and I managed to reduce them to the meekest of behaviour without any violence whatsoever. Do you still read the *Iliad*?'

'Of course I still read it, *Didáskale*,' replied the King. 'Every evening.'

'Well, then? Who did Achilles send as an envoy to the chiefs of the Achaeans? Was it not perhaps his old teacher Phoenix? And since you are the new Achilles, it goes without saying that I am the new Phoenix. Let me go, I tell you, and I guarantee I will succeed in bringing those blockheads to see reason.'

Leonidas was so decided that Alexander felt unable to deny him this moment of glory and gave him the job. He then sent his delegates off on a ship flying flags of truce, their mission to negotiate the surrender of the city. Understandably anxious, he went into his tent at the end of the causeway to await the outcome. But time passed and nothing happened.

Towards midday Ptolemy entered, his face dark and solemn.

'Well?' Alexander asked. 'What is their response?'

Ptolemy gestured to follow him outside, and from there he pointed to the highest towers of the city of Tyre. Five crosses had been placed up there, each with a blood-covered body nailed to it. Leonidas's was clearly distinguishable because of his bald head and his skeletal limbs.

'They tortured and crucified them,' said Ptolemy.

Alexander was dumbstruck, paralysed by the sight before them. His face darkened just as the sky did, black clouds deepening the intense darkness in his left eye.

Then, suddenly, he let out a cry, an inhuman howl that seemed to come from his very innards. The raging fury of Philip and the ferocious barbarism of Olympias exploded within him at one and the same instant, unleashing a blind and devastating rage. But the King immediately regained his composure, from somewhere he found a solemn and disturbing calm, like the calm of the sky before the storm.

He called Hephaestion and Ptolemy to his side. 'My weapons!' her ordered. Ptolemy nodded to his adjutants who replied, 'At your service, Sire!' and they ran off to get things ready and to dress him in his most shining armour, while another brought the royal standard with the Argead star.

'Trumpets!' Alexander ordered again. 'Give the signal for all the towers to attack!'

The trumpets blared and shortly afterwards the din of the battering-rams hammering the walls and the hissing of the missiles launched from the catapults and the *ballistae* resounded across the gulf. Then he turned to his admiral: 'Nearchus!'

'At your service, Sire!'

Alexander pointed to one of the assault towers, the one nearest the walls. 'Take me up there on to that platform, but in the meantime take the fleet out, break into the harbour and sink all the ships you meet.'

Nearchus looked up at the ever-darkening sky, but he obeyed and had himself transported together with the

King and his companions on the quinquereme flagship. He immediately gave orders to lower all the sails and to take all the masts down, then he hoisted the battle standard and raised the anchors. From all the one hundred ships of the fleet there now came the rumble of the drums beating out in unison the rhythm for the rowers and the sea boiled with foam in the wind and the stirring movement of a thousands of oars.

The flagship reached the platform under a rain of projectiles thrown from the heights of the walls. Alexander jumped from the gunwale, followed by his companions, and they all entered the tower, rushing up the stairs between each floor in an inferno of dust and shouting, in the deafening din of the battering-rams crashing into the walls, in the strident, continuous, rhythmic calling of the men as they kept time with the swing of the wood.

Suddenly he appeared at the very top just as the sky, black as pitch now, was torn asunder by a dazzling flash of lightning. For an instant the spectral pallor of the crucified envoys was illuminated, together with Alexander's golden armour and the vermilion splash of his standard.

A bridge was lowered on to the battlement and the King, followed by his companions, set off on his attack, flanked by Leonnatus, who was armed with an axe, Hephaestion, his sword unsheathed, Perdiccas, bearing a long spear, and Ptolemy and Craterus, resplendent in shining metal. The King was immediately recognizable because of his own dazzling armour, the white crests on his helmet, the red and gold standard, and the archers and all the other defenders of Tyre tried to pick him out. One of the assault team, a Lyncestian by the name of Admetus, threw himself forwards, anxious to display his courage before the King, and was cut down, but Alexander took his place immediately, wielding his sword left and right and crushing enemy soldiers with blows from his shield, while Leonnatus cleared the way on his right flank with the devastating force of his cleaver.

The King was already on the battlements and threw a Tyrian to the sea below while he cut another one open from the chin to the groin and proceeded to throw a third one down on the other side, to the houses below. Perdiccas ran a fourth one through with his spear, lifted him up like a harpooned fish and threw him into a group of his fellow soldiers as they approached. Alexander shouted ever louder now, dragging the torrent of his own soldiers behind him, and his fury reached its climax, almost as though it were fed by the rumble of the thunderclaps that shook both sky and earth from the celestial heights to the infernal abyss. He advanced along the battlement, unstoppable now, running now, heedless of the rain of arrows and iron bolts launched by the catapults. He ran towards Leonidas's crucifix, not far from him as he charged on. The defenders lined up to push him back, but he knocked them aside as though they were puppets, one after another. Leonnatus, with his immeasurable energy, struck out blindly in the ruck with his axe, causing sparks to fly from the Tyrian shields and helmets, shattering swords and spears into fragments.

Finally the King found himself under the cross where a catapult had been positioned with its crew. He shouted:

'Take control of this catapult and use it against the others! Get this man off that cross! Get him down!' And while his companions took control of the small square, he himself spotted a box of tools next to the catapult and grabbed a pair of pincers, leaving his shield to crash to the ground.

An enemy archer took aim at that precise moment from just twenty feet away and pulled his string tight, but then a voice rang out in the King's ear – it was his mother's voice, full of anguish, calling out to him: '*Aléxandre!*' And, miraculously, the King spotted the danger. In a flash he pulled his dagger from his belt and threw it at the archer, planting it firmly into the man's throat, into the hollow between his collarbones.

His companions formed a wall with their shields and he extracted the nails, one by one, from the tortured limbs of his teacher. At that moment he saw before his eyes the naked limbs of another old man one bright afternoon at Corinth – Diogenes, the wise man with peace in his eyes, and his soul melted in his heart. He murmured, '*Didáskale . . .*' and somehow Leonidas heard the word and his vital force, all gone now, returned for an instant, just long enough for him to move slightly and open his eyes.

'My boy, I am afraid I did not manage . . .' Then he collapsed, truly dead now, in Alexander's arms.

Suddenly the sky was rent open above the city and the sea, the earth and the small island full of shouting and blood, were all flooded by the torrential rain, by a tempest of wind and hail. But the elements could do nothing to extinguish the fury of the warriors. Outside the harbours, in the raging, foaming waves, the Tyrian fleet was engaged in a desperate battle with Nearchus's powerful quinqueremes. In the city the defenders retreated from house to house, road to road, fighting on their very thresholds to the bitter end.

Some time towards evening the sun created an opening in the clouds, illuminating the dark waters, the crumbling walls, the carcasses of the ships drifting off to sea, the bodies of the drowned. The last pockets of resistance were soon quashed.

Many of the survivors sought refuge in the sanctuaries, embracing images of their gods, and the King gave orders for these people to be spared. But it was impossible to control the soldiers' thirst for revenge against the Tyrians they captured on the streets.

Two thousand of them were crucified along the causeway. Leonidas's body was burned on a pyre and his ashes sent to Macedon where they were buried beneath the plane tree. It was in the shade of that tree that he used to teach his pupils, when the weather was fine.

56

ALEXANDER GAVE ORDERS for the fleet to proceed south-wards and to take the disassembled war engines to Gaza, the last stronghold before the desert which separated Palestine from Egypt.

Ten ships were sent to Macedonia to enlist new men as replacements for those who had fallen in taking Tyre. It was in this period that the King received a second letter from King Darius:

> Darius, King of Persia, King of Kings, Light of the Aryans and Lord of the Four Corners of the Earth, to Alexander, King of Macedon, Hail!
>
> I want you to know that I fully appreciate your valour, and the good fortune the gods have been most liberal in granting you. Once again I propose that we should become allies and even relatives.
>
> I offer you the hand of my daughter Stateira and if you accept I will grant you dominion over the lands extending from Ephesus to Miletus, *yauna* cities, up to the river Halys, as well as a gift of two thousand silver talents.
>
> I advise you not to challenge fate, because it is a fickle companion and might just turn its back on you at any moment. Do not forget that should you wish to continue your expedition then you will be an old man

before you have crossed the full extent of my empire, even without engaging combat. Remember too that my territory is protected by enormous rivers – the Tigris, the Euphrates, the Araxes and the Hydaspes, all of them impossible to cross.

Think well on it, and take the wisest decision.

Alexander had it read to his war council and at the end asked, 'What do you think? How should I reply?'

No one dared suggest to the King what he should do and no one spoke, apart from Parmenion, who, because of his age and his prestige, felt he had the right to express his point of view. All he said was, 'I would accept, if I were Alexander.'

The King lowered his head as though wanting to reflect on that statement and then replied, coldly, 'So would I, if I were Parmenion.'

The old general stared at him in pained surprise; it was clear he was profoundly offended. He stood and walked away in silence. Alexander's companions looked at one another dumbfounded, but the King simply continued, his tone composed and calm.

'Of course, General Parmenion's point of view is understandable, but I imagine you all realize that Darius is in fact offering me nothing, apart from his daughter, which I have not already conquered. On the contrary, he asks me implicitly to relinquish all of the provinces and all of the cities east of the Halys which have cost us so much. We will go on ahead. We will take Gaza and then Egypt – the oldest and richest country in the entire world.'

So he replied to the Great King with a curt rejection

and set off marching along the coast, while the fleet, led by Nearchus and Hephaestion, proceeded in convoy.

Gaza was a well-appointed fortress, but its walls were of brick and it stood on a clayey hill some fifteen stadia from the sea. The commander of the stronghold was a black eunuch by the name of Batis, very brave and loyal to King Darius – he refused to surrender.

Alexander therefore decided to attack and rode round the walls to see where he might be able to dig pits and where the engines might best attack the bastions. Both of these matters were complicated by the sandy ground which surrounded almost the entire hill.

As he was thinking, a crow passed overhead and let a tuft of grass it was carrying in its claws fall on to his head. The bird continued on towards Gaza, where it perched and soon found itself stuck in the bitumen which had been used to cover the walls and which had melted in the heat of the sun.

Alexander was struck by this scene and asked Aristander, who now followed him everywhere like a shadow, 'What does all this mean? Is it an omen from the gods?'

The seer lifted his gaze towards the burning disc of the sun and then looked with his pinpoint eyes at the crow struggling with its wings stuck in the glue-like bitumen. The bird gave another tug and finally managed to free itself, ripping out some feathers and leaving them trapped on the walls.

'You will take Gaza, but if you do it today, you will be wounded.'

Alexander decided to fight anyway, so that his army would not think that he was afraid of an omen of pain, and while his teams of miners set to digging tunnels under the walls to bring them down, he led a frontal attack on the city along the ramp that rose up to the city.

Batis, counting on his favourable position, came out with the army and counterattacked violently, lining up his Persian soldiers together with ten thousand Arab and Ethiopian mercenaries, men with black skin whom Alexander's soldiers had never seen before.

Even though his old wound from Issus still caused him some pain, the King took his place in the front line with his foot-soldiers and sought a direct clash with Batis, a black giant gleaming with sweat as he valiantly led his Ethiopians.

'By the gods!' shouted Perdiccas. 'That man has certainly got balls, even if he has been castrated!'

Alexander used his sword to mow down the enemy soldiers who challenged him, but then a catapult crew at the top of a tower spotted his red standard, the crests of his helmet and his shining armour and took aim.

Far off, up in another tower, in the palace at Pella, Olympias felt the mortal danger and sought desperately to cry out: '*Aléxandre!*' But her voice would not carry through the ether, blocked as it was by a bad omen, and the bolt was let loose from the catapult. It hissed through the stagnant air and hit its mark, passing through Alexander's shield and his breastplate and planting itself in his shoulder. The King fell to the ground and a group of enemy soldiers rushed to finish him off and strip him of his weapons, but Perdiccas, Craterus and Leonnatus drove them all back with their shields and ran many of them through with their spears.

The King, twisting in pain, cried out, 'Call Philip!'

The physician came immediately. 'Quick! Out of the way! Out of my way!' and two bearers put the King on a stretcher and swiftly carried him from the battle.

Many saw him mortally pale with the heavy bolt protruding from his shoulder and so the rumour spread that the King was dead and the army began to waver against the enemy attack.

Alexander realized what was happening from the shouts and cries that reached his ears: he took Philip's hand – his physician was running alongside him – and said, 'I have to return to the front line – pull out the bolt and cauterize the wound.'

'But that won't be enough!' exclaimed the doctor. 'Sire! If you go back down there you will die.'

'No. I have already been wounded. The first part of the omen has come true. The second part remains to be fulfilled – I will enter Gaza before sunset.'

They were at the royal tent now and Alexander repeated, 'Extract the bolt now. That is an order.'

Philip obeyed, and while the King bit the leather of his belt to stifle his cries, the physician cut his shoulder with a surgical instrument and extracted the point of the bolt. The blood flowed copiously from the wound, but Philip immediately took a red-hot blade from a brazier and plunged it into the cut. The tent filled with a nauseating smell of burning flesh and the King let out a long moan of pain.

'Sew it up,' he said through his clenched teeth.

The doctor sewed, stemmed the flow of blood, and applied a tight bandage.

'And now put my armour back on.'

'Sire, I beg you . . .' Philip tried to make him see reason.

'Put my armour back on!'

The men obeyed and Alexander returned to the battle-field where his army, disheartened now, was losing ground to the enemy thrust. This despite the fact that Parmenion had called out another two battalions of the phalanx in support.

'The King is alive!' shouted Leonnatus in his thunderous voice. 'The King lives! *Alalalài!*'

'*Alalalài!*' replied the soldiers and they started fighting again with renewed vigour.

Alexander again took up his position in the front line, despite the fierce pain, and he pulled the rest of the army with him, amazed as they were by his sudden reappearance, as if they were being led not by a human being, but by some invincible and invulnerable god.

Their opponents were soon overrun and pushed towards the gates of the city. Many of them fell wounded and subsequently died simply because they failed to reach safety on the other side of the walls.

But while the gates were being closed and the Macedonians shouted their victory cry to the skies, a soldier who had seemed to be dead suddenly threw off the shield that was covering him and thrust his sword deep into Alexander's left thigh.

The King ran the man through with his javelin, but he collapsed immediately after this final effort, racked by pain from the wounds he had received.

For three days and nights he was consumed by a raging

fever while his men continued to dig ceaselessly into the depths of the great tumulus on which the city of Gaza rose.

Barsine came to visit on the fourth day and she stood there looking at him for a long time, moved by the reckless courage which had led the young man to bear so much pain. She saw Leptine weeping sadly in a corner, then she moved over to her and kissed her lightly on the forehead before leaving, silently as she had entered.

Alexander regained consciousness that evening, but the pain was unbearable. He looked at Philip, who was sitting by the side of the bed, his eyes red with so many sleepless nights and said: 'Give me something for the pain . . . I cannot bear it. I think I am going mad.'

The doctor hesitated, then, on seeing the King's face contracted, almost distorted by the stabbing pains, he realized just how much he was suffering. 'The drug I am about to administer,' he said, 'is a most potent one and as yet I do not know all of its effects, but you cannot bear this pain for long without going out of your mind, so we must take the risk.'

At that moment they heard the distant noise of the walls of Gaza collapsing, thanks to the pits which had been dug under them, and soon came the shouting of the soldiers engaged in furious combat. The King began mumbling, as though completely out of his mind, 'I must go to them . . . I must go . . . give me something to calm the pain.'

Philip disappeared and returned shortly afterwards with a small jar from which he extracted a dark substance with a most intense smell. He took a little of it and handed it to the King, 'Swallow it,' he ordered, while only the look in his eyes gave away just how apprehensive he was.

Alexander swallowed the substance his doctor had ordered and waited, hoping the pain would desist. The noise of the fighting from the walls provoked a strange and growing feeling of excitement, and, gradually, Alexander's mind began to fill with the ghosts of great warriors from the Homeric epic he had read every evening since adolescence. Suddenly he stood up: the pain was still there, but it had changed now, it was something different and indefinable – a cruel, driving force which filled his breast with a dark, ruthless wrath. The wrath of Achilles.

He walked from the tent as though in a dream. In his ears he heard the words of his physician begging him, 'Do not go, Sire, you are not well. Please stay here.' But these were words that made no sense. He was Achilles now and his duty was to run to the battlefield where his companions were in desperate need of his help.

'Prepare my chariot,' he ordered, and his adjutants, astounded, obeyed. His gaze was absent and glazed, his voice metallic, almost toneless. He climbed up on to the chariot and the driver whipped the horses, guiding them off towards the walls of Gaza.

He lived everything that followed as though he were in some sort of nightmare. All he was aware of was the fact that he was Achilles, driving victorious once, twice, three times around the walls of Troy, dragging behind him in the dust the body of Hector.

When he came to himself he saw his driver pulling on the reins and bringing the chariot to a halt before the ranks of the assembled army. Behind him, tied to the chariot by means of two straps, he saw a body which had been reduced to a bloody mass. Someone explained to him that it was the body of Batis, the heroic defender of Gaza who had been brought to Alexander as a prisoner.

He lowered his gaze in horror and left the scene as quickly as he possibly could, moving in the direction of the sea. There the pain returned, and, sharper than ever now, it racked his exhausted limbs. He returned to his tent in the deep of the night, overwhelmed by shame and remorse, and still tormented by the sharp pains in his shoulder, his chest and his legs.

Barsine heard him moaning in a pain so deep and desperate that she had to go to him. When she arrived, Philip made a gesture telling Leptine to leave them alone.

She sat on his bed, dried his brow which was shining with sweat and moistened his cracked lips with chilled water. When he embraced her and pulled her to himself in his delirium, she dared not push him away.

57

PHILIP WASHED HIS HANDS and began changing the dressings and the bandages on Alexander's wounds. Five days had passed since the massacre of Batis and the King was still in shock because of his actions.

'I think you were under the influence of the drug I had given you. Perhaps it relieved your pain, but it unleashed in you other forces beyond your control. I had no way of knowing . . . no one could have foreseen it.'

'I attacked and tortured a man who was unable to defend himself, a man who merited respect for his valour and his loyalty. I will be judged for this . . .'

Eumenes, sitting alongside Ptolemy on a stool on the other side of the bed, stood up and moved nearer. 'You cannot be judged in the same way as other men,' he said. 'You went beyond all limits, you had frightful wounds, you withstood pain that no one else could ever have borne, you were victorious in combat that no one else would ever have dared engage in.'

'You are not like other men,' continued Ptolemy. 'You are of the same stamp as Hercules and Achilles. Now you have left the conditions and the rules that govern the life of ordinary mortals behind you. Do not torment yourself, Alexander, for the truth is that if Batis had taken you as his prisoner, he would have inflicted even greater atrocities on you.'

Philip in the meantime had finished cleaning the wounds and changing the dressings and he gave his patient an infusion to help calm him and soothe the pain. As soon as Alexander had dozed off, Ptolemy sat down near him, while Eumenes followed Philip out of the tent. The physician understood immediately that the secretary had something to tell him in private.

'What's wrong?' he asked.

'We have received bad news,' replied Eumenes. 'King Alexander of Epirus has been killed in an ambush in Italy. Queen Cleopatra is beside herself with grief and I do not know whether to give her letter to the King.'

'Have you read it?'

'I would never open a sealed letter addressed to Alexander. But the messenger gave me all the news.'

Philip thought for a moment before replying. 'I would say it's better if we don't give it to him. Physically and mentally he is in a delicate state. This news would only lower his spirits even further. It's best if we wait.'

'Until when?'

'I will let you know, if you trust me, that is.'

'I trust you. How is he really?'

'There is and there will continue to be much pain, but he will come out of it. Perhaps you are right, perhaps he is not an ordinary man like the rest of us.'

And Barsine too suffered much in this period, in the grip of remorse for having betrayed the memory of her husband. She simply could not forgive herself for having succumbed to Alexander, but at the same time she was aware of how much he was suffering and she wanted to be with him. She still had her old wet nurse with her, an elderly woman by the name of Artema who of course knew her well and had noticed how much she had changed recently and how preoccupied she appeared to be.

She went to her mistress one evening and asked, 'What is your torment, my girl?'

Barsine lowered her head in silence and cried silently.

'If you don't want to tell me, I cannot make you,' said Artema, but in truth Barsine felt the need to confide in a friend.

'I have succumbed to Alexander, Artema. When he came back from the battle I heard him crying out and groaning, tormented by that immense suffering, and I could not resist. He has been good to me and my sons and I felt duty bound to help him at that moment ... I went to him and I wiped the sweat from his brow, I caressed him. For me he was simply a young man burning up with fever, racked by nightmares, by images of blood and horror.' Artema continued to listen, intent and thoughtful. 'But suddenly he pulled me to himself and embraced me with an irresistible force and I knew not how to refuse him. I don't know how it happened ...' she murmured, her voice quavering. 'I do not know. His pain-racked body seemed to emanate some mysterious perfume and his feverish gaze had an unbearable intensity.' She burst into tears.

'Do not cry, my child,' Artema consoled her. 'You have done nothing wrong. You are young and the life that is left in you will reclaim all its rights in full. What is more, you are a mother living through a time of war and with your children you have fallen into the hands of foreign enemies. Instinct will lead you to seek a union with the man who has power over everyone and can protect your sons against all dangers.

'This is the destiny of every beautiful, desirable woman – she knows that she is an item of prey and she knows that only by offering love or succumbing to man's impulses can she hope for salvation and protection for herself and for her offspring.' Barsine continued to cry, covering her face with her hands. 'But Alexander truly is a most handsome young man who has always shown great kindness of spirit and respect in your regard, who has shown that he deserves your love. You are suffering now because there are two deep and terrible sentiments living within you at one and the same time – the love for a man who no longer exists, a love which has no reason to survive but which refuses to die nevertheless, and the unconscious love for a man whom you reject, because he is an enemy and in some way caused the death of the husband you loved. You have done nothing wrong. When a feeling grows within you, don't repress it, because there is nothing which happens in the hearts of mankind which does not come from the will of Ahura Mazda, the eternal flame, origin of every celestial and terrestrial fire. But remember, Alexander is not like other men. He is like the wind that passes and disappears. And no one can imprison the wind. If you know that you cannot bear separation, then do not succumb to love.'

Barsine dried her eyes and went out into the open air. It was a fine moonlit night, and the rays of the white disc drew a long wake of silver over the still waters. Not far off was the King's pavilion and the flames of the lamps projected his solitary, troubled shadow on the wall. She walked seawards until the water reached her knees and suddenly she thought she smelled his fragrance and heard his voice whispering, 'Barsine.'

It was not possible, and yet he was there behind her, close enough for her to feel his breath.

'I had a dream, I don't remember when,' he said quietly, 'and the dream was that you gave your love to me, that I caressed you all over your body, that I took you gently. But when I awoke I found only this in my bed.' And for a moment he held up a handkerchief of blue byssus before letting it fall and be swallowed up by the waves. 'Is it yours?'

'It was not a dream,' replied Barsine without turning round. 'I came to you because I heard you crying out in your suffering and I sat next to your bed. You embraced me with such strength that I knew not how to reject you.'

Alexander put his hands on her hips and turned her round to face him. The moonlight bathed her face in an ivory pallor and it shone in the depths of her dark gaze.

'Now you may do so, Barsine. Now you may reject me while I ask you to take me into your arms. In a matter of a few months I have suffered and inflicted all sorts of wounds, I have lost all thoughts of my youth, I have touched the bottom of every abyss, I have forgotten that I ever was a child, that I ever had a father, a mother. The fire of war has scorched my heart and I live every instant seeing death riding by my side, yet death never manages to strike me. It is in those instants that I know what it means to be immortal and this fills me with amazement and with fear. Do not reject me, Barsine, now that my hands can finally caress your face, do not deny me your love, your embrace.'

His body was as scarred as a battlefield – there was no part of his skin that was free of scratches, scars, or grazes. Only his face was wonderfully intact, and his long hair fell softly around his shoulders, framing his countenance with an intense and poignant grace.

'Love me, Barsine,' he said, pulling her to himself, holding her to his chest.

The moon disappeared behind the clouds as they advanced from the west and he kissed her with passion. Barsine responded to that kiss as though she had suddenly been enveloped in the flames of a fire, but at that very same moment in the depths of her heart she felt the vice-like grip of a dark despair.

*

The army set off again on its march towards the desert, just as soon as the King was well enough to travel. After seven days they came to the city of Pelusium, gateway to Egypt, on the eastern side of the Nile delta. The Persian governor, aware that he was completely isolated, surrendered and handed over the city together with the royal treasure.

'Egypt!' exclaimed Perdiccas as he looked over the seemingly endless landscape from the towers of the fortress – the slow waters of the rivers, the waving heads of the papyruses along the banks of the canals, the palms loaded with dates as big as walnuts.

'I never really believed it actually existed,' said Leonnatus. 'I thought it was just one of the tales old Leonidas used to tell us.'

A girl wearing a black wig, her eyes made up with bistre, her body wrapped in a linen gown so tight she almost seemed naked, served the young conquerors palm wine and sweetmeats.

'Are you still sure you cannot bear the Egyptians?' Alexander asked Ptolemy, who could not keep his eyes off the beautiful young maid.

'In truth I'm not so sure any more,' replied Ptolemy.

'Look! Look out there, in the middle of the river! What are those monsters?' Leonnatus suddenly shouted, pointing to a place where the water seemed to be boiling and there were glimpses of scaly backs which shone in the sun for a few instants before disappearing.

'Crocodiles,' explained the interpreter, a Greek from Naucratis by the name of Aristoxenus. 'They're everywhere, and don't forget it – swimming in these waters can be extremely dangerous. So be careful because . . .'

'And those things over there? Look at those!' shouted Leonnatus once again. 'They look like enormous pigs.'

'*Hippopotamoi* – that's what we Greeks call them,' explained the interpreter.

'River horses,' said Alexander. 'By Zeus, I do believe Bucephalas would feel offended if he knew that we call these beasts horses.'

'It's only a figure of speech,' replied the interpreter. 'They're not at all dangerous because they feed on grasses and weeds, but they can overturn boats with their enormous mass and anyone who falls into the water is then potential prey for the crocodiles.'

'A dangerous country,' said Seleucus, who up until that moment had been admiring the spectacle in silence. 'And what do you think will happen now?' he asked Alexander.

'I do not know, but I believe we might be welcomed in friendship, if we succeed in understanding this people. They give me the impression of being kind and wise, but most proud.'

'That's right,' Eumenes confirmed. 'Egypt has never tolerated any external domination and the Persians have never understood this fact – they have always installed a governor with mercenary troops at Pelusium and all this has achieved is to cause revolt after revolt, all of them subsequently suppressed with violence.'

'And why should things be any different for us?' asked Seleucus.

'They could have been different for the Persians as well, if they had respected the Egyptians' religion and if the Great King had let them invest him as Pharaoh of all Egypt. In a certain sense it's all just a matter of form.'

'A matter of . . . form?' repeated Ptolemy.

'Quite,' said Eumenes. 'Form. A people who live for the gods and for life after death, a people who spend enormous wealth just to import incense to burn in their temples certainly confers great value to matters of form.'

'I think you're right,' said Alexander. 'In any case, we shall discover whether you are soon enough. Tomorrow our fleet should arrive, after which we will go up the Nile to Memphis, the capital.'

Nearchus's and Hephaestion's ships dropped anchor at the mouth of the eastern branch of the delta two days later, and the King and his companions travelled up the Nile to Heliopolis and then Memphis while the army followed by land.

They paraded along the great river before the pyramids, which glinted like diamonds under the sun at its height, and then before the gigantic sphinx, crouched there for millennia to guard over the sleep of the great pharaohs.

'Herodotus writes that thirty thousand men took thirty years to build it,' explained Aristoxenus.

'And do you think that is true?' asked Alexander.

'I think so, even though in this country they tell more stories than any other part of the world, simply because so many of them have been accumulated over the years.'

'Is it true that in the eastern desert there are winged serpents?' Alexander asked again.

'I do not know,' replied the interpreter. 'I have never been there, but it is certainly one of the most inhospitable places on earth. But look, here we are now, approaching our moorings. Those men you can see there in the front line with shaved heads are the priests of the temple of Zeus Ammon. Treat them with respect – they might be able to spare you much trouble and much blood.'

Alexander nodded and prepared to disembark. The first thing he did on stepping on to dry land was to approach the priests reverently and ask to be taken to the temple to pay homage to the god.

The priests looked at one another and quietly

exchanged a few words before replying with polite bows; then they set off in procession towards the grand sanctuary, singing a religious hymn, accompanied by the sound of flutes and harps. As they came to the colonnaded atrium, they spread out in a fanlike formation, as though inviting Alexander to enter. And Alexander did enter, on his own.

The sun's rays penetrated through a hole in the ceiling and then passed through a dense cloud of incense rising from a golden incense-burner positioned at the very centre. The rest of the temple was barely visible in the darkness. Alexander looked around – the temple seemed to be completely deserted and in the midday silence the noises which came from outside seemed to be completely absorbed by the forest of columns supporting the cedar-wood ceiling.

Suddenly the great statue appeared to move – its ruby eyes shone as though animated by some internal light and a deep and vibrant voice resounded through the great columned chamber.

'The last legitimate sovereign of this land was forced to flee into the desert twenty years ago and he has never returned. Are you perhaps his son, born far from the Nile, the son we have been waiting for for years?'

At that moment Alexander understood everything he had ever heard about Egypt and about the spirit of its people and he replied, his voice firm and solid, 'I am.'

'If you are him,' continued the voice, 'then prove it.'

'How?' asked the King.

'Only the god Ammon may recognize you as his son,

but he speaks only through the oracle of Siwa, which stands at the heart of the desert. That is where you must go.'

Siwa, Alexander thought. And he recalled a story his mother had recounted when he was a child – the story of two doves set free by Zeus at the beginning of all time. One had alighted on an oak tree at Dodona, the other on a palm tree at Siwa, and from these places prophecies had begun to be pronounced. She had also told him that she had first felt him move in her belly when she had gone to the oracle at Dodona and that his next birth, a divine birth, would come to pass when he visited the other oracle, at Siwa.

The voice faded and Alexander came out of the great dark chamber, reappearing into the sun in the midst of a joyous exultation of hymn-singing and music.

The bull Apis was led into his presence and the King paid homage to him, crowning his brow with garlands, then personally offering a sacrifice of an antelope to the god Ammon.

The priests, greatly impressed by his reverence, came to him and offered him the keys to the city. Alexander's immediate reaction was to order restoration works on the temple, which here and there was somewhat run down.

58

THE JOURNEY TOWARDS the remote oasis at Siwa began a few days later, when Alexander's wounds appeared to have healed completely. One part of the army marched northwards, while another followed with the fleet. The point fixed for their meeting was in the lagoon not far from the westernmost branch of the Nile delta.

When Alexander arrived there he was very much taken with the wide bay and the island covered with palm trees, sheltering it from the northerly winds and by the wide strip of flat ground which ran behind the beach.

He decided to set up camp there and organized a celebration together with his companions and his army for the success of their expedition and the way they had been greeted peacefully in Egypt. Before the supper degenerated into an orgy, Alexander wanted his friends to listen to some musical performances by Greek and Egyptian artists together with a piece of dramatic bravura from Thessalus, his favourite actor, who gave a masterful interpretation of Oedipus's soliloquy from *Oedipus Coloneus*.

The applause had not yet died down when a visitor for the King was announced.

'Who is it?' asked Alexander.

'A rather strange man,' said Eumenes, looking somewhat bewildered, 'but he claims he knows you very well.'

'Oh yes?' said the King, who was in a good mood. 'Well then, bring him to me. But what is it that's so strange about him?'

'You'll see for yourself shortly,' replied Eumenes and he moved off to fetch the visitor.

As the visitor made his entrance a buzz ran through the entire theatre, accompanied by a few laughs, and everyone's gaze turned towards him. He was a man of about forty, completely naked except for a lion's skin, just as Hercules was said to have worn, with a club in his right hand.

Alexander barely managed to stifle his own laughter at this signal homage to the figure of his ancestor, and, making considerable effort to keep a straight face, asked, 'Who are you, O stranger and guest, who so resembles the hero Hercules, my ancestor?'

'I am Dinocrates,' replied the man, 'a Greek architect.'

'Those are strange clothes for an architect,' said Eumenes.

'What matters,' declared the man, 'is not how one dresses, but the plans one is able to propose and eventually realize.'

'And what plans do you have to propose to me?' asked the King.

Dinocrates clapped his hands and two young men appeared and proceeded to unroll a large sheet of papyrus at Alexander's feet.

'By Zeus!' exclaimed the King. 'What on earth is it?'

Dinocrates was visibly satisfied at having captured the King's attention and began to explain: 'It is indeed an ambitious project, certainly worthy of your greatness and your glory. What I intend to do is to sculpt Mount Athos into the figure of a colossus which bears your features, and this is what you see represented in the drawing before you. In his open hand the giant will hold a city which you will found personally. Is it not extraordinary?'

'Ah yes, it most certainly is extraordinary,' said Eumenes, 'but I wonder if it is feasible.'

Alexander observed the grandiose drawing which depicted him as tall as a mountain with an entire city in his hand and he said, 'I am afraid it might be a trifle beyond my capabilities . . . and then, if I ever had any intention of commissioning such an enormous statue, I would contact an extremely good young sculptor I met when I studied at Mieza with Aristotle. His name is Chares and he was a pupil of Lysippus. I hear tale that one of his dreams is to build a giant of bronze some eighty cubits high. Do you know him?'

'No.'

'It matters not, but in any case I do have a project to suggest to you.'

'So you don't like this idea, Sire?' asked the disappointed architect.

'It's not that I do not appreciate it. It simply seems to be a little . . . too much. My project, on the other hand, can be got under way tomorrow, if you feel that you want to take it on.'

'I most certainly would be honoured, Sire. All you have to do is say the word.'

'In that case follow me,' and the King invited him out

into the open and they walked towards the shore. It was a fine summer's evening and a crescent moon was reflected in the still waters of the bay.

Alexander took off his cloak and spread it on the ground: 'There ... what I want is a plan for a city in the shape of a Macedonian cloak, like this, all of it arranged around the bay here before us.'

'Is that it?' asked Dinocrates.

'That's it,' replied the King. 'I want you to start tomorrow at first light. I must leave here on a journey and when I come back I want to see the houses already standing, the roads already paved, the jetties of the harbour already constructed.'

'I will do what I can, Sire. But who will provide the funds?'

'Eumenes, my secretary general, will deal with all that,' said Alexander, and then he turned to walk back to his tent, leaving the bizarre architect alone in the midst of the deserted plain with his club and his lion skin. 'And make sure you do a good job!' he shouted.

'One last thing, Sire!' shouted Dinocrates in return, before the King rejoined his friends at the banquet. 'What will be this city's name?'

'Alexandria. Its name will be Alexandria, and it will be the most beautiful city in the world.'

*

Work began very soon and Dinocrates, having taken off his lion skin and put on some decent clothes, proved to be up to the job, even though other architects who had been following the expedition for some time were very envious of the fact that the King had entrusted such a commission to a stranger. But Alexander often acted out of instinct, and he was rarely wrong.

There was only one episode which cast something of a shadow over the founding and building of Alexandria. Dinocrates had drawn up the plan of the city, then he had positioned his instruments to mark the layout on the ground. Chalk was used to trace the perimeter, the main roads and the secondary roads, the areas to be used for the main square, the market and the temples. At a certain stage, however, the chalk ran out and, unable to complete his work, he had the army commissariat provide him with sacks of flour to complete the layout. He then asked the King to come and see so that he might have at least an idea of what Alexandria would look like, but while the King was on his way together with his seer Aristander, a flock of birds landed and began pecking away at the flour, wiping out part of the markings.

The seer immediately noticed that Alexander was rather perturbed by the incident, as though it might be a bad omen for him, but he quickly put the King's mind at rest: 'Do not worry, Sire. In fact this is an excellent omen – it means that the city will be so rich and prosperous that people will come here from all over, looking for work and sustenance.' Dinocrates, too, felt relieved by this interpretation and set to his work with renewed vigour, all the more so because in the meantime the chalk had arrived.

That night the King had a beautiful dream. He dreamed that the city had grown, that everywhere there were houses and palaces with wonderful gardens. He dreamed that the bay, protected by the long island, teemed with vessels at anchor unloading all types of goods from all parts of the known world. And he saw a causeway reaching out to the island where a high tower stood – a gigantic tower which spread light in the darkness for the ships approaching Alexandria. And he thought he heard his own voice asking, 'Will I ever see all of this? When will I return to my city?'

The next day he recounted the dream to Aristander and asked him the same question, 'When will I return to my city?'

Aristander turned his back to Alexander at that very moment because a sudden weight descended on his heart, the saddest of premonitions, but quickly he turned once more to face his King and with a tranquil expression on his face said, 'You will return, Sire, I promise you. I know not when, but you will return . . .'

59

THEY SET OFF WESTWARDS with the sea to their right and the limitless desert to the left, and after stopping just five times they reached Paraetonium. This was an outpost which functioned as a meeting-point for the people, in part Egyptian and in part Greek, who came from the city of Cyrene, and the nomadic tribes of the interior – the Nasamones and the Garamantes.

These tribes had split the coast up into sectors, and whenever a wreck took place it was looted by those tribes in whose sector the ship went down. The survivors were sold as slaves at market in Paraetonium. It was said that some two hundred years previously the Nasamones has crossed the mysterious, endless sea of sand and that they had reached, on the other side, an enormous lake populated with crocodiles and hippopotamuses with trees of every type which bore fruit in all the seasons. It was also said that this region housed the cave of Proteus – the god of many forms who lived among seals and who was able to predict the future.

Alexander left part of the army at Paraetonium, under Parmenion's command, to whom he also entrusted Barsine. He went to say goodbye to her the evening before his departure, taking a gift – a necklace of gold and enamel which had once belonged to a queen of the Nile.

'There are no jewels worthy of your beauty,' he said, as he placed it around her neck. 'There is no splendour which can compete with the light in your eyes, there is no enamel which can ever equal the magnificence of your smile. I would give any riches to be able to sit before you and watch you smile. It would give me more joy than kissing your lips, than caressing your hips and your breasts.'

'A smile. That is a gift Ahura Mazda took from me some time ago now, Alexander,' replied Barsine, 'but now that you are setting off on such a long and dangerous journey, I know that I will worry constantly and I know that I will smile when I see you once more.' She kissed him lightly on the lips and then said, 'Come back to me, Alexander.'

The army moved on with a reduced contingent now and Alexander, followed by his companions, set off into the desert in the direction of the sanctuary of Zeus Ammon after having loaded up with water and supplies in sufficient quantities, carried by a hundred or so camels.

Everyone had advised the King not to undertake the journey in midsummer because of the unbearable heat, but he was now convinced that he could face and over-come any obstacle, recover from any wound, challenge any danger, and he wanted his men to be equally aware of this conviction. Following the first two legs of the journey, however, the heat really did become unbearable and the men's and the animals' water consumption increased to the point where there were concerns over their ability to reach Siwa safely.

To add to their troubles, on the third day a sandstorm

broke out, severely testing the men and the animals and completely wiping out the road. After hours and hours of unbearable torment, the cloud of sand cleared and all they could see around them was the infinite, rolling extent of the limitless desert – the stones marking the route had disappeared and there was no other sign of which direction they should take. And the men, walking, sank into the increasingly hot sand to the point where their exposed feet and legs began to suffer burns. They had to wrap material from their tunics and their cloaks right up to their knees, just so that they could keep on going.

On the fourth day many of them began to despair and it was only the King's example which kept them going. Alexander was at the head of the column, on foot just like the humblest of his soldiers, and he always drank last and was happy to eat just a few dates while making sure that everyone had what he needed to survive. In this way he gave all his men sufficient energy and determination to continue.

On the fifth day the water ran out and the horizon was featureless as usual – no sign of life, not even a blade of grass, no shadow of a living being.

'And yet there are people out there,' said the guide, a Greek from Cyrene who was black as coal and whose mother was almost certainly Libyan or Ethiopian. 'If we were to die out here, the horizon would suddenly fill up as if by magic – men would appear like ants from all directions and in no time at all our bodies would be left, stripped of everything, to dry up in the desert sun.'

'A truly pleasant prospect,' said Seleucus, who was just behind them, barely managing to keep up and struggling onwards with his Macedonian wide-brimmed hat on his head.

Just then Hephaestion noticed something and called to his companions, 'Look over there!'

'They're birds,' confirmed Perdiccas.

'Crows,' explained the guide.

'Even more pleasant,' complained Seleucus.

'But it's a good sign,' replied the guide.

'You mean because our carcasses won't go to waste,' said Seleucus.

'But no . . . it's a good sign. It means we are close to an inhabited area.'

'Close for someone with wings, but for us, on foot and without food and water . . .'

Aristander, also walking nearby, suddenly came to a halt: 'Stop!' he ordered.

'What's wrong?' asked Perdiccas. Alexander also stopped and turned towards his seer, who had sat down on the ground and pulled his cloak over his head. A gust of wind blew across the dunes, the sand shining like molten bronze.

'The weather is changing,' said Aristander.

'By Zeus! Not another sandstorm, please!' said Seleucus in desperation. But the gust of wind became stronger and began blowing away the stifling air, bringing with it a vague hint of the freshness of the sea.

'Clouds,' said Aristander, 'there are clouds on their way.'

Seleucus exchanged looks with Perdiccas, as if to say, 'He's delirious.' But the seer really could feel the clouds approaching and it was not long before the grey weather front appeared from the north, darkening the horizon.

'Let's not get our hopes up too high,' said the guide. 'As far as I know it never rains here. Let's start walking again.'

The column set off again into the blinding light, towards the south, but the men kept turning round to look at the clouds as they advanced from the north, ever darker, rent now and then by spasmodic flashes of lightning.

'It may never rain here,' said Seleucus, 'but there's plenty of thunder.'

'You have very acute hearing,' replied Perdiccas. 'I can't hear anything.'

'It's true,' the guide agreed. 'There is thunder. It won't rain, but at least the clouds will provide us with shelter from the sun and the temperature will become bearable.'

An hour later the first drops of rain thumped into the sand and the air filled with the intense and pleasant smell of damp dust. The men, who had been at the end of their tethers, their skin burned, their lips cracked, seemed to go out of their minds – shouting, throwing their hats in the air, opening their dry mouths to capture even just a few drops before they were absorbed into the burning sand.

The guide shook his head, 'You would all do better to save your breath. The rain evaporates in the sun even before it touches the earth and it returns upwards to the sky in the form of a light mist. And that is all we will have.' But even before he had finished speaking, the sparse drops had turned into a light rain and then into lashing sheets of water that fell heavily in the midst of lightning and crashing thunder.

The men stuck their spears in the sand and tied their cloaks to the shafts to gather as much of the liquid as possible. They put their helmets and their shields on the ground, concave side up, and very soon they were able to drink. When the shower finished, the clouds continued across the sky, less dense and compact now, but still enough to provide them with shade for their march.

Alexander had said nothing up until that moment and he continued, lost in his thoughts, as though following some mysterious voice. Everyone turned to look at him, convinced now that they were being led by a superhuman being who would always survive wounds and adversity that would have killed anyone else, a being who could make it rain in the desert and who could even have flowers grow there, should he so wish.

*

The oasis at Siwa appeared on the horizon two days later at dawn. Across the blinding reflection of the sand, the men saw a strip of an incredibly lush green colour. They shouted enthusiastically at the sight, many of them crying on seeing this triumph of life in the midst of that infinite, arid landscape. Others gave thanks to the gods for having saved them from a terrible death, but Alexander continued his silent march as though he had never doubted that they would reach their goal.

The oasis was immense, covered with palm trees laden with dates and nourished by the wonderful spring which gurgled at its very heart. The water was as clear as crystal and it reflected the dark green of the palms and the age-old monuments of Siwa's ancient and mysterious religious community. The men threw themselves into the water immediately, but the physician Philip began shouting, 'Stop! Stop! The water is very very cold. Drink slowly, take small sips.' Alexander was the first to obey, thus setting an example for the others to follow.

What they all found difficult to believe was the fact that they were expected – the priests were lined up on the steps of the sanctuary, preceded by their ministrants, who waved censers which smoked with incense. But by now the events of their journey had convinced them that anything might happen in this land.

The guide, who also functioned as their interpreter, translated the words of the priest who welcomed them with a cup of fresh water and a chest of ripe dates. 'What do you want of us, O guest who comes from the desert? If you ask for water and food you will find them because the law of hospitality is sacred here.'

'I ask to know the truth,' replied Alexander.

'And of whom do you ask these words of truth?' the priest inquired once again.

'Of the greatest of all the gods, of Zeus Ammon, who lives in this solemn temple.'

'Then return to the temple tonight and you will know what you wish to know.'

Alexander bowed and moved over to his companions,

who were setting up camp near the spring. He watched Callisthenes put his hands in the water and splash it on his forehead.

'Is it true what they say? That in the evening it warms up and then at midnight it is actually lukewarm?'

'I have another theory. In my opinion the spring water is always the same temperature – it is the air temperature which varies incredibly, so that during the day, when the air is very hot, the water seems very cold. While at night, when there is a bit of a chill in the air, the water feels warmer and even lukewarm at midnight. It's all relative, as Uncle Aristotle would put it.'

'Quite,' said Alexander. 'Have you had any more news about his investigations?'

'No, only the things I have already told you about. But we will certainly have more news when the ships return with the new recruits. For the moment it seems he has found some trace of Persian involvement, but I already know what he would say if he were here.'

'So do I. He would say that of course the Persians were interested in having my father assassinated, but even if they didn't do it, they would spread word that they had so that future Kings of Macedon would think twice about undertaking hostile action against them.'

'That is indeed most probable,' Callisthenes agreed as he put his hands into the spring once more.

Just then Philip the physician arrived. 'Look at what the men have found,' he said, holding up a large snake, its head wrinkly and triangular in shape. 'One bite can bring death in an instant.'

Alexander looked at it. 'Tell the soldiers to be careful

and then have it embalmed and sent to Aristotle for his collection. And do the same thing if you see any interesting plants, or anything with unusual properties. I will give you a letter to accompany everything.'

Philip nodded and moved on with his snake, while Alexander sat at the edge of the spring and waited for evening to fall. Suddenly he saw Aristander's reflection appear in the water before him.

'Do you still have that nightmare?' asked the King. 'That dream about the naked man being burned alive?'

'And you?' asked Aristander. 'What nightmares trouble your mind?'

'Many . . . perhaps too many,' replied the King. 'My father's death, the death of Batis, the valiant soldier I dragged behind my chariot around the walls of Gaza, the ghost of Memnon, who appears between myself and Barsine every time I hold her in my arms, the Gordian knot which I cut with my sword rather than undoing and . . .'

And he stopped, reluctant to continue.

'And what else?' asked Aristander, staring into his eyes.

'A rhyme,' replied Alexander, lowering his gaze.

'A rhyme? Which rhyme?'

Very quietly the King sang it:

> 'The silly old soldier's off to the war
> And falls to the floor, falls to the floor!'

Then he turned his back and continued to look at Aristander's reflection.

'Does it have some special significance for you?'

'No, it is only a rhyme I used to sing when I was young. My mother's nurse, old Artemisia, taught me it.'

'In that case pay it no heed. As for your nightmares, there is only one way out of that,' said Aristander.

'And what would that be?'

'Become a god,' replied the seer. And as soon as he spoke his image dissolved into the water because of the frantic movements of a tiny insect on the surface, desperate to escape death in the jaws of some predator.

*

At nightfall Alexander crossed the threshold of the great temple, illuminated within by a double row of lamps hanging from the ceiling and one great lamp on the floor which spread a flickering glow over the colossal limbs of the god Ammon.

Alexander looked up to the savage gaze of the giant, his enormous curled horns, like a ram's, his ample chest, his strong arms hanging at his sides, his clenched fists. He thought again of the words his mother had said to him before he left: 'The oracle at Dodona marked your birth, another oracle, in the middle of a burning desert, will mark for you another birth and another life which will last for ever.'

'What do you ask of the god?' all of a sudden came a resounding voice from the forest of stone columns which supported the roof of the temple. Alexander looked around, but saw no one. He turned his gaze to the enormous ram's head with its great yellow eyes crossed by a black slit – was this then truly a manifestation of the divine?

'Is there still anyone . . .' he began. And the echo responded, 'Anyone . . .'

'Is there still anyone among those who killed my father whom I have yet to punish?'

His words died out, refracted and deformed by the thousands of crooked surfaces in the temple, and there was a moment's silence. Then the deep, vibrant voice resounded again from the giant's chest – 'Take care! Measure your words, for your father is not a mortal man. Your father is Zeus Ammon!'

The King came out of the temple deep in the night, after having listened to the answers to all of his questions, but he did not want to return to his tent among all his soldiers in the camp. He crossed through the palm gardens until he found himself alone on the edge of the desert, under the infinite expanse of the starry sky. Then he heard someone approaching and turned to see who it was. Eumenes was standing there before him.

'I would rather not talk just now,' Alexander said, while Eumenes continued to stand motionless, 'but if you have something important to tell me, I will listen.'

'Unfortunately it is bad news which I have carried with me for some time now, waiting for the right moment . . .'

'And you think that this is the right moment?'

'Perhaps. In any case I cannot keep the news from you any longer. King Alexander of Epirus has been killed in battle, ambushed by a horde of barbarians.'

Alexander nodded gravely, and while Eumenes walked away he turned once more to the infinity of the sky and the desert, and cried in silence.

ALEXANDER: THE ENDS OF THE EARTH

The story of Alexander concludes with *Alexander: The Ends of the Earth*, the final volume of Valerio Massimo Manfredi's bestselling trilogy

Turn the page to read the first chapter . . .

1

THE KING SET OFF again across the desert, taking another route that led from the Oasis of Ammon directly to the banks of the Nile near Memphis. He rode alone for hours and hours astride his Sarmatian bay, while Bucephalas galloped alongside wearing no halter or tack at all. Alexander had understood just how long their journey was going to take, and he sought to spare his horse whenever possible, keen to preserve its strength and vigour.

The march took three weeks under the baking hot sun and they suffered much before the thin green line marking the fertile banks of the Nile came into view. However, Alexander seemed to be immune to exhaustion, hunger and thirst, so immersed was he in his thoughts and in his memories.

His Companions tried not to disturb these reveries because they realized he wanted to be alone in the midst of those endless, desert spaces, alone with his feeling of infinity, with his anxious dreams of immortality, with the passions of his soul. Only when evening fell was it possible to approach the King, and occasionally some of his friends would enter the tent to speak to him and keep him company while Leptine bathed him.

One day Ptolemy took him by surprise with a question

he had been wanting to ask his King and friend for too long: 'What did the god Ammon tell you?'

'He called me "son",' replied Alexander.

Ptolemy picked up the sponge that had fallen from Leptine's hand and returned it to her, 'And what did you ask him?'

'I asked him if all of my father's murderers are dead or whether any of them have survived.'

Ptolemy said nothing. He waited for the King to come out of the tub and then placed a towel of clean linen over his shoulders and began rubbing him dry. When Alexander turned, his friend looked firmly and deeply into his eyes and asked him, 'So do you still love Philip, your father, now that you have become a god?'

Alexander sighed, 'If you weren't here before me now, I would say that this question had come from Callisthenes or Cleitus the Black . . . give me your sword.' Ptolemy looked at him in surprise, but he did not dare reply. He simply unsheathed his sword and held it out. Alexander took the weapon and cut the skin on his arm with the sharp metal point so that a bright red rivulet started running down it.

'What is this, Ptolemy, if it is not blood?'

'It is indeed blood.'

'Quite. It is not the *icor* which is said to run through the veins of the celestial gods,' he continued, reciting from Homer. 'Therefore, my friend, try to understand me, and if you love me then put an end to these pointless gibes.'

Ptolemy understood and apologized for having spoken in that way, while Leptine washed the King's arm with wine and put a bandage on the wound.

Alexander saw that his friend was truly sorry and invited him to stay for supper, even though there was not much to eat – dry bread, dates and some rather sharp palm wine.

'What are we going to do now?' asked Ptolemy.

'We will travel back to Tyre.'

'And then?'

'I do not know. I think Antipater will send me news on what is happening in Greece and our informers will let us know what Darius is planning. At that stage we will take our decision.'

'I know that Eumenes has given you the bad news regarding your brother-in-law, Alexander of Epirus.'

'Yes, he has. My sister Cleopatra will be beside herself with grief, and my mother too, for she loved her brother very much.'

'But I am sure the greatest grief will be your own. Am I not right?'

'Yes, I believe you are.'

'What was it that brought the two of you so close together, apart from your family ties?'

'A great dream we shared. Now the entire weight of that dream lies on my shoulders. One day we will invade Italy, Ptolemy, and we will annihilate the barbarians who killed him.'

He poured some wine for his friend and then said, 'Would you like to hear some poetry? I have invited Thessalus to keep me company.'

'Indeed I would. Which poems have you chosen?'

'Works by a variety of poets, all of which are about the sea. These endless sands around us remind me of the great spread of the sea, and then all this dryness makes me long for it.'

As soon as Leptine had cleared away the two small tables, the actor entered. He wore a stage costume and had make-up on his face – bistre around his eyes, his mouth lined with minium, a red dye to create a bitter expression, like those of the masks from the tragedies. He strummed some subdued chords on his lyre and began:

> O breeze, breeze of the sea,
> That wafts swift galleys, ocean's coursers,
> Across the surging main!
> Where will you bear me, the sorrowful one?*

Alexander listened in the deep silence of the night, enchanted by the voice that was capable of any intonation, capable of resonating through all human feeling and passion, capable of imitating the very wind and the crash of thunder.

They sat up until late in the night listening to the voice of the great actor as it mutated through every shade of feeling, wailing through the tears of women, or rising proud as he gave voice to the heroes. When Thessalus finished, Alexander embraced him, 'Thank you,' he said, his eyes moist with emotion. 'You have evoked the dreams that will come to me this night. Now go and rest – we have a long march ahead of us tomorrow.'

Ptolemy waited up a little longer to drink some wine with Alexander.

'Do you ever think about Pella?' he suddenly asked.

---

* Euripides, *Hecuba* (lines 444–445), translated by E. P. Coleridge (1938).

'Do you ever think of your mother and your father, of the days when we were boys and we rode all over the hills of Macedon? Of the shining waters of our rivers and our lakes?'

Alexander considered the question for a moment and then replied, 'Yes, often, but it's as though they are distant images, like things that happened many many years ago. Our life is so intense that each hour is like a year.'

'This means, then, that we will grow old before our time, does it not?'

'Perhaps, or perhaps not. The lamp which burns brightest in the room is the one that is destined to burn out first, but all those present will remember just how beautiful its light was during its heyday.'

He pulled the door of the tent to one side and accompanied Ptolemy outside. The sky over the desert was filled with a myriad stars and the two young men lifted their eyes to look.

'Perhaps this too is the destiny of the stars that shine brightest in the celestial vault. May your night be a peaceful one, my friend.'

'And yours too, *Aléxandre*,' replied Ptolemy, as he moved off towards his tent on the edge of the camp.

*

Five days later they reached the banks of the Nile at Memphis, where Parmenion and Nearchus were waiting for them. That same night Alexander saw Barsine again. She was staying in a sumptuous building that had belonged to a pharaoh and her apartments had been arranged on the upper floors. In the evening the northerly winds brought to these rooms a pleasant coolness as they stirred the blue byssus curtains, as light and delicate as butterfly wings.

She waited for him, sitting on an armchair decorated with gold and enamel friezes, dressed in a light gown in the Ionian style. Her black hair with its violet highlights lay loose over her shoulders and she wore light make-up after the Egyptian manner.

The moonlight and the light of the lamps hidden behind alabaster screens mingled in an atmosphere perfumed with nard and aloe, glowing with amber reflections from the onyx tanks full of water, on the surface of which lotus flowers and rose petals floated. From an openwork screen of stylized ivy branches and gliding birds, came the quiet, gentle music of flutes and harps. The walls were completely frescoed with ancient Egyptian pictures representing scenes in which naked maidens danced to the sound of lutes and tambours before the royal couple on their thrones, and in a corner there was a large bed with a blue canopy supported by four columns of gilded wood with capitals in the shape of lotus flowers.

Alexander entered and looked long and ardently at Barsine. His eyes were still full of the dazzling light of the desert, his ears rang with the sacred words of the Oracle of Ammon, his whole body emanated an aura of magical enchantment: the golden locks falling on his shoulders, his muscled chest with the scars it carried, the changing colour of his eyes, his slender, nervous hands with their blue veins. Over his naked body he wore only a light *chlamys*, held loosely on his left shoulder with an ancient silver buckle, an age-old inheritance of the Argead dynasty, and he wore a golden ribbon around his forehead.

Barsine stood up and immediately felt lost in the light of his gaze, 'Aléxandre . . .' she said as he pulled her into his arms and kissed her lips, as full and moist as ripe dates. He pulled her down to the bed and caressed her hips and her warm, perfumed breasts.

But suddenly the King felt her skin go cold and her limbs stiffen under his hands; a menacing air permeated the room, alerting all his warrior's senses. He turned quickly to face the imminent danger and found himself being attacked head on by a body running towards him. He saw a hand raised as it brandished a dagger, he heard a wild, strident cry reverberate around the walls of the bed chamber, and he heard Barsine cry out in grief and in pain.

Alexander quickly pinned the aggressor to the floor, twisting his wrist and forcing him to release the weapon. He could have massacred him there and then with the heavy lamp holder he had instinctively grabbed, but he had recognized the young fifteen-year-old – Eteocles, Memnon's and Barsine's eldest son! The boy struggled and turned like a young lion caught in a trap, shouting all sorts of insults, biting and scratching now that he was unarmed.

The guards burst in, having heard the scuffle, and they took hold of the aggressor. The officer in command understood immediately what had happened and called out, 'An attempt on the King's life! Take him below and have him tortured before he's executed.'

But Barsine threw herself crying at Alexander's feet, 'Save him, my Lord, save my son's life, I beg you!'

Eteocles looked at her with contempt written all over

his face and then, turning to Alexander, said, 'The best thing for you to do is to have me killed, because I will try again and again . . . a thousand times until I succeed in vindicating the life and honour of my father.' He was still shaking, partly because of the excitement and agitation of the scuffle, and partly because of the hatred burning in his heart. The King gestured to the guards to leave.

'But, Sire—' protested the officer.

'Out!' said Alexander. 'Can't you see he's just a boy?' and the man obeyed. Then the King turned once again to Eteocles, 'Your father's honour is fully intact. He died because of a fatal disease.'

'It's not true!' shouted the boy. 'You had him poisoned and now . . . now you're trying to take his woman. You are a man with no sense of honour!'

Alexander moved closer and repeated, his voice firm, 'I admired your father; I considered him my only worthy adversary and I dreamed of one day fighting him in a duel. I would never have had him poisoned; when I have to deal with my enemies I do so face to face, with sword and spear. As for your mother, she has made of me a victim because I think of her every waking moment; I am tormented by the thought of her. Love has all the strength of a god, love is irresistible and invincible. Man knows neither how to avoid it, nor how to escape it, in the same way that ultimately man cannot avoid the sun and the rain, birth and death.'

Barsine sobbed in a corner, her face hidden in her hands.

'Have you nothing to say to your mother?' the King asked.

'From the very instant you first laid hands on her, she has no longer been my mother, she is nothing to me now. Kill me, I tell you, it is in the best interests of both of you. Otherwise I shall kill you and I will offer the blood of both your bodies to my father's soul, so that he may find peace in Hades.'

Alexander turned to Barsine, 'What shall I do?'

Barsine dried her eyes and composed herself, 'Let him go free, I beg you. Give him a horse and provisions and let him go. Will you do this for me?'

'I warn you,' said the boy once more, 'that if you let me go I will speak to the Great King and I will ask him for armour and a sword so that I may fight in his army against you.'

'If this is the way it must be, then so be it,' replied Alexander. Then he called the guards and issued orders for the boy to be given a horse and provisions before being set free.

As he walked away towards the door, Eteocles sought to hide the violent emotions gripping his soul, as his mother called out to him. The boy did stop for an instant, but then he turned his back once again, crossed the threshold, and went out into the corridor.

Barsine called out again, 'Please wait!' Then she went to a chest and out of it pulled a shining weapon together with its scabbard. She rushed into the corridor and held it out to her son, 'It is your father's sword.'

The boy took it and held it close to his chest, and as he did so burning tears flowed from his eyes and made tracks down his cheeks.

'Farewell, my son,' said Barsine, her voice quavering.

'May Ahura Mazda protect you and may your father's gods protect you too.'

Eteocles ran off along the corridor and down the stairs until he came to the courtyard of the palace, where the guards placed a horse's reins in his hands. But just as he was about to leap astride the animal, he saw a shadow emerge from a small side door – his brother, Phraates.

'Take me with you, I beg you. I won't stay here, a prisoner to these *yauna*,' and Eteocles hesitated as his brother continued to plead with him. 'Take me with you, I beg of you, I beg you! I don't weigh much, the horse will manage both of us until we find another one.'

'I cannot,' replied Eteocles. 'You are too young and then . . . someone must stay with our mother. Farewell, Phraates. We will see each other again as soon as this war is over, and I will free you then.' He held his tearful younger brother in a long embrace, then he leaped on to the horse and disappeared.

Barsine had witnessed the scene from the window of her bed chamber and she felt herself wither at the sight of her fifteen-year-old boy galloping off into the night to face the unknown. She cried disconsolately, thinking of just how bitter the fate of human beings can be. Just a short time before she had felt like one of those Olympian goddesses painted and sculpted by the great *yauna* artists, and now she would gladly have changed places with the most humble of slaves.

DISCOUNT OFFER

Purchase any of these four paperbacks from www.panmacmillan.com for just £4.99 each.

£1 postage and packaging costs to UK addresses, £2 for overseas.

Heroes   The Oracle   Spartan   Tyrant

To buy the books with this special discount

1. visit our website, www.panmacmillan.com

2. search by author or book title

3. add to your shopping basket

4. use the discount code **VM** when you check out